# THE
# OBEDIENT
# ASSASSIN

# THE OBEDIENT ASSASSIN

A NOVEL BASED ON A TRUE STORY

## JOHN P. DAVIDSON

**DELPHINIUM BOOKS**

HARRISON, NEW YORK • ENCINO, CALIFORNIA

THE OBEDIENT ASSASSIN
Copyright © 2014 by John P. Davidson

First Edition

*Jacket and interior design by Greg Mortimer*

Library of Congress Cataloguing-in-Publication Data is available on request.

ISBN 978-1-88-328558-6

14 15 16 17 18 RRD 10 9 8 7 6 5 4 3 2 1

*For*
*Cezar Moreira Sanchez*

# ONE

The men could see the car coming on the road for a long time. It would appear on a rise, then disappear, a black sedan moving through the landscape of white limestone hills. The road was a rough track. Jeeps came that way and trucks, mules, and wagons, but a car was rare.

It was cold that afternoon, the temperature hovering near freezing. Rafts of slate-gray clouds marched south. As far as one could see, the ground had been stripped of anything that would burn; brush, trees, and even weeds had been cut down or ripped up. Tin cans radiated out from the old farmhouse and the entrenchments dug along the ridge. The smell of rotting garbage and human excrement filled the air. Across the valley, on the opposite hillside, the Loyalist camp looked like stone-age dwellings dug into earth. Occasionally, soldiers the size of ants would appear, and a lone voice would echo through the cold dry air. Or, with a resonant metallic snap, a loudspeaker would come on and one of the Loyalists would drone on about General Franco saving Spain and how the Republican Army was filled with *comunistas y maricones*—Communists and queers. The sound of gunfire was desultory and usually distant—the pow-pow-pow of a rifle or the staccato of a machine gun.

Lieutenant Mercader lay huddled on his cot in a low stone shed that stank of sheep. He heard the car arriving, the voices of men talking excitedly. *"Es una dama con su joven."* It's a lady with a boy.

Women didn't come to the front, not even peasant women trying to sell food. The lieutenant was cold and exhausted, but he put his feet to the ground and reached for his steel-frame glasses. The shed was filled with gloom, the sound of snoring. When he pulled the tarpaulin from the opening, he saw the Peugeot, elegant despite the crust of white mud, sliding into the farmyard. As he watched, his mother got out of the car. Tall, as tall as most men, she was imposing and inevitable with her shock of white hair. As she walked to the farmhouse, she wrapped a black shawl around her head. She knew the protocol. She would see Commander Contreras first.

The lieutenant considered going to the car to talk to the little boy, his half-brother, sitting in the back. Instead, he let the tarpaulin drop and returned to his cot to wait, pulling the wool blankets over his boots and up to his chin. The ache of shame lay like a chunk of ice in the pit of his stomach. His face rigid, his eyes moving rapidly from side to side, he thought of the words he would say, the hard truths that must be told. Shivering, listening to one of the junior officers snore, he inserted a hand into his pants to scratch at the lice feasting in his pubic hair.

After a while, voices came from the farmhouse, the sounds of departure. She was talking to Commander Contreras, saying goodbye. Then, as was inevitable, she stood at the opening to the shed. "*Hijo, ven! Es Caridad, tu mama.*" Son, come! It's Caridad, your mother.

"*Voy,*" he answered, his voice deep and hoarse.

With a blanket wrapped around his shoulders, he pushed the tarpaulin aside and stepped out of the shed. He studied her face for signs of grieving and saw the flush in her cheeks from drinking brandy at the commander's fireside.

"Here," she said, handing him a pack of cigarettes.

"Where did you get them?"

"Barcelona."

"How?"

She shrugged, refusing to commit.

"What are you doing here? What do you want?"

"Is that how you greet me?"

He didn't answer. The expression on his face did not change.

"I wanted to see you. We have to talk."

"About?"

"I need to tell you about Pablo."

"I know what happened. What can you possibly say?"

"We have other things to discuss."

"What?"

"Where can we talk? In private?"

"Not here. In the car?"

"No, there is the chauffeur and Luis."

"Then come this way. It isn't nice, but nothing is."

He led her down a path through the farmyard and around the corner of the barn. The men, trying to get out of the north wind and looking for privacy, had been shitting against the wall. So much shit accumulated, Contreras ordered them to find another place. Now the dung was dry, frozen, and relatively odorless. Dead rats hung from a wire fence, a warning to their surviving brethren.

She snapped open her handbag to withdraw a second pack of cigarettes, offering him one along with a small box of wax matches. He lit hers, then his, taking a deep breath. "This will make my head spin."

"What is the ration?"

"Two a day."

"Keep these as well. There are more in the car."

Mother and son, they stood in the cold, smoking. Crows cawed in the distance. The black shawl wrapped around her head suggested a peasant woman in mourning, but her back was too straight and there was something innately haughty about the cut of her lips and her prominent cheekbones. She took a deep breath, exhaling audibly through her nostrils. Her eyes drifted over the holes pocking the plot of ground next to the barn, trying to decipher the mysterious rectilinear pattern, slowly understanding that there had once been an orchard. The soldiers had cut down the trees for firewood, then come back to dig up the stumps to burn, too.

He turned to face her. "So, tell me about my brother."

"You said you knew."

"I said you were wasting your time if that was why you came. But now that you're here, tell me. I want to hear your version."

Her eyes moved, appraising him, looking for a way past the anger. He was twenty-two, aged by the war, fully a man. His cheeks were hollow, his lips chapped and red. Though dirty and tired, he was handsome with his thick auburn hair. He had her looks, his olive skin shading into the faintest lavender beneath deep green eyes.

"Tell me," he insisted. "How did they kill him?"

"It was a disciplinary action. Pablo disobeyed orders. He knew the rules. You don't leave bodies in a public place after a political execution. You never leave a body on the street. What Pablo did was no small thing."

"They could have warned him."

"They did. They warned him. He was seeing a woman who belonged to POUM, a suspected Trotskyist. They told him to break it off, but he refused."

"That was Alicia. He was in love with her."

"He put himself above the cause."

"You didn't defend him?"

"What could I do? I wasn't there. The orders had been given."

"With all of your connections, all of the strings you pull, you let your comrades make an example of Pablo? You let this happen?"

She laughed, the silent bitter gesture of a laugh. "I didn't *let* it happen. You overestimate my power."

His voice choked as tears stung his eyes. "Is it true they strapped him with dynamite? Is it true they marched him in front of a tank? Tell me, is it true?"

"Yes."

"They had him run down like a dog. They gave him a sporting chance, then crushed him in the dirt like a miserable cur."

She nodded.

"I want to hear it from you."

"Please, Ramón! This is cruel."

"He was my brother!"

"He was my son!"

He looked away. The wind was blowing; a crow, its black wings ruffling, had landed on the fence to peck at one of the dead rats. "The shame. His. Ours. He had to be shitting his pants with terror. And all of his comrades watching!"

She met his eyes, her own blurring with tears. "You have to understand. He was going to be punished. The decision had been made and I could do nothing. Everyone was watching me, waiting for me to break. But no, I held my head up. All I could control was my own behavior. I made the ultimate sacrifice and kept silent. I proved my loyalty beyond a doubt and now they owe me."

"What are you doing here? What do you want?"

She tossed away the end of her cigarette. "You know this is a lost cause."

"If we lose to Franco, we'll be without a country."

Her chin lifted, indicating the entrenchments. "Those are Spaniards you're shooting at on the opposite side of the valley. They're like you, no different. They're hungry, scratching at their own flea bites, freezing in their own shit. This is a revolution we should have won. This is archaic, rooting in the mud. You don't turn people into revolutionaries by shooting at them. You indoctrinate them. We would have won had it not been for Trotsky, splitting the left, setting the people against each other."

"I know about Trotsky. You needn't preach to me."

"You have to understand that the fight has moved on; a bigger war is coming."

He shuddered, feeling the cold once more. "What do you want from me?"

Her eyes settled on his. "I have been given an opportunity. I'm leading a mission that will change the course of history. I am second in command. It's a great honor for all women. I've come here with an assignment for you."

"As you see, I'm engaged in fighting a war."

"No, you have to listen to me. This is undercover, intelligence. Our orders come directly from Stalin."

"How did this plum fall into your hands? Is this a reward for your loyalty?"

"Perhaps in part."

"Who is first in command?"

"Colonel Eitingon. Leonid."

He laughed. "Of course, Eitingon! Hasn't he done enough to us?"

"What do you mean?"

"He left you when you were pregnant. I remember your misery."

"I behaved like a bourgeois girl. He did what he could. He never left us. He helped us. He paid for you to go to school."

"He abandoned you."

She winced, shaking her head. "That isn't true."

"That's his bastard sitting out there in the car."

"Leonid wanted to stay with me."

"But he had two wives, two families. Walking out on Papa the way you did, dragging all of us to France, you ruined our family."

"I had to leave Barcelona. I was dying on Calle Ancha, and I didn't know it."

"I don't trust you."

"Ramón, you want to hate me, but we're alike. You have so much to gain, but you must face the truth. We have to think beyond Spain."

"Without our country we have nothing. We'll be like the Gypsies, the Jews, wandering from place to place."

"That's why we have to win the bigger war. Ramón, we have to think ahead. I can take you out of all this. Tonight in Barcelona, you will have a hot bath and a good meal. You can see Lena. You'll sleep in a warm bed, and in France . . ."

"France?"

"Yes, Paris. We would leave tomorrow. What I am offering you is something far better than this, perhaps something glorious."

"What is the assignment?"

"I can't tell you. Not here. But you will know soon enough. Trust me!"

He shook his head. "No, I'm sorry. No, never."

# TWO

**A**s the train crept toward the tunnel at Portbou, Ramón watched a strip of beach and the cold gray water of the Mediterranean slide along beside the railroad tracks, wondering when he would see Spain again, whether he would ever return to Barcelona. He felt ridiculous dressed in a wool suit that was too small, as if he were a schoolboy traveling with his mother. Caridad sat across from him knitting, her fingers moving quickly, pulling the black yarn, the needles clicking softly. He didn't know how she'd managed to coerce him to leave the front, much less convinced him to get on the train.

They had fought for hours in the wretched farmyard with the dried human feces plastered to the wall and the dead rats hanging on the wire fence. He had been adamant, certain that he wouldn't go with her. He was entrenched, engaged in a battle. But she had argued him into submission, appealed to all of his vanity, his fears, dug her fingers into the tender places of vulnerability that only a mother knew. She told him she needed him and knew what was best for him, had sources of information and contacts he could never imagine. And in this way, the afternoon had passed, the two of them fighting, smoking her cigarettes, the crows pecking at the dead rats. Occasionally, there was gunfire in the distance, the metallic voice on a megaphone decrying the Republican soldiers as *comunistas y maricones*. The day waned, a cold breeze blowing from the north. As the sun set, a line of pink ran between the gray clouds and the dun-colored horizon. In the end, it was the cold that had driven him into the car with her, the fundamental desire for warmth.

Now, after they had spent three hours on the train, the light dimmed as they entered a tunnel, a wall of rock replacing the view of the Mediterranean. In a familiar transition, a reminder of all their crossings into France, the train groaned and shuddered in the dark. Then the wheels rolled freely and they came to a halt at the platform on the French side of the tunnel. Ramón glanced at his mother, who was putting her knitting away. She looked fashionable in a wool suit, with a stole of martens around her shoulders, each biting the tail of its predecessor.

While Ramón pulled the suitcases from the overhead rack, she gathered up her handbag and a small case. By the time he found a porter, she was on the platform buying cigarettes at a kiosk. The station at Cerbère was small, and, it being the south of France, was open to the cold salt air and the sound of the gulls. As if drawn by a magnet, Ramón walked out to look up at the rugged foothills of the Pyrénées tumbling down to the Mediterranean. He felt the presence of Canigou, the sacred mountain looming out of sight.

The year before the war broke out in Spain, the spring when it felt as if life was still beginning, he had hiked up through the groves of orange and lemon trees at the base of the mountain. As he climbed, the vegetation changed, the mountain air becoming cool and dry, the intense sunlight burning his skin as he rose higher through pine and fir thickets, the snowy peak above glistening white against a cobalt blue sky. He had slept on a bedroll, looking up at the constellations and galaxies of stars wheeling in the night sky. In the afternoons, he looked south toward Spain, the smell of orange blossoms wafting up to mingle with the scent of pine and fir in the thin mountain air. He spent a week exploring the flank of the mountain, drinking icy water from the rushing streams and eating bread and ham he bought from peasants he met along the way. On one of the last days, he encountered an Englishman, outfitted with climbing equipment, who led him up one of the steep ravines to the lip of the glacier.

Standing outside the station, he remembered those days and wished that was where he was going. Then, feeling the call of duty, he went back inside, where he found Caridad sitting at a table in the café, reading a Paris newspaper and smoking a cigarette, a pot of tea before her. "Where did you go?" she asked, glancing up at him.

"Nowhere," he answered, pulling out a chair.

He watched as she exhaled two thick streams of smoke from her nostrils, drawing it voluptuously into her mouth, her lips scored with faint vertical lines.

"Still angry?" she asked in an amused tone of voice, expelling another cloud of smoke.

"Who said I was angry?"

"You've been pouting since we left Barcelona."

He looked away.

"You know, a man speaks up, says what's on his mind. It isn't my fault that you couldn't find Lena. You shouldn't put the blame on me."

"We could have waited another day."

She shook her head, narrowing her eyes into a slight grimace. "No, *mi hijo*, we couldn't wait. We have an important meeting to-morrow in Paris."

"What time tomorrow?"

"After we get in."

"And who will be there besides Eitingon?"

"His chief. Others."

"Are they coming from Moscow?"

She frowned slightly. They were speaking Catalan, but everyone spoke Catalan along the border.

"Where are they coming from?"

"Don't ask so many questions. You will find out when you need to know."

A waiter brought the menu and set a small pitcher on the table.

Ramón looked at it with wonder. "Milk? We didn't even ask for it."

She smiled. "Yes, and cream and butter and plenty of meat. You'll see. You won't be sorry you came."

She touched the sleeve of his jacket with her long fingers, recalling how she'd watched him starving as a baby, his tiny hands clutching desperately at the air, looking into her eyes with panic. He couldn't eat. A mysterious disease, marasmus, afflicted infants after the war. She had tried everything, including seven different wet nurses. Finally, in an act of desperation, a stroke of genius, she had soaked horse meat in cognac, knowing that he needed something strong, that she wouldn't let him go.

She smiled sadly, rubbing the fabric of his jacket between her fingertips. "Don't worry, we'll get you a new suit in Paris. This one is threadbare and no longer fits you."

On the night train to Paris, they shared a compartment with four other passengers, whose presence precluded a conversation between Ramón and his mother, allowing him to pretend he was traveling alone. From the seat opposite Caridad's—across this small distance—he observed her, the way she jerked impatiently at the yarn she was knitting, the way she smoked, lighting one cigarette from the end of another. Everything about her—her self-absorption, her patronizing regard for others—grated on his nerves. She had always been knitting, even when he was a boy. It was a way to stay calm, like fingering the beads of a rosary. He watched the tips of the needles and the thread, wondering if it would be a sock, the sleeve of a sweater.

He finally made himself look out at the French landscape rolling past as dusk fell, at the sere winter fields, the olive groves and small stone villages; the train rocked at a steady clip, the constant and rhythmic clicking of the rails constant. That morning he had been standing in the small tiled vestibule of Lena's parents' building, impatiently ringing the bell for apartment 3C. He was so close, he could see her deep brown eyes, the way she would laugh when she realized he was there. But the buzz of the doorbell went unanswered. Again and again he rang, then he walked out to the sidewalk, looking up at the windows of the corner apartment. The building was on one of those small squares sprinkled throughout Barcelona, once pristinely manicured, now shabby, littered with trash. It was ten in the morning. Where was she? Her mother and sisters? He went to the café where he often waited for her, where he could watch the front door of her building. With the minutes slipping past, he drank a *fino*, then, unable to believe that he would really miss her, wrote an awkward note on a napkin that he slipped into her mailbox.


As night fell, the passengers in the compartment began turning on their reading lamps, the window becoming a mirror that looked in rather than out, a reflection accompanying the compartment, the passengers swaying slowly.

"*Permiso, permiso.*" He stood, making his way to the door of the compartment. "*Pardon! Pardon, si'l vous plaît.*" Swaying, touching the walls of the narrow corridor, he walked to the end of the car, a tremendous rush of noise and cold air greeting him as he stepped out onto the platform, the locomotive hooting in the distance. He was walking back, against the motion of the train through another car of compartments to the bar car. He avoided the Spaniards—it was occasionally difficult to tell Fascists from Communists—and, speaking French, asked for a brandy and then, as if a second thought, writing paper, which he took to one of the small tables at the back of the car. Lighting a Gauloises, he stared at the blank page for a moment before writing, *Querida Lena*.

She was his *novia*. There had been many other girls, but that was only expected. It was important that he be able to teach Lena about sex after they married.

*Recibiste la nota que te dejé esta mañana? I rang the bell to your apartment again and again, and can't believe that I missed seeing you—if only for a moment. I was in town for one night and left early this afternoon for Paris. I'm on the train now, sitting alone with a brandy, thinking of you. You might laugh when you read that I am with my mother. I can't tell you what we're doing because I still don't know. And I can't tell you how she talked me into this. I find her infuriating but somehow impossible to refuse. She is so certain about everything, so sure that she's right. She said there was nothing she could do to help Pablo, that all of the decisions had been made, etc. etc. I don't know when I will come home, but I will write to you often. I would ask you to come to Paris, but I know how your parents feel, that they would never agree. My darling Lena, I hope you think of me often. Te adoro, R*

He folded the sheet of paper, slipping it into his breast pocket. After finishing his brandy and smoking a second cigarette, he went back to the compartment, where most of the lights had been turned off, and Caridad, in her corner next to the window, was sleeping, her head back, her mouth slightly open.

In the morning when he woke, she was applying lipstick. They went to the dining car for coffee and bread, and were once more sitting in the compartment as the train approached the outskirts of Paris. He watched as she powdered her face and fretted with her hat, driving a long pin through her hair. Glancing up from a small round mirror, she looked at him anxiously. "Now, you won't be churlish with Leonid, will you?"

"No, Mother, I promise to behave."

"I don't want sarcasm. This is very important. He's giving us a great opportunity. Do you understand?"

"Yes. I understand."

"There he is," she said, waving at a man standing on the platform.

By the time Ramón had gotten their bags, Caridad was outside, embracing Eitingon. Ramón hung back, a bit embarrassed and sad for his mother, who was holding on too tight, squeezing too hard. He winced as she threw her head back to gaze ardently into Eitingon's face.

Holding a gray homburg in one hand and wearing a black top-coat with a collar of Persian lamb, the Russian looked like a rich banker rather than a revolutionary. He had thick black hair, pleasant gray-green eyes, and a romantic-looking scar on his chin. Replacing his hat, giving the brim a slight tug, he gave Caridad a last squeeze, then, laughing, held out his hand to Ramón. "My boy, I hardly recognized you out of uniform," he said in French.

"And I could say the same of you," Ramón answered, also in French.

Eitingon blinked, noticing the coolness, then forged on, clapping Ramón on the shoulder. "Well, you look splendid, handsome as ever."

"Thank you, sir. You look quite well yourself."

"Let me help you with that." He picked up one of the suitcases and led them outside to the waiting car, scattering the pigeons on the sidewalk. It was cold in Paris, and the traffic whirling around the Gare de Lyon was much heavier and faster than any in Barcelona. A driver helped stow their luggage in the car's trunk, then the three settled in the back of the car, Caridad sitting between the two men.

"Well, are we ready?" Eitingon asked.

"I'm not sure," said Ramón. "I still don't know what we've come for."

"Ah, your mama is being very strict with you," Eitingon said, gripping Caridad's gloved hand in his own. "And the children?" he asked her. "Luis? You got them settled?"

"Yes, with family in the country near Ripollet. It's a lovely farm. They'll be safe."

Eitingon gave the driver an address, then the car lurched out onto the street. Despite his misgivings, Ramón felt his spirits lift when the Seine came into view, stunningly beautiful, iconic. On the opposite bank, a long row of apartment houses uniform in height and proportions looked down upon the cold silvery river where a tug was pulling two flat barges upstream. They crossed a bridge to the Boulevard St.-Germain, the gray sky fragmented by the bare black limbs of the chestnut and plane trees. Eitingon pointed out Café de Flore and Les Deux Magots for Ramón, then began to tell him about the dinner he'd had the night before. "You can't imagine guinea hens roasted so tenderly," he said, his French seasoned with a slight Russian accent, his grammar slightly askew. "The hens were so succulent, so simple. I'll take you, a modest little restaurant no one knows about. The cheeses and wines, perfectly selected. And the carrots! They were sautéed in olive oil, with slivers of those black olives from Nyons, garlic, and parsley. The colors were beautiful."

"I know that dish. It's Provençal."

"Yes, of course you do. I don't suppose you've had the chance to cook anything?"

"There's nothing to eat in Spain."

"Well, it's all here. The markets are brimming, you'll see."

They turned onto a street lined with apartment buildings, the façades forming a wall capped with mansard roofs. The one they entered was much like the others. Ramón waited with the luggage while Eitingon and his mother went up in the cage, their voices echoing above like the chattering of birds. When Ramón got off on the fifth floor, a door stood open to a flat. Caridad and Eitingon were sitting on a sofa in their coats, talking and smoking cigarettes, pale yellow sunlight coming through the glass doors to shallow balconies.

"I think it will be fine," Caridad was saying.

"Ah, Ramón! I should have helped with the luggage!"

"That's all right. The lift is so small." He took in the flat, the high ceilings, the ornate moldings, the parquet floors that squeaked beneath his feet. "This is quite grand," he said, stepping out onto the balcony for a view of the city all gray and silver and black, the stone buildings smudged with soot, the only color the red clay chimney pots with ribbons of smoke trailing up to the leaden sky.

"What do you think?" Eitingon asked when Ramón came in for a cigarette.

"One could be comfortable here."

"It's only temporary. You and Caridad will have your own flats."

"And what is it that we will be doing?"

Eitingon smiled.

"There's a meeting this afternoon?"

"Ah, yes, my friend Pavel Sudoplatov has come from Moscow to inspect the team your mother and I have put together. He's quite congenial, a lovely chap. When I dropped by his office at the Kremlin, he couldn't have been more charming. It was my dear fellow this, my dear fellow that. And that was just at the time when anyone who had been in Spain was suspected of being a Trotsky sympathizer. Everyone else in the Kremlin was creeping around frightened they're going to get caught in one of those internal purges and end up before a firing squad. Everyone in Moscow is suspected of being a Trotsky sympathizer. Everyone's suspect—especially if you've been in Spain.

"But Pavel was sitting pretty. He had his secretary serve tea, then started telling me about this assignment, got it straight from Stalin and Beria. Said he was called into Stalin's office with Beria, looking the villain with that horrible monocle and pencil-thin mustache. Stalin starts pacing around the room as if he's alone, gazing out the windows and reflecting upon the state of the world, Hitler, Germany, the coming war. Then Stalin sits down at his desk, and suddenly sits up straight as if he's been goosed in the ass or received an electric shock. 'The Trotsky problem must be solved,' he announces, or something like that. Trotsky mustn't split the Left in an international war the way he did in Spain. They gave Pavel the assignment and promoted him, made him director of the Foreign Department at the NKVD. Pavel's a clever fellow, made his reputation as an assassin when he rigged a box of chocolates as a bomb. Some greedy bastard thinks he's opening a present and, kaboom, it explodes in his face."

"You mentioned a team?"

"Ramón, you understand about Trotsky, that he has to be eliminated?"

"Yes, I understand."

"Did you ever run into David Siqueiros in Spain?"

"The Mexican painter?"

"Yes, that's him."

"I heard about him. He was famous on the front for his uniforms."

"Yes, well he's an artist and quite the peacock," Eitingon agreed. "He designed his uniforms and had them made in New York. But he's also a brave soldier, a hero of the Mexican Revolution."

"I know his reputation."

"He's going to lead a strike against Trotsky in Mexico. We'll provide the money and he'll assemble a small army of men. The conclusion is foregone, a fait accompli."

"Where in Mexico?"

"A suburb outside the capital city, one of those Indian names."

"Coyoacán," said Caridad.

"That's it. Trotsky's living in a house there that belongs to Diego Rivera. Siqueiros knows the place. All of those Mexican painters are pals, or at least they know each other. And, of course, Caridad knows Mexico. She's been there, understands how the Party operates, and she knows all of the Mexicans who fought in Spain. The whole operation has simply fallen into place one piece after another."

"And will I be part of this small army in Mexico?"

"No, nothing so crude." Eitingon looked to Caridad as if for guidance.

"We need someone to infiltrate Trotsky's organization here in

Paris," she said. "With your French and English, you can fit in easily."

"You will work as an undercover agent for the GPU," Eitingon assured him. "It's, how do you say, a plum as these things go."

"And you and Caridad will be running the operation?" Ramón asked.

"That's right. You'll have to be careful not to be seen in public with Caridad. She's well-known to Trotskyists. But at the moment, the Fourth International is so screwed they wouldn't know their own mothers."

"The Fourth International?"

"Trotsky's organization," Eitingon answered.

"I see, as if the Third International has been replaced."

"The cheek, suggesting that the Soviet Union is no longer the revolution! Not many have heard of the Fourth International, and if we're successful, not many will. Trotsky's son was running the Fourth International here in Paris and it seems the poor chap had to have an appendectomy. You know how it is when you're sick, how you always want to be with your countrymen, with people who speak your language. So, Sedov—that was his name, Lev Sedov— checked into a clinic here in Paris that's run by White Russians. He had the surgery, a routine affair, and was recovering splendidly. Two days later, he died of mysterious causes." Eitingon winked for Ramón's benefit. "Silly bastard used a French alias at the clinic, thought the Russians wouldn't get on to him. But then we already knew he was there. His secretary is one of our operatives."

"You had someone inside?" asked Ramón.

"Yes, an excellent fellow, a student at the Sorbonne. Anthropology, I believe. His code name's Étienne. You'll meet him."

"If you have him, why do you want me? I thought my job was to get inside?"

Eitingon and Caridad glanced at each other again. "Étienne isn't working for us," Caridad explained.

"He isn't GPU?"

"Yes, but he's not our agent. We aren't informed of all of the operations under way in Paris. And we need someone unknown who can go to New York and Mexico. We will want you in Trotsky's house in Mexico so that we know what he's doing."

Eitingon clapped his solid hands together, rocking forward on the sofa. "Well, I'm sure you want to wash up and rest a bit. I'll come back at two and we'll go over to the Hotel Lutetia to see Pavel."

# THREE

Outside, the cold winter air smelled of wood smoke and roasting chestnuts. On the opposite side of the street, a peasant in a dark blue smock, his face red and grizzled, was selling live chickens from the back of a truck, while two women stood smoking cigarettes, waiting for a dog to defecate. Eitingon and Caridad walked quickly ahead, arm in arm. Following on the narrow sidewalk, Ramón had one of those sudden and dreamlike feelings that made his scalp prickle, as if he had fallen through time and was once more a boy in Toulouse, homesick and out of place, following in the wake of Caridad and Eitingon, hoping they wouldn't forget him.

Ramón stopped in his tracks on the narrow sidewalk. He had taken a wrong turn, regressed. Eitingon and Caridad were unaware of him, talking, and moving away. And from this distance, he saw that they were no longer young, Caridad no longer beautiful. With her white hair, tailored suit, and the fur stole of martens wrapped around her shoulders, she looked like a dowager of some sort, a person to be contended with, but not a woman who fell in love. She was aging more rapidly than Eitingon, who, though stout and bearlike in his overcoat, retained his virility, vivid complexion, and dark shining hair.

"Is something wrong?" Caridad asked, stopping to wait for Ramón.

"No, no, I'm coming."

He was in Paris. The cold air smelled delicious. An old man pushed a wheelbarrow filled with coal; a concierge slowly polished the brass on a door. Men at the counter of a café talked over cups of espresso and glasses of wine. They knew about the war in Spain, and that Hitler was massing his troops just across the border. But France was at peace.

As they turned a corner, the Hotel Lutetia rose above the street, a Beaux Arts wedding cake with layer upon layer of rich icing. As they entered, a man stood up from one of the overstuffed chairs facing the door. He was tall, had thick black hair, a long narrow aristocratic face, and an aquiline nose. He looked very dramatic in uniform, a gray cape, jodhpurs, and riding boots. As he embraced Eitingon, the cape opened, revealing the scarlet silk lining. He kissed the Russian on both cheeks, then, clicking his heels together, bent down to kiss Caridad's hand. "And this is Antonio Pujol, my *compañero* and aide de camp," he said, introducing the man at his side. A Mexican Indian, Pujol had pockmarked cheeks, a flattened nose, and thick lips. "Antonio is a Marxist prodigy, with a remarkable understanding of theory. And he's also a fine artist. I found him in the market in Mexico City."

As Ramón was introduced to Siqueiros, he noticed the sharp cut of the painter's lips, the oddly sensuous, almost feminine mouth. Siqueiros insisted that he had met Ramón. "*Sí, claro! Conozco muy bien el hijo de Caridad.*"

"So what is this about?" Siqueiros said to Eitingon. "What is it that Sudoplatov wants?"

"He wants to see the team we've assembled."

"But we can't assemble our team here," Siqueiros objected. "We have to do that in Mexico."

"He wants to see us," said Eitingon.

"Ha! You mean he wanted a junket to Paris!"

"Perhaps that, too. But should anything go wrong, God forbid, Sudoplatov has to be able to say that he came to inspect his team. You know how methodical Stalin is. Everything has to be done by the rules and everything on the list has to be checked and double-checked."

Siqueiros switched into French as they started for the elevators, telling Eitingon and Caridad how he'd been rushing around Paris, going to galleries and seeing friends—Braque, Léger, Picasso. Ramón, all the while, studied the hotel. The paneling in the elevator was a dark polished wood, the carpet in the hallway a deep royal blue.

On the fourth floor, they walked down a long corridor to one of the identical white doors that punctuated their passage. Eitingon knocked and an aide let them into the foyer of a large suite; they waited a few moments to be escorted into a drawing room where a fire was crackling in the hearth and pale yellow silk-draped windows looked out at the cold gray sky. Sudoplatov came into the room as he made the last adjustment to his French cuffs. Wearing a navy pinstripe suit with a white shirt and white silk tie, he had deep-set brown eyes, regular features, a strong nose, and the square jaw of a film star. He embraced Eitingon, kissing him upon each cheek, then his mouth. They spoke warmly in Russian for a few moments, then he turned to Caridad. *"Enchanté,"* he said to her, kissing both of her cheeks. *Enchanté*, he said to each of them, which was the extent of his French.

Eitingon stood at Sudoplatov's side, making the introductions, saying a few words about each of them. As Ramón shook Sudoplatov's hand, he remembered the box of chocolates exploding, that the Russian had once had nothing but his youth, daring, and ingenuity. Now as director of the NKVD's Foreign Department, he oversaw the GPU.

Everyone was lighting cigarettes and chatting while a tray of small glasses of eau-de-vie went round the room. The gathering might have been a small cocktail party had there not been a sharp undercurrent. Beneath the hum of conversation Sudoplatov turned to Eitingon. "She looks well," he said in Russian. "I'm surprised she's still with us. She isn't bitter?"

"No, a loyal comrade. She's proven that. No one more so."

"The handsome young man is her son?"

"Yes."

"The family resemblance is striking. They have the same eyes." Sudoplatov took a deep drag from a cigarette, his nostrils flaring. "Should we begin?"

"Of course. How do you want to proceed? Should I translate for the others?"

"Not necessary and so tedious. They know the plan, don't they? I'm the one who needs to hear it. I may ask them questions as we go along."

"As you wish. I will explain so they won't feel uncomfortable."

Sudoplatov took another drag of the cigarette, then stubbed it out as Caridad and Ramón settled on a sofa. Siqueiros took an armchair, Pujol standing just behind him.

"Now, my dear Leonid, tell me about Operation Mother," Sudoplatov said in Russian, pronouncing the last with the appropriate degree of irony.

As Eitingon and Sudoplatov proceeded, Ramón had the sensation of doors sliding shut. Other than the occasional *da* or *nyet*, the language was impenetrable to him. He wondered how difficult it would be to learn Russian. He had no memory of learning French. For him, Spanish, Catalan, and French were all the same on the inside. Shifting from one to another was subtle and effortless, a response to exterior circumstances, to people. English, which he had learned in the first grade at a British school in Barcelona, felt different in some fundamental way he couldn't quite describe. A shift into English started some place deeper, took longer to reach the surface.

Ramón smoked a cigarette and finished his eau-de-vie, looking up when Eitingon translated a question about Trotsky's residence in Mexico for Siqueiros. Siqueiros, who had been languishing in boredom, accustomed as he was to being the center of attention, responded to the attention like a dry plant to water. Of course he knew the exact house, which belonged to friends, and no, he didn't think it should be a problem. Like every house in Mexico it had a wall, but, as walls went, it wasn't very high or sturdy.

"How many men will you need?" Eitingon translated once more.

"Twenty should be enough."

And would Siqueiros be able to assemble the men?

Siqueiros shrugged. "Of course. If there is money, there will be no problem."

Eitingon and Sudoplatov entered into a longer discussion that Ramón followed by watching their faces and listening to the tone of their voices. At one point, Sudoplatov appeared to be unhappy, asking several sharp questions, but in the end he relented.

"He wants to know if you're satisfied with the plan," Eitingon told Caridad.

"Yes." She nodded and smiled at Sudoplatov. "Tell him yes."

A burning log popped in the fireplace.

"And the operation is fail-safe?"

"Yes," Caridad answered. "Exactly as Stalin ordered."

# FOUR

Eitingon picked up an oyster from the bed of ice and slid it into his mouth, closing his eyes to taste the cold ocean waves and appreciate the exquisite texture. He gave his head the slightest shake, then took a swallow of the Sancerre to wash away the faint metallic taste of the oyster. "These *Portugaises* are very good. Should we have another dozen?"

"Yes, but I wish we'd ordered a different wine."

"Yes, this is modest. We'll drink the Pétrus with the *civet de lapin*."

The restaurant was Eitingon's discovery, a storefront with a zinc bar and paper tablecloths, a proprietor chef who wore a white toque and shouted at his daughter when she didn't serve the plates fast enough.

"Here, suffer the last of this," Eitingon said, filling Ramón's glass. He wanted to loosen Ramón's tongue, to find out what he was thinking. He took another swallow of wine, remembering the old stone farmhouse outside Toulouse, a ruin with the vines and arbor. Records playing on a wind-up gramophone, they had eaten at a table beneath an oak tree. Caridad was such a beauty. He assumed she was a wealthy Spanish bohemian, looking for a new life with her children in France.

"You know about Pablo," said Ramón.

Eitingon studied Ramón's face.

"He didn't deserve such a death. I don't understand how she let that happen."

Eitingon looked down at his wineglass, which he turned slightly on the table. "What could she do? She wasn't there. Pablo left a corpse on the street."

"A father," he hesitated, biting his bottom lip. "A father would have saved his son."

"Perhaps. You can't be sure. Caridad knew she was being watched, that her loyalty was being tested."

"And she passed the test."

"And this is her reward. I wasn't there, so I couldn't help her. But I could give her this assignment."

Eitingon glanced away, then took a deep breath and exhaled. He had a vivid memory of Ramón in Toulouse. A week or so after Caridad had driven him from the house with her histrionics, he had gone back to see if there was anything he could do. The other children had somehow drifted away, but Ramón, at his mother's side, attempting to attend to her, had that shell-shocked look, that haunted gaze of soldiers who had been in battle.

"Caridad isn't an easy person," he said.

Ramón laughed.

"How old were you when we met in Toulouse?"

"Ten, more or less."

"What do you remember?"

"Everything, I suppose."

"Do you blame me for what happened?"

Ramón blinked. "No, should I?"

"She was angry at me. She would have said things. I know I made mistakes. I didn't understand how sheltered her life had been. I thought she was another sort of woman, had had a more worldly life. And then . . ." He hesitated. What had happened had been so appalling he couldn't imagine what that time had been for Ramón, an ambulance coming to the house, neighbors standing at the gate.

Eitingon gave his wineglass another turn. "I think religion was the problem for Caridad."

"Religion? She's an intellectual, an atheist."

"Not then. She kept talking about the church. That's what she kept saying, that she was lost because she had abandoned the church. She's a complicated person. Ramón, all of this Marxist theory, dialectical materialism is mumbo jumbo to me."

"Yes, to me as well. On the front, anytime a group of soldiers got together, they would argue about who was a Stalinist and who was a Trotskyist. And, of the two, who was the true Marxist. And then there were all of the arguments about all of the socialist organizations in Catalonia and which of them were Trotskyist."

"And what did you make of it?"

"I didn't listen to the arguments that much. As far as I'm concerned Lenin was the father of the revolution."

"And Trotsky?"

"Perhaps he was the spoiled son who made trouble when Lenin chose Stalin to be his successor."

Eitingon shrugged. "For Caridad, Marx and the *Manifesto* is like Holy Scripture. You know she wanted to become a nun?"

"Yes, but her parents made her marry Papa because he was rich."

The sounds of pots clattering came from the kitchen.

"Ramón, I did some things wrong, but I hope you don't blame me."

"No, I was sorry when you left. Particularly after Thorez came." Ramón shuddered with distaste. "He was cold and distant."

"I don't imagine Maurice Thorez was much fun, but I suppose that's what she needed."

"You mean all that theory. I guess I'm not smart enough for it."

"You're smart enough. Theory just doesn't interest you."

Eitingon urged Ramón to take the last oyster, then pushed the tray of ice and shells aside. "We need to talk about your assignment."

"Yes, I don't really understand what I'll be doing."

"The beginning is the most difficult. We have to study the situation and wait for the right opening. You need to start thinking about your cover."

"I thought you would assign me a new identity."

"It's much better if you create your own, something you're comfortable with, something you like."

"How do I do that?"

"Stay as close to the truth as you can. If you invent too much, then you forget and get confused. For example, you have Caridad in your life. So whoever you become might have a mother who interferes, who smokes too much, perhaps she knits. At the core, that will have truth for you. You can be who you want, just as long as your story fits together. It has to be sturdy enough to hold up under pressure. You must remember it in your sleep and be able to cling to it should you be tortured. But let's not dwell upon the negative."

He poured more wine in their glasses. "How good is your English? Could you pass for an Australian or American?"

"Not with my accent."

"You can't be Spanish. That would wave red flags."

"I could be South American, from Argentina or Chile."

Eitingon put the wine bottle down in the center of the table and looked fixedly at Ramón. "No, if they hear Spanish they'll suspect you're from Spain. You must blot Spain from your memory and the Castilian language from your identity. You've never been to Spain. You don't know a word of the language. Your mother tongue is French."

"So, I'm from France."

Eitingon thought for a moment. "But if you're from here, where is family? Friends? What schools did you attend? No, you can't be a Frenchman," he reasoned. "It might work in New York or Moscow, but it obviously won't work in Paris. You must come from another French-speaking country."

"Morocco? Algiers?"

"Do you feel like a Moroccan? An Algerian?"

Ramón's spine stiffened. "No, please! I'd rather not."

"I didn't think so. How about Belgium! That's the ticket! It's just north of France, the way Spain is just south. You can be Belgian.

That will explain your lack of family in Paris and any little discrepancies in your accent."

Ramón looked into the distance, imagining the implications of his new nationality. "And what about Trotsky?"

Eitingon waited.

"I suppose I must learn all about Trotsky if I'm going to be one of his adherents."

"No, no, no. You're not going to be one of them. That world is too small. You're not going to be like them, but acceptable to them as someone quite different. In fact, you should be from a world they don't know."

They finished a second round of oysters and watched with interest as the owner's daughter presented the bottle of Pétrus. Eitingon tasted it, blinked both eyes, then handed his glass to Ramón. "Yes," Ramón concurred. "It's excellent."

The stew arrived on a large white platter, in a rich and fragrant sauce containing small translucent onions, slices of carrots, and a sprinkling of parsley. "This rabbit tastes as if it lived on wild thyme," said Ramón after they started eating.

"Yes, it probably did. Remember the rabbits in Toulouse?"

"How could I forget?"

"What about your name? You might want to keep your initials. It's much easier with monograms and such. Something with an *R*? Robert?"

"My first name is Jaime—Jaume in Catalan."

"Well, then, something with a *J*."

"Jacques is a name I've always liked. I had a little friend named Jacques when we lived in Toulouse."

"Jacques suits you very well, but you should get rid of those steel-rim glasses. They make you look like a soldier or a German factory worker."

"You know what I would like to be," said Ramón. "I've always wanted to be an aristocrat."

Eitingon, knife and fork poised in midair, smiled at the young man, pleased that he wasn't an ideologue like his mother. "An aristocrat? Now that's antithetical."

"Antithetical to what?"

"To Marxism, Stalinism, Trotskyism for that matter."

"But there are natural aristocrats, people who are superior, who are simply born that way?"

"My dear Ramón, that's exactly what aristocrats tell us, that they are our betters because of the blood running through their veins. Because of their pedigree."

"But you know what I mean."

"Yes, I suppose so—that some people are exceptional, naturally superior." He cut a piece of the rabbit, pushing it through the sauce. "If that's what you want, posing as an aristocrat has a certain genius. Nothing would be more foreign to Trotskyists. You could be an aristocrat estranged from your family in Belgium, a black sheep on his own in Paris."

"Yes, and of course I like good food and wine."

# FIVE

Ramón lay in bed, thinking about Lena. He had sent her three letters from Paris but had yet to get a response. He knew that something must be wrong—in addition to Barcelona being a war zone.
Lena wouldn't let him worry. But if she hadn't gotten his letters,
if she thought he had disappeared . . . if she imagined that he was
being inconsiderate, then she would be angry. She had a temper,
much like her mother's, and remembering her mother, Doña Inez,
he could imagine the old woman hiding his letters, wadding up
the message on a paper napkin that he'd stuffed into their mailbox.
Doña Inez had always disapproved of him and done everything possible to direct Lena toward more suitable young men.

Staring at the ceiling, his eyes settled on a cloudlike stain near
the cornice that trickled down the opposite wall. He got out of bed,
pulled a robe over his pajamas, and put on his slippers. He went into
the bathroom, then out into the hallway, and down the staircase to
the flat just below his. The sound of a man's voice came through
the door. He listened until he was sure it was a radio broadcast, then
tapped on the door. "*Es Ramón*," he called through the door.

The sound of the radio stopped, a dead bolt shot, then a second.
The door opened as far as the chain allowed. Caridad peered out,
her eyes moving from side to side.

"I'm alone," he said in Catalan.

She shut the door to remove the chain, put down her pistol, then
let Ramón in. Her flat was almost empty. There was a radio set,
a rocking chair, a cigar burning in a saucer, various ashtrays and

cups, newspapers and journals. "You're smoking a cigar?" he said, wrinkling his nose.

"When I'm knitting. I don't have to keep stopping to light cigarettes. There's coffee if you want," she said, returning to the rocker and her knitting.

He picked up a pack of cigarettes, lit one, then went into the kitchen where an espresso pot sat on the stove. He tapped the chrome pot to see if it was hot, then struck a kitchen match to light the burner. "Is there anything to eat?" he asked.

"There's a box of soda crackers."

"No cheese? No butter?"

"This isn't a café."

He finished his cigarette, running it under the tap to extinguish it, then placed several crackers on a saucer next to his cup. When a wisp of steam began spiraling out of the spout of the espresso pot, he poured the thick, syrupy coffee into a small white cup, stirring in two spoonfuls of sugar. His mother glanced at him as he returned with his coffee and plate of crackers. "You slept late," she said, her needles clicking rapidly

"Don't tell Leonid. I'm supposed to be at the gymnasium."

She shifted her tongue in her mouth but refrained from speaking, her eyes riveted on the needle tips.

"Is that Cuban?" he asked, indicating the cigar.

"Yes."

"I was thinking about your family in Cuba."

"Your family, too," she answered, not quite glancing at him. "You are a del Rio as much as a Mercader."

She had told about the del Rio family in Cuba—the vast sugar-cane plantations in Cuba, the legions of servants, the fiestas, the beautiful horses and carriages. Her life had a mythic, perhaps fantastic quality that defied conventional logic. Had her parents really left Cuba to come to Barcelona so that she could learn penmanship from the sisters of Sagrado Corazón de María? The convent was famous for penmanship. The nuns taught their students to form perfectly rounded letters. Women of the highest class throughout the Spanish-speaking world recognized the handwriting.

He brought his cup to his mouth, closing his eyes slightly as he took a first sip. "Were the del Rios in Cuba aristocrats?" he asked.

Her needles stopped clicking as she reached for her cigar. "They were aristocratic."

"And very rich?"

"Yes, at one time."

"But not aristocrats?"

"They didn't have titles, if that's what you mean."

"Were your parents rich when they came to Barcelona?"

She took a puff from the cigar. "They probably thought they were rich. They were both spoiled. I doubt they knew anything about money."

He studied her, trying to reconcile the woman smoking a cigar with the stories about her past. Under the tutelage of the sisters, she discovered her religious vocation. She would have entered the convent and become a nun had Pablo Mercader not happened by while she was standing in front of her school with the other girls. He was the most conventional of men, as predictable as a clock. He spent his days walking back and forth from the family house to the family offices, both on Calle Ancha, the wide commercial street that ran parallel to the waterfront. He had never diverged from his well-beaten path until the day he saw Caridad, who stood out from the other girls, a head taller, her long hair as black as a raven's wing, her eyes green. He was almost twice her age, twenty-seven, yet he followed her home. The next day he was waiting in front of the school. For days he followed her until he summoned the nerve to speak. For a year he walked her home before asking her to marry him. Surprised that he didn't recognize her religious vocation, she declined his offer until her parents intervened. The del Rios wanted the alliance with the wealthy Mercader family.

"And the Mercaders," Ramón asked. "What happened to the money?"

"Your uncle stole it. You know that. Nicolas was the oldest and took control after the old man died. He sold the textile mills and went to Buenos Aires."

"No one could stop him?"

"They didn't know. He was going to invest in textile mills in Argentina and send money back to Barcelona. Everyone waited and waited, but the money never came."

"And no one did anything?"

"In the end, it was too late. And you know how your father is."

Ramón bit into a cracker, wishing for butter and jam.

"Why all these questions about the past?" she asked.

"Eitingon says my new identity should make sense. I'm wondering if it makes sense for me to be an aristocrat."

She nodded, her eyes focused on her needles, her lips moving as she counted stitches. "You're still Belgian?"

"I'm estranged from my family. I'm not sure why."

"You married the wrong woman. That will always do it."

# SIX

A new fedora on the back of his head, his overcoat folded over his lap, Eitingon sat in a chair near the ring watching Ramón spar with the Québécois, their jabs and feints informed by the multiple rhythms of the gym, the sound of a speed bag, a rope rhythmically tapping the floor. The Canadian had a thug's face and was fifteen pounds heavier.

"Ramón! Up! Up!" the coach was saying. "Left, left, right!"

Ramón wasn't terribly powerful, but he was quick and lean, sweat glistening on his olive skin. He danced in, jabbing with his left, then swinging with his right, he took a punch in the face. He staggered backward as the bell clanged, blood trickling from his nose.

"Here," Eitingon said, wiping away the blood.

Ramón tipped his chin, looking up at the ceiling while Eitingon packed his nose with a bit of cotton. Ramón was breathing heavily, his chest rising and falling, his forearms resting on his thighs, the large gloves dangling between his legs. He accepted the water bottle from Eitingon and drank, his Adam's apple rising and falling.

"Enough?" asked Eitingon.

Ramón frowned, not understanding what he meant.

"Had enough?"

Ramón shook his head. "I'm not going to quit because of a nosebleed. I'll go another round."

When the bell clanged once more, he stood up, rubbing the back of a glove across his mouth, and returned to the center of the ring. He knew he wasn't going to hurt the Canadian, but Ramón resolved to box smarter. Concentrating, biting his bottom lip, he jabbed at his opponent, feinting and fading away as he swung. They were both panting when the bell clanged again.

"Well done, Alonzo," Ramón said in French, clapping a glove on his opponent's shoulder. "That was a good thump you gave me."

He let Eitingon remove his gloves, accepted a towel, pressing it to his nose, then raised a water bottle to his mouth.

"You looked good!" Eitingon said.

Ramón smiled ironically then hung his head to catch his breath.

Ramón led the way to the locker room, where Eitingon removed a folded sheet of paper from his suit coat. "Are you ready?" he asked.

"Yes, I suppose. Let me put on my glasses."

"You have three minutes."

Eitingon consulted his stopwatch then waited as Ramón went down the list of French kings and the dates of their reign. The lists were growing longer and more complicated, but after two minutes, Ramón handed the paper back and began to recite what he'd just read.

"Very good," Eitingon said. "Your memory is remarkable. I don't understand why you did so badly in *prepa*."

Ramón shrugged. "I had a bad attitude and the cops wouldn't leave me alone."

"Now, some laps in the pool."

Ramón squinted at him, pushing back his damp hair from his forehead. "Laps? I thought Trotskyists were intellectuals, not sporting fanatics."

"No matter. I want you in top form mentally and physically. You might have to memorize documents quickly. We don't know what sort of physical challenges you might face. But tell the truth, you're enjoying this, aren't you?"

Ramón smiled. "Yes, I suppose I am."

The locker room smelled of sweat, liniment, wet towels, and soap. Ramón sat down on a bench to take off his plimsolls, then stood to undress. He was neither modest nor immodest. He was simply physical, a physical being. Except for pubic hair and beneath his arms, his body was almost hairless. To Eitingon, his skin looked satiny, his veins a coppery green beneath the surface. Naked, a towel over his shoulder, Ramón pushed through a heavy door to the pool, an echoing tile chamber of water, chlorine, and moving shadows. "Swim a few laps to warm up, then we'll check your times," said Eitingon.

Ramón made a face as he dropped into the shallow end of the pool, then pushed off. He looked strong but swam without style. When he stopped, he complained that his arms were tight from boxing.

"Yes, that's why we're doing this." Eitingon took out a stopwatch. "Now, let's get your time for a hundred meters. Next, we make it lower."

Ramón took a long hot shower then lit a cigarette at his locker and dressed leisurely, enjoying the feel and smell of his new clothes, the fine cotton underwear, the soft wool of his trousers. The morning out was cold and gray. "If you're going to pose as a Belgian aristocrat living in Paris, then you must not only look and dress like an aristocrat, you must also know the city," Eitingon said as they walked to the tailor's shop. The names of the streets and bridges, the arrondissements, the great monuments and parks, the Métro, the markets, and cafés, Ramón must know it all.

They stopped at a *zinc* for a coffee, a glass of white wine, and a smoke. The tailor's shop was nearby on one of the small streets behind St. Michel, a modest establishment that felt warm and inviting. The proprietor, Monsieur Emile, greeted them by name, bringing out two suits in progress, the pieces of fabric held together with large white stitches. Ramón put on the first suit and stood before the mirror while the tailor and an assistant moved around him, marking the fabric with chalk, pinning the seams to make small adjustments. "When these are finished, we'll need two for spring and summer," said Eitingon.

"For the summer in France?"

"Yes, and perhaps the tropics."

"Then a very light wool. Like this, perhaps," he said, pulling down a bolt of cloth. "Very fine wool properly spun and woven can be as cool and comfortable as cotton. It's what the Arabs wear in the desert."

Eitingon felt the fabric in a thoughtful way, moving it between the tips of his fingers. "Tell me, Monsieur Emile, what would . . . let's say, a young aristocrat have in his wardrobe? What would be authentic?"

"Ah, that would depend entirely upon the young man and the family," said Monsieur Emile, touching his thick mustache in a thoughtful way. "Of course, he would have suits for each of the seasons, heavy woolens for winter, lighter for the fall. And clothing appropriate for the various hours of the day. At least one smoking jacket for the high season, a white dinner jacket for summer and spring. A morning suit for weddings. Perhaps tails, but not necessarily. Then, of course, all of the furnishings—overcoats, raincoats. The trench coat has become very popular. Sweaters, shirts, scarves, hats, gloves, neckties. Pajamas, a robe, a dressing gown, slippers. And shoes. Shoes and boots that would be made to order. If he hunts, that is a wardrobe unto itself."

"This would be a significant investment?"

"Yes, but an investment made over time. Everything wouldn't be new. In noble families a young man might wear clothing that had belonged to uncles, his father, older brothers. If a jacket is of excellent quality and is one of many, then it will last forever. Quality is always what matters. Quality, not quantity."

"What about jewelry?" asked Ramón.

"Jewelry!" Monsieur Emile's eyes grew larger, verging upon alarm. "Discreet! It must be very discreet. Either gold or silver—perhaps a ring, but a ring only if it has special meaning, never decoration. Cuff links, studs, a cigarette case, and a lighter. Rarely gemstones and never diamonds."

"And if the young man is a playboy?" Ramón suggested.

"That might be a different matter. Most men of fashion look to the Prince of Wales as the beau idéal, but the nobility aren't necessarily fashionable. They believe they are beyond style, but, as you may have observed, there is always a certain tension between the world of fashion and the aristocracy."

Outside a fine mist had started to fall. "And what about luggage," Eitingon said as they stepped onto the sidewalk, avoiding two adolescent girls in overcoats strolling by, their arms linked, their shoulders pressed together in companionship. "You're going to need suitcases and probably a trunk."

"I like pigskin, and they say it lasts longer than calf."

"Well, prowl around and see if you can find something in the secondhand shops. Sudoplatov has given us carte blanche, but it wouldn't look right if everything you own is new." The Russian glanced at his wristwatch.

"Anything else?" asked Ramón.

"What do you mean?"

"That I should be doing. An assignment?"

"No, no, just familiarize yourself with the city, think about your new identity." Eitingon cocked his head, fixing Ramón with a look. "Is something the matter?"

"I don't feel as if I'm doing much."

"This is the waiting phase of the assignment, and that can be the most difficult time. You're an actor preparing for a great role. Don't worry, you'll eventually have your hands full." Eitingon smiled. "Anything else?"

"No, that was all."

"Then I will see you later."

Eitingon tugged the brim of his hat and shrugged deeper into his overcoat. Ramón watched him walk down the street, turning at the first corner. He knew better than to ask where he was going. He often didn't know what Eitingon and Caridad were doing or where they were. Collaborating with other agents? Reviving their old romance? The GPU was an opaque and secretive world, a series of cells, one separated from the next, all suspicious of the others. One never knew who might be an agent or whether one might be under surveillance.

Ramón had a persistent uneasy feeling. He had no sense of having joined an organization. No one had sworn him in as Soviet agent; no one had given him a secret badge or an identification card. Perhaps it was the nature of undercover work, but he felt excluded and alone, shut off from important information.

Left to himself, he strolled down to the river and walked along the quays, observing the barges. He would focus on becoming Jacques Mornard.

The air felt cold and liquid, the day full of possibility. He considered going down the steps to the footpath beneath the embankment where couples would occasionally make love. Everywhere he looked—in doorways, on park benches—Parisians were making love. He stopped at a balustrade, his attention captured by a fisherman, his line an angle to the pole, a reflection in the water. Because of the mist, the scene had a granular quality like that of a photograph. He told himself he would wait patiently until the man got a strike, raised the pole, pulled line. Like an unnoticed shadow, he would share the man's vigil. But then, as if waking from his own reverie, he started for the Boulevard St.-Germain.

St.-Germain-des-Prés was beginning to feel like home to him. Eitingon had told him about the famous cafés, which ones attracted artists, which ones were frequented by intellectuals and writers. In the winter, the cafés were enclosed with sheets of plastic, which made them feel like tents.

On his own, he had found a café where young women would sit at the tables for hours, nursing their *consommation* while waiters hovered. The girls were like him, works in progress, creations of self-invention. They scrimped to put together one outfit for the season—

a hat, a coat, a dress, gloves, and shoes they would wear day after day. When a girl was lucky, she attracted a man to buy her a meal and a glass of wine. For a bit more, she would go to a hotel nearby.

Ramón enjoyed listening to the girls talk about their clothes. Each had a special waiter who took an interest in their romances, who advised and mothered them. The waiter would groom a girl, allow her to linger at a table—conduct a little business on the side.

Remembering Eitingon's instructions, he went into an antique shop near the École des Beaux Arts where he found a silver cigarette case with the initials JM.

"Sterling?" he asked the clerk.

"Plate but it hasn't worn through. No one would know the difference."

He bought the case, transferring cigarettes from the package in his pocket. A handsome set of brushes caught his attention. "Those are sterling," the clerk said. "The backs are sterling; the bristles are set in ivory."

Ramón nodded. "I'll consider them another time."

He opened and closed the case, admiring it as he walked. Entering the café, he saw a girl with red hair who looked chic in a soft green hat, a green scarf, and gloves. She was playing with a little Japanese fan in a coquettish way, opening it and closing it before her face.

"Jacques Mornard," he said, offering her a cigarette.

"What a pretty case!"

"Thank you, my father in Brussels gave it to me. It's a family heirloom." He lit her cigarette, thinking he might take her to a hotel until he noticed that her teeth were rotten.

"Brussels?" she asked, opening the fan. "Are you Belgian?"

"Yes."

"You sound Provençal, like a friend from the South."

"Of course. I spent summers there as a boy. My mother's family had a place near Toulouse."

"That explains it."

"What is your waiter's name?"

"Bruno."

"Does he take good care of you?"

She smiled from behind the fan. "Oh yes, he is very kind. He is my family here in Paris."

# SEVEN

The voice came and went, falling beneath a persistent whining sound as if being drowned out by a siren. A dark layer of gray smoke hung in the room, clamping down on the atmosphere of anxiety, fear, and fatigue. Caridad sat by the wireless, hollow eyes staring straight ahead, focused on the strangely impassive voice rising and falling, speaking monotonously in Catalan. Holding a yellow pencil in her left hand, she took notes on a pad cradled in her lap. Eitingon stood at one of the two desks, speaking Russian into the telephone receiver.

"What are they saying?" he asked in French, lowering the receiver from his ear.

Caridad glanced up at him as if waking from a dream. "The names of streets," she answered. "Intersections in Barcelona."

"Where bombs have hit?"

"I don't know yet. I can't tell."

Ramón concentrated on the voice, listening intently for the streets near Lena's intersection. The Italian bombers, SM.79s and SM.81s, had been hitting Barcelona every three hours for two days. He pictured the formation of the planes, the silhouettes against the sky. He could hear the steady and distant drone of the engines, followed by a high-pitched whistling, a moment of appalling silence, then the terrible thud, the deafening explosion, waves of shock pounding the air, the stinging debris, the clouds of smoke rising above the wailing sirens.

As civilians, Ramón and Pablo had fought side by side in Barcelona when the city rose up against Franco's generals who tried to topple the Republican government in Catalonia. Families, friends, neighbors, and workers took to the street, fighting from block to block and barricade to barricade. It had been a glorious triumph of the people. Labor unions took over factories. Workers distributed arms, food, and clothing. For a brief time, it seemed that Spain would throw off the oppression of church, aristocracy, and army.

Now, two years later, Fascist bombs rained down: firebombs, gas bombs, and delayed-fuse bombs that would pass through roofs and building before exploding within, causing the maximum lateral damage mere inches above the ground.

"This is a repeat of Guernica," said Eitingon. "They're bombing civilians, hitting the working districts hardest. They're not even bothering with military targets. The Republican Army doesn't have anti-aircraft guns, no air cover."

"Guernica on a bigger scale," Caridad amended.

Cause and effect, an arithmetic chain of events unfolding, pitting Fascists against Communists. Leon Blum, the Socialist prime minister of France, opened the border to Spain; the Soviets shipped supplies across the border to the Republican Army in Barcelona, and now Mussolini was bombing the city into submission.

Unable to sit still, Ramón got up and walked to the window, pulling back the shade. It was odd to see people below, Parisians, strolling along the sidewalks, odd that it was a sunny March afternoon, still cold and a bit blustery. Eitingon had furnished the front room of the flat as an office—two desks, a telephone, a large black typewriter, the wireless, filing cabinets, and a heavy dark green floor safe. French, Russian, Spanish, and English newspapers were scattered around the room, stacked in drifting piles on the floor. Ashtrays overflowed. Cups and saucers covered every horizontal surface.

Ramón hesitated, then picked up his overcoat and headed toward the door. Caridad looked up, the yellow pencil poised in her hand. "You're leaving?"

"I can't sit here anymore," he answered in Catalan. "I'm going to Barcelona to look for Lena."

She frowned, not trusting what she'd heard. "You can't do that. The roads are closed. There's no way in."

"There's always a way. At least I can try."

"Leonid," she raised her voice, switching into French. "Ramón is leaving for Barcelona."

"What's this?"

"He's going to rescue his sweetheart."

Eitingon lowered the telephone receiver.

"I have to go," Ramón explained. "I can't sit here any longer."

Eitingon nodded, a serious expression on his face, then he smiled kindly. "Ramón, your impulse is noble, but Caridad is right. The roads are closed, the trains aren't running. How would you get there?"

"I don't know. I could catch a ride. Someone has to be going. I can walk if I must. At least we know the border is open."

"And if you managed to arrive, where would she be?"

"At home with her family."

"What part of the city?"

"The Eixample," answered Caridad. "It's a rich neighborhood, relatively safe. The area stands out on aerial maps. Fascists don't bomb the rich if they can help it."

"Then she's probably safe," said Eitingon.

"Yes, but I have to see her. I have to be sure." Ramón opened the door, starting out.

"You're acting like a fool," cried Caridad. "I won't allow it."

Eitingon put down the telephone, going to the door. "Ramón, it isn't a good idea, and we need you here."

"To do what?" His face flushed red with frustration and anger. His eyes were staring. "I've been waiting for months. I never know what's happening. You never tell me anything."

"Yes, waiting is difficult, but Caridad and I have been working our connections. We've been in touch with comrades in New York. Something is about to break and we'll need you here. We can't tell you exactly what's going to happen, but you're an important part of the operation. We're counting on you."

"I can't stay. I have to look for Lena."

Caridad stood up abruptly, her pad of paper falling to the floor. "If you leave," she shook the yellow pencil at him, "we'll report you to our superiors as insubordinate."

Eitingon wheeled on her. "Don't say that! Don't threaten him! He'll listen to reason." He turned back to Ramón and said in a calm voice, "We have comrades in Barcelona, GPU agents. I'll get in touch with them now."

"How? The phone and telegraph lines are down."

"They have a shortwave radio in Barcelona. We can send a message through an agent in Toulouse. It will take a while, but this will be far faster than you trying to go down there. We'll know something in a day or two. If you leave Paris now, it could be a week before you find out what has happened. Now, what is her address? Tell me her address and I'll telephone Toulouse. If her building hasn't been bombed, will that be enough information to satisfy you?"

"She could have been in a café," Ramón objected. "Or on the street."

"Yes, but for the moment. Can you sit still for the moment?"

Ramón tipped his head, a forlorn expression on his face, then shrugged off his coat.

For three days, he listened to reports of the bombing and pored over newspaper reports. The grip of anxiety loosened when he learned through the GPU agent in Barcelona that Lena's building was undamaged. The Eixample was barely hit. Caridad had been right, the Fascist bombs fell primarily on working class districts.


The trees were beginning to bud when Caridad summoned Ramón to her apartment. Eitingon was there, and both he and Caridad seemed excited; they had finally found what they wanted—a young woman, one of Trotsky's followers who was coming to Paris for the Fourth International meetings. She would arrive in Paris the first part of June, which gave Ramón a bit less than six weeks to completely inhabit his new identity as Jacques Mornard.

Not only did Ramón have to get Jacques's story straight, but he had to invent a story for everyone in his family. What did his father do in Brussels? What was his mother like? Did he have brothers and sisters? What were their names and what did they do? Where did they live? If his parents were wealthy aristocrats, they would need to live in an exclusive area at the right address. There was every possibility that one of the Trotsky delegates would be from Brussels and ask these kinds of questions.

Eitingon warned Ramón that all of these details and all of these stories had to remain consistent. Ramón couldn't make things up as he went along or he would forget what he said and trip himself up. He should write down all of the details, commit them to memory, then burn his notes.

To complicate matters and as an incentive for Ramón, Eitingon decided that Jacques Mornard should own a car. Ramón had never owned or purchased a car and was thrilled at the prospect. In addition to all of his research, he began looking for a suitable automobile—something a bit elegant but not flashy.

"Her name is Ageloff, Sylvia Ageloff," Caridad said at a subsequent meeting. "She comes from a rich family in New York, wealthy Jews who fled Russia before the revolution. They're very cultured, very well educated. She speaks Russian, French, and of course English."

"She's a Jew?" Ramón asked.

"Don't worry about that," said Caridad. "If she's Jewish, she can't expect you to introduce her to your family or friends."

"How did you find her?"

"Through the editor of a Stalinist paper in New York. His secretary knows her. She's also older than you. Twenty-seven."

"I'll give myself six years and say I'm twenty-nine."

"She's an intellectual. She has an older sister who travels to and from Mexico as a courier for Trotsky, and a younger sister who worked as one of his secretaries. The editor's secretary in New York will escort her to Paris. She will arrange the introduction."

# EIGHT

Sylvia Ageloff was studying French in the Hotel St. Germain when the front desk called to say Mademoiselle Weil was there to see her. *"Oui, oui! Très bien!"* Sylvia said, unable to think of the words to say *send her up*. She'd taken French in high school, but nothing would come back when she needed it. "One minute," she called, when she heard Ruby knock.

When she opened the door, Ruby, standing in the hall, had struck a pose to show off the black-and-white polka-dot dress she was wearing with a broad-brimmed black straw hat. Her eyebrows were plucked to pencil-thin lines and her large lips painted bright red. "How do I look?"

"Oh, very nice. Very glamorous."

"And look at you!" Ruby exclaimed. "Such a bookworm! Here you are in Paris studying your old French textbook!"

"Well, I want to learn some French."

"But you have to be with people who speak it. You'll never do it holed up in your hotel room, though this isn't bad. Not bad at all." Ruby strolled to the window, pulled the drapes to look across the Rue du Bac at the row of tall narrow façades, the stone stained almost black, the rows of balconies and windows setting off opposing and complementary rhythms. "Are you having fun?"

"Yes. Very much," Sylvia answered. She didn't consider Ruby a true friend, so she found it odd having her in the room, and it had been odder still sharing a cabin with her on the ship coming over. "And you?" Sylvia asked. "Have you been having fun?"

"My sister has shown me the most divine time."

"Is Corinne here in Paris?"

"Yes, off with some of her glamorous friends. She's been so generous, but I can't tag along the entire time. So, I thought I'd see if you
wanted to go out."

"I suppose I could do something."

"I know! Corinne gave me a letter of introduction to a man here
in Paris. I think he might be some sort of aristocrat. She said he was
very attractive. Let's call him."

"Ruby, I didn't come here to meet aristocrats."

"I'm not sure that's what he is, but let's call him. Let me use your
phone!" She picked up the receiver and made a face for Sylvia's benefit while she waited for the hotel operator. "Do you speak English?"
she asked. "Yes, I want to call out."

She gave the operator a number and a moment later was introducing herself, saying that she was at the Hotel St. Germain. "You
do? Really? You live that close? Yes, well, I'm here with my friend.
Let me ask her."

"He's just a few blocks from here and wants to come over."

"Ruby, I don't know."

"He sounds so French. I'll go down and meet him, and if he's attractive, I'll give you a call."

Ruby freshened her lipstick, touching the corner of her mouth
with the nail of her little finger. "How do I look?" she asked, turning to Sylvia.

"You look fine, very pretty."

Sylvia tried to go back to her book but Ruby had broken her con-
centration. She waited for Ruby to call so that she could say she really wasn't interested, then, as the time passed, began to think that
Ruby had forgotten her altogether. Finally the phone rang.

"Sylvia, you have to come down. I'm serious. If you don't come
down, I'm coming to get you."

"Oh Ruby!"

"Please!"

"I'll be there in a few minutes." Sylvia put her book aside and stopped to glance at the mirror. She was fair and slim. She felt pretty until she put on her glasses, which, despite the pale blue translucent frames, weighed upon her as a handicap. She occasionally dispensed with her glasses when meeting an attractive man—a dubious strategy that made the man blurry and her squinty—but she was confident that she wouldn't be interested in anyone Ruby knew. She ran a comb through her hair and applied fresh lipstick.

As she walked into the lobby, she felt a little shock of recognition when she saw a man sitting in one of the armchairs, smoking a cigarette. For a moment she thought he was someone from her past, or that he might be an actor she'd seen on the stage in New York or in a film. Sylvia found it vaguely reassuring that he was wearing glasses, a pair of tortoise-shell horn-rims. Ruby was sitting at his side, her eyes shining with pleasure. He rose as Sylvia approached, making a little bow. "Ah, you're the other girl from New York."

She nodded, taking in the accent and his casual, elegant clothes.

"And you're from here," said Sylvia, resisting the urge to take off her glasses.

"I live in Paris, but no, not from here. I was just telling Ruby that I'm Belgian, but you would never guess where I was born."

"Not Brussels?"

"No, it's more complicated. Tehran."

"Is your family Persian?" She smiled.

"Do I look Persian? No, my father was ambassador there. But you didn't come to Paris to hear such things."

Sylvia noticed that his English sounded formal and a bit old-fashioned, as if he had learned it from a textbook. "Did you go to school in England?" she asked. "You speak English so well."

"No, my parents sent me to an English primary school in Brussels. I don't have the chance to use it so often, and if you listen long enough, you'll encounter some rusty spots. I was just asking Mademoiselle Weil what she'd seen of Paris. It's a beautiful day and my car is on the street. Nothing would give me more pleasure than to show you a bit of the city."

Ruby was nodding eagerly, but Sylvia, sensing something, a connection between the two, decided not to interfere. "No, thank you. I'd better not."

"Sylvia!" Ruby complained.

"You're very kind, but I'm not free."

"Sylvia!" Ruby hissed at her, taking her arm and pulling her aside. "What are you doing?"

"Go ahead. You'll have fun."

"But I can't go alone. I don't know him. Please, do this one last thing for me."

Sylvia looked at Jacques pretending to ignore the exchange and, for some mysterious reason, found herself compelled to say, "Okay, but I have to go up to my room to get my handbag."

When Sylvia returned, Jacques led the way out to a gleaming black Citroën. Knowing how flirtatious Ruby was, Sylvia insisted on sitting in back, assuming she would be quickly forgotten. The interior, the tan leather seats, smelled liked saddle soap. The day was warm, the pattern of light and shadows on the street swaying gently beneath the trees. "Ah, pardon!" Jacques said as the car lurched abruptly from the curb. He smiled at Sylvia in the rearview mirror. "The clutch is new, a bit stiff I'm afraid."

From the backseat, she watched St.-Germain-des-Prés pass by, catching a glimpse of an ancient square down a small side street, a pocket of smaller, darker buildings. Compared to Paris, New York had no past. Sylvia was aware of the layering of time in Paris, the great freight of history bearing down on the present, threatening to break through the scrim of her perceptions.

Turning onto one of the broad rectilinear streets that Haussmann had cut through the medieval heart of the city, suddenly they were crossing a bridge, the towers of Notre Dame leaping up before them in all their Gothic gloom. Slowing the car to a halt, all of them craning their necks to the windows, Jacques pointed out the flying buttresses and the gargoyles.

They crossed the Ile de la Cité then turned west on the Rue de Rivoli, passing a gray stone flank of the Louvre, then the open expanse of the Jardin des Tuileries before arriving at the Place de la Concorde, a vast square paved in stone. Sylvia felt the cool spray of mist from the fountains blowing in the breeze, beading the windshield, the silhouette of the Egyptian obelisk rising to be echoed by the Eiffel Tower in the far distance. Jacques pointed out the Petit Palais, the Grand Palais, and the Hotel Crillon; then, leaving the parklike area, they were heading up the Champs-Élysées, the traffic becoming thick and loud, the Parisians blowing their car horns incessantly, the air growing dense with exhaust fumes. All of the traffic merged in a great gyre rotating around the Arc de Triomphe, which stood apart and impassive like an enormous packing crate. Jacques maneuvered the car from lane to lane until breaking free of the centrifugal force; they went sailing off onto a tree-lined avenue lined with stately houses that led them into the leafy calm of the Bois de Boulogne. "This is quite peaceful, almost like being in the country," Jacques said as they watched a group of young women in riding habits cantering past on horses, the hooves raising powdery little echoes of dust.

Leaving the park, they crossed the Seine once more, then drove up along the Left Bank, returning to the St. Germain-des-Prés where rows of café tables beneath plane trees beckoned to them. This was the Paris Sylvia had dreamed of. This was summer, heightened by that feeling, that reality that war was coming, that it was all about to change, that it would never be the same again. With the dusty afternoon light filtering through the trees, Jacques looked at home in his suit, the young women reflected in his dark glasses.

Struggling with French, Sylvia and Ruby marveled as he spoke to the waiter, disappearing into that other language and culture, becoming someone unknowable. But he wanted to make it all accessible to them. He knew the right apéritif to drink on a warm summer afternoon. He had that thing called *savoir faire*. Perfectly barbered and scented, the shadow of beard visible beneath his fine olive skin, he was European down to the tips of his nicotine-stained fingers. But beneath the languor, he was alert, tightly wound, and finely tuned—almost as if there were two people occupying the same skin. When he spoke about his family, it was with an inaudible sigh, a deep hurt. "My mother, you would have to know her to understand. She's beautiful and charming and forceful. I love her but hate what she stands for. She's from a noble family in Brussels and is intent on perpetuating the aristocracy."

"And your father?"

"He is from a family of merchants, wealthy but not aristocrats. Of course, they disapprove of the way I live here in Paris. It's an old story. I'm the third son. The money I have from the family isn't enough, so they think I should have a rich wife or a career to earn money."

"And what would you like to do?"

His lips tightened and suddenly he looked grim. "That's the problem. I'm not suited for anything."

"But there must be something you love doing."

"Yes, but it's difficult to get a job as an alpinist."

"Mountain climbing?"

"You see, it isn't really a career unless you are famous for your exploits, climb the north face of the Eiger like the Germans. The truth is, I haven't had the chance to climb so very much, just enough to get the taste."

"It isn't frightening?"

"Exhilarating. The higher you go, the more difficult it is, but also the more beautiful. Everything is clean and pure. It's just you and the mountain, unless you're with a team." He laughed. "But I like sports and am studying journalism. Perhaps that will lead to something."

"Does your family worry about what's happening in Germany?" Sylvia asked.

"Of course, everyone worries. Hitler is a fool and perhaps a madman, but what can anyone do? He uses the hatred of Jews to his advantage. Everyone is anti-Semitic. It's a fact of life. Even my parents, if they saw me sitting here in this café with two attractive Jewish girls from America, they would very much disapprove."

Sylvia laughed to mask the little sting of bigotry. "Isn't that rather archaic of them?"

"Everything about nobility is archaic. But that's their problem because I do what I want. I hate politics. I hate hearing about politics. I take people for what they are."

He signaled to the waiter for the *addition*. The day was coming to an end. Dusk was falling. It was the blue hour, the sky turning to indigo then cobalt. Birds flocked into the treetops, and somewhere in the neighborhood church bells tolled. Jacques paid the bill and grew distracted and remote as they left the café.

"I can walk to my hotel," Sylvia offered. "It's just a few blocks."

Jacques smiled sadly. "This has been so pleasant, I hate for it to end."

"Yes, we've had so much fun," Ruby agreed.

Again the smile that suggested a fundamental sadness, perhaps the dread of being alone. "I don't want to monopolize your time, but I know a perfect little restaurant, the sort of place Americans such as yourselves would never find on your own. The cuisine is superb. If you've no other commitments I would like to invite you to dinner this evening. I can take you to your hotel. Everyone can rest a bit, refresh themselves, then I'll return at a proper time."

Ruby looked to Sylvia.

"You would be doing me a favor," Jacques entreated.

"Oh, Sylvia! We have to!" Ruby exclaimed.

· · ·

That evening, Sylvia dressed with care, choosing a tailored navy skirt and jacket, with a white blouse that tied at the neck. She studied her reflection with her glasses, then without, her image becoming softer, the lines blurring. Jacques wasn't the sort of man she had gone out with in New York. He wasn't an intellectual who cared passionately about ideas and politics. He was as an archetype she recognized from movies and books, an aristocrat, a rich playboy. He had to know countless people in Paris, and, if Ruby was any sort of indication, he was attractive to women in a superficial way. She turned her face slightly for a more flattering angle. For a moment her mind went still, then, giving herself a small shake, she decided he wasn't her sort.

Nevertheless, at dinner, after a glass of wine, she removed her glasses to look prettier in the candlelight. Jacques talked about Paris, barely glancing up when Eitingon and Caridad came in to take a table across the room.

Jacques was telling Sylvia and Ruby about the best places to hear jazz, the most exciting shows, but food was his favorite topic. When the waiter came, he discussed the menu and wines at length. He knew the recipes, what made the various dishes special. He spoke with confidence that there was a correct way to eat and drink, that these quotidian things in life were fundamentally important. When their plates came, he insisted on carving the chicken, handling the cutlery like surgical instruments.

"There's so much to see in Paris," he said. "Of course, you have to go to Montmartre for the very best view of the city. But when you say Montmartre, most people think of the Moulin Rouge, but the view from Sacré Coeur is sublime and there are wonderful little streets and small excellent cafés. It's like a village up there. Indeed, it is a village. I can pick you up in the morning at eleven. There's so much to do and it would give me so much pleasure."

# NINE

She pulled a strand of black yarn from the skein, keeping her eyes on the tips of her quickly moving knitting needles, not looking at him. "No news from Lena?"

"Just a note, finally."

"What does she say?"

"That she wants to stop writing for a while."

"Why?"

"It's too difficult, she says. Her mother gets upset when my letters arrive."

"And how do you feel?"

"I don't like it, but if that's what she wants . . ."

Caridad sighed, raising an eyebrow as she reached for a cigar. "So, the Weil girl is leaving. That will make things different."

"Yes, I'm sure Sylvia will be timid without Ruby along as a chaperone."

"Where are you taking her?"

"Versailles, to see the château."

Caridad nodded. "It will give you a chance to get the Citroën out on the road. And Americans love palaces."

"Is that true?"

"That is my understanding." She glanced up at him. "So now the real work begins."

"The real work?"

"The seduction," she said.

"Oh yes, that."

"How will you proceed?"

"It shouldn't be difficult. She studied psychology. I'll confide in her the problems I'm having with my difficult mother."

The right corner of his mother's mouth lifted in the precursor of a smile. She took a puff from the cigar and peered into the smoke as she blew it out. "Do you have any hint that she might suspect you?"

"Of what?" he said, waving his hand at the smoke.

"Of deceiving her."

"If I keep arriving in a cloud of cigar smoke, she's going to suspect that I'm having an affair with a man." He brushed a piece of imagined lint from the navy blue *JM* monogrammed on his cuff, wondering if maroon wouldn't have been better for the pink shirt. "She doesn't have a high opinion of aristocrats. In her mind, I could hardly be worse than what I've claimed to be."

"But that doesn't mean she won't fall in love with you."

"No, of course not."

"Does she guess that you're so much younger?"

"No, I seem to be aging rapidly."

"And where will you take her to dinner tonight?"

"I thought that small place on Vieux-Colombier."

"It's a shame she wears glasses. She has no *chic* whatsoever."

"She doesn't care about fashion. She's an intellectual, a bit like you, Mama."

# TEN

Their heels clicked on the parquet as they strolled through the royal apartments at Versailles, their reflections floating through the clouded glass of the immense gilt mirrors. Sylvia moved slowly, stopping to read long passages in her Baedeker. When they came to an exit, Jacques went out to one of the great staircases to smoke a cigarette. He missed Ruby, chatting away mindlessly, flirting. But now he would focus on Sylvia. He sensed that he needed to go very slowly, that to get her attention he would have to offer her a puzzle.

He turned when he heard her coming. She was carrying her guide, wearing high-heel sandals and a yellow cotton dress. "I'm sorry I took so long," she apologized. "I didn't mean to keep you waiting."

"You didn't. We can stay as long as you want."

"The château is beautiful, isn't it?"

"It is a gloomy place for me."

"Really? With all of those chandeliers and mirrors?"

She gazed up at him, holding her right hand against the glare of the sun, her face reflected in the dark lenses of his sunglasses. "Do you want to see the gardens?"

"It's getting rather warm. I believe I saw a café when we drove through the village."

"Yes, that's fine with me. I've seen enough."

They walked to the parking lot then drove down the long narrow lane lined with plane trees, a plume of white dust rising in their wake. In the village, they stopped at the sidewalk café, where they chose a table in the shade. He placed their orders then lit a cigarette. "I suppose Versailles and the revolution are more interesting for someone with your family history."

"What do you mean, my family history?"

"Ruby told me how your family fled Russia before the revolution, that the Ageloffs were a rich family in Russia."

Sylvia laughed. "That's preposterous."

"It isn't true?"

"I can't imagine where Ruby got that."

"She's not a close family friend?"

"No. I don't really know Ruby all that well. She was a friend of my sisters until they quarreled about politics. She stopped speaking to them when they accused her of being a Stalinist, but then she started calling when she heard I was coming to Paris."

"And the Ageloffs weren't wealthy Jews. They didn't flee Russia?"

"Far from it. My father was from a small village in the Ukraine. He arrived in New York in the late 1890s, long before the revolution. He was a young boy, penniless and all but illiterate. He still doesn't speak English very well."

"But you're well educated."

"Yes, it was important to him because he had so little. I don't know how he learned."

"He's still alive?"

"Yes, of course, but there's a funny story about him. He built an apartment building that opened just before the market crash in 1929. Whenever anyone mentions the Ageloff Towers, someone invariably says, 'Oh yes, Ageloff. He jumped off his skyscraper when the market crashed.'"

"Was it a skyscraper?"

"Yes, I suppose you could say that."

"He arrived penniless but built a skyscraper?"

"He'd gotten into the construction business. He's been successful."

"It must be true what they say about America, that anything is possible."

"He was always good with numbers, and he wasn't afraid of taking risks. And I suppose he was lucky."

"Yes, luck is important," Jacques agreed.

He took a swallow of the wine when the waiter brought it, a nicely chilled rosé. Sylvia did the same. "May I see your glasses?" he asked, holding out his hand.

"My glasses?"

"I want to look at the frames."

She removed her glasses and handed them to him. "They're very nice," he said after examining them. "The blue brings out the blue of your eyes. I don't think we have them like this here in Europe. Do you hate wearing them?"

Sylvia smiled bravely. "I don't think any girl wants to wear glasses."

"I rather like mine. I think they make me look intellectual, which, of course, I'm not. But it's different for a man. Have you tried dark glasses?"

"No, I never have."

"Here, try mine," he said, handing his glasses to her. He laughed when she pulled them to her eyes and recoiled in surprise. "My lenses must be stronger."

"Or at least different," she agreed.

"But let me see how you look. Close your eyes if you need to. Yes, that's nice. You should consider getting a pair of sunglasses. They make you look like a film star."

"A film star? Jacques, be serious," she said, removing the glasses.

"But I'm serious. I'll take you to my optician in Paris."


As they drove back toward Paris, Jacques tuned in a radio station that played the occasional American song. Both of them smiled, and hummed along with Fred Astaire singing, "Nice Work If You Can Get It."

*Holding hands at midnight,*
*'Neath a starry sky*
*Nice work if you can get it*
*And you can get it—if you try*

Jacques seemed quite happy until they reached the outskirts of Paris, then he fell silent, letting Sylvia see the shadows surrounding him, letting her wonder. "I'm afraid you might be tired of my company," he said when he stopped the car in front of her hotel. "But I wonder if you would have dinner with me again tonight. There's something troubling me. I believe you understand me, that I can talk to you with confidence."

Of course, Sylvia agreed. That evening they walked from the hotel to the restaurant, Jacques looking particularly handsome in a dark pinstripe suit. He held Sylvia's chair for her, ordered an apéritif, and discussed the menu with the waiter. Finally, settled into their own pool of candlelight, he let his eyes roam across Sylvia's face, then took a deep breath and sighed. "I don't know how to tell you this. I'm afraid you won't think well of me, that this might be the last time I see you."

She tipped her head to one side.

"The truth is I've made a mistake, a very large mistake in my life, and I don't know where to turn. I've told you about my mother, that I'm very close to her. I've always done everything I could to please her."

"Yes?"

"You must understand that the world I come from is very different than yours. We aren't free the way you are. What your father did could never happen in Brussels. We're always aware of the past. History guides us in everything. We always feel this obligation to family."

"Yes, I think I understand."

"When I was younger, too young to know better, my parents selected a girl for me to marry. Yes, Sylvia, it is still done that way. The girl wasn't from the nobility, but my parents wanted an alliance with her family for business reasons. She is a very nice girl but not interesting, at least not to me."

He studied his hands resting on the table before him, then took a cigarette from his case and lit it. "Well, I did what my parents wanted and married her. I tried to please everyone, but in the end I couldn't." He smiled sadly. "Here, the civilized thing would be to take a mistress. Marriage is about family and property. Romance is something else. But I want to be loved for myself and to love some-one who understands me. That's why I'm here in Paris."

"Yes?"

"I've asked for a divorce, but she refuses and my parents have taken her side. They say I'm being immature, that I have to keep my end of the bargain."

"Your end of the bargain?"

"Yes, that's how they think."

"Are there children?"

"No. If there were I could never leave. And meeting someone like you, someone who is free, I now realize that I must."

"You can't stay married to a woman you don't love. Your parents have to understand. They can't stop you, can they?"

"They can stop the money," he replied.

"You're still young. You're well educated. You can start a career."

"You don't know what it's like for us here in Europe, so burdened by the past, history, hemmed in by all of these traditions. *Change, start*—those are not words that mean the same thing for us. We see life in a different way."

"But if you're unhappy then you must change. There are always exceptions. We only have this one life. We have so little time, we have to make the best of it."

He placed his right hand over her left and gripped it. "Sylvia, I'm so glad I've met you."

# ELEVEN

It gives your appearance a bit of dash," Jacques said, studying Sylvia's reflection in the mirror. He'd selected a small straw hat, lacquered white, that sat jauntily to the right side of her head.

"You don't think it looks like a plate?" She smiled.

"No, not at all. It is the size of the smaller one. The saucer."

He turned to the saleswoman and started speaking rapidly in French. Sylvia understood the words *drôle, gamine, mignonne*. For Jacques, it seemed only natural to take Sylvia shopping. Sylvia knew nothing about fashion, and he'd had spent so much time listening to the girls at the cafés talk about clothes, he could guide her to the right shoes, the perfect belt. He'd taken her to a hairdresser for a stylish short cut, and, with his guidance, she'd started tying a small silk scarf round her neck and rolling up the short sleeves of her blouses the way she'd seen boys do.

"Yes, the hat gives you flair," he pronounced, taking out his billfold, the saleswoman nodding in agreement.

Sylvia's friends staying at the Hotel St. Germain noticed the handsome, well-dressed Frenchman arriving each morning at eleven, bringing Sylvia's mail from the American Express office. He would smoke a cigarette while he waited for her, then escort her out to the black Citroën to whisk her away.

Imagining she would hear brilliant speeches and debates, Sylvia had come to Paris to observe the Fourth International meetings, but following the murder of Trotsky's son, the secretary of the organization, Rudolf Klement, had decreed that no more than two people would meet at a time—a sure way to discourage infiltrators. There would be no congress, no general meetings in Paris, and almost nothing for Sylvia to observe.

Happily, Jacques was there to entertain her, planning outings, taking her to restaurants, to museums, and concerts. He bought her thoughtful presents—a bouquet of violets, chocolates, a small basket of ripe plums. He did nothing abrupt that would startle her, but listened closely to what she said and praised her intelligence, insight, and sympathy. He occasionally alluded to the future in a wistful way, gazing into her eyes a moment longer than necessary.

"Sylvia, someday I want to show you the Pyrénées. Did you know there are glaciers? Yes, that far south, great flows of ice that sparkle in the sun. That's where I go mountain climbing. The villages are beautiful, the food and wine superb. There's nothing more satisfying than climbing to the top of a peak, and looking down on the world. But Sylvia, if you came along, I wouldn't need to climb. We would stay in small inns, take long walks, sleep like angels."

At the Hotel St. Germain, Walta Karsner, noticing Jacques and the change in Sylvia's appearance, was the first to congratulate Sylvia on taking a lover.

"Walta!" Sylvia laughed, blushing a deep pink.

"Sylvia, this is Paris. It's what you're supposed to do." A Californian, Walta rarely did what was expected of her. She had grown up in a wealthy family of Methodists in Sacramento, but went to Barnard College in New York, where she married a Columbia student who was both a Jew and a Communist. She tended not to see boundaries where others did.

"I'm sorry to disappoint you, but Jacques isn't my lover."

"Why ever not? He's very sexy."

"Yes, Jacques is charming, but he's really not my type."

"What do you mean?"

"He's not an intellectual."

"Who cares? He's very handsome, and, you know what they say about Frenchmen."

"What do they say?"

"They'll kiss you in places American men wouldn't dream of."

"Walta!"

"That's what they say."

"Well, it doesn't matter. He has no interest in politics or the things I care about. He's not very reassuring about Hitler, and I don't think he knew that Franco's troops had cut Spain in half."

Walta's husband, Manny, and the other men attending the Fourth International meetings showed little interest in Jacques, but Walta was always eager to be in his company. She spent a morning with them, exploring the leafy gravel paths in Père Lachaise, looking for the tombstones of Chopin, Balzac, Proust, and Bernhardt. Afterward, Jacques took them to lunch and a swimming beach he knew on the Marne.

Lying in the sun, wriggling the toes of her long white feet, Walta watched Jacques on the diving board. He was focused, self absorbed, his body perfectly proportioned, the muscles gliding smoothly beneath the olive skin.

"How did you meet him?" Walta asked.

"A girl from New York."

"He reminds me of boys who went to Stanford. You know, rich, athletic."

"Yes, he trains every morning at a gymnasium," said Sylvia.

"What kind of training?"

"Boxing, swimming, fencing."

"He must be wonderful in bed."

Sylvia smiled but said nothing.

"I'm always hearing that intellectuals make better lovers, more imaginative and sensitive. But some of them are so cold, and at least athletes realize they have bodies."

"I suppose."

"Oh, Sylvia, please don't tell me that you haven't."

"Walta, the situation is complicated."

Walta was silent for a moment. The diving board bent and re-bounded with a hollow wooden sound; Jacques sliced through the green water to surface, his hair close to his skull.

"You mean it's him?" Walta said, giving Sylvia a pitying look.

"No, of course not, but . . ." Sylvia heard the hesitation, the catch in her own voice. ". . . we're very different."

"Oh brother!" Walta groaned, rolling onto her stomach.


Ramón looked around his flat with dismay, wondering how he could possibly bring Sylvia there. The rooms—one bedroom, a bath, a foyer, living room, dining nook, and small kitchen—had come furnished with an ugly brown sofa, a green armchair, a bed and chest of drawers, a battered dining set. He had no rugs or drapes, nothing to make the place seem like a home—much less a love nest. Ramón knew how to cook but regarded home decoration as treacherous territory, filled with mysterious rules and the opportunities for many faux pas.

A lamp? He needed a lamp or two. Or three. The overhead lighting was harsh.

Curtains and a rug? He wouldn't know where or how to start. He couldn't ask Eitingon or Caridad for help. Their flats looked worse than his, filled with battered office furniture. Perhaps he could find candlesticks for the table, a picture of some sort to hang on the wall.

He would invent some sort of story as to why Jacques Mornard lived in such a place. There had been a fire. All of his possessions were destroyed. He needed a few framed photos of family members and friends, something to indicate a life, at least one photo to place on top of his chest of drawers. The bed? He would ask the concierge where to buy linens and how much to pay.

In the most intimate way, he found his identity as Jacques Mornard to be inhibiting. Seduction came naturally to Ramón. Flirting was a diversion, a pastime. Like most Spanish men, he put his *novia*

Lena on a pedestal, but other girls were fair game. He and Sylvia had reached that delightful phase of suspense when something had to happen. Wherever they looked, they saw couples kissing—on bridges, in doorways, on park benches—men and women locked in deep, soulful kisses. Paris was working its spell. Sylvia looked at him in a different way. She retreated into herself, waiting for him to follow. He was an expert at reading these signs, but now he was self-conscious and observed himself as well as Sylvia.

"This is temporary," he explained, the first time he took her to his flat. "I lived with a friend from Brussels who had one of those big flats filled with all sorts of antiques and family things. I never needed anything except my clothes, and now that he's moved back to Brussels, I'll have to get my own things."

Indeed, the rooms were bare, bereft of photographs, books, and art—the usual clues to an identity. Sylvia noticed the riding boots and crop in one corner of the bedroom, picked up the hairbrushes he'd found in an antiques shop and had engraved with his initials. "Do you like those?" he asked, coming behind her as she rubbed his fingers across the carved letters. "They belonged to my grandfather. The bristles are set in ivory, the backs are solid sterling."

As he leaned forward, she turned, looking up into his eyes. He removed her glasses, then his. "I've been wanting to do this," he said as he kissed her. "I don't know why I've been hesitating."

When he kissed her she responded warmly. "Sylvia, perhaps we shouldn't."

"No, it will be all right. I want to."

As he unbuttoned her blouse, he felt a little wave of triumph, that he was succeeding, advancing his agenda. She let the blouse slip from her shoulders, lightly freckled, her skin white and soft when he reached behind her to unhook her brassiere. When she turned away shyly, he made himself busy for a moment by pulling back the bedspread, then going to the windows to close the shutters, dimming the afternoon light. When next he looked, she was beneath the sheet, blond head propped against the pillows.

"Do you need something?" he asked.

"No, only this."

Smiling at her, he undid his necktie, then sat down on a chair to remove his shoes. "You look so pretty. Making love in the afternoon . . ."

"Seems a little wanton . . ."

"That was not what I was thinking."

Unbuttoning his shirt, he went into the bathroom, washed his hands, then rubbed a bit of toothpaste across his teeth. Returning in a navy blue robe, he sat beside her on the edge of the mattress and put his hands on her shoulders as he leaned down to kiss her. After a moment, she slipped toward the middle of the bed so that he would lie down beside her. He removed his robe and pulled back the sheet to touch her breasts, tracing his fingertips across her skin.

He imagined he might feel distant making love to her; he had done that, had sex in a mechanical way. So, as they made love, he was surprised by how in tune they were and by the rush of affection he felt for her.

Afterward, she watched as he lit a cigarette. "Walta was right."

"About what?"

"She said Frenchmen make excellent lovers."

"But I'm Belgian."

"Yes, of course."

He touched her collarbone, a touch of affection.

"Everyone thinks I'm your mistress."

"That I'm keeping you?"

"No, not that. They think I'm your lover."

"Do you care?"

"Not really." She was silent for a few moments, watching him smoke, finally deciding. "Would you like to go somewhere?"

"Yes, of course," he answered. "But where?"

"There's going to be a meeting of the Fourth International at a village outside Paris. It's all very top secret, the only general meeting when everyone will see each other. Would you like to come?"

"If it's so secret, can I be there?"

"I'll ask. I think it will be fine. Everyone knows who you are."

"Which village?"

"Périgny. Old friends of Trotsky's have a house there, Alfred and Marguerite Rosmer."

"Will it be boring?"

"Probably. But Walta and Manny are going. We could all drive together."

"I suppose. When is it?"

"Soon. I'll check the date."

"Yes, I'll go, but promise it won't be too boring."

# TWELVE

Somewhere out in the woods, a cuckoo called, making a hollow knocking sound that underscored the silence of a country day, as did the clank of each cowbell and the buzzing of every fly. It was hot, almost three in the afternoon. Dressed in a suit and sunglasses, he stood next to a hedge of rhododendron, smoking cigarettes, mopping his face with a handkerchief as drops of perspiration trickled from his armpits down his side.

A large rumpled man was speaking in a heavy German accent, droning on about security threats to the Fourth International and rumors that GPU agents were attempting to infiltrate, while at his side stood Étienne, a boyish-looking man, with wide-set eyes and a sensitive mouth—the perfect face for betrayal.

"Who is the German?" Jacques whispered when Sylvia walked over to take his arm.

"Rudolf Klement," she whispered back. "He's the secretary. He's in charge."

"Ah!"

"You look restless."

"Yes, this is tedious. You know how I hate politics."

A man near the front raised his hand to ask a question. They were in the garden at the side of a stone farmhouse with a shingled roof. The gathering might have been a faculty party or a parish meeting. "Madame Rosmer asked if you were my fiancé," Sylvia whispered.

"Who?"

"Jacques, you really must pay more attention. Alfred and Marguerite are our hosts."

"I'm sorry. It's just so hot."

"We'll leave for Paris soon."

"It's getting so warm in the city. I want to get away."

"Yes, we'll leave soon."

"No, I mean get away from Paris. I was thinking how pleasant it would be in the Pyrénées, where I know a lovely little hotel run by a family. We could eat excellent food, hike during the day, and sleep under blankets at night."

"That sounds divine," Sylvia said, squeezing his arm. "Could we invite Walta and Manny?"

"We can, but do we really want them?"

"It would be easier for me to tell my family I was going if we were chaperoned."

Jacques rolled his eyes.

The meeting was finally coming to an end. Marguerite Rosmer, a stout woman wearing a black straw hat and a black-and-white floral dress, approached them. She had a cheerful face, lively blue eyes, and a capacious bosom. "We're having tea and refreshments," she said to Sylvia in careful, school English. "I hope you can stay."

"I'm afraid we must get back to the city," Sylvia answered.

The older woman turned to Jacques and spoke rapidly in French.

"What was that about?" Sylvia asked after Marguerite left them.

"Nothing, really. She was asking about my family."

They started toward Jacques' car, collecting Walta and Manny along the way. Driving back into Paris, Sylvia told them about the Pyrénées—the villages, the food, the trout pulled from icy streams.

"Oh yes!" said Walta.

"That sounds fine, but we can't travel the way you do."

"What do you mean, Manny? We'll drive down together."

"Walta and I can't afford to stay in fancy hotels and eat in first-class restaurants."

"Don't worry," said Jacques. "The hotels are modest. You'll be our guests."

"No, Jacques, you always grab the check, which is damn generous of you. But we need to pay our own expenses. If we go, we stay in hotels we can afford. You can't make all the decisions."

"But I'll buy the wine. I can't stomach bad wine."

# THIRTEEN

**B**ut has she fallen in love?" asked Caridad. She was knitting rapidly, now red yarn with the black.

Ramón helped himself to the pack of cigarettes on the table. Eitingon was sitting in an armchair, reading a newspaper. "No, I suppose not," Ramón admitted. "Not yet, at least."

Caridad pulled a strand of the black yarn impatiently. "You have to make her fall in love with you. If not, you can't control her. You need absolute control."

"I hate to hurt her."

His mother's lips curved into the slightest smile. "Hurt her?"

"Break her heart."

"Don't be a fool. This is a war. Countless people are being killed. Countless more will die."

"She's so unsuspecting."

"You're giving her a wonderful time, a romance, something to remember Paris by." She continued knitting, frowning at the needles and yarn. "It's too bad she wasn't a virgin."

"I didn't think she would be."

"Has she said anything about her lovers?"

"Not directly, but there is a professor in New York she talks about."

Caridad pulled a longer strand of red, then held up what was becoming a small sweater with horizontal stripes. "It isn't gratification that seduces a woman, it's mystery. Isn't that right, Leonid? It's not what you give, but what you hold back."

Eitingon glanced over from the newspaper. "Yes, of course."

"What are you suggesting?"

"Sylvia isn't a schoolgirl. She's an intellectual. You're going to have to do something interesting to get her attention."

"Like what?"

"You could disappear."

"Disappear?"

"As myopic as she is, that shouldn't be difficult. That would give her a puzzle, a mystery."

"Do you mean leave Paris?"

"No, but make it look as if you did. You have to keep an eye on her. But you let her simmer, cook. When she's ready, you come back for her."

"But how do I disappear?"

"You invent something. You have a family emergency in Brussels. You can write Sylvia from there through one of our comrades in Brussels. You'll know from her letters what she's thinking. You pay one of the clerks at her hotel to tell you what she's doing. You observe her at a distance. You follow her from time to time. It will be interesting, a little game to play."

"That sounds cruel."

"Yes, doesn't it?" She continued to knit as she gave the matter more thought. "But if you want your disappearance to have the greatest impact, you should prime her, set her up for it. Plan something special for her to anticipate."

"I've been telling her about the Pyrénées. We've been planning to go away."

"That should do it."

"But what if I ran into her by chance? We'll be in the same city, the same arrondissement."

"You know her habits, where she goes and when. You should be able to avoid her as easily as you can follow her." Caridad shrugged her shoulders. "And if you encountered her, you would think of something. You had just returned and were coming to see her."

"And if she looks for me here at our building?"

"She doesn't have a key to the door downstairs. We tip the concierge. She won't talk."

"Well, I suppose."

"Of course. Think of all the time and money you'll save."


Now that Jacques and Sylvia had the mountains in mind, Paris was intolerable. The streets were hot and dusty. Parisians were leaving in droves. Getting away was the only sensible thing to do. Already dressed for a holiday—Sylvia in a loose cotton skirt Jacques had picked for her; Jacques in white cotton trousers and a linen shirt—they strolled down Boulevard St.-Germain to meet Walta and Manny and plan their journey.

Dusk had settled. Yellow lights hung in the trees over the café, a favorite gathering spot for the Fourth International. As they approached, they saw Walta and Manny and other familiar faces, then felt a distinct chill in the air.

"Oh, Lord!" said Walta. "You haven't heard. You didn't get the note I left at the hotel."

"Heard what? We've been to dinner."

"Rudolf Klement is missing."

"Who?" asked Jacques.

"You saw him at the meeting at the Rosmers'. He's the secretary of the Fourth International."

"He isn't missing," Manny said angrily. "He's been kidnapped by the GPU."

"We don't know that yet," Walta objected.

"We're talking about Rudolph," Manny insisted. "He's never late. He didn't show up at the office yesterday or today. Something happened."

"He's not at his apartment?" asked Sylvia.

"Tom and I went by his place. The door wasn't locked and his dinner was waiting on the table. The evening paper was next to his plate, last night's paper. He never touched his food. It looks as if he was about to eat when someone knocked at his door."

"The GPU snatched him," said another man. "If he's not being tortured, he's already dead."

"You've notified the police," Jacques asked.

"There's nothing they can do."

Perhaps it was their arrival, or perhaps it was mere coincidence, but the group began to break up. Feeling the presence of danger, Sylvia sank down into the chair beside Walta. Jacques took the one beside hers and signaled to the waiter.

"Well, what now?" asked Walta.

No one answered.

"Are you still going to the Pyrénées?"

Sylvia and Jacques looked at each other. He shrugged, tipping his head as if toward an exit. "I want to get away."

"Yes, we might as well go," said Sylvia. "All of us. There's nothing we can do here."

# FOURTEEN

Her heart racing, Sylvia woke in the middle of the night certain that someone was in her room. Groping in the dark for her glasses, she was about to scream when she felt a man's hand cover her mouth and heard Jacques whisper. "Ssshh! It's me. Don't be afraid." The mattress gave and the springs squeaked as he sat down beside her.

"Oh!" she let out a gasp of relief. "I was so frightened."

"No, no, no. It's only me."

"Jacques, what are you doing here?" Everything was blurred, soft with sleep—pillows, sheets, nightgown.

"Ssshh! I couldn't leave without telling you."

"Leave? Where are you going?" she asked, reaching out for the lamp.

"No, don't turn on the light. I don't want to disturb you. I'll be gone before you know it."

"Gone?" she said, pushing up on her elbows.

"Brussels. My parents have been in an accident. I have to leave immediately."

"Jacques, were they hurt?"

"My brother came to get a surgeon and we're leaving now. It's very bad. The chauffer was killed, and my mother may have to have her leg amputated. Somehow, my father wasn't injured."

"Oh Jacques!"

"I know, our trip to the Pyrénées . . ."

"That doesn't matter. When will you come back?"

"I'll write as soon as I can."

"Do you want me to come there?"

"No, of course not." He held her for a moment, then was gone before she was fully awake, the door closing behind him.

Later, when she woke again, Jacques's appearance and departure felt eerie and dreamlike.

"How did he get past the porter and the desk clerk?" Walta asked when Sylvia called to say they would have to postpone their trip.

"They must have been asleep."

"But they lock the door to the street. And you lock the door to your room."

"I don't know," Sylvia answered. "Perhaps Jacques tipped the porter."

"But why would his brother come all the way to Paris to get a surgeon if it was an emergency? There must be good surgeons in Brussels."

"Maybe it was a special surgeon. Or perhaps their surgeon was here in Paris."

"Why wouldn't his brother telephone or send a wire?"

"Walta, why so many questions?"

"It just sounds strange."

"I know, but I'm sure Jacques can explain when he comes back."


Ramón climbed into the car, deciding that it was perfect cover, an old gray Peugeot that gave him a clear view of the entrance to the Hotel St. Germain. The car smelled like the rotting raffia of the upholstery, and there was a suspicious-looking pint bottle filled with a golden liquid that proved to be motor oil. He sorted through the glove box and found a map of France tucked above the sun visor.

Waiting there, he felt invisible. Should Sylvia come his way, he would hold the map in front of his face—a strategy that was simple but effective. He had noticed, however, that city people like Sylvia rarely looked into cars to identify the occupants; whereas the natives of small towns, who expected to know everyone, always tried to identify the people in passing vehicles. Seeing was a function of habit and expectation.

Shortly after eleven, Sylvia and Walta came out of the Hotel St. Germain, Sylvia wearing a white short-sleeve blouse, the sleeves rolled up as he instructed, a small scarf tied at her neck. They stopped on the sidewalk to talk, then Walta reached out to touch Sylvia's shoulder and they both laughed. Observing them, Ramón experienced a surprising flash of resentment—that Sylvia was proceeding without him, that she showed no signs of needing him. He had felt the rupture of his daily life and missed the routines he'd established with her.

Glancing at his wristwatch, he guessed that she was going to the American Express office to get her mail. As Sylvia and Walta turned the corner, he got out to follow. He stood in a doorway when the women stopped to part ways, then Sylvia went on to the American Express office. Ramón slipped into another empty car—Parisians so rarely locked their cars—and was waiting when Sylvia came out, carrying her mail. He knew that she would go to her favorite café. There she would sit at one of the shady tables fronting on the sidewalk, order a café au lait, and read her mail.

From yet another parked car, he watched as she opened an envelope, and was sure it was his letter she was reading when she put her hand to her mouth in shock. He had labored over the description of his parents' accident, how they had been driving in from their country estate to spend a day in Brussels when his father told the chauffeur to stop the car so that he could urinate, a realistic touch, he thought. His father was standing next to the road when a twelve-ton truck hit the parked car, killing the chauffeur instantly and injuring his mother, who was now in critical condition, waiting to learn whether the surgeons would amputate her leg. Sylvia's silent gesture of shock gave him a sense of satisfaction, followed immediately by twinges of remorse.

Ramón had asked Sylvia to write to him in Brussels in care of a Madame Gaston, a family friend, explaining that with his parents in a state of crisis they must be discreet. Madame Gaston sent Sylvia's letters back to Paris and mailed his replies back from Brussels with a Belgian postmark.

Their letters went back and forth, settling into a steady correspondence. Ramón made a habit of following Sylvia to the American Express office; he would then walk slowly behind her to the café. Watching Sylvia from a distance, he couldn't know for sure what she thought or felt. He felt a flash of anger when the possibility that Caridad's little scheme might backfire crossed his mind, that his disappearance might cause him to lose Sylvia. Sylvia wasn't like other women. She was the antithesis of Caridad. Sylvia wrote warm and affectionate letters. His spirits lifted when he saw her handwriting on an envelope, the dark blue ink on the delicate onionskin envelope that made a crinkling sound when he opened it. In the meantime, he received nothing from Lena.

With Paris emptying *pour les vacances*, with shops and restaurants closing, the city took on a mournful abandoned air. He felt a bit disconnected, ghostlike. When he saw an item in *Le Monde* about Rudolf Klement, for a moment he couldn't connect the rumpled, professorial man he'd seen speaking in a garden in Périgny with a torso stuffed into a large suitcase floating in the Seine. The newspaper said that Klement's head, arms, and legs had been so cleanly severed that the authorities suspected the work of a surgeon.

"Is this us?" he asked, passing the newspaper to his mother.

She read the notice. "What do you mean, us?"

"The GPU? Did we do that?"

"Leonid and I knew about Klement, but he wasn't our target."

"Why make it so grisly? Why chop up the body like that?"

"It's efficient."

"The only way to get his body into a trunk?"

"Well, yes, but as Stalin has demonstrated, if you instill terror in people, you don't have to lock them up or kill them. They will do what you want."

"Was Klement such a threat? He didn't look like one to me."

Caridad studied Ramón for a moment as if she were perplexed. "He was a key figure in the Fourth International. What he looked like is of no importance."

# FIFTEEN

Later that day, from a distance, he observed Sylvia's reaction to Klement's death. She looked anxious and weary. All of her brightness was gone, the vitality. She had taken on a grayish pallor, a fearfulness that made him want to reach out to her. He was so close to her, he could reach out so easily. He felt terrible deceiving her.

Then, four days later, like a weird echo, her letter came back from Brussels.

*Shocking, terrible news! The police found Rudolf Klement's body floating in the Seine. I can hardly bear to write this, but whoever killed him (Stalin's henchmen, everyone says) cut off his arms, legs, and head and stuffed him in a suitcase. I no longer know what I'm doing here in Paris and must make some decisions about going home. I had a letter from my boss saying he can only hold my job until September 15, then I will be replaced.*

*I would feel better if I only knew where you were and what had happened. You've become such a mystery to me. I thought I saw you today. It was such a vivid and strange sensation.*

*Have you heard that new song? I'll be seeing you in all the old familiar places. It's strange how haunting a song can be! But truly, I wonder if I will see you again. My family has been writing, urging me to come home. They're very worried about what's happening here in Europe. I think I might be able to stand the greater uncertainties if I only knew about you. With much love, Sylvia*

After reading the letter, he walked to the garage near his flat where he kept the Citroën. He was sick of following Sylvia around, playing a silly game of his mother's devising. He had no plan other than to go for a drive, to get out of the city. But being in the car was a tonic—the feel of a hot breeze coming through the windows, shifting gears, the power of the engine. He'd thought vaguely of returning to Versailles but found himself on the road to Lyon, drawn in some inexorable way, as if each mile he drove was another reason not to turn back, as if a plug had been pulled and water was rushing down a drain.

It was August, the time when one is meant to leave Paris, to get away. He would treat himself to a night in Lyon. He knew the restaurant where he would dine, the dishes he would order. He would stroll around, walking past the culinary school where he studied, find a little hotel where he could sleep.

From his car, he began to see glints of river in the distance, the terraced vineyards climbing up the hills. Farm trucks sat beneath shade trees next to the road, filled with tomatoes and peaches and plums. He thought of Provence, the fields of lavender, the groves of olive trees. The scent became stronger, the pull of the South, the gravity of home.

Stopping on the edge of Lyon to buy gasoline, he counted his francs—enough for an expensive meal and a night in a hotel—or enough for three or four days if he was careful. He drove into the city, following the spires of the basilica, then parked on the street near the restaurant he remembered liking. He studied the menu in the window for a few minutes, then walked toward the basilica, strolling along the Rhône—or perhaps it was the Saône—as dusk fell and the streetlamps and shop lights came on. When he saw a telephone office, he hesitated a moment. He knew Caridad would start looking for him, but he couldn't bear the thought of hearing her voice, her assumption that he would do what she wanted, her voice hectoring and badgering him. No, he would not call her. He had to shut her out in order to listen to himself. He had come this far. That was his decision, and now he felt whole and free again.

He bought bread and sausage, which he ate sitting in the Citroën, studying a road map. Lyon was a bit out of the way, too far east. But he could drop down to Aix then head back along the Riviera to Perpignan and eventually Cerbère. He asked a man to point him toward the road to Aix then started south. The traffic was light but slow, mostly trucks trundling along at fifty kilometers an hour. He passed through Valence, stopping on the outskirts of Aix near a gas station where he slept in the backseat of the car. When he woke, listening to the insistent drone of cicadas in the trees, he felt as if he were once more a boy in Toulouse.

He got the car gassed up, found coffee and bread, then started east through Languedoc-Roussillon, the landscape becoming increasingly wild and rugged, the road winding and turning. The sun was strong, the air hot, dense with the smell of motor oil and melting tar, the scent of juniper, rosemary, and pine. At intervals, small, carefully cultivated valleys came into view with vineyards, olive groves, and lavender fields, followed by wild and rugged terrain, craggy boulders and ridges, stony hilltop villages. He saw gulls and sensed the air changing, then, coming over a ridge, in the distance he glimpsed the white, snowcapped peak of Canigou floating spectral in a misty band of blue haze that lay between land and sky. His breath caught at the sight of the mountain; the road dropped down from the ridge, the Mediterranean came into view, reflecting the curve of the earth, the swells rising and falling, marking the passage of time. He was close to home, Barcelona, just hours away.

The train station at Cerbère felt oddly quiet at two o'clock in the afternoon. "Barcelona?" the man in the ticket window repeated. "No, there's nothing for Barcelona."

"Nothing?"

"The border is closed."

"And for cars?"

"As well. There's a war, you know."

Outside, on the street he saw a Gypsy leading a dancing bear on a chain. The man, dressed in flashy black pants and shirt with a rakish black hat, looked weathered and weary. The bear, a metal collar around its neck, was filthy, its heavy coat matted and dusty. Ramón lit a cigarette, offering the pack to the Gypsy, who took two, saying one was for a friend.

"Where do you cross the border?" Ramón asked in Catalan.

The Gypsy lifted his chin and pointed inland toward the foothills with his pursed lips.

"In a car?"

"Walking or on horseback. There are paths."

"Do you mean the crossing at Puigcerdà south of Toulouse?"

"No, much closer. There's a dirt road that goes through the forest. When it starts up into the hills, you see an opening for a trail into Catalonia."

Ramón got back in the car, starting north on the blacktop until he saw a well-used dirt road that ran inland toward the hills. When he found the trail, he drove back to the train station in Cerbère, parked the Citroën, and flagged a taxi, calculating that the chance of the car being stolen or vandalized would be greater on a dirt road so close to the border.

He paid the taxi driver, then started down the rocky trail. He needed a bath and a shave, but he looked relatively respectable in a white shirt and pair of gray slacks. He was in Catalonia once more, three hours from Barcelona by car or train. He stayed on the trail till it came to a dirt road, where he turned back toward the coast. When he saw a woman in a battered straw hat hoeing in a garden next to a farmhouse, he stopped to ask for water. Wiping her brow, a smudge of dirt on her cheek, she brought him a tin cup from the well. She was in her forties, her face lined and faded, her lips chapped. Despite her age and a certain heaviness that emanated from her body, he could see her prettiness.

"Water tastes better on this side," he said in Catalan, wiping his lips.

"You came from France?"

"Yes, just now on the path. But I'm a native of Barcelona, trying to get home."

"You weren't there during the aerial attack?"

"No, but I hear it was bad."

She nodded gravely.

"Do you know anyone who goes that way? I would pay for a ride. I had to leave my car on the other side."

She considered, looking into the distance. "What day of the week is it?"

"Wednesday, I believe. Or is it Thursday? I've been on the road."

"Don Tomas should be going. He goes every Thursday to sell his cheese at the market on Friday. He stays with his daughter in the city."

"And where can I find Don Tomas?"

"The next house on the road. Tell them that Matilda sent you."

Ramón thanked her for the water and continued walking. He saw goats grazing in a field before the house came into view, an old Peugeot truck in front of a low stone shed. A man wearing a straw hat and a dark suit was loading enamel buckets into the back of the truck. A black-and-white collie barked at Ramón and ran toward him, alternately cowering and wagging his tail. The man hushed the dog, then pushed his hat back to get a better look at the stranger approaching. Ramón mentioned Matilda, that he was hoping for a ride to Barcelona and would be happy to pay.

The man shook his head. No, he wouldn't take money. They were going anyway.

"For the gasoline," Ramón was saying when the farmer's wife appeared from the house in a flowered dress and a straw bonnet.

"Jaume, it's just for petrol. It's only fair."

Bustling to get away from home, she was carrying a black handbag, a covered straw basket, a large tin can filled with flowers, and a lumpy package wrapped carefully in wrinkled brown paper and string. In France, Ramón had imagined that his country was dying, but, as ever, the farmer and his wife were going to the city, taking their cheese to the market. Ramón took the basket and flowers from the woman and offered to help load the buckets of *recuit*, soft, creamy cheese.

In the truck, he was afraid they would ask too many questions, but when he said he had been living in France with his mother, they assumed that she was French and that he had dual citizenship. They were far more interested in talking about their daughter who had married a medical student in Barcelona. "A good boy, a brilliant student," the farmer said.

"But an anarchist," the woman worried.

"So many were anarchists in Catalonia."

"And they'll pay the price with Franco."

Ramón sat by the door, his arm out the window, the woman in the middle beside her husband. It was dark by the time they reached Barcelona. The headlights picked out piles of rubble, wooden barricades, shattered storefronts, and abandoned cars. The streets were almost empty, pedestrians hurrying along as if pursued. The farmer and his wife insisted on taking him to Calle Ancha, the wide commercial street that ran parallel to the waterfront.

He stopped at a pharmacy to buy a toothbrush, then walked to his father's building, noticing the gaping hole across the street. He still had the key he'd carried since he was thirteen, which still opened the heavy, battered wooden door. He switched on the sickly overhead light in the black-and-yellow tile foyer, the same pallid yellow as old piano keys. The stone flags of the curving staircase sagged with age, the light above dying as he reached the landing. He pressed the button on the wall plate for the next landing and continued up another flight, stopping in front of 2B, raising the heavy brass knocker shaped like a dolphin and tapping firmly.

His father before him had grown up in the apartment, and he had been born there. After what seemed a great while, he heard his father inside coming from what sounded like a great distance.

A dead bolt snapped back, then the door opened. "Ramón!" The name followed a sharp inhalation of air. *"Ay, hombre, que gusto!"*

Tall, his head bald, his shoulders rounded, his father looked older and sadder. He had tied a black band of ribbon around his left sleeve and draped a white sheet over the vestibule mirror. He offered his hand, then embraced his son. "Come in. What are you doing here? Can you stay?"

"For the night, if you don't mind."

"The house is empty except for me. Your old room is waiting for you."

A lamp burned in the long hallway to the kitchen. He led the way to the back of the apartment, his carpet slippers whispering on the worn tiles. "I sit in here," he said, referring to the kitchen, which had never been meant to be seen, much less lived in. Everything was utilitarian and roughly made, worn by decades of use. A bare bulb hanging from a chain cast a greenish glow. A rocking chair had been positioned near a window for the sea breeze. A radio, newspapers, an ashtray, and cigarettes waited on a small table within easy reach. A small bowl of water on the floor belied the presence of a cat.

"You must be hungry. Would you like an egg? An egg and bread?"

"Something to drink, perhaps. A sherry?"

"Yes, of course. *Un fino.*"

He pulled a bottle from a shelf and dusted off a small clear glass.

"Won't you have one with me?"

The old man looked surprised. "Yes! Why not?" He filled a second glass, raising it to Ramón, who patted his own sleeve to indicate the black ribbon.

"Is that still for Pablo or for more recent deaths?"

"Oh yes." He glanced down at the ribbon. "For Pablo but so many others. And so many still to come. You noticed the building across the street? Or what was once a building?"

"Of course. I couldn't miss it."

"It was frightful, the bombing. Three days, every three hours. Forty tons of explosives they dropped, the constant sirens. I sat here and waited. What could I do? Most of the time we had no electricity, no lights or water. During the day, I could go down the stairs to talk to my neighbors, but at night I sat and rocked."

He took a sudden and quick swallow of the sherry, emptying the small glass. "It will be so much worse under Franco. I'm glad I'm old. I won't have to live through much of it."

"How many years do you have now?"

"In December I complete seventy."

Ramón nodded, tacitly agreeing that that was indeed many years.

"The last I heard you were on the front in Aragon. Then I lost track of you."

Ramón drank his sherry. "I've been in Paris."

"With Caridad?"

"Does that surprise you?"

"No, why should it?" He raised his eyebrows and shoulders in unison; there was nothing he could do. "You always had to take care of her, even as a little boy."

"I never thought of it that way."

"Is she still working for the Soviets?"

"Yes. I as well."

"And how is that, working for the Soviets?"

"It's limbo. You never know where you are, always waiting."

"I won't ask what it is you're doing." He filled their glasses again. "Well, the alternatives . . . You must be hungry."

"I haven't had much for the last day or so, being on the road."

"Marta made tuna with vinegar and onions."

"She still comes in?"

"Not so often now."

"Do you mind?" Ramón asked, going to the old icebox and opening the door.

"Of course, you are the chef. Make what you like. I'm afraid you won't find much to work with."

Ramón removed a saucer from the top of a bowl to examine the tuna. "This will be fine. You must have crackers."

"Yes, there in the bread box—where they always are."

He ate from the bowl, scooping the tuna onto crackers with a fork.

"You're going to Ripollet?"

"Ripollet?"

"To see Montserrat and your brothers."

"No, I hadn't thought of it, but I will now that you mention them. I've come to see Lena."

"Ah, the young Miss Imbert. You still feel that way?"

"Yes, of course. Some things don't change."

"And what about her?"

Ramón grimaced. "I'm not sure; that's why I had to come. She sent a postcard in March to say she had survived and didn't want me to worry about her. But she had almost stopped writing before then and nothing since."

"Ah, and so you worry."

"I would have gone to her tonight, but I needed a bath and a change of clothes. I hope I can find something here."

"Look in the cupboards in your old room. I'm not sure what's there."

Ramón finished the tuna, then went down the hall through the parlor where there were framed wedding photographs, the ugly vase that never broke, the heavy green sofa where his father pretended to sleep when Ramón was a boy, letting him riffle his pockets for coins and draw faces on his bald head. The air was heavy with the Mediterranean, the sounds of the docks. The room he'd shared with his brothers was filled with mementos of the past, discarded books and games, old clothes and photographs; a home that had been shattered, then, in bits and pieces, became a refuge for the children. Pablo Mercader, so much older than Caridad, was like a grandfather to his children.

Ramón opened the cupboard. One of the shirts folded and

stacked on a shelf looked as if it would fit, as did a pair of trousers that he held up to his waist. He went back to have another sherry with his father, then lit the hot water heater and took a long bath, scrubbing his nails, lying in the milky water until it grew cold.

In the morning, he went to a barbershop for a shave and haircut, then bought a single red rose from a woman selling flowers from a tin bucket. Smelling of talcum and hair tonic, carrying the rose, he walked toward the Eixample, the grid of streets where the corners of the blocks were rounded off, making octagons rather than rectangles. Before the war, sidewalk cafés with awnings and umbrellas had made the intersections seem like little parks, but many of the storefronts were boarded up and trash littered the sidewalks. As if it were a winter morning with a cold wind blowing, people walked quickly, hurrying from the disaster. On every block or so, families loaded furniture and household belongings into old trucks and cars. A gull perched on a pile of rubble.

The Imbert family lived in Passeig de Gràcia, one of the more affluent sections of the Eixample. He climbed the steps to their building but stopped as he was about to press the bell to their apartment. Someone was playing a piano, somewhere in the building. He stared at the name Imbert next to the vertical column of buttons. Then he went back out and down the steps to the street, where he lit a cigarette and leaned against the fender of a car, looking up at Lena's window. He would will her to come out. He would send powerful thoughts that she couldn't resist.

The time passed slowly. He thought of Sylvia in Paris and wondered what she was doing. He smoked a second cigarette, then a third. A church bell rang nearby. A flock of nuns moved down the sidewalk, medieval in black robes and starched white wimples. He wondered if they were from Sagrado Corazón de María, the convent where Caridad had acquired her perfect penmanship. She and Eitingon would be furious with him for disappearing, which gave him a delicious feeling of satisfaction. Let them rant. Let them rave.

He was in Barcelona to see his *novia*. He paced around the intersection, keeping a constant eye on Lena's door. Then, finally, when he thought it would never happen, the door opened and Lena appeared.

She stopped when she saw him, her eyes lighting up. "Ramón!" His name came in a dramatic rush, as if someone had struck the strings of guitar. "What are you doing here?"

"I brought you a rose, but you must mind the thorns. The woman didn't have tissue to wrap it in."

"But why didn't you ring the bell? When did you get here? You're supposed to be in France."

He smiled, giving her the flower.

"Why didn't you let me know you were coming?"

"I didn't know. I was driving to Lyon and suddenly I had to see you. I didn't stop or turn back. I didn't have a change of clothes. I just kept coming." What he claimed for his credit, following his heart, was what he would pay for with Caridad.

"Has something happened?" he asked. "You stopped writing and then, when I got here, I was afraid you wouldn't see me."

"Why wouldn't I see you?"

"I don't know. Perhaps I wanted to surprise you."

Looking up, she studied his face in her earnest way. Her dark chestnut hair was parted on the side like a schoolgirl's. She had gray eyes, long lashes, and thick black brows. Her lips were a deep rose color, a bluish touch of lavender. Putting his arms around her, he could smell soap and the freshly ironed starch in her white cotton blouse. Her silky hair against his cheek was fragrant. Her body, her flesh was softer than Sylvia's. These were older and more familiar sensations that threaded through his life, linking present and past, making sense of his history. They embraced for a moment, then she took a deep breath, pushing away. Looking up at him, she squinted as if trying to adjust her vision.

"Lena, has something happened?"

She compressed her lips, shaking her head. "No, Ramón. Not here. I can't do this."

"But we have to talk."

"Do you want to come in?"

"No, there's that café around the corner. Is it still there?"

"But I can't stay," she warned.

They walked to the café. Anxious, his mouth gone dry, he couldn't think what to say. Sitting down at the table across from him, she shook her head in a puzzled way.

"Lena, I . . ." he began.

"Ramón, you've been gone for months and months. And before that . . ."

"Yes, the war, it's a terrible time."

"But you're in France now."

"The war is bigger than Spain."

"You're there with your mother?"

"Yes." He had to send a telegram.

"What do you want from me?"

"What I've always wanted—to marry you."

"Do you want me to come to Paris with you now? Is that why you're here?"

He hesitated. There was Sylvia to think of, Eitingon and Caridad. "No, not now. That wouldn't work."

"No, of course not." She looked away as if for a moment she had thought of someone or something else.

"But when the war is over . . ."

She shook her head. "Ramón, you're"—she paused, looking around and lowering her voice—"you're working for the GPU. Isn't that true?"

"Yes."

"Don't you understand what that means? I can't leave my family. We're too deeply rooted here. This is my life."

"But after the war."

"We would never be able to come back. When the Republic falls, Franco will start rounding up Stalinists in Catalonia to march them in front of firing squads. It's already happening in the South."

"I'm not a Stalinist."

"Then why are you working for the GPU?"

"It's an important mission, an opportunity."

"In the end, it won't matter why or what you believe. You won't be able to come back to Spain. Not openly. Not to live."

"There are places where we could live."

She bit her bottom lip, then let it go with a little fluttering puff of exasperation.

"Magdalena, is there someone else?"

"No. Yes. It has nothing to do with you. I had to stop living in the past."

"Who is he?"

"You don't know him and it wouldn't matter. He would be a good husband, a good father. I'm not in love with him, not yet, but I hope someday I might."

Lowering his eyes, he noticed her hand on the table beside the rose, her chubby fingers with the long, rounded nails. As he reached out, her hand curled up and pulled away.

# SIXTEEN

Sylvia felt she was entering hostile territory when she stepped off the train in Brussels. Moreover, she felt lost without Jacques. He would know where to go, the perfect little hotel, a charming café. But without him, the city was stale and dreary, sweltering in the August heat. She checked into a commercial hotel near the train station, washed her hands and face, then sat down on the side of the bed and gave the hotel operator the number Jacques had given her for Madame Gaston. As she waited for the call to go through, Sylvia imagined Madame Gaston as a kindly, pleasant-looking woman, a faithful family retainer, perhaps the nanny who had raised Jacques.

She sensed something wrong the moment she heard Madame Gaston's voice. Rather than French and genteel, she spoke English with a German accent that was curt, even suspicious. "Jacques Mornard?" she said as if she were confused. "Jacques Mornard?"

After muffling the phone to confer with another person, Madame Gaston came back on the line and told Sylvia to meet her at a café near Sylvia's hotel.

The woman who arrived had sallow skin, gray, oily hair, and was carrying a big cheap handbag. "So, you are Miss Ageloff," she said, sitting down at Sylvia's table. "You look like you might do him some good."

"I'm sorry. I don't understand what you mean."

"You know what he's like. He's a rich playboy. You're not exactly his sort, are you, dearie?"

Sylvia's felt the blood come to her face as if she had been slapped. Was the woman remarking that Sylvia was a Jew? Sylvia chose to defend Jacques and disregard the slight.

"He has good qualities. Are you a friend of the family?"

"A friend of his family? Oh no, they're far too grand for the likes of me. He's a friend of my son. They trained together."

"Trained for what?"

"Officer training. Jacques didn't tell you he was in the army?"

"No, it never came up. He's been writing to me but suddenly the letters stopped. I started to worry that he wasn't well. He said I could call you if I needed to see him."

"And you took the train all the way to Brussels to find him?"

"I needed to get out of Paris."

"Well, he's not here. He went to London on family business. How long will you stay?"

"Just tonight."

"He might return tomorrow. Call me tomorrow and I should know something. I will investigate."

"What time should I call you?"

The woman observed Sylvia in a shrewd way, her arms wrapped around the large handbag resting in her lap. "I don't know. In the afternoon."


Sylvia walked to the main square but the soaring Gothic arches failed to lift her spirits. She returned to her hotel room, where she spent dismal hours trying to read, thinking how different Brussels would be with Jacques. That night, when she finally slept, Sylvia had frightening, fleeting dreams that left her exhausted and uneasy. She ate breakfast in the hotel dining room, where the coffee was weak, the rolls stale. She watched the clock until it was time to check out of the hotel, then telephoned Madame Gaston.

"Sorry," Madame Gaston said in her curt way. "He's still in London and won't be back anytime soon. I don't know when he'll return."

After the line went dead, Sylvia placed the receiver in its cradle. She sat on the edge of her bed, feeling lost and confused. Nothing made sense to her. She had to consider the possibility that Jacques was lying to her, but she couldn't understand what possible motive he might have. She wanted to talk to her sisters or to someone she knew and trusted. She finally stood up and looked around the room to make sure she hadn't forgotten anything, then picked up her small suitcase. She had come looking for Jacques. Now, she understood that he had disappeared. She left the key at the desk and walked to the train station.

# SEVENTEEN

Ramón watched the front of the building for a few minutes from the car, then got out to cross the street, letting himself into the heavy timber doors with his key. He noticed the curtain move slightly in the concierge's window, then he switched on the light in the stairwell, which did little to dispel the gloom or his mounting sense of dread as he climbed the stairs, the stone treads scooped out by the passage of time, the countless passage of footsteps. As he reached Caridad's landing, the light went out. He hesitated for a moment, then found the light switch for the next landing and went up to his apartment. He was empty-handed except for a rumpled brown paper bag that held the razor, toothbrush, and toothpaste he'd bought, an old shirt, and a pair of trousers he'd brought from his father's flat. He inserted his key into the lock, felt the bolt move, then swung the door open to a scattering of notes on the floor, a mute blast of Caridad's anger and frustration.

Moaning, he squatted down on his heels to gather up the pieces of paper marked with the distinctive penmanship, the letters perfectly rounded. The rooms were warm and stuffy with the summer heat. He opened a window, pulled the shade, then went into the kitchen to draw a glass of water. Sitting down in the living room, he lit a cigarette as he read through the messages.

*Hijo, where are you?*

*Ramón, has something happened? C*

*Ramón, what is happening? Let me know where you are.*

The messages built to a crescendo of anxiety and anger, then they stopped. Reading through them, despite their hectoring tone, he almost felt sorry for her, but then his twinge of guilt reignited a flash of anger. He sat still for moment, finishing the cigarette, gazing around the flat, then, facing the inevitable, got up to go downstairs to her door.

He listened for a moment to the din of her radio, then tapped the signal they had agreed upon—two quick knocks, then a third. He heard scrabbling at the lock then she flung the door open. "Oh, my God! It's you. Finally. I've been insane with worry."

He flinched as she tried to embrace him. "Don't," he said. "Don't do that. You're angry. Go ahead!"

She stepped back from the door. "Come in!" she said, closing the door. "Where have you been? Where in God's name?"

"Barcelona. Home."

"Barcelona? You went there? What were you doing?"

"I did as you said. I disappeared."

"Disappeared?"

"I followed your orders."

"You were supposed to disappear to that girl, not to me!"

He shrugged.

"Give me that cheek, and I'll give you the back of my hand."

"I'm here. Isn't that what matters."

"What were you thinking?"

"I wasn't really thinking, not at first. I was sick of all this, waiting, following Sylvia around. I went for a drive and just didn't stop."

"And the car?"

"It's outside on the street."

She turned away from him, going to the ashtray beside her rocking chair where a cigarette was burning. Windows were open but the room was choked with smoke. She was wearing a housecoat, her gray hair loose, her face bereft of makeup. Turning back upon him, she asked, "What was in your mind?"

"Nothing. I didn't plan to go, but then I was on the road going south and wanted to see Lena."

She brought both hands to her face, rolling her eyes heavenward. "You fool! You idiot!"

"I'm back. I'm here now."

"I had to fight Leonid tooth and nail to keep him from reporting you."

"Report me to who?"

"Our superiors, the GPU. Sudoplatov. You were AWOL."

Ramón blinked. "AWOL?"

"You've taken money, a great deal of money. The clothes, the car—you're living like an aristocrat. Do you think the GPU would let you walk away?"

"Eitingon wouldn't report me. He likes me. He always acts as if I'm his son or something."

"He does like you, but he follows orders. He only sticks his neck out so far. He has to make this mission work. Don't you understand what's happening in the world? Can't you look around and see? Spain is a small taste of what's coming everywhere. We're on the brink of catastrophe. Franco is nothing compared to Hitler. The Fascists will crush us like fleas. Eitingon knows this very well. He's scrambling to stay upright, to find his footing. He won't let you endanger that. This mission is what he has. It's all that any of us have. You, me—without this mission, we have no place in the world, no work, no money, nothing to do. Do you understand? Are you listening?"

"Yes, I'm listening."

"Rudolf Klement? You know what happened to him. They opened his veins and drained his blood in his bathtub. Then they carved him up like an animal, like a pig, packed him up, and threw him in the river."

She stabbed out her cigarette and lit another. "I know you blame me for not saving Pablo but I'm only a woman. I don't have much power. I can't protect you. And now I see the same thing happening again. Pablo wouldn't give up that girl. Alicia. He didn't follow orders. And now you go chasing after Lena."

"No more. That's over."

"Why?"

"Doña Inez convinced her she has to marry a rich man."

"That Fascist bitch."

"She's not a Fascist. No more than your mother was. She wants Lena to have a good life."

"And Sylvia? What about Sylvia? You know she went to Brussels?"

"She did what?"

"She called Madame Gaston, and, of course, Gaston sent us a wire. Sylvia showed up in Brussels, looking for you."

"And what happened?"

"Gaston met her at a café, told her you had gone to London on family business. She's back in Paris. We're keeping tabs on her."

Ramón lit a cigarette of his own, then went to the window to look down at the Citroën waiting on the street.

"What are you going to do about Sylvia? You have to put this right. You can't lose her. She's your way in."

He felt a kind of sadness thinking of Sylvia, a tenderness in his heart. "Yes, Sylvia. I'll make it right."

# EIGHTEEN

Sylvia received two more letters from Jacques, neither satisfactory. She crumpled up the second letter and threw it on the ground. Both had been written before her meeting with Madame Gaston. Sylvia didn't want letters; she wanted Jacques to come back. She wanted to know what was happening. She hated the feeling that he had simply disappeared, that he might have lied to her.

She considered booking her ticket to New York, but, after the heat of summer, Paris regained its old charm. The light became deeper and softer. In the mornings and evenings, a delicious chill crept into the air, the first intimation of autumn. Shops and cafés were opening, women appearing in their new outfits for the season. She was returning from an art gallery when she walked into her hotel and noticed Jacques sitting in a wing-back chair, the cigarette in his left hand, the horn-rim glasses, the elegant tweed jacket, a ribbon of smoke spiraling toward the ceiling. She hesitated when he rose to embrace her.

"Sylvia! Sylvia?" he said, coming toward her.

She shook her head.

"Sylvia?"

She turned and walked out of the hotel. She started down the street. Without thought, she walked to the Seine with Jacques at her side. He had the grace not to speak, to wait until she was ready. The chestnut and plane trees had started to turn shades of yellow and red. The river gleamed silver, etched with sinuous lines of currents beneath the surface. Beyond the booksellers' kiosks, with Notre Dame rising on the far bank, she finally stopped and asked for his handkerchief. She removed her glasses to blot her eyes, then sniffed soundly. "I felt frightened when I saw you. I don't understand but it was a sensation going up my spine."

"A fright?" His eyes stood still behind his lenses, moving only to search her face.

"Jacques, what happened? I went to Brussels. I saw that woman, Madame Gaston."

He nodded slightly, an all but imperceptible sign of assent.

"She said you had gone to England."

"No, I'm sorry. She didn't tell you the truth."

"What is the truth?"

"Sylvia, I can't explain my family to you, and I can't explain what happened. It's too complicated, too strange. It's so strange, I just can't tell you. But you have to know that you're very important to me, unlike anyone I've ever known. Being away from you, I missed you so much. I don't want to think about a future without you."

"What about your family?"

"They know about you."

"How?"

"They have their spies."

"And your wife?"

He winced a bit. "Yes, that came as a surprise, painful. She's interested in another man. She's decided not to wait for me."

"Oh, I'm sorry."

He shook his head. "It's for the best. I want to make some changes. I can't get away from my family altogether, but I'm going to get a job. A friend says he can get me started as a correspondent for L' Auto, a Belgian sports journal."

"Jacques, that's wonderful."

"I won't make much money. We'll be poor like everyone else."

"But it's a start."

"But now, Sylvia, I'm back and you have to trust me." He opened his arms, and she allowed him to fold her in. Her tears came freely, wetting the breast of his shirt. "Oh my God!" She laughed, pulling away, wiping her eyes with her fingers. "I imagined the most terrible things."

"Sylvia, I'm in love with you," he said, feeling the truth of the words as he said them. "I want to marry you."

She laughed again. "Marxists don't believe in marriage."

"If you don't believe in marriage, what do you do when you feel this way?"

"You tell your friends and the world that you are husband and wife. We don't need a judge or a rabbi to say that we are married. That's between the man and woman."

"But I'm not a Marxist."

"And now you tell me," she said with a smile. "I'm proud of you. And don't worry, you'll like having a job."

"I don't know about that, but come, let's get you something to drink. You're trembling. I think a *marc* would be appropriate."

# NINETEEN

It was cold now—November, the ninth day. The limbs of chestnut and plane trees were bare. It was the blue hour; twilight slowly drenched the streets from slate to indigo. Blinking back tears, she walked away from the newsstand, pulling the fur coat closer. Looking down at the sidewalk, she expected to see shards of shattered glass, to hear it crunch beneath her feet. She didn't understand the black-and-white photographs covering the front pages of the newspapers when she first looked at them. In one photograph, a street looked so empty it might have been someplace in the American West. A merchant, too dazed to move, stood in front of a shop. Because glass is transparent, she couldn't see in the photograph that the shop windows were shattered, couldn't see the piles of glass on the sidewalks.

Skimming headlines and captions, the meaning sinking in, she felt her connection to the poor Jew whose shop windows had been shattered. There were no limits, no separation; that was the message. A seventeen-year-old Jew kills a Nazi foreign officer in Paris and a day later Nazis shatter the windows of every Jew in Germany.

She fished in her purse for keys as she approached her building, letting herself through the heavy timbered door that closed with a solid thud behind her. The flick of the blue-and-white check curtain in the concierge's window made her feel uneasy, observed. She pressed the electric switch for light and started up the cold stone stairs worn by so many footsteps. As the dim bulb went out behind her, she pressed another switch on the landing. She fumbled for a second key, letting herself into the flat, which was filled with afternoon shadows, the smell of cigarette smoke and coffee. She had been there for a little over a month, and the rooms still looked alien.

Removing her kid gloves, she went into the bedroom, where, in the long cupboard mirror, she caught a glimpse of herself, a woman in a fur coat and a felt hat, a scarf tied at her throat as Jacques liked. He'd given her the coat, apologizing that it was possum rather than beaver or mink. He'd found it at a *troc*, assuring her that fashionable women in Paris looked for bargains in the secondhand clothing shops. A rip in the silk lining had to be mended, but the furs were nicely worked, the pelts still supple. She'd brought nothing for cold weather and was now wearing the suits, sweaters, and skirts that Jacques had selected for her.

She hung the coat in the cupboard, removed her hat, and went back into the living room, where the rented typewriter stood waiting on the table. In the small kitchen, she put a match to one of the two burners that blossomed into blue flames, the familiar smells of sulfur and gas making her miss her two sisters, the big apartment they shared in Morningside Heights. She had been happy that summer in Paris, but now she was beginning to understand what it meant to be a foreigner. She became increasingly aware of how little she understood, that terrible things happened in Europe.

The water in the kettle was coming to a boil when she heard footsteps on the landing, Jacques's key in the lock. Rushing to him, she burrowed into the protection of his cashmere topcoat, wrapping her arms around him and holding tight.

"Here, here, what's this?" he said, taking her by the shoulders and holding her back.

"I just saw the news from Germany before coming in. I didn't know until just a few minutes ago."

"Oh yes, the Jews."

"At the kiosk on the corner, looking at the papers, I was . . ."

"Yes, of course, you're upset. That's what the Nazis want. I'm sorry I couldn't warn you. Did you buy a paper?"

"I couldn't stand to bring it home. It's too ghastly."

"Sylvia, let me take off my coat."

"Have you been smoking a cigar?"

"No, one of the fellows in the office smokes."

She followed him as far as the bedroom door, where she poured out her feelings about Hitler until the kettle started to whistle.

"Sylvia."

"Yes?"

"The kettle. You must try to not let this get to you. That's what they want."

"Yes, I know." She went to the kitchen. "I'm making tea. Do you want a cup?"

"No. I've just had coffee."

"You stopped on the way home?"

"Yes, I had coffee with a friend."

"Anyone I know?"

"A woman I saw in the street, someone from Brussels. An older woman."

"You've lived here so long, I always think we'll run into some of your friends. Funny we never do."

He turned to smile at Sylvia. "Darling, give me a few seconds to collect myself. I'll be with you in a moment."

She made her tea. When Jacques came out of the bedroom, he was wearing a dressing gown and slippers, smelling of soap and water and fresh cologne, his thick hair still damp where he had combed it. "Don't you want to be comfortable?" he asked, lighting a cigarette.

"I thought I would work for a while. I find it reassuring when I'm upset."

"Do you have to use the typewriter?"

"No, I can work in longhand. I'm still making notes for my article."

"Bring your tea and sit with me on the sofa. Yes, that's much better."

"If I were a proper French wife, I could make your supper."

"You'll never be French, but I could teach you a recipe or two."

"My sisters and I always had Clemmy to do the cooking. Isn't that silly for three young women. Clemmy's from Alabama and makes the most divine fried chicken and biscuits. She'll cook for you when we're in New York." She sipped her tea, watching as he took up one of his sporting papers. "How was work today? What did you do?"

"Nothing very interesting."

"But tell me, I'd like to know."

He smiled at her fondly. "I pulled some stories off the wire and rewrote them to send to my chief in Brussels."

"What were they about?"

"What was what about?"

"The stories."

"Sports. Why do you want to know?"

"I'm just interested."

"Really, Sylvia, I never realized having a job meant one had to talk about it constantly."

"It's normal that a wife should want to know about her husband's work. I was thinking I might drop by your office one day—just to see. We could go to lunch."

"It isn't in a nice sector. You might not like being there."

"What is your office like?"

"Oh, I don't know, the usual thing. Drab and dingy."

Watching the way he stubbed out his cigarette and picked up a magazine, she sensed that she was making him uneasy. She finished her tea, then went to the table where she had a pad and a stack of books next to the typewriter. She was reviewing a book on the uses of projection and transference in Freudian analysis, an assignment Jacques got for her when she announced that she would have to go back to New York if she didn't start making money.

"You know, this would be much easier if I could talk to the editor," she finally said.

Jacques looked up from his journal. "I explained that to you. He thinks I'm writing the article. If he knew you were doing the work, then it's doubtful he would give me the assignment."

"But he doesn't think you are a psychologist?"

"No." He hesitated as if he wanted to say more, do more to make her happy.

"Then what difference does it make? Couldn't he just assign it to me?"

"He could but I don't know that he would." He smiled, searching for more to say. "Isn't the money good?"

"Yes, the fee is extremely generous. Too generous. I can't imagine what sort of publication is paying so much."

"A scholarly journal, don't you think?"

"No. They usually don't pay anything at all."

"No?"

She saw that he didn't really know, that there was no reason to press him. "I would have a better idea of what they want if I knew what the journal is."

"Just do your best, Sylvia, and let's not look fortune in the teeth."

She sat still for a moment, then closed the book and got up from the table. She knew he wanted to protect her, but at times she felt confined. And it was hard to escape the fact that her being Jewish would make life difficult for them. And that made her terribly sad.

# TWENTY

M y boy, it's marvelous news," said Eitingon in his Russian-flavored French, spreading a sliver of the foie gras on a toasted slice of bread. "She's known to be an enchantress, and if you win her over, you can dispense with Sylvia."

"Dispense with Sylvia?"

"You find her tedious, don't you?"

Ramón recoiled inwardly. He didn't find Sylvia tedious. He found it odd and annoying that Eitingon would think so.

"Of course you're reluctant to toss aside what you've spent so much time winning."

Ramón wanted to get up from the table and walk away, but he was there to make peace, to smooth things over.

"Go ahead." Eitingon urged him to try the foie gras. "It's ambrosial. Be sure to get some of that lovely jelly on top." He took a swallow of the Château Latour and watched the younger man lean forward.

"Nice, isn't it?" said Eitingon.

"Who is the enchantress?"

"Frida Rivera, the wife of Diego. She's a direct link to Trotsky in Mexico. She's arriving in Paris any day now."

"And why do you say she's an enchantress?"

"She's famous for her conquests. Rivera is a great womanizer, sleeps with everyone. And she does the same. They're quite the pair."

"What brings her to Paris?"

"She's Mexico's delegate to the Fourth International Conference," Eitingon said and laughed.

"She's a militant?"

"I hardly think so. Rivera fancies himself a politician but he's an amateur. After he was kicked out of the Party, he went over to the Trotskyists and became a great hero to them when he got President Cárdenas to give Trotsky a Mexican visa. Rivera gave Trotsky and his entourage a house and made a show of embracing the old Russian."

"And why would Rivera's wife come here as a delegate to the Fourth International?"

"She's coming for an exhibition of her paintings."

"Is she an artist?"

"Yes, in a minor sort of way." Eitingon helped himself to more foie gras, inadvertently transferring a bit of the duck gelatin on the back of his hand to the scar on his chin, giving it a gloss. "She's been in New York, where she captivated the press and all of high society. The newspapers and magazines wrote about her every move, calling her the surrealist woman."

"I wonder what they meant?"

"You know about the surrealists?"

"Of course. Salvador Dali is Catalan."

"Yes, sorry. Well, at any rate, Frida Rivera is having an exhibition here. You must attend the vernissage. That will be the perfect way for you to meet her."

# TWENTY-ONE

Enchantress, he kept thinking, enchantress. He dressed with extra care for the evening—his navy blue suit, a beautiful white shirt of the finest cotton, a silk tie in an orange-and-green geometric pattern with socks to match, his favorite cologne. He'd hesitated over the socks, but decided that a flash of unexpected color would be just the thing for surrealists.

On the way to his car, he did as Caridad said and stopped to buy flowers. "Get the biggest bouquet of flowers you can find," Caridad told him. "Red roses are the best. That will get her attention. For someone like Frida Rivera no gesture is too large."

He thought a prop would boost his confidence, but as he drove through the city he felt a twinge of guilt about Sylvia. He didn't like misleading her and leaving her alone. He would have much preferred staying at home with her. The flowers on the seat began to annoy and make him feel uneasy. The gallery, Pierre Colle, was on the Right Bank on a small street—Rue de Cambacérès just below the conjunction of the boulevards Haussmann and Malesherbes. By the time he arrived, flakes of snow drifted through the car's headlights. He parked and, carrying the bouquet, walked along Cambacérès until he came to the gallery where a placard in the window announced—*Mexique.*

Inside, the gallery, filled with people and smoke, looked like a greenhouse with tall tropical plants, pieces of primitive sculpture, what appeared to be colorful Mexican toys, and large black-and-white photographs. Jacques saw a familiar face across the room, a bald head and large blazing eyes. Realizing it was Picasso, he suddenly felt foolish with the roses, as if he were a messenger. He considered hiding the bouquet beneath his coat, but, deciding that to be impractical, he did his best to minimize the roses by carrying them at his side like a wet umbrella.

Eitingon had shown him a photograph so he recognized Frida Rivera standing alone and perhaps momentarily lost. She had braided her black hair and a thick scarlet ribbon into a crown. A scarlet cloak was wrapped around her shoulders; a cascade of ornate gold necklaces and embroidered fabric fell to a long black skirt that swept the floor with a stiff white ruff.

Burdened by the roses, he glanced down at one of the displays, his eyes settling on a small, brightly painted shadow box in which a trio of skeletons wearing sombreros played a guitar, accordion, and trumpet while two more skeletons, a man and woman, danced in the foreground. It was a cheerful domestic scene, amplified by two mirrors set into the sides of the box. His eyes drifting to a small painting, he blushed as he recognized the woman gazing out at him, naked, a strange object—her own head?—coming out of her vagina. She lay on a bed in some state of agony he couldn't comprehend, yet her facial expression was contemplative; the eyebrow exaggerated, batlike; the individual hairs above her mouth picked out to make a boy's pubescent mustache.

"Ah! *Quel surprise!*" a woman exclaimed behind him. It was Marguerite, an acquaintance of Sylvia's, a Parisian and a Trotskyite. She looked chic in a gray Chanel suit. "Jacques Mornard! And where is Sylvia this evening?" she asked in French.

He leaned forward to exchange kisses, one cheek then the other. "Sad to say Sylvia's working, slaving away on these reviews she's writing."

"At this hour?" the woman asked, giving him a skeptical look.

"Yes, a deadline. The editor suddenly wants several reviews at once, and the money is too good to say no. Sylvia's so independent. She's afraid of being kept."

"Americans!" the woman said and laughed.

"Yes, Americans," he agreed.

She glanced in a pointed way at the roses all but dragging on the floor. "You intend to meet Frida? Or perhaps she's a friend?"

"Ah, these?" He held the flowers up as if he'd forgotten them. "Sylvia asked me to bring them. She hated to miss this evening. Her sister knows the Riveras in Mexico."

"Look, that's André Breton talking to her. Do you know him? The man with the leonine mane."

"No. And who is that at his side?"

"Marcel Duchamp. He looks like a saint, doesn't he? His face is so gaunt and ascetic. For a genius, he's said to be very kind. Are you going to the dinner?"

"Dinner?"

"No one received an invitation. Breton was supposed to make the arrangements and did nothing. Frida's furious with him. People are stopping at a bistro just at the end of the block. You should go if you like."

She departed, leaving Jacques alone to observe Frida Rivera moving through the party. He considered presenting the roses, but they weighed him down like an albatross. Hoping no one would notice, desperate to unburden himself, he skulked out of the gallery for the street.

"Flowers?" He held them out to a passing woman who shied away. "Roses?" he said to a second woman, who avoided him as if he were mad.

He finally deposited the bouquet in a trash can and went into a *zinc*, where he had a cigarette and a brandy. By the time he ventured out, the crowd from the vernissage was moving down the street toward the bistro, Frida Rivera bringing up the rear, limping slightly beneath her great skirt.

She was pushed up against a very tall, soigné blonde in the crowded entrance of the bistro. When the blonde turned away,

Jacques offered his silver cigarette case. *"Puta!"* She said to him. *"Estas putas ricas no van a comprar nada. Ni una cosa! Nadita!"*

Whore! These rich whores aren't going to buy anything. Not a thing! Not the smallest thing.

She accepted the cigarette, then, smoothly shifting gears, she placed her small ringed hand on his, leaned toward the lighter, pausing to look up from the trembling flame into his eyes. He recognized the move as a cliché, yet felt his cock stir against his expensive underwear, responding to transgression, the blatant signal. The mustache was real; the black bristles gave her the mouth of an adolescent boy, the upper lip curling slightly in a sneer. He saw the comprehension in her eyes, that they were in perfect communication, then realized he had slipped.

*"Parlez vous Anglais?"* he said.

She looked at him more closely. *"Pero eres español."*

"No, Belgian."

She exhaled, squinting against the smoke, then met his eyes again, raising possibilities, posing questions, starting a conversation that was sexual rather than verbal. "You're not French?"

"No. I'm from Brussels."

"An intellectual? An artist?"

"No."

"That's good. I'm sick of artists and intellectuals, all the big *cacas.* You know Breton?"

"No."

"Then who are you? Why you wasting time here?"

"Friends said I should meet you."

"These people know me?"

"Your reputation. They know me."

"What reputation? That I'm some kind of big *puta?*"

"That you're not like anyone else."

She looked away as if she'd heard another voice, as if he'd lost her. Then, turning to him, she dropped the cigarette on the floor, pulling back her skirt to step on it with the toe of her small boot. "Stay here," she said, putting her hand on his arm and pressing firmly. "I'll come back."

She disappeared in the crowd for several minutes, then returned to Jacques. "Okay, let's go."

"You don't have to stay?"

"No one will notice if I'm not here. None of these *pinche pende-jos* cares about a *chicua* from Mexico. They're all here for each other." She pulled her red cloak closer as they stepped outside. "We need a taxi."

"I've got my car."

"Is it far?"

"No, just half a block."

"I'll wait while you get it."

Jacques trotted down the street to the Citroën, then circled the block. "Where are we going?" he asked when she got in.

"Montmartre, a small street, Rue Junot. I'll show you when we get there. You can find Montmartre?"

"Of course. It isn't far."

She looked out the window as they drove, not bothering to speak, making him miss the kind of easy conversation he and Sylvia would have, the shared observations and references, the threads of other conversations weaving together to make a life. He was no longer sure where home was, but, for a moment, he yearned to be there.

In Montmartre, Frida guided him to Rue Junot, then a house, with a shining black door and tall windows looking out on a front garden. A foyer with black-and-white marble squares on the floor led to a salon with floor-to-ceiling books and long, moss-green velvet drapes. The lamplight was soft; the air smelled of flowers and leather and the embers of a fire smoldering in the grate. Removing her cloak, she went to a table where a collection of liquor bottles stood on a tray. "Brandy?" she asked.

"Yes, please. Whose house is this?"

"An American woman, rich but not a bitch. She saved me from that pigsty Breton calls home. You can't believe how Breton and his wife live, a filthy little apartment. They stayed with us for three months in Mexico when he came looking for Trotsky. Diego's not a rich guy, but at least our houses are clean and the food is good. We took them everywhere, introduced them to everyone in Mexico. We loaned them our cars and chauffeurs. We treated them like royalty, all the time Breton saying I must come to Paris, that little Frida was a surrealist without even knowing. If I would come to Paris, he promised to organize an exhibition for me at the best gallery there.

"I didn't care about being a surrealist or having a show in *pinche* Paris, but little *tonta* that I am, I believed him, shipped my paintings from New York, got on a ship, and came all the way to this *pinchismo* place. And what did Breton do? *Nada! Nadisma!* He didn't bother to get my paintings out of customs, didn't get a gallery. I was supposed to sleep in a tiny bedroom with his little girl.

"And then he drags in all of that junk he bought in the markets in Mexico to show with my paintings, children's toys, and his photographs. You can't even see my paintings. If it hadn't been for Duchamp, nothing would have happened. Duchamp's the only one around here who's got a foot on the ground. You know Marcel Duchamp? You must have seen him at the gallery. He's the *novio* of the *dueña* of this house."

"What did Breton want with Trotsky?"

"If Stalin says art has to be realistic, what are surrealists going to do? Everyone is a Marxist. Trotsky is the only place to go."

She settled on a sofa and accepted a cigarette. "Here, come sit with me." She looked him over. "You're very *guapo*."

"I'm what?"

"Don't tease. You know what I'm saying. How old are you? Twenty-five? I don't often sleep with such handsome young men. My husband Diego is a fat old pig."

"You intend to sleep with me?"

"Isn't that why you're here?"

Dutifully—he knew how to play the game—he picked up her hand, pressing it to his mouth, then turning it to kiss the inside of her wrist. "Wait!" she said, rising from the sofa. "I have to make pipi."

She went into the next room, closing the door behind her. He lit another cigarette and got up to look around, stopping to pour another brandy, paging through a portfolio of charcoal drawings. After what seemed an age, the door opened but rather than come out, she called him into the room, which was dark except for a candle burning next to the bed where she lay propped against pillows, her black hair falling down one shoulder, her nipples two black roses beneath a thin muslin nightgown.

She watched, her eyes dark and gleaming, as he sat on the edge of the bed at her side. As he leaned forward, he thought of Sylvia, her blue eyes, the trust. She wouldn't understand what he was about to do, but he had no choice. *Que puto soy yo*, he thought. This was his job.

## TWENTY-TWO

A nd?" asked Caridad. "Will she help you?"

"Perhaps. Perhaps not. It's difficult to tell."

"Why not? She liked you well enough."

"But that means nothing to a woman like her. She used me as a toy."

"What does she say about Trotsky?" asked Eitingon.

"She had a long letter from him. Something happened in Mexico but she won't talk about it. Whenever I mention him, she changes the subject."

They were in Eitingon's flat. Caridad looked ashen after making countless telephone calls and smoking countless cigarettes. Catalonia had fallen—Tarragona, Barcelona, Girona. It would be only a matter of weeks before Franco's troops took Madrid. Half a million Spanish refugees were pouring over the border into France.

Ramón believed that Lena would be safe. Her father had kept his distance from the Left and maintained alliances with Franco's machine in Barcelona. But in the chaos of a war zone there were always accidents and mistakes. One never knew what would happen. The wrong people were killed.

Ramón felt as if the earth were trembling beneath his feet, as if an avalanche had started as he was climbing a mountain. He listened as Caridad placed yet another call to Perpignan, trying to find a Party operative who could tell her what was happening on the border with Spain.

Eitingon stood up and began pacing back and forth across the room. "What do you want to do?" he asked Caridad when she hung up.

"I want to see the children. Jorge is old enough to take care of himself, but Montserrat and Luis are too young for this. I want to go to Ripollet."

"I'll drive you," said Ramón.

"What about Sylvia?" said Eitingon.

"I'll tell her I have to go to Brussels to see Mama. I won't be gone long."

"Ramón, don't forget you've broken with your family. We don't want to lose Sylvia. At this point, that's all we have. And you couldn't get across the border." Eitingon got up and started to pace. "All of this is taking too long. We've spent months and we're still in Paris, no closer to Mexico."

"Is Sudoplatov unhappy?" asked Caridad.

"No, not yet. But we need to show signs of progress."

"We've had to wait for Siqueiros," said Caridad. "There's no point in going to Mexico without him. How often have we told him this? He won't take orders. He doesn't listen to us."

"Of course he won't. Siqueiros is an artist, Mexico's greatest hero." Eitingon stopped at a window, parting the curtain to look out. "But we chose him. The plan is ours. Our heads are on the chopping block."

"Should we replace Siqueiros?" asked Caridad.

"No, that would send the wrong signal to Moscow, draw their attention. They aren't thinking about us—at least not yet. The war in Spain will be over soon, and David will have to go back to Mexico."

"Speaking of going back," Ramón interjected, "Sylvia's still threatening to leave."

Caridad and Eitingon looked at each other. "What do you think?" he asked.

"Let her go," said Caridad. "Tell her you will follow. We might as well start moving toward Mexico."

"I'll need a Belgian passport. I can't use my Spanish passport."

"We'll have one forged. That's not a problem." She shook a cigarette from a pack to light from the end of one burning in an ashtray.

• • •

Walking back to the flat, Ramón thought of Lena. She and her family would suffer hardships in Barcelona but thousands would be executed, the blood would pour, bodies scraped into mass graves. Hundreds of thousands Spaniards would be displaced.

Caridad had seen it coming. She told him what was going to happen the day she appeared at the front in Aragon. Now she was walking half a block ahead of him on the sidewalk, a precaution should they encounter Sylvia coming from the flat.

It was cold out, gray, but spring would come, the tiny acid green buds making a haze on the trees. He had been in Paris a year and what he had pretended—to be a resident—had become a reality. He felt divided, as if he had become two people. He had told the story of Jacques Mornard and the aristocratic family in Brussels so often that it was as real as his past in Spain. He looked at the Parisians he met on the street, studying their faces, wondering how they could go calmly about their business. Surely they felt the tremors of their own coming avalanche.

He stopped at an outdoor flower stall to buy a small bouquet of violets for Sylvia. He avoided looking at the newspapers on the kiosk as he approached his building, fishing keys from his pocket. He opened the heavy wooden door to the street, stepping into the cold interior of the building. The blue-and-white check curtain in the concierge's window flicked to the side, revealing for a moment the woman's eyes. He'd tipped her generously to assure that Sylvia—*l'Américaine, sa femme*—didn't learn that his mother was also living in the building. "Ah, the wife, the mother. It is not a good situation," the concierge surmised. "Well, what she doesn't know . . ."

He switched on the light for the first flight of stairs, then for the second. Caridad would by now be in her flat, lighting a cigar, heating water for coffee. As he opened his door, he heard Sylvia typing. She looked up, removing her pale blue glasses.

Did she seem distant? Cold?

"I brought you a gift," he announced, "a little bouquet of violets.

They're very humble but sweet."

"You thought of me."

"Of course, I'm always thinking of you."

Noticing the thick airmail envelope on the table and that she didn't come to greet him, he felt a different variety of anxiety sweep through him, the fear that she had seen through his charade.

"You went out for the mail." He leaned down to kiss her cheek. "Anything interesting?"

"A letter from my sisters."

"What do they say?"

"The usual. They're worried about Germany and think I should come home."

"Yes, that is the usual." He went into the bedroom to hang up his coat, then to the kitchen to get a small glass of water for the violets. "I'm pouring a glass of wine. Would you like some?"

"No. Not yet. I have more to do."

He sat down on the sofa with his wine, lighting a cigarette. "Darling, come and sit with me. I've missed you."

She looked up from her work. "Just a moment. Let me finish this one sentence."

"No, please. We need to talk."

He held out his hand as she joined him, taking hers in both of his. "That's better. You know, these are not just words that I say. I really did miss you."

She moved closer to snuggle against him.

"I wish you wouldn't work so hard. It must be something about Americans. It doesn't seem natural."

"I'm sorry, Jacques. It's just that . . . You wanted to talk about something?"

"Perhaps your sisters are correct. Perhaps it's time you leave."

"But Jacques, what about us."

"Paris is safe for the moment but we shouldn't take chances."

"And what about my work?"

"Yes, there's also that. I happened to speak to our editor today. He says he won't be needing any more reviews."

"Why not? Isn't he happy with them?"

"I asked him, but he was evasive so I knew something was wrong. I assume it has to do with what's going on in general."

Sylvia looked stunned, taken aback. "Jacques, what will we do?"

"I will follow you, of course. You're my wife. I'm your husband. We'll be together."

She smiled but with hesitation. "But what would you do in New York?"

"The World's Fair starts in New York before long. A friend told me the French Pavilion needs people who speak English. That's a possibility."

"Oh, Jacques, that would be wonderful. You'd like New York. It's not Paris, but we could be happy there."

"It will take a while for me to arrange my documents. I could follow you in a month or two."

"But you would come? You wouldn't disappear again?"

"Darling, I never disappeared."

# TWENTY-THREE

Sylvia slipped back into her old life—the large apartment near Columbia University she shared with her sisters, a job as a social worker at the Welfare Department—but she was a changed woman. In her mind and in her heart, she was married to Jacques Mornard, a Belgian aristocrat. She wrote him almost every day, and rushed home every evening to look for his letters and always smiled as she read, "My Darling Blonde Bird." He was having difficulties with his visa in Brussels, where his father was once again interfering. The jobs at the French Pavilion were for French citizens only. But there was always the possibility of freelancing in the United States for one of the European papers.

After two months, Sylvia received a wire from Jacques saying that he would sail soon. Suddenly she noticed that it was spring and life would be glorious. A crossing took six days. He could be there in a week or ten days.

She began planning a dinner party for his first night in town. She would invite all of their New York friends they had seen in Paris. Clemmy would make a special dinner—a leg of lamb, scalloped potatoes, green beans, and floating island. To prepare for Jacques's arrival, Sylvia bought a new dress and had her hair cut and styled. To hurry the time along, she made a long list of chores. The apartment had to be cleaned, floors waxed, the windows washed. She bought champagne and stocked the liquor cabinet, planned outings to entertain Jacques.

When another telegram arrived from Jacques saying his ticket had been canceled, Sylvia sat down on the floor and cried into her hands. For a moment, she felt a wave of anxiety, that he might disappear again. When his letter arrived, he expressed his own disappointment.

The opening of the World's Fair came as a reminder of Jacques's absence. Spring turned to summer, long, hot weeks of waiting. On August 23, Stalin signed a nonaggression pact with Hitler, confirming the worst fears of Sylvia and her friends about the Soviet Union. On September 1, Nazi troops invaded Poland.

Sylvia felt that giant doors were slowly swinging shut and Jacques would be trapped on the opposite side of the Atlantic. Then, the first week of September at eleven on a Saturday morning, Sylvia's sister Ruth answered the telephone in the apartment. "It's for you," she said, handing Sylvia the receiver. "I think it's Jacques."

Sylvia took the telephone receiver, her hand trembling. Something had to be terribly wrong for him to make a transatlantic call. Sylvia said hello in a small, fearful voice.

"Sylvia, it's Jacques," he said, his voice happy.

"You sound so close—like you're just around the corner."

"I am. I'm at the Hotel Marseilles on 103rd Street."

"You're here? In the city?" This couldn't be right. When he arrived, she would meet him at the dock and wave to him through the streamers as he came down the gangway. When he arrived, she would have days to prepare.

"You're on 103rd Street?"

"The Hotel Marseilles. I just checked in. Shall I come there? Or why don't you come here?"

"Why didn't you let me know you were sailing?"

She felt left out, somehow cheated.

"Sylvia, I sent you a wire."

"You did? It never arrived."

"Well, you know a war has started. Do you want me to come there? Or would you like to come to the hotel? I have all sorts of wonderful news."

Sylvia glanced around the apartment, which was in a state of disorder. "I'll come there."

"Well, hurry. I can't wait to see you."

She wanted time to think, to have her hair done. She wanted days and days of happy anticipation, but she took a quick shower, applied her makeup, and put on a white pique sundress that had a small bolero jacket. Entering Jacques's hotel, she noticed then ignored an odd impulse to ask at the front desk when Mr. Mornard had checked in. But all of her uneasiness evaporated when Jacques opened the door to his suite, his tie loosened, the sleeves of his shirt rolled up. Here was Jacques, handsome and so appealing. "Finally," he said, taking her in his arms, kissing her.

A large trunk stood in the middle of the living room. Through the bedroom door she could see suitcases lying open on the bed. "Let me look at you," he said. "Your hair is different."

"I had it waved, and it's grown out. Don't you like it?"

"I liked it better the way you had it in Paris, but we can always have it cut again."

"Yes, however you like it. I'm just glad you called today or you would have missed me. We're going away for the weekend tomorrow, taking a group up to our family's lake house. Of course, you have to come."

"Sylvia, I just arrived."

"It's a big holiday here, Labor Day weekend. No one stays in town. You'll have fun. Walta and Manny will be there. You can relax and recover from your trip. There's no way I can get out of going."

"Well, if you insist. Are you hungry? I thought I would have lunch sent up, a bottle of Champagne to celebrate. I have to tell you my news! You know all the difficulties I was having because of my father."

"Yes, problems with your visa."

"Well, Mama finally came to my rescue. She gave me ten thousand dollars and told me to buy a new passport."

"A fake passport?"

"Wait!" He went into the bedroom and returned with a leather envelope that contained a stack of bills and a Canadian passport, which he opened to the photograph.

"It looks just like you."

"It is, silly. That's my photograph. But look at the name."

"Frank Jacson?" She tried a French pronunciation.

"Jackson," he corrected

"But they left out the *k*."

"Yes, an error, an odd spelling, but the *Jac* is just as you write it."

"This is illegal."

"It's only a document, a technicality."

"Must I call you Frank?"

"In Mexico, you should probably refer to me as Frank Jacson, but, of course, I will still be your Jacques."

"Mexico?"

"Yes, that's the other part of my news. Mother arranged for me to work for a great friend of hers. Peter Lubeck is a financier who specializes in commodities. He's opening an office in Mexico City and has hired me to be his assistant. He believes the war will create tremendous competition for raw materials from Latin America. It's a great opportunity for me. He plans to make a killing."

"Isn't that profiteering?"

"Sylvia, don't be a goose! Someone will make money on the war. That's the way it always is. Lubeck's paying me fifty U.S. dollars per week and giving me a letter of credit. And you're going to join me in Mexico as soon as I get settled."

"When do you leave?"

"I'm not sure. I have to wait for Lubeck, but I think I'll be here for about a month. I thought I'd rent an apartment in the Village. He's paying my expenses, but I don't want to spend a fortune on a hotel."

"Greenwich Village?" She was surprised that he sounded so familiar with the city.

"Yes, in Paris didn't you keep saying that St.-Germain reminded you of Greenwich Village?"

"I might have. I don't recall."

"Of course you did. Lubeck has an associate who can set me up there."

"It's a long way from my apartment."

"You'll stay with me. A wife's place is with her husband. And while I'm thinking of it, I want you to keep some money for me." He had started to count out hundred-dollar bills. "Here is three thousand dollars. I want you to hold it for me."

"Why don't you put it in the hotel safe?"

"I won't be here that long, and I want you hold it."

"What will I do with it?"

"Whatever you wish. I trust you completely."


Jacques stayed in New York for a month. That first weekend, he and Sylvia went to the Ageloffs' lake house in the mountains north of the city. The place had a ramshackle charm with screen porches on both floors looking out at the water. Jacques lay in his bathing trunks on the wooden dock in front of the house while the others listened to the radio and talked about the war. England had started to evacuate civilians from London, and the Nazis were invading Poland. For exercise, Jacques rowed the Ageloffs' dinghy, making the small boat jump beneath the oars.

September flew past in a blur for Sylvia. Suddenly, almost as abruptly and mysteriously as he had arrived, Jacques was leaving. Sylvia accompanied him to Grand Central Terminal, a second taxi filled with Jacques's luggage. It was a crisp October day, and he looked particularly good in sunglasses, a tweed jacket, a green-and-black striped silk tie, and charcoal-gray wool slacks. Distracted, he watched the city pass, then, as if recalling Sylvia, he covered her hand with his. "It won't be long. You'll come down in December."

"Yes, I hope so."

"Don't worry about money. I'll pay for everything. But try to come for a month or two."

"I'm not sure I can get that much time away. This is a new job."

"Can't you ask for a leave?"

"I can ask," she said and laughed, "but that doesn't mean I'll get it."

"Well, I wish you could just quit your job and move down with me, but we had better see how the situation works out there. I know I seem impatient, but I don't like to be without you."

In the train station, Sylvia and Jacques followed a line of porters carrying his bags across the great echoing hallway. The crowds, the commotion, and the hurry were already pulling them apart. Jacques was intent on his tickets, on getting his luggage properly checked, and passing out tips. She followed him onto the train to his compartment. She heard the porter calling "All aboard! All aboard!" and felt the car jerk beneath her feet as Jacques kissed her goodbye. He stood on the stairs as the train began to move and she walked along the platform. He was still waving to her, smiling as the train disappeared into the dark tunnel.

# TWENTY-FOUR

The volcanoes soared over the mountain valley, the white, snowy peaks blazing against the pure blue sky. They were much higher than Canigou, far more imposing. A curl of smoke spiraled above the cone-shaped volcano, its companion voluptuously elongate, a woman lounging on her side. Beneath these two monsters, these thrilling deities, rose the domes and spires of the city next to an expanse of lake, a tranquil mirror reflecting the heavenly blue. The valley was shaped like an oval cup, the earth a dry pinkish color sutured with uniform lines of blue-green knots of maguey plantations.

After a long train trip from New York to Texas, Ramón had caught a Pan Am flight in Brownsville and wasn't prepared for the sudden arrival in Mexico City and the astonishing view. The mountain light was incandescent, the atmosphere radiant. He gave himself a week to settle in and find his way around, then went to work, telephoning Frida Rivera and, after a series of calls, received an invitation to dinner—*la cena*—at three-thirty in the afternoon.

As he stood deliberating over his suits and jackets, he thought of Frida. He'd seen her among Sylvia's friends in Paris, which had made him anxious with Sylvia present, to be moving in the same circles. Then Frida withdrew in a mysterious way. Something happened. He hoped she might help him in Mexico, but she was confusing, like everything in Mexico. The weather seemed to pass through several seasons in the course of the day. Early mornings were as crisp as October in Paris. A warm and soft spring commenced at eleven. By midafternoon, full summer in the south of France was blazing.

And evenings could be quite cold. He finally decided to dress for summer, the hour of the *cena*, choosing a light navy blazer.

His eyes narrowed as he approached the black Ford sedan—a step down from the Citroën—waiting for him beneath the porte cochère of the Hotel Montejo. He tipped the doorman, and, after a moment to adjust his rearview mirror, pulled out onto Paseo de la Reforma, Mexico's grandest boulevard, which, modeled upon the Champs-Élysées in Paris, was almost as much park as avenue with allées of trees, cascading fountains, heroic monuments, and revolving traffic circles. He thought of Sylvia when they went for a drive that first day in Paris. She would love Mexico. She was so good at reading guides, figuring things out. Unlike Paris, Mexico City was thriving, filled with Europeans fleeing the war. Rich Americans, denied the usual pleasures of Mediterranean holidays, filled the luxury hotels where Latin orchestras played rumbas and cha-chas in bars and rooftop dinner clubs.

The twenty-minute drive to Coyoacán took him through Tacubaya and Mixcoac, old villages that had become suburbs. Coyoacán felt distinct and somehow exclusive. It still appeared to be a mountain village with cobblestone streets. The zocalo, like every zocalo in Mexico, had its church and municipal palace, but here village life had been idealized with beautiful beds of flowers. He found the address Frida had given him in a new area beyond the zocalo where wide streets laid out in a grid were named after European capitals. It being three in the afternoon, time for the midday meal, the village was all but empty and a motionless quiet prevailed.

A *chófer* waited in a pale green Studebaker sedan in front of 45 Londres. As Jacques parked, an enormous Mexican with froglike eyes came out of the house, carrying a dish covered with a pink dish towel. He was wearing a ten-gallon Stetson and a revolver in a holster that made him look larger still. The driver leapt out to open one of the back doors, taking the dish, as the Studebaker's springs gave beneath the man's weight.

After the Studebaker drove away, Ramón got out of the Ford and crossed the street, noticing raw adobe bricks stacked on top of the cobalt blue wall. A maid answered the door, admitting him to rooms filled with deep shadows and a gathering of life-size papier-mâché figures. To one side, large doors opened onto a garden, where the cobalt walls were lined with flowering plants and fruit trees. Women's voices came from what he suspected was the kitchen, then Frida appeared, a shadowy figure moving slowly through the dining room. With her long hair falling loose down her back, she looked convalescent in an embroidered blue-and-red tunic, carrying a small blue-green glass in one hand. Noticing the slight limp, he remembered the leg withered by polio, the scars on her abdomen.

When he leaned forward offering to kiss her, she shook her head and cut her eyes, indicating the presence of servants. "Was that your husband who was just leaving?"

"Oh! You saw Diego?"

"I was surprised. You said he was divorcing you."

"Yes, but he's not divorcing Blanca, our cook. He came to get her duck mole. Lupe, his first wife, no his second, taught Blanca the recipe so he feels he has a rightful claim."

"That sounds complicated."

"Not very. It's his favorite dish. Did he see you?"

"I don't think so."

"That's good."

She winced at the stronger light as they walked out to the garden, where the air was filled with the fragrance of geraniums and orange blossoms. A large green parrot squawked in its cage at the end of the garden away from the table set for lunch beneath the frangipani tree. "So, everything changes?" he said.

"*Todo! Y todo jodido!*"

"That bad?"

"I love Diego but he's a sadistic pig. I get home from Paris sick as a dog. My spine is killing me. I need another surgery, and Diego announces he's divorcing me. It's the old one-two punch for little Frida. Nick, the guy I love in New York, had just told me he was getting married. Then Diego tells me I'm getting a divorce. Pow! Pow!"

She put her hand on his forearm. "You want a *copita*? *Que bruta soy yo!* I'm drinking brandy, a lot of brandy these days. But there's wine and whiskey. Or tequila. I have a special tequila you should try."

She rang a small silver bell for the maid, and, after telling the woman what to bring, led him to chairs made of bamboo and canvas. In the sunlight, her complexion had an unhealthy yellow tinge, and her facial hair, the black mustache and eyebrow, had lost its luster.

"Why does he want a divorce? Did he find out about the man in New York?"

"Diego doesn't give a reason. He says," she paused, wiggling four fingers in the air to make quotation marks, "that it's merely a legal convenience, the modern thing to do. That's what he told *Look* magazine." She took a swallow from her glass. "Diego's a big dope. He's like a circus ride for all the rich bitches that come down here. Paulette, you know the little tramp's wife. What's his name? The little tramp?"

"Chaplin?"

"Yes, Paulette moved into the San Ángel Inn across the street from Diego's studio. Diego's sleeping with her and his assistant, an American girl."

She stopped speaking when the maid returned with another brandy, a tequila, and small bowls of salted nuts on a small tray of hammered silver. Finishing the brandy in her hand, she took the one on the tray. "You might want some lime in the tequila, but try it without to see what you think. Yes, the taste is different but not as bad as that damned absinthe."

She drank steadily through the meal, putting a spoon into the clear broth of the soup but eating nothing. The food and seasonings were strange to Jacques, the corn tortillas a crude kind of crêpe. A small plate of rice flavored with a green herb followed the soup, then a stuffed chili pepper in a tomato broth. As the pièce de résistance, the cook brought out duck covered with a thick sauce that looked like mud. "Really? Chili peppers and chocolate?" Ramón said, discreetly scraping the sauce to the side.

After the maid served coffee and flan, Ramón mentioned Trotsky. "So, this is where he lived. I'm surprised he could fit into this house."

"Why do you say that?" she asked in a belligerent tone, beginning to slur her words. "This isn't a mansion, but it's bigger than it looks. My father built this house."

"Of course, but Trotsky would have his entourage—secretaries and guards, all sorts of people."

She nodded once and then again. "I think Diego found out about Trotsky while I was in Paris."

"You and Trotsky?"

She shrugged. "I didn't have a choice. Diego, that pig, was sleeping with my sister, and that was the real kick in the gut. Cristina means more to me than anyone. She's my heart, my soul. The only way I could repay Diego was with his hero *chavitos*."

"His what?"

She tapped her chin. "You know, little goat. Trotsky has his little beard. He's an old-fashioned guy. He couldn't just have sex, he had to fall in love with me, make a big drama so his wife catches on. Diego suspected something. He's such a cheat he always suspects. The minute I left for New York, Diego squeezed the sorry truth out of Cristina. That's what was going on when I was in Paris. That's what I couldn't tell you. There I was, Mexico's delegate to the Fourth International, a hero to all the Trotskyists!"

"When did Trotsky move out of this house?"

"While I was in Paris. Diego didn't confront Trotsky but they both knew. The old man wanted to start paying rent, but Diego refused. So Trotsky got out. He's in an old place a couple of blocks from here."

"Have you talked to him?"

"Why so much interest in Trotsky? Are you here to kill him?"

"No, of course not. Do I look like an assassin to you?"

"Someone will kill him. Every fool knows that."

"Who says?"

"Everyone. But not me. I'm keeping my distance." She pulled a shawl around her shoulders. They'd lost the sun in the garden, and it was immediately cold in the shade.

Leaving, Jacques asked about the papier-mâché figures he'd noticed coming in. One of them, a woman with long blond hair and red lipstick, was wearing a low-cut gown and a sparkling necklace. Another, a man, wore a badge, a gun, and boots. "Villagers here in Mexico make them. The blond girl is a rich *gringa*, maybe a whore. And he's a sheriff. Villagers make them to burn on feast days. Sometimes they're modeled on specific people."

"They burn them in effigy?"

"Yes, they're called Judases. Diego and I collect them."

The light was fading as Jacques got in his car. Why had she asked that question? Was he there to kill Trotsky? Did she as an artist feel compelled to say and do what was inappropriate? He started the engine, then idled along, two, three blocks and he was on the edge of the village, the houses becoming marginal, the cobblestones ending. Twilight, the melancholy time of day. A eucalyptus tree towered before him, rising above a wall like the sail of a great schooner. In the distance across the valley, the volcanoes stood, their flanks a deep somber blue against the paler sky, the snowcapped peaks turning pink in the fading sunlight.

A masonry wall ran along the street, dwarfing the Ford until he turned left onto Calle Viena, a rutted dirt track, where, looking up and back he could see a machine-gun turret and concertina wire bristling on the front wall of the compound. Two Mexican policemen stood on the street in front of a guard station, a small brick hut that had just been built. Across the street was a *milpa*, a corn patch. Somewhere close by a rooster crowed, and in the distance a donkey was braying. He turned left onto Viena and drove to the end of the wall, and the block, where a row of cypress trees marked the dry bed of a river. There was nothing beyond. This was the end of the city, the edge of Coyoacán.

# TWENTY-FIVE

"Sí, *claro! Claro!*" said David Siqueiros. Sitting at a desk, telephone receiver resting on his shoulder, he had his boots propped in a bottom drawer. Rather than his cavalry uniform, he was wearing a brown leather jacket smeared with paint, an olive-green turtleneck sweater, and a pair of rough canvas dungarees. His dark hair had grown longer; parted in the middle, it emphasized the length of his face, his pale skin and full lips. Listening, amused, his green eyes moved from Eitingon to Caridad to Ramón, then settled upon Antonio Pujol, who conveyed a Mayan patience, his face a mask, the nose flattened, the cheeks pocked, the thick lips slightly curled as if pressed up against a window pane. Siqueiros held up two fingers to Pujol and tipped his mouth toward him. The younger man shook a Lucky Strike out of a pack, stood to pass the cigarette to Siqueiros, rattled a wax match out of its box, and struck it.

They were in an apartment Siqueiros kept in the Zona Rosa. He'd given the place to Caridad and Eitingon to use as an office, but he behaved as if it were still his. And he had taken a telephone call during a meeting.

Caridad, her lips pressed in a straight line, looked down at her quickly moving knitting needles, giving the black thread an angry pull. Jacques sat on a battered green leatherette sofa.

"*Amilcar, te aviso tan pronto que sepa, pero la comisión es segura. Voy a pintar esa pared.*"

Siqueiros continued speaking, lighting the cigarette, blowing a plume of smoke toward the ceiling. "I'm sure the commission will come through, and as soon as it does I'll give you a ring. You will be the first to know, I promise."

Caridad gave Eitingon a pointed look and stubbed out a cigarette as Siqueiros rang off.

"What is it?" Siqueiros asked in French, dropping his jaw and shoulders in an expression that was entirely Gallic.

"My dearest David, was that a reporter?" Eitingon asked in French.

"Yes, Leonid, the arts editor at *La Opinion*, Amilcar Lopez."

"Given the secret nature of our mission," said Caridad, "might it not be wise for you to avoid the press?"

Siqueiros smiled at her. "Contrary to what you might think, if I suddenly dropped from sight, it would only arouse curiosity. The best camouflage I have is to stay in the public eye."

"But perhaps you can avoid giving interviews while we're working," Caridad suggested.

Siqueiros leaned back in his chair, comfortable with his position. He had the lease to the apartment. The telephone was his. He was the one who knew where all trip wires were hidden in the Mexican Communist Party—who was a Stalinist, who was Trotskyist, who hated whom. Siqueiros was the one who had the charisma to recruit and lead a group of men into an illegal armed assault. "If you like I can have the telephone disconnected. That way reporters won't bother me here."

"No, no, no!" Eitingon said, holding up the flat of his palm. "It would take far too long to get another."

"Surely the Party has some pull at the telephone company," said Ramón.

"Of course, the Party runs the unions for both telephone companies."

"Never mind," said Eitingon. "Even with all of David's influence, it could take months to get another line."

"As it is, we're behind schedule," Caridad complained. "We don't have a schedule. I don't like being the scold, but if we don't set deadlines and work diligently we'll never accomplish anything."

"Where is the plan for the house?" asked Siqueiros. "How many guards are there, how many policemen, how many machine guns?

Is there a siren? We can't plan an attack without this information."

"Ramón is cultivating Frida Rivera and thinks she will help."

"Fridita," Siqueiros scoffed, looking at Ramón. "What do you make of Señora Rivera?"

Thinking, Ramón lit a Lucky Strike, dropping the wax match in a cup. "She knows everything. And everyone."

"But will she *do* anything?" Siqueiros smiled. "No, my young friend. I've known Frida since she was an adolescent. When Diego was a Stalinist, Frida was a Stalinist. When he was a Trotskyist, she was a Trotskyist. She has no political beliefs of her own, no conviction." Siqueiros laced his fingers together, letting his eyes rest upon Ramón. "Why don't we just shoot the old man?"

"No, the Kremlin has very clear guidelines," Caridad lectured. "We have to wage a campaign in the press to convince people that Trotsky is a terrorist and a traitor. You know Stalin's philosophy: first the moral assassination, then the physical. We have to shift the blame away from the Kremlin."

"It was a joke," said Ramón. "He was making a joke."

"What about the wall around the house?" Siqueiros mused, bored with the political discussion.

"A few sticks of dynamite will do the trick," Eitingon suggested. "Blow a hole and send your men in before Trotsky's guards have recovered from the shock."

"We still have to know who's inside, how they're armed."

Eitingon glanced at Ramón. "What about Sylvia? I trust you've kept her on the string."

"Yes, of course."

Eitingon frowned, thinking for a moment. "Get in touch with her to see how soon she can come. She may be the only way you get into the house. She's the key we need."

# TWENTY-SIX

Watching Sylvia come down the stairs of the Pan Am plane, Jacques felt a wave of pleasure, which he saw reflected in her face, the eager wave, the kiss blown from her fingertips. She was wearing her sunglasses and carrying the possum coat over her arm. He was delighted to see her; he couldn't deny his feelings. Caridad and Eitingon might despise Sylvia for being gullible, but the possum coat summoned another story, a history he had with Sylvia, the reality that she considered him her husband. She cared for him and the things he had given her. Eagerly and happily, he moved toward her, putting Caridad and Eitingon out of mind. To play this role, to make love to Sylvia, to share a bed, he joined her in her innocence.

"You didn't really need to bring your fur," he said as they went to claim her luggage. "It's not that cold here."

"But it's cold in New York. I had to wear something going out to Idlewild, and it will probably be cold when I go back."

"Let's not think about that," he said, putting his arm through hers.

After claiming her bags, he led Sylvia and a porter to the yellow Buick roadster, explaining how he had traded in the black Ford sedan. Driving into the city, Sylvia observed the small, somber people with swarthy skin, jet-black hair, and sharp features. Wearing sandals, straw hats, and what appeared to be white pajamas, the men drove horse-drawn carts and burros loaded with towering bundles of sticks and great sacks of charcoal. Women in heavily embroidered dresses appeared to be cooking on open fires along the road.

She had heard a great deal about the city from both of her sisters, and from artists in Paris and New York who rhapsodized about the light and colors in Mexico. Jacques pointed out the snowcapped volcanoes, saying he had climbed Popocatépetl, the one shaped like a pyramid.

"It looks enormous, and such a terrifying name."

"Yes, it's Aztec. I didn't quite make it all the way to the top," he confessed. "The altitude is something here, and I wasn't acclimated. The other one is Iztaccíhuatl, the sleeping woman."

Jacques made a point of driving down Reforma, which, but for the occasional burro, looked Parisian. They passed the American Embassy on their right, made a U-turn at one of the big traffic circles, and pulled beneath the porte cochère of the Hotel Montejo. "Remember, you're Mrs. Jacson," he said as they walked into the hotel, which seemed very Mexican to Sylvia. The floors were red tile, the walls white stucco, the ceilings crossed with heavy, darkly stained beams.

Knowing that Sylvia would want time to bathe and collect herself, Jacques said he had to run a quick errand for his chief, Mr. Lubeck. He walked the three blocks to Calle Hamburgo, which ran behind the hotel through the Zona Rosa, and climbed the stairs in the Edificio Ermita to Siqueiros' apartment. He tapped on the door, slipped his key into the lock, and let himself into the office, which was dense with smoke. Eitingon was on the phone, speaking Russian. Caridad looked up, closing the file she'd been reading. "And did your little blond bird appreciate the yellow Buick?" she asked.

"Yes, the Buick is a great success," he said, sitting down on the green leatherette sofa, wondering if his Mother was jealous of Sylvia.

Caridad's eyes narrowed. "Is something the matter?" she asked.

"No, nothing."

"Leonid, Ramón's wife has arrived," Caridad announced as Eitingon hung up the receiver.

He smiled at the younger man, his eyes alive with interest. "What are your plans? Your immediate plans."

"The usual—show her the city, sweep her off her feet. I thought I might take her dancing at Ciro's tonight."

"Ciro's?" Caridad repeated. "Isn't that a bit glamorous for someone like Sylvia?"

"I don't know. She might enjoy it."

"Where is she now?"

"At the hotel. We're going to the Bellinghausen to dine. It's nearby. She can stretch her legs a little."

"And what about Trotsky?" asked Caridad

"I have to wait till she says she wants to see him. I can't suggest it."

"No, of course not," Caridad agreed. "What if she doesn't want to go?"

"She will. Sylvia never wants to miss anything. Both of her sisters have made the pilgrimage. It's a family ritual."

Eitingon cautioned him not to show the slightest interest in Trotsky. "That's something about Jacques we established in Paris. You don't want to pressure her about anything."

Ramón reminded Eitingon and Caridad that there were still a few details they hadn't worked out. Sylvia would want to know where his office was and a telephone number where she could call.

Eitingon grimaced. "These little details, we don't want them tripping us up. Now that she's arrived you must be careful about coming here."

"She thinks I have a normal job. I'll have to come here more than ever."

"Perhaps it's a mistake to keep her in a hotel so close," said Eitingon,

"Would she follow you here?" Caridad asked.

"No."

"Give her the address but change one digit," said Eitingon. "It won't matter if she telephones. I never answer in Russian."

Jacques walked back to the hotel, stopping in the lobby at the house phone to call Sylvia. "Are you starving?" he asked.

"Yes, but I'm not quite ready. Why don't you come up?"

"I need to take care of something at the desk. I'll see you down here. Hurry! I'm famished."

When Sylvia stepped out of the elevator, Jacques was standing near the front desk looking at a newspaper. "There you are!" he smiled. "The restaurant's just a few blocks from here. I thought you'd like to walk."

He led her out the front doors to Reforma then around the corner and into the Zona Rosa, explaining that in Mexico, the main meal, dinner, was served between two and three and that afterward, everyone took a siesta. Stores and offices closed and didn't open again until five, when workers returned to their jobs and stayed until nine or ten.

Jacaranda trees covered with purple blue blossoms lined the narrow streets in the Zona Rosa. Two ragged little boys with shoeshine boxes fell into the step with them, saying, "*Señor, dejenos lustrar los zapatos! Señor, porfavor! Un pesito, un pesito.*"

An Indian woman sat on the sidewalk, her back against a building, a little girl at her side, her open hand out, propped on her knee. "*Limosna,*" she murmured as they passed, her eyes staring into space. "*Limosna!*"

Jacques guided Sylvia into the restaurant and exchanged a few words in Spanish with the mâitre d', who led them briskly through a dining room of raspberry-pink stucco walls and white linen table clothes to a partially covered patio. Rafts of cigarette and cigar smoke floated up into the limbs of a ceiba tree along with the thrum of voices punctuated by the clank and clatter of forks and knives. An army of waiters in white jackets moved through the room. One held Sylvia's chair while another unfurled a white linen napkin to place in her lap. "I feel like we're in a movie about Mexico," she observed, leaning forward happily.

"Yes, the restaurant is supposed to resemble a Mexican hacienda, very traditional. Famous bullfighters, film stars—all sorts of Mexican celebrities come here—politicians, stars of radio shows, and journalists."

"Do you see anyone you know?"

He glanced around, his lips compressing briefly. "No. No one. I'm still too new to the city." His opened the large menu before him. "I think we should have a daiquiri to start."

"Will I be all right? What with the altitude?"

"One shouldn't hurt you."

As Jacques summoned their waiter to ask for their cocktails, Sylvia opened her menu. She recognized a few of the words—*taco, tortilla, chile*—but the rest was indecipherable. "What's this?" she asked Jacques. "S-E-S-O-S," she spelled the letters out.

"*Sesos,*" he pronounced the word in Spanish, glancing at his menu. "Brains, calves' brains. They're very rich, sautéed in butter. I don't think you would like them."

"Jacques, have you already learned Spanish?"

"Spanish?"

"You spoke to the maître d' when we came in and to the waiter."

He realized that she was right and wondered if he was being deliberately careless. "Just a few words," he answered. "If you speak French then Spanish just comes to you."

Jacques offered Sylvia a cigarette which she declined, and lit one for himself. When their daiquiris came, Sylvia talked about the things she wanted to see—the Chapultepec Castle, the Palace of Fine Arts, the National Museum of Art, the Floating Gardens of Xochimilco, Teotihuacán and the Pyramid of the Sun. "I'd love to fly over to Acapulco for a weekend and lie on the beach. Wouldn't that be lovely, to swim in the Pacific and get a tan?"

"Yes, but remember, I'm a workingman. I don't know how many holidays Mr. Lubeck will give me."

"Oh yes, Peter Lubeck! And when will I meet him?"

Jacques gazed at her, a slight frown flickering across his features. "Sylvia, I don't think that would be quite the thing."

"But as your wife, I should meet your boss."

"I'm sorry to tell you, but Mr. Lubeck doesn't approve of our marriage."

"Doesn't approve?"

"He's very Catholic, very traditional. Someone told him we weren't married by a priest or judge. That and he thinks you're a Communist."

"But I'm not. Didn't you tell him?"

"A follower of Trotsky, a sympathizer—it's all the same to him. But Sylvia, don't let this spoil anything. I must warn you that the support for Hitler is very strong here. But it isn't anti-Semitism so much as a dislike for the United States."

"Mr. Lubeck isn't a Nazi, is he?"

"No, of course not. If he met you, I know he would see your virtues. It's the way we were married he disapproves of."

# TWENTY-SEVEN

As they walked through the cavernous and echoing spaces filled with the blue smoke of incense, the murmur of prayers, and the slanting rays of sunlight, stained shades of blue and red and green, Sylvia kept stopping to consult her guide, a serious-looking book the size of a hymnal with an oxblood-red cover, filled with maps and long historical sections in fine print. With her handbag draped in the crook of her right arm, her weight resting on her left foot, her right canted forward, she would stand reading for minutes at a time, oblivious to the devout Indians shuffling past in shawls and *serapes*.

"Did you know the Spanish built this cathedral on the ruins of the Aztecs' main temple?"

"No, I had no idea." Jacques reached for his cigarettes. "Incense, it smells like cat pee."

"Darling, you probably shouldn't smoke in here."

"No, I suppose not. But with all this smoke . . ." He felt impatient, wondering why she had to stop and read. Why couldn't she just look at what was in front of her?

She raised her head and smiled, pushing her glasses back. "Would you like to go? Are you getting hungry?"

"Yes, the smell of incense always brings back unpleasant memories."

They drove the few blocks to an American restaurant Jacques knew that occupied a sixteenth-century Spanish mansion across from the Alameda. "It's like a big drugstore," Sylvia said as they walked through a pharmacy and newsstand to the dining room, where the waitresses were dressed like Mexican Indians in long, colorful cotton gowns. Sylvia asked for a club sandwich and opened the guidebook once more. "This is so interesting," she said after reading a bit. "Mr. Terry says that the Aztecs sacrificed people at the temple where the cathedral is. Thousands of people would watch. The priests would blow conch-shell horns and beat drums, then, just as the sun came up, they would slice open the chest of their victim, rip out the heart, and hold it up to the light. They believed the sun wouldn't rise if they didn't perform the sacrifice."

"Sylvia, that's ghoulish."

"No, this is interesting. The priests and nobles would cook and eat the bodies of the victims."

She stopped to eat part of her sandwich. "Oh, listen to this. The Spaniards were appalled when they discovered that the Aztecs practiced cannibalism."

"Yes, of course."

"They destroyed the Aztecs' temples because they were cannibals, then made them convert to Catholicism where the sacrament involves eating the body and blood of Christ. How's that for confusing?"

After lunch, they took a brief stroll through the Alameda, a long formal garden with gravel paths, statues, and fountains. Sylvia wanted to visit the Palacio de Bellas Artes, but it was closed so they drove out Reforma past their hotel to the Chapultepec Castle, which stood on a hill, looking back toward the cathedral.

After climbing many flights of steps and walking through the living quarters of the emperor and empress Maximilian and Carlota, they found themselves on a terrace where Sylvia opened her guide and began to read. "Maximilian was a Hapsburg, did you know. I don't quite understand what he was doing in Mexico, but he was executed after four years." She read a bit more then looked down at Reforma. "Carlota, his wife, was terribly jealous. They had the boulevard built so she could watch his carriage come and go from the palace on the Zocalo. She wanted to make sure he didn't stop along the way."

. . .

The following morning, while Jacques was knotting his tie, Sylvia put a call through to Trotsky's secretaries in Coyoacán. Jacques listened as she identified herself, mentioning her sisters Hilda and Ruth. When she hung up, she said she had been invited for tea at four. "I thought they would be busy but they want me to come this afternoon."

"At four," said Jacques. "That's fine. I'll be free then."

She hesitated for a moment, uncertain how to proceed.

"Is there a problem?"

"Yes, I don't think you should come."

He looked at her reflection in the mirror. "Because of Mr. Lubeck?"

"No, do you think I would be that petty?"

"Then why?"

"Hilda and Ruth, everyone says the Stalinists here are doing everything possible to get Trotsky deported. The slightest infraction of the law could threaten Trotsky's status. I can't do anything that might endanger him."

"I don't understand what you're saying."

"You're here on a forged passport. I don't think you should go to the house."

"Because of my passport?"

"It probably wouldn't matter, but still . . . you needn't drive me. I'll take a taxi or catch the trolley."

"No, I'll take you. I won't have you running around the city alone." He finished adjusting his tie and put on the jacket of his suit. "I have to go to the office but I'll be back in time to go to Coyoacán."

When Jacques returned, Sylvia was dressed and ready to go, quietly excited to meet one of the great heroes of her life. For fear of making Jacques feel excluded, she talked about other things as they drove to Coyoacán. "This village was on the edge of the lake," she said as they drove through Tacubaya. "This village, the next one, and Coyoacán were all on the edge of the lake when the Spaniards arrived."

With the breeze wafting through the windows of the car, she tried to imagine the blue water, the boats coming and going, the Aztec city larger and more beautiful than any in Europe. The Spaniards had begun draining the lake when they invaded, and as the city grew in population the lake had all but disappeared. The air was rich with exotic smells. People and livestock wandered along beside the road.

She was charmed when they arrived in Coyoacán with its cobblestone streets and immense stone walls draped with bougainvillea. Jacques showed her the zocalo with its municipal palace, church, and gardens, then proceeded to Calle Viena, where Sylvia let out a small gasp when she saw the walls, topped with concertina wire, guard towers, and machine-gun turret. "Oh, it's a prison."

"More like a fortress, I'd say."

A drowsy Mexican policeman leaned against the raw brick hut that stood on the street between the fortress and a field of corn. Across the valley, the volcanoes loomed against the sky, a curl of smoke rising above El Popo. Jacques parked the Buick at an angle toward the wall, jumped out to get Sylvia's door, and walked her to the entrance, a fortified steel door set into the wall next to a metal garage door shut tight. When she rang the bell, a metal slot opened in the door. She gave her name, and a moment later, an electric lock on the door buzzed; the door opened a couple of inches, followed by the sound of a heavy iron bar scraping concrete. The door finally swung open to a view of a black Dodge and a bit of green garden beyond.

Jacques watched Sylvia disappear inside, then glanced up to the wall where a young man with rusty brown hair stood, holding a bolt-action Springfield rifle. Sensing a flicker of interest, Jacques nodded, then returned to the Buick. Leaving the door open, he turned on the radio and tuned in a Glenn Miller song. He smoked a cigarette, then got out of the car and took off his jacket as if he were too warm. Aware that the guard was watching, he went to the front of the car, where he put his right foot up on the bumper to retie his shoelace. He checked his left shoe, then began a tour around the Buick to inspect the tires. He was tapping the third tire with the toe of his shoe when a voice came from above. "How do you like the Buick?"

He looked up and smiled at the young man. "It's a good car but not as responsive as the Citroën."

"You're not from the States?"

"Canada. What about you?"

"New York. My old man drives a Buick."

"Does he?"

"I'd rather have a Packard."

"They're said to be good. I've seen a couple here in Mexico."

The young man shifted the rifle then looked down on his side of the wall to check if he was being observed.

"What's your name?" asked Jacques.

"Sheldon. Sheldon Harte, but a lot of the Mexicans call me Roberto."

"Why is that?"

"That's my first name, Robert. Robert Sheldon Harte. And I guess Sheldon's sort of hard for them to pronounce. E-sheldon," he said to demonstrate.

"Yes, I see what you mean."

"Everybody here has a couple of names, code names, aliases, noms de guerre. They take new names when they join the movement. Funny, the Jews always take Christian names, but never the reverse."

The young man looked down again, and after a moment another guard appeared, a large, strapping man with black hair, prowlike nose, and a square jaw. He'd tied a red bandana round his neck and wore a big revolver in a holster hanging from a wide leather belt. Jacques nodded his head, then went back to his car. He had accomplished what he wanted. Next time, they would know he was Sylvia's husband.

After an hour and a half or so, the reinforced metal door opened and Sylvia stepped out onto the street looking radiant. "You had a nice time," Jacques said, helping her into the car.

"Yes. Yes, I did. You'll never guess who's here. Do you remember the Rosmers? Marguerite and Alfred? We went to their house for that meeting in Périgny. They both remembered you, Marguerite, especially. She wanted to know about my handsome aristocratic husband."

"And what did you tell them?"

"That you were waiting for me outside. I explained about your passport."

"What did they say about that?"

"Nothing, really. I invited them to have dinner with us one evening. I hope you don't mind."

"No, not if you want them."

She assured him the Rosmers were thrilled by the invitation. They'd been living for months in a tiny little room at the back of the garden and had brought the Trotskys' grandson from France. He was orphaned when Sedov was murdered. Alfred and Marguerite stayed to help him get adjusted. Now they couldn't go back to France.

"If you want them, I'm pleased. We can entertain them at our hotel."

"I also volunteered to help in the office. I need something to do while you're at work, and Trotsky is desperate for help. He's fallen behind on his biography of Stalin, and his publisher in New York won't send money until Trotsky sends more chapters. And he can't work on the chapters because he has to take magazine and newspaper assignments for the ready cash. It's a vicious cycle."

"Trotsky doesn't have money?"

"I can come out on the trolley. They said I'd be perfectly safe. Marguerite takes the trolley all the time."

"You want to come here and work for Trotsky? What would you do?"

"I'm not sure. He's writing the first draft of the biography in Russian. I suppose I could proof the English translation as it comes back. Or I could help with the research. Do you mind?"

"No, and don't worry about taking the trolley. I come out here on business so it won't be a problem."

## TWENTY-EIGHT

And so Jacques became a presence at the gate of 45 Calle Viena. He would drop Sylvia off, disappear for an hour or two to call on investors in San Ángel, the neighboring suburb, then return to wait for her. He made a point of not asking her questions—how many guards there were, who worked in the house—but he listened carefully, remembering the names, slowly putting together a roster.

"Oh yes, Sheldon," Alfred Rosmer said in French as he held out his glass for Jacques to fill with champagne. They were in Jacques and Sylvia's suite at the Hotel Montejo. Jacques had found two good bottles of champagne and arranged for the hotel kitchen to send up canapés and prepare what he hoped would be a simply roasted chicken that they would eat in the dining room. Rosmer took a sip from his glass, then wiped his gray drooping mustache. He had spent so much of his life arguing politics, first as a syndicalist then as a leader of the Communist Party in France, he found it a relief to be with this young businessman who could afford so many good things in life.

"Sheldon doesn't really fit in with the other men," said Rosmer. "I'm not sure what it is."

"Sheldon Harte?" said Marguerite. "He's a romantic. He came to Mexico with romantic notions about writing a play. And he's from a wealthy Park Avenue family, while the other men are working class."

"But I think it's more than that," Alfred replied.

"What would it be?"

"I'm not quite sure, so would rather not say. Marguerite, what was that story about Sheldon and the wheelbarrow?" he asked.

Marguerite Rosmer's face lit up. A stout woman—plump to her husband's thin—she had a jovial, shrewd face, full cheeks, and a large bosom. She became amused, telling how Sheldon, just after arriving, gave away the key to the front gate while he was on guard duty. One of the Mexicans working on the renovation of the house kept coming and going with a wheelbarrow, and Sheldon, deciding it was too much trouble to keep opening the gate, finally handed him the key.

Marguerite started to laugh, then, seeing the blank expression on Sylvia's face, she explained. "His job was to guard the gate, not give the key away." Marguerite dabbed at her eyes.

"And the one who wears the red bandana?" asked Sylvia.

"That's Jake Cooper, a different sort altogether," Alfred said. "He's a truck driver from the American Midwest. His parents were Jewish immigrants, terribly poor. The Teamsters union sends men down to work as guards for Trotsky. They're all volunteers." Alfred took out his pipe to chew on. "They come and go; some are better than others. But Trotsky has never worried about security. After a revolution and a civil war he's not easily threatened."

After dinner, as Jacques was opening a bottle of wine, Sylvia asked Alfred about the book he was planning to write. "Yes, Moscow under Lenin," he said, "those first seven years."

"If Lenin had lived, would everything be different?" Sylvia asked.

"We want to think that. I gave years of my life to Lenin, but, in truth, he was the source of some of the problems we have now. He concentrated too much power in the Party and the Central Committee. He was so intent on defeating the Czar that in some ironic and unconscious way he created a dictatorship in the Czar's image. Trotsky kept warning Lenin, and Trotsky was right. That was the crux of his disagreement with Lenin in those early years. Trotsky wasn't without flaws, but he had remarkable vision."

"But you won't join the Fourth International?" said Sylvia.

As if to gather his thoughts, Alfred took out his tobacco pouch and loaded the bowl of his pipe. "Trotsky is an old friend, a man I admire. But no, something for me changed when I was expelled from the Party in '24."

"When was it that Trotsky changed?" asked Jacques, returning to the table.

"Trotsky? Change in what way?" said Alfred.

"Turn away from Marxism and the revolution."

Alfred raised his eyebrows. "But my dear boy, I'm not sure what you're talking about. Trotsky never deviated from Marx or Lenin."

Jacques opened his mouth to speak but caught himself. He focused his attention on pouring the wine as Alfred gave a brief disquisition on Marxist theory, saying that Marx had always believed that for a workers' revolution to succeed, it had to be an international movement. Otherwise, economic surpluses would be wasted on nationalistic wars over markets and raw materials. It was Stalin who initiated a policy of revolution in one country, decreeing that the Soviet Union would no longer support revolutionary movements in other countries.

Jacques focused on the wineglasses and gave no sign that he was listening. Alfred pressed the tobacco down in the bowl of the pipe with his thumb and struck a match, then leaned forward as if seized by a thought.

"Did you follow what happened in Spain?" he asked.

Jacques blinked away the impulse to say that he was there, that he was a Spaniard who knew all there is to know about the war in Spain. Instead he shook his head. "No, I'm afraid not."

"Ah well, then it's a topic for another evening."

# TWENTY-NINE

Sylvia's thoughts flew to Madame Gaston as she replaced the telephone receiver in its cradle. She felt as if the earth had suddenly dropped beneath her, that sudden strange sensation in her stomach as when Jacques took a dip too fast in the yellow Buick. She returned to the table near the front door where she was working. One of the secretaries was typing, the keys of the large black machine clattering, while in his office, Trotsky was speaking into his Dictaphone machine, the Russian phrases and words coming through his open windows and open door as if he were addressing a crowd of thousands rather than writing a book. She tried to focus on her work, but after a few minutes, she got up and walked back through the dining room and out onto the patio to look for Marguerite.

The Rosmers had a room at one end of a row of small rooms that had been built along the inside wall of the garden for the guards and secretaries. Marguerite came to her door in a housedress, her long, graying hair falling down her shoulders. "Sylvia, you're agitated. What's wrong?"

"I just called Jacques at his office and a woman answered."

"Yes." Marguerite nodded. "His secretary."

Sylvia shook her head. "When I asked for Frank Jacson, she said I had a wrong number. I called back and got the same woman. She'd never heard of Frank Jacson or Jacques Mornard."

"Perhaps you called the wrong number," said Marguerite, stroking her long hair flat against her chest.

"No, I'm sure it was the right number. I've called it two or three times and Jacques has always answered."

"But you know what the telephone system is here, two different companies for one city. It's absurd. Calls always get mixed up."

"No, that's not it."

Sylvia stopped, not sure where she was headed, not wanting to betray Jacques's loyalty. "This sort of thing has happened with Jacques in the past. I've sensed there was something he wasn't telling me. You know, his fake passport, and he won't introduce me to his boss."

"Do you think he has another woman?"

"No." They were standing in the shade of the eucalyptus tree, the sounds of the village drifting over the wall.

"Then what is it?"

Sylvia took a deep breath, then glanced over her shoulder to make sure no one was listening. "I think he's working as an undercover agent."

Marguerite was facing the house, so that she saw the patio, the door to the dining room. Trotsky's voice came from his office. "You think Jacques is working for the GPU?" Marguerite whispered.

"Oh, good Lord, no. If I did, I . . ." Sylvia couldn't think what she would do. "Jacques is not a Stalinist. He's not even a Communist. I think he's working for the English."

"Well, it's possible. Everyone has spies in Mexico because of the war. France, Germany, the Soviets. The town is full of spies." She stepped closer, lowering her head. "But you have to find out. You have to know who Jacques is."

"But how?"

"Go to his office."

"I could never do that. Jacques doesn't want me to meet his boss, and he would be furious if he thought I was spying."

"Wives always spy on their husbands. It is their job. Choose a time when you're sure he won't be there. You don't have to go *into* the office. There will be a sign on the door; you can make discreet inquiries in the building."

"Marguerite, it would be such a betrayal."

"Yes, but you must have your peace of mind. You must assure

yourself. No doubt it is nothing. Being in this house with all of the guards and the guns affects one's imagination, makes one anxious. But you must investigate."

Sylvia returned to her desk, where she kept thinking about Jacques—how he had disappeared from Paris. When it was time to leave, she gathered up her belongings and put on her dark glasses. Jake Cooper was on the wall above her; Sheldon Harte manned the metal door in the garage that opened to the street.

"Going now?" Harte said, moving the heavy iron bar propped against the door, pressing the electric switch that released the lock. He glanced through the peephole then pushed open the door.

Outside, the sight of Jacques standing by the Buick was reassuring. This was the man she knew and loved. He was talking to Otto Schüssler, one of Trotsky's secretaries.

"Ready?" Jacques smiled when he saw her. His lips were red and chapped from the dry air and mountain sun. Beyond him, above the city, a wisp of smoke rose from the cone of Popocatépetl. At its side, snow covered the flank of the sleeping woman.

Jacques flicked away the cigarette and went around to open the car door for her. "Otto's girlfriend is coming from Germany," said Jacques.

"Otto, that's wonderful." Sylvia smiled. "What's her name? When will she arrive?"

"Her name is Gertrude, but I call her Trudy. Soon! Next week, I think."

"I'm glad she could get out of Germany," Sylvia said as they drove away.


The following morning as they finished breakfast, Sylvia asked Jacques if he was going to the office. They were in the hotel dining room and Jacques, having just lit a cigarette, was putting the tip of a finger to his tongue to remove a fleck of tobacco.

He frowned. "Why do you ask?"

"No reason. Wives just like to know what their husbands are doing."

"Mr. Lubeck and I have a meeting downtown."

"What kind of meeting?"

"Sylvia, you know I can't talk about work. We're buying commodities for the war."

She let the matter drop. After he left, she spent an hour and a half waiting nervously in the suite. She wasn't like Marguerite. She wasn't French, didn't think that men had lovers and that wives should spy. And why, married to a man like Alfred, would Marguerite believe that? Sylvia felt she should trust Jacques, that to doubt him undermined the marriage. But the seed of doubt had already taken root. She had to return to New York soon, and she couldn't leave without knowing.

Downstairs, the morning was brilliant. The thin mountain air was crisp and had the sharp smell particular to the city, a blend of shoeshine polish and exhaust fumes. She turned the corner into the Zona Rosa and walked quickly to avoid the little boys and the Indian woman sitting on the pavement with her child. A house full of furniture came toward her on the backs of Indians dressed in white—a sofa, stuffed chairs, tables, a desk, a chest of drawers. The Indians moved down the street, each bent over, leaning into the cloth straps that went around their foreheads to support their loads. A moving company, Jacques had explained to her; that was how it was done in Mexico.

When she came to Calle Hamburgo, a cross street, she began looking for the Ermita building at 820 Hamburgo. Having imagined Jacques working in a modern office or bank building, she was all but certain there was some mistake when she saw the crude metal placard saying "Ermita" on the side of a stucco apartment building. Surely, this wasn't where Lubeck, an international financier, had his office. But with the war, perhaps there was a shortage of proper offices.

She scanned the street for Jacques's yellow Buick, then, her heart beating faster, went into a small dark lobby that had red clay tiles on the floor. Jacques had written #203 after Edificio Ermita on the sheet of notepaper from the hotel. As she started up the stairs she heard voices and smelled food cooking. People obviously lived in the building, but glancing down the first hallway she saw placards on the doors for offices. When she arrived at 203, the sound of children playing came through the door. Jacques couldn't have a family in Mexico. It was simply impossible. Emboldened, she knocked. After a few moments, a young Mexican woman with a baby in her arms opened the door just wide enough to look out. Fumbling for her high school Spanish, sure that she was on a fool's errand, Sylvia asked for Frank Jacson. The woman frowned, shrugging her shoulders.

"Do you speak English?" asked Sylvia.

"*Un poco.*" The woman held up thumb and index finger to indicate a small amount.

"Do you know Frank Jacson?" asked Sylvia.

The woman shook her head, shifting the baby in her arms.

"Or Mr. Lubeck? Peter Lubeck? He has an office here."

The names meant nothing to the woman.

Sylvia turned away. She went back down to the street and studied the sign in front of the building. Nothing made sense to her. Was Jacques an undercover agent? Did Peter Lubeck even exist?


At the hotel, her hands were trembling when she picked up the phone and asked the hotel operator to put a call through to the house in Coyoacán. "I'll come there," said Marguerite. "I'm just catching a ride into town with Jake Cooper. I'll have him bring me to your hotel. You can tell me everything when I arrive."

Sylvia paced back and forth in the suite until she heard Marguerite at the door. "Now, what is all of this?" said Marguerite. "There has to be an explanation. Jacques is a lovely man. You can't jump to conclusions."

"I'm not. I did as you said and went to investigate. I found what should have been his office, but there was a Mexican woman living there with her children."

"Do you think Jacques has a family here?"

"No, of course not. He just arrived."

"You know men do these things. Did you describe Jacques to her?"

"She didn't understand English that well, but his name didn't mean anything to her."

"I had better go. I'm older and I speak more Spanish. I'll sort this out."

Waiting for Marguerite, Sylvia went into the bathroom. Believing in the restorative powers of water, she washed her face and hands, combed her hair, and applied fresh lipstick. Putting on her glasses, she studied her reflection for a moment, then removed them. Tilting her face slightly to one side, she realized that she wasn't sure she was truly attractive to Jacques. If she only knew, if she was only sure that she was pretty, she could be sure that Jacques loved her.

Marguerite returned, looking pleased with herself. "Sylvia, it's just as I said, a silly misunderstanding. Jacques is in 205, not 203."

"Did you see him?"

"No, I didn't even go in the building. A man was working out front, a concierge. I described Jacques and his car, and the concierge knew exactly who I meant. Lubeck as well, an older *extranjero*."

"Jacques wrote down the wrong number?"

"A simple mistake. You were afraid he was lying to you, but it was all a misunderstanding."

# THIRTY

Beyond Coyoacán and San Ángel, the road passed a flow of black lava that lay on the earth, a blister of tar fifty feet high and three miles long. Orchards and gardens climbed the slope of the valley, giving way to scrub forest and patches of burned timber. Children stood in front of adobe hovels, watching as the yellow Buick passed. Ramón was driving with Eitingon beside him on the front seat. Caridad sat in the back, looking determined, ready for a confrontation when they found Siqueiros. She was sick of his antics, his attitude of noblesse oblige. In order to prick her, he was always attacking Ramón. "Where is the map of the house?" Siqueiros would say. "I have to know what's on the other side of the wall."

He was always harping on Ramón's failure to get into the house. What was wrong with Ramón? Why couldn't he control Sylvia? *La fea*, Siqueiros called her, the ugly. Like most Mexican men, Siqueiros thought women should be voluptuous and fleshy, and they certainly shouldn't wear glasses. *La jamona*, he called Sylvia, the old maid. Perhaps *la jamona* was unsatisfied.

Caridad and Eitingon had done all of the delicate work of creating the correct political climate for Trotsky's assassination. They had conducted purges at the Communist papers. *El Popular* and *La Voz de Mexico* were now howling for Trotsky's deportation, calling him a Fascist, a terrorist, and a traitor. Yet Siqueiros dragged his feet. He wanted to talk about disguises and aliases as if he were putting on a theatrical performance. He took orders from no one and certainly not Caridad.

Ramón slowed the car as they entered the village of Santa Rosa, a small gathering of adobe huts, a one-room school, a municipal building. Siqueiros had told them to look for the third lane after Santa Rosa. They would cross a ravine then turn right next to a tall paling of prickly pear. When Ramón stopped to open a gate, the quiet of the countryside settled upon them, the sound of a breeze.

"Are you sure this is right?" asked Caridad.

"Yes, according to David's directions."

She crimped her lips, looking away.

The dusty white road curved around the side of a hill, pebbles and small stones crunching beneath the tires. A small adobe house was coming into view when a Thompson submachine opened fire. Puffs of dust followed a long-legged yellow dog racing across a plowed field below the house until, with a yelp, the dog flipped, tumbling into a bloody corpse.

"*Ay, pinche perro!*" cackled a man's high-pitched voice.

"*Hijole!*" another cried. Two men standing below the house turned away from the field, one of them swinging the machine gun over his shoulder. The Arenal brothers, Siqueiros' studio assistants and brothers-in-law, moved with a familial looseness. The one carrying the machine gun, Leopoldo, sported a tan zoot suit, a long jacket with enormous shoulders, baggy trousers nipped at the ankles. Luis wore paint-splattered blue coveralls and a new straw hat, the sort that children or country bumpkins bought in the market.

"Fools! Fools and troublemakers," Caridad hissed as David Siqueiros emerged from the adobe structure. Ramón stopped the Buick next to a gray Packard. Siqueiros' wife, Angelica, was sitting with her little girl on a blanket they'd spread beneath a big cottonwood tree. The land sloped away below the house. In the distance, beyond a patchwork of dun-colored fields, the tiled domes and spires of San Ángel and Coyoacán sparkled in the afternoon sun. Off to the left, the city rose only to be dwarfed by the snowcapped volcanoes.

"*Bienvenidos!*" Siqueiros greeted them. "*Bienvenidos a nuestro escondite.*" Welcome to our little hideout.

A beer bottle in his left hand, he went around to open the door for Eitingon, behaving as if they'd arrived for a party. Draping his right arm over Eitingon's shoulder, he insisted that they see the inside of the house, which he persisted in calling his *escondite*. The house was unfinished and had neither electricity nor plumbing. The first room had a metal cot and a cheap wooden table of the sort one can buy at any market, and four equally cheap chairs. The second room had another cot and an easel standing in front of two windows looking out on the valley. Wearing an emerald-green cowboy shirt and a child's belt decorated with pieces of red glass, Antonio Pujol lay on the cot, reading a Mexican comic book.

"Look at the view!" Siqueiros insisted. "I rented the house from a man in the village. I told him I'm going to teach art students here."

"Your *escondite*," Caridad pronounced the word as if picking it up with tongs, "isn't going to be much of a secret with people firing machine guns out here."

"Nobody will remember a little gunfire six or eight months from now."

"Not six, not eight," she replied. "Closer to three. The operation has been scheduled for May."

"Who scheduled it?" Siquieros asked, swiveling toward Eitingon. "I still don't have a map of the house."

"We got it," said Eitingon, switching from Spanish to French, pulling one of the chairs out form the table. "Can we talk here?"

"As you like," Siqueiros replied in French, sitting down along with Caridad.

Eitingon took a long envelope out of his coat pocket and unfolded a carefully drawn blueprint. "Here's the entrance on Viena." He tapped the paper. "The gate opens into the old garage. A path runs up to the house, which is shaped like a T. The top of the T runs along the exterior wall next to the river—a library, a dining room, and a kitchen. The base of the T is made by three rooms in a row that extend into the lot—Trotsky's office, his and his wife's bedroom, and a third bedroom for the grandson. Behind them there's a larger garden and a patio."

"Yes, yes. It's very clear."

"And here is the eucalyptus tree you see from outside." Eitingon indicated a small circle. "Along this back wall they've built four small rooms that face into the patio. That's where the guards sleep and the old French couple. With only four guards, there are probably never more than two on duty at night. One would be at the front entrance, the other in the machine-gun turret on the wall above."

"Where did you get this?"

"Ramón."

Siqueiros looked up at Ramón standing in the doorway, his shoulder against the frame. "How did you get it?"

"I befriended one of the guards, a young American. I've met him a couple of times at night in town, took him drinking. Even took him to a whorehouse."

"Which one?"

"The Kit Kat Klub," Jacques answered.

"But that's a cantina, not a whorehouse."

"A whore was there."

Siqueiros laughed. "And you made this drawing there?"

"No, just a sketch that I refined."

"Do you think this is accurate?"

"Yes, and I'll know more soon enough. I'm sending Sylvia home to New York. She's the reason I haven't been in the house."

"Sudoplatov wants the strike in mid-May," Eitingon interjected. "The May Day parade will be an anti-Trotsky rally. Hitler will invade France a week or two later, the middle of May. The execution should occur at the same time."

"So Trotsky will get pushed off the front pages."

"Exactly. But can you be ready by then?"

"Yes, I have most of the arms, and I know the men I want. I still have to find some police or army uniforms so that we can take them by surprise." He looked to Ramón. "Do you think you could get that guard to open the gate?"

"Possibly."

"If we don't have to go over the wall, we can be in and out before they know what happened." He leaned down to look at the map of the house. "We position a machine gun next to the tree to pin down the guards, then surround Trotsky's bedroom. It will be like shooting an old trout in a barrel."

# THIRTY-ONE

She blotted the red lipstick carefully, then narrowed her eyes, stepping back to study her reflection in the mirror above the vanity. Hoping for an improvement, she removed her glasses, but she didn't feel good about the evening. It was her last night before leaving, and she wished they weren't going to a nightclub. But Jacques insisted they go out.

"I'm afraid I look frumpy," she said, walking into the living room of their suite, where Jacques, in a white dinner jacket and black bow tie, was sitting on the sofa.

"Sylvia, you mustn't say that." He studied her for a moment. "You look lovely."

"But this dress!"

"You always like blue."

"But it's out of style."

"No one in Mexico will know. And don't worry, we'll get you some new evening gowns in New York. That's something to look forward to."

He got her possum coat from the closet. "We're going to have a wonderful time at Ciro's. You'll see, it's very glamorous."

In the elevator, she fretted with her dress, then stopped worrying it with her fingers, telling herself that her nerves were frayed because she was leaving. She dreaded living once more in New York with her unmarried sisters, spinsters in the making. She feared that her life at this hotel, with its garden filled with flowers and its brimming fountains, would become a dim memory. It all hung in the balance. It all depended on Jacques, who draped the fur around her shoulders as they walked out to the porte cochère, where the yellow Buick was waiting. The night air was crisp, the traffic on Reforma beginning to subside. "I hope he'll be all right. I hate leaving just now," Sylvia said as Jacques started the car.

"Do you mean Alfred?"

"Yes, Alfred."

"He should be fine. It's probably nothing serious," Jacques said, wheeling the car out onto the avenue.

"But if it isn't serious, why have surgery? Why not wait until he gets to New York? It must be urgent."

"They haven't told you what kind of surgery?"

"No, but you know how old-world they are. So proper."

"Perhaps it's a rupture. That's something common for men his age, and it's not all that serious."

He pressed the lighter in the dash and handed her his silver case. "Do you mind?"

She extracted one of the cigarettes, then noticed that unpleasant smell as tobacco and paper hissed against the red-hot coil of the lighter. Reforma, with all the rows of trees lining the esplanades and pedestrian promenades, was almost like a forest. The *peseros*, the shared taxis that cost a peso, the oldest and cheapest cars, sped back and forth, stopping to let passengers in and out. Poor people, Indians, walked next to the street, carrying large bundles on their backs, holding children by the hand. Watching them, she felt homesick, confused as to where home was. Jacques looked so happy and handsome. Happy because she was leaving? Because they were going to a famous nightclub? Sometimes he seemed so childish to her. He couldn't see past the glamorous nightclub to the weeks, even months of separation. How could he be happy on this of all nights?

As they arrived at the club, she resolved to shake off her uneasiness. She would be what he wanted, gay and lively. Chauffeurs stood next to the large shining automobiles lined up in the street. As they walked in, the sound of an orchestra playing "Begin the Beguine" came through doors at the far end of a stately hallway, lined with columns and paved with squares of black-and-white marble. She waited as Jacques checked her coat and again as he gave his name to the maître d', who led them into a large circular room where dancers revolved beneath massive tiers of chandeliers and clouds of smoke rose from the tables and banquettes that surrounded the dance floor. "Look!" said Jacques, nodding toward one of the murals that decorated the room. Someone had painted immense naked women lounging voluptuously in some sylvan glade, their thighs, buttocks, and breasts displayed as if on a banquet table. "Are those Rivera's?"

"Oh, Lord! They must be! Poor man! I heard he'd been reduced to this."

"Poor man? What do you mean? This is the best nightclub in Mexico!"

"He was an artist and a revolutionary. He was trying to lift the masses. Now he's entertaining the rich. Look, these women aren't even Mexican."

"His Mexican peasants would be out of place here."

"Jacques, that's what I'm saying."

"I don't understand your point."

"There are probably some in the kitchen," she said ruefully.

They proceeded, following the maître d' to a banquette that, like all the other banquettes and tables, had its own small lamp, casting its own little island of light. "Look at those people down there. We should be closer to the dance floor. I'm going to ask for a better table."

"No, I'm happy here. I don't want to be too close."

"Well, if you insist." Jacques signaled to a waiter.

"I think I'll have a Gibson," said Sylvia.

"Are you sure? Isn't that a bit strong?"

"I like the sound of a Gibson. I'll be a Gibson girl. Look at that woman's necklace! Do you think those are real emeralds?"

"They must be. Shall we dance?"

"Not just yet. Let's have our drinks and take in the atmosphere. This is quite extraordinary. I feel like I'm in Hollywood."

"Then you're having fun."

She put her hand on his, giving it a soft squeeze. A girl passed carrying a tray of cigarettes, cigars, and mints. Then another followed selling orchids. Jacques insisted on buying Sylvia a corsage, apologizing for not having had one sent to the hotel. She finished her Gibson, then they went out onto the dance floor. The song was relatively slow, a foxtrot. She didn't much care for dancing as a rule, but she pressed her face against Jacques's dinner jacket, inhaling the faint scent of his cologne, his body guiding her. Once she fell into the rhythm, it came naturally, shuffling along with this herd of rich people, turning slowly in a circle. She preferred the slow romantic songs, "Blue Moon," "Red Sails in the Sunset," "Chasing Shadows." They sat out the faster, Latin songs.

She had a second drink, then a third, which made the evening feel remote and somewhat unreal. When she walked into the women's lounge, she heard German voices and the sound of weeping. A woman was sobbing, dabbing at her eyes with a handkerchief while two others offered comfort. "*Schoen, shatzie, schoen,*" one of them was crooning. The women were in their thirties, beautifully dressed and groomed. When they saw Sylvia, they closed ranks and had disappeared by the time she came out of one of the stalls.

She sat down at one of the vanities for a moment, studying her face, the faint band of freckles across her cheekbones, her wide mouth. She wondered what it would be like to be beautiful in an absolute and objective way. Were her doubts about Jacques really doubts about herself? She touched up her lipstick, then went back out to find their table empty. She was tapping her fingertips on his cigarette case when she noticed Jacques on the dance floor with a young woman. Talking in an animated way, he tipped his head back to laugh, giving the girl an extra little spin.

A wave of jealousy washed over Sylvia. The girl was younger and prettier; she had beautiful dark hair and lovely white shoulders. She and Jacques looked so comfortable together—they had to know each other. He had come to the club to see her. At the end of the song, he stood holding her hand, then made a slight bow before returning to Sylvia.

Sylvia attempted to smile, to behave as if nothing had happened, but she was at sea. "Who was that?" she asked.

"Just a girl. She saw me sitting at our table alone and invited me to dance."

"She doesn't have a name?"

"She must, but I didn't ask." Jacques managed an awkward half smile.

The orchestra started to play once more, a tall blond woman in a gold lamé gown coming to the front of the stage. "Like the beat beat beat of the tom-tom," she sang, "when the jungle shadows fall."

The song was familiar but why were prologues always so difficult to recognize? Why didn't they sound like the rest of the song? As the melody commenced, the glittering crowd resumed its rhythmic shuffle, the romantic gyre turning slowly. *Night and day, you are the one.*

"You don't mind that I danced with her. She's here with her aunt and uncle and doesn't have a partner."

"Poor child, and how kind of you! You looked like you knew each other. I was sure of it."

Jacques laughed. "I've never seen her." He lit a cigarette then signaled for their waiter. "You aren't jealous?"

"No, I'm not jealous. What do you think of me? But I am tired. I'd like to go to the hotel now. I'm leaving tomorrow."


They didn't speak in the car driving back to the hotel. The silence was toxic, like the jealousy hardening her heart, twisting her mind.

She was being swept away by something she couldn't see or control. And everything Jacques said, every innocuous utterance—*Poor dear, I know you're tired*—inflamed her imagination. She held her tongue until he closed the door to their suite behind them.

"Who was she?" Sylvia said, slapping her clutch on the back of the sofa.

"Who?"

"You know who I'm talking about? The girl at the club."

"Sylvia, I have no idea. I never saw her before. And I'll never see her again."

"Is she your mistress? Is that who you were seeing before I arrived? Is that where you go when you disappear? You've been seeing her all along, haven't you? I've known something was wrong from the beginning. Did she follow you here from Paris?"

Jacques laughed uncertainly.

"Tell me! I want to know the truth! She's your mistress! What's her name?"

"Sylvia, listen to yourself. You're not making sense."

"You wanted to go to Ciro's so you could see her. Or you wanted her to see me so she wouldn't be jealous."

"That's crazy, Sylvia. If I had a mistress I was hiding, would I arrange for her to come to the same cabaret? Would I get up and dance with her while you went to the loo? That makes no sense."

Sylvia hesitated.

"Does it?" he pressed her. "Does that make sense?"

Sylvia took a deep breath, started to speak, then shuddered. Bringing her palms to her face, she began to weep uncontrollably as she once had in Paris. He put his arms around her, stroked her back gently, cooing to her. "Sylvia, Sylvia, I know I have my flaws, but I love you. Why can't you believe that?"

She shook her head, then pulled away, hiccoughing, trying to regain control of herself. She accepted his handkerchief, then dried her eyes, still wincing from her pain.

"Do you want a nightcap? Something to make you sleep? Of course you're exhausted and anxious, the night before a long journey. We should have stayed in, had a quiet dinner."

"No, I don't want something to make me sleep. I want you to tell me the truth. I don't care about the girl. That was crazy. But I know something is happening that I don't understand. I've sensed it from the beginning."

His eyes went very still.

"Jacques, who are you? I don't know who you are. Is there a Mr. Lubeck? What are you doing here? I see you and I hear you. And I love you so much, but I'm afraid I'm losing my mind."

Jacques looked lost, hollow. He removed his glasses and rubbed his eyes, then, shaking his head, he spoke in a very low, quiet voice. "Sylvia, please don't say these things to me. I am your husband." He hesitated. "My life, the world I come from has fallen apart in ways you can't understand. The only future I can imagine is with you in New York. That's all I have."

She started to cry again but in a different way. The storm was subsiding. He put his arms around her. "Darling, let's go to bed. Everything will be all right."

"You won't disappear again?"

"No, I won't disappear. I promise. I love you. I may be able to come to New York. We're going to finish our business here, and perhaps I can find a job in New York. We can have an apartment, a real life together. That's what we want, isn't it?"

"Yes, of course," she agreed, desperate to believe him.

"Let's go to bed. It's our last night for a while."

When he went into the bedroom, she was sitting at the vanity, rubbing cold cream into her face. "Jacques." She raised her eyes to his in the mirror.

"Yes?"

"There's one more thing I want you to promise."

"Yes, whatever."

"While I'm gone, I don't want you to go to Coyoacán."

"To Coyoacán? Do you mean to the house?"

"Yes, I don't want you around Trotsky."

"I haven't even met the man. I have no interest in him. What are you thinking?"

"I don't know why exactly, but I don't want you going to the house while I'm gone. I have a strange feeling about this."

"What if Marguerite and Alfred need something?"

"They have friends there. They'll be fine. You can see them here in the city."

"I don't understand."

"I don't care if you understand. Will you promise not to go? Will you please promise me?"

"Yes. Yes, I promise."

She began to wipe the cold cream from her face, leaning closer to the mirror, noticing the shadows beneath her eyes. She hated the shadows, wished they didn't exist.

# THIRTY-TWO

Admission, when it came, was sudden and effortless. The electric lock snapped, the heavy iron bar scraped against concrete, then the reinforced steel door opened into the garage where a station had been set up for the guards in the right bay—a desk with an office chair and a high stool that could be pulled up to the peephole. "Mrs. Rosmer said you should wait in the garden," Jake Cooper explained as he let Jacques in. "She says there's no reason you should stand on the street."

A straw chair waited for him. He unbuttoned his jacket and sat down, lighting a cigarette, crossing his legs in the style of American men, his right ankle resting above his left knee. A flagstone path ran parallel below the front wall, leading to the open doors of the library, the clatter of typewriters; bougainvillea cascaded over the roof of the little porch to make a bower above the door. A narrow strip of brilliantly green grass separated the path from the wing of the house that extended into the garden, three rooms each with a romantic little balcony a foot above the ground, a curved ornamental railing with French doors.

After a moment, a high-ranking Mexican officer in jodhpurs, tunic, and riding boots emerged from the bougainvillea to stride down the path to the gate. Beneath a visor cap, his face was soft and somehow feminine, a dark mole just beneath the left corner of his mouth. He glanced at Ramón and nodded briskly. As he was going out, Sheldon Harte waved from the machine-gun turret on the front wall above the library door. "You're here for Marguerite?" he called.

Jacques nodded affirmatively and smiled. "I'm taking her to see Alfred."

He finished his cigarette, then, realizing that Jake Cooper was speaking to someone on the street through the peephole, Jacques got up, pretending to stretch his legs. Hands in pockets, he strolled over to inspect the beds of daisies and ferns beneath the little balconies. The first of the three rooms was Trotsky's office; part of his desk was visible through the French doors. The next room was filled with shadow, a bed covered with an Indian blanket, sunlight coming from high windows on the opposite wall. The third set of French doors looked into the boy's room, a single bed, a child's desk, model airplanes suspended by wires from the ceiling.

Checking to make sure he was unobserved, Jacques moved to the end of the wing, rounding the corner of the house with the intention of locating an exterior entrance and the rooms for the guards at the back of the compound. A breeze moved through the boughs of the eucalyptus tree above, rippling the raft of sunlight and shadows floating upon the ground. There was the scent of eucalyptus and wood smoke, the diffuse and distant sounds of the village. Sheltered by walls and the tree, the garden felt like a little corner of paradise.

For a moment Jacques didn't notice the man standing with his back to the house, facing some sort of wire cage. But then, sensing another presence, he turned. Heart skipping, Jacques recognized the distinctive face that, with the goatee, round gasses, and high forehead, looked like that of Mephistopheles. Satan. That Trotsky wore a blue peasant's smock and held a white rabbit he had pulled from a raised hutch made him that much more sinister. The men looked at each other, arrested in a moment of stillness, then Jacques—wishing he had no knowledge of what lay ahead—bowed ever so slightly and retreated from the shade of the eucalyptus to the strip of lawn and his chair.

By now, Marguerite Rosmer's procession through the library could be heard, her fluty voice bidding the secretaries farewell, collecting good wishes for her husband. She emerged wearing her one good dress, the navy blue, carrying her handbag and a straw basket covered with a dish towel. "Ah! *Mon cher*, there you are!" she piped in French, letting Jacques rescue her from the burden of the basket. "I made Alfred some of my chicken soup with none of those *chiles* he detests. I see Jake let you in. So much nicer than sitting on the street like a peon."

She spoke to Jake Cooper in English, asking the whereabouts of Natalia Sedova—as everyone referred to Madame Trotsky. Once more on the street, Jacques held the door of the Buick for Marguerite, then put the basket in the back of the car, making sure the jar of soup stood upright.

"And Alfred?" Jacques asked, sliding behind the steering wheel.

"Much better, thank you."

As he started the car, she opened her black leather purse, which exhaled a history of face powders, hand creams, mints, and medicines. He sensed she was about to bring out a letter from Sylvia, but it was an embroidered handkerchief he'd given her on an outing to the Indian market in Toluca. She and Alfred had to pinch their pennies so tightly, and she had been delighted with the knots of silk violets that ran along the border.

By some unspoken agreement, neither she nor Jacques mentioned Sylvia, who had been gone less than two weeks. He was sure Sylvia had extracted some sort of promise from Marguerite to keep him away from the house. But with Alfred in the hospital, it was too great a sacrifice for Marguerite to forgo Jacques's assistance, not to mention the pleasure of his company. So many in the house needed rides to one place or another, and so often Trotsky's cars weren't available, or the Ford was being repaired.

"Did I tell you I moved from my hotel to the Shirley Courts?" Jacques asked.

"The what?"

"It's very modern, an American motel."

"Motel?"

"Motor hotel. A hotel for cars."

"Wouldn't that be a garage?"

"It's most convenient with a car. You can pull right up to your door without going in and out of a lobby."

"I think I've heard of that kind of establishment, a place married men take their mistresses."

"But this is very wholesome, a family place. Mr. and Mrs. Shirley have a son who's interested in mountain climbing."

"Well, a motel! I would like to see it."

"I'm not sure that would be wise. Mr. Shirley might not like my bringing a beautiful married woman."

He pressed the cigarette lighter and rolled down his window. "Who was that at the house just now? A Mexican army officer. A colonel, I would think."

"That must have been Colonel Sanchez, head of the secret police in Mexico. To look at him you wouldn't think it, but Mexicans tremble when they hear his name. He's very powerful."

"What was he doing there?"

"He comes to the house on a regular basis."

"Really?"

"Yes, President Cárdenas made Colonel Sanchez personally responsible for Trotsky's safety when he first arrived in Mexico. By now, the Colonel drops by as if he were an old friend of the family."

They were halfway into town when she said, *"Regarde l'éclair!"* as a bolt of lighting flashed in the dark clouds clustered against the volcanoes. "The rainy season is about to start. Last year, we arrived just at the end of the season—so charming, quite exotic. Every evening there's a dramatic storm—like in an opera. Lightning and thunder crashing. You think it's the end of the world, then—poof!—it's over."


The French hospital was in the Condesa, an enclave of wealthy European Jews where four- and five-story Art Deco apartment buildings sprouted up around a bare, almost treeless park. The exterior of the hospital was white as was the interior, halls white and clean, smelling of ether and disinfectant. Alfred was growing restless in the second week of his convalescence. Jacques took the older man's hand in his, kissing him on the cheek. At Marguerite's bidding, he procured bowl, spoon, and napkin for the soup, then left the Rosmers to themselves. He wanted a moment alone to go over what he had seen at the house in Coyoacán, but instead found himself thinking about Sylvia.

It had been easy to comfort her, to take her in his arms, to dream with her about the life they would have in New York. But beneath her hysteria, at some level she understood what was happening. He worried that some day she would feel betrayed, but there was nothing he could do, and never had been, to alter the course of events. Whether or not Ramón provided the floor plan, Siqueiros would storm the house.

He smoked his cigarette in front of the hospital, thinking that the park and the buildings looked raw and ugly, that it was a mistake trying to re-create Europe in Mexico.

He had finished the cigarette and was holding the car door for Marguerite when Sheldon pulled up in Trotsky's big black Dodge. "Look!" said Marguerite. "There's Natalia Sedova. She's come to see Alfred."

Trotsky's wife sat in the back of the Dodge with her grandson Seva. The boy got out first, looking pale and vulnerable in his school uniform, a white shirt, black shorts, and long black socks. "Marguerite!" he called. "Mr. Jacson!"

Natalia Sedova followed, a thin woman with gray hair and a sad, long face, holding a coffee can filled with daisies, ferns, and a frond of bougainvillea from the garden. Ramón wanted to turn away, to protect himself from the sight of this woman, but Marguerite was hugging the boy. "We almost missed you," she said to Natalia Sedova. "I didn't know you were coming. Alfred will be so glad to see you."

"He isn't too tired for another visit?"

"Not at all. He'll be delighted."

"I don't believe you've met Sylvia's husband, Frank Jacson," said Marguerite, turning to include Jacques.

Natalia Sedova offered her hand, her thoughtful gray eyes studying his face. "I've heard a great deal about you from the Rosmers. And from Seva. You've been very kind to include my grandson in your outings with Marguerite and Alfred."

Jacques felt a stab of remorse. Unable to speak, he could only smile, then looked down, putting a hand on the boy's shoulder. "We've had some fun, haven't we, Esteban?"

"Yes, sir," the boy said, turning to smile up at Jacques.

"And do you know Mr. Harte?" Natalia Sedova asked. "Sheldon is here from New York, helping us for a while."

Jacques smiled, and the two men shook hands as if they'd never spoken.

The encounter pleased Marguerite. "Such a good person," she remarked, settling into the Buick.

Jacques stepped on the ignition. "Her eyes are so sad," he said in an involuntary, wondering voice. "I've never seen such sad eyes."

"Yes, but it's only natural when someone kills your children."

# THIRTY-THREE

Row after row, eight abreast, thousands of Mexicans marched down Reforma. Many looked Aztec or Mayan, with straight black hair and sharply sculptured features. Plumbers, carpenters, electricians, painters, the rank and file of the Communist Party in Mexico, they carried cardboard placards demanding that Trotsky get out of the country. *Afuera Trotsky!* Trotsky, get out! They walked silently, their faces so impassive, it might have been a funeral procession but for the trucks with loudspeakers that passed at regular intervals bearing large pictures of Trotsky looking satanic with his white goatee, eyes glaring intensely through his spectacles, a harsh metallic voice ringing from big cone-shaped speakers. "Trotsky is a traitor and terrorist!" the voices would cry from the distance, grow painfully loud, then fade away as the trucks moved on. All the while, the shuffling of the workers' feet on pavement remained soft and constant.

To the casual observer, the May Day parade was a stunning turnaround. Trotsky had been a hero to peasants and workers when he arrived in Mexico, and now he was an archvillain. To Jacques, the parade was a demonstration of Eitingon and Caridad's prowess. They had brought the power of the Kremlin and Comintern to bear upon the Communist Party of Mexico. Moving behind the scenes, never showing their hand, they purged the Communist newspapers in Mexico, replacing the editors and writers who had accepted the presence of Trotsky. Brought to heel, the Communist press mounted a campaign against Trotsky, all but calling for blood. Trotsky was not a friend of the worker. He was a terrorist and a Fascist.

Eitingon and Caridad had applied the same sort of pressure to the largest and most powerful labor unions in Mexico, which were Communist-run. Union bosses had turned out twenty thousand Mexicans to protest against Trotsky. Eitingon and Caridad had their hands on the levers of power and were pulling all of the elements of their plan into alignment. Everything was running according to schedule. The attack on Trotsky would take place soon. It was the first of May; Hitler's troops had invaded Denmark and Norway. France, the Netherlands, and Belgium were next. The free world would watch in horror as a Fascist dictator marched through Western Europe. Hitler would provide all the cover needed for Stalin to settle an old score.

After the parade finally passed, Jacques got in his car and started for Coyoacán. He would have preferred not going on that particular day, but Marguerite had asked him, and he feared it would look strange if he didn't appear.

As Jacques pulled up in front of the house, lightning flickered in the dark clouds clustered against the volcanoes. He recognized Julia and Ana, the women Siqueiros had hired to spy on the house. Dressed like peasant girls, they were flirting with the policemen in front of their hut. They had rented cheap flats on the next street, where they entertained the police, pumping them for every last detail about their post.

Jacques waved to Jake Cooper in the machine-gun turret, then heard the electric lock snap open as he approached the reinforced door. The heavy metal bar scraped against cement; Sheldon opened the door, stepping aside, his eyes wide in the dim light of the garage.

"What are you doing, letting me in like that?" Jacques asked in a low voice.

"I heard your car. I knew it was you."

"You have to be careful."

"Marguerite had to go out, but Hansen wants to see you."

"Me? Why does he want to see me?"

"I don't know, but he said to send you in. He's in the library."

Walking up the flagstone path, Jacques felt as if some greater gravitational force were taking hold of him, a strong ocean current that would drag him out to sea. The doors to the library stood open, a waiting trap. As he stepped beneath the bower of bougainvillea, he removed his dark glasses, his eyes and mind working rapidly, taking notes for Siqueiros. The room resembled a battlefield command station, spartan, improvised, orderly with unfinished plank floors, thick adobe walls plastered a deep mustard color, bare lightbulbs hanging on long cords from the rafters of the ceiling. There were two desks and a worktable, two big black typewriters, filing cabinets, a telephone, a map of Europe, and a small bookshelf filled with volumes of an encyclopedia.

Jacques had imagined the room so often, assembling a picture from bits and pieces of information. He was surprised to find it empty, except for Joe Hansen, who sat at the desk toward the back of the library. He gazed up from a typed document, studied Jacques for a moment, then got to his feet. Wiry and of moderate height, Hansen was like a character from the Wild West, his dark blond hair cut badly by a Mexican barber, pale blue eyes, and a prominent Adam's apple riding above the knot of his tie and the frayed collar, a holstered pistol hanging from a wide leather belt.

"Marguerite asked me to give you this," he said, handing Jacques an envelope. "I've seen you outside. I don't think we've met."

"Yes, I know who you are."

"The Old Man wanted me to talk to you. He keeps hearing about you and has begun to wonder what it is you're doing here."

Jacques felt his mouth go dry. "I'm in Mexico on business. My wife, Sylvia, introduced me to the Rosmers."

Hansen frowned. "What about this false passport?"

"Yes, I had to buy a Canadian passport in Paris. I'm Belgian but couldn't get a passport there."

"Why was that?" Hansen asked, crossing his arms.

"A problem with my family, a legal difficulty."

"By legal, do you mean criminal?"

"No." Jacques recoiled a bit as if offended. "I don't believe this is your business, but I was commissioned as an officer in the army. Later, after I was discharged, my family pulled strings to have me recalled so I wouldn't leave the country. I was eventually cleared but with the war and all, my visa was tied up in red tape. Buying a passport was a matter of convenience, nothing more."

Hansen chewed on that for a moment, nodding. "The Old Man also wants to know about your politics."

"I stay clear of politics."

Hansen gave a slight shrug. "Well, I'll let you get on your way."

Leaving, Jacques found Sheldon waiting in the garage. Thunder rumbled in the distance. The tin roof above ticked as the afternoon sun abated. The area smelled of dust and oil and tires and grease. A straight-back chair, a clipboard, and a stack of old magazines suggested the monotony of waiting.

"What did he want?"

"Nothing. He had a note from Marguerite for me."

"Why didn't he give it to me?"

"I don't know." Jacques took out his cigarette case, offered one to Sheldon, and took another for himself. As he lit their cigarettes, he observed the young man's hand tremble slightly. Jacques put a hand on his shoulder and gave it a reassuring squeeze. "Can you get away tonight?"

He nodded. Yes.

"Come to the Shirley Courts. I'll bring you home."

"When should I come? Is seven too early?"

"No, that's good. Now, you'd better let me out."

He watched Sheldon move the heavy iron aside. The door opened to the smell of rain coming across the valley.

# THIRTY-FOUR

With rain sheeting down the windows and the electric lights flickering overhead, Caridad looked haggard, her mouth a thin red line of lipstick she was quickly blotting away with the butt end of a cigarette. "It's tomorrow night, then?"

"Yes. Tomorrow is a Friday. Is there any reason it shouldn't be on a Friday?" Eitingon asked. "Anything special about the schedule at the house?"

He looked around the table.

The time had finally come.

"Ramón?"

"No, I think the guards have the same schedule."

"And David, you have your men ready?"

"Yes, but they're restless. Ten or eleven days is a long time to wait when you don't know what you're waiting for."

"And we still go in at four a.m.?"

"Unless there's a reason to change."

"I'm having the men gather in three groups at different houses," said Siqueiros. "I'll make the rounds, give them instructions, pass out the uniforms, but someone needs to be at each of the houses to make sure they don't wander off."

"Ramón?"

"Yes, I can do that."

"And I'll do another," said Eitingon. "One of the Spaniards can hold down the third."

Eitingon slid the map of the house to the middle of the table. "Let's go over it again to make sure we're all in agreement." He pointed out where the cars would park, one on Churubusco next to the dry riverbed, another on Abasola, and a third on Viena. "We approach on foot."

"Bloody dogs are going to bark."

"That can't be helped."

"What time should Julia and Ana start the fiesta for the cops?" asked Siqueiros. "They've got enough tequila and mescal to float a boat."

Caridad looked to Siqueiros. "How long does it take to get a cop drunk?"

"Twenty minutes." He laughed.

"No, seriously. If we want them dead drunk at four in the morning?"

"Tell the girls to start the party at ten o'clock. You can't predict how fast anyone is going to pass out."

Siqueiros turned to Ramón. "And your friend will open the gate for you?"

"He will, if he's there."

"That's a big fucking if. Can't you find out?"

"If I ask too much, he'll get nervous. Anyway, the schedule could always change at the last minute. I'm more worried that one of the other guards will be up in that machine-gun turret on the front wall. That could turn into a firefight."

"We would still win."

"Yes, but with a lot of blood."

"What are the chances?"

"Unlikely. One of the other guards is sick and has been sleeping through the shift from midnight till dawn."

"If we have to go over the wall, we'll have dynamite, grappling irons, and rope ladders. But if the gate opens, then we're in and out within minutes."

"When do you give the men their assignments?"

"Not until tomorrow night. Three of the boys will set up a machine gun behind the trunk of that eucalyptus tree to keep the guards pinned down, while four of us with machine guns position ourselves at Trotsky's windows. No one will hear anything until we start shooting. Some of the men will stay out front to take care of the cops and the guard."

"Remember, this is the room where the boy sleeps," Ramón said, pointing to the floor plan. "You'll have to go through there to get to the Old Man's room, but there's no reason to hurt the boy. Just let him run off or hide under his bed. And this room back here is where the Rosmers sleep. I don't want them hurt."

"Are you getting soft?" Siqueiros asked.

"No, but there's no reason to hurt them."

"Ramón and I aren't going in," said Eitingon. "As soon as the gate opens we leave. He'll drive me back into town. Caridad and I are on the six-thirty flight to Brownsville. You and your men can use Trotsky's cars to get away."

"What about Sheldon Harte?" Ramón asked. "What happens to him?"

Siqueiros made a pistol with his index finger and thumb, then pulled the trigger.

"No," said Ramón. "You can't kill him."

"If we leave him, he'll identify you. Your picture will be in every post office in Mexico and the United States by eight o'clock the next morning."

"Then let's go over the wall."

Eitingon looked at Caridad, pushing his hand through his hair. "No, we're not going over the wall unless we have to, and we won't kill the guard. David, you can take him with you when you leave. Make him drive one of the cars. We'll implicate him. The cops are going to suspect him anyway. It will look like an inside job, like Trotsky's men turned on him. Stalin will like that."

"Then what happens?"

"We'll stash him for a couple of months. By then we'll be drinking vodka and eating caviar in Moscow. He can sell his story to the newspapers." Eitingon rubbed his eyes and looked around the table. "Anything else? Any questions?"

Ramón wondered about the future as he drove to the Shirley Courts. The only thing that made sense to him was to be with Sylvia in New York. He surely couldn't see himself in Moscow; a winter there would be worse than prison. Returning to Spain was out of the question as long as Franco was in power. His sister and brothers were in Toulouse, hoping the war would wash over them.

That night in bed, he tossed and turned. He dreamed that he heard a loud metallic clanking noise coming toward him, a familiar sound he couldn't identify. Then he looked down to see the sticks of dynamite strapped to his chest.

He stayed at the motel the next morning until the Arenal brothers came by in a panel truck to pick up the crate of "engineering equipment" he'd been keeping in the storage room at the Shirley Courts. Then, to kill time, he walked to the apartment on Hamburgo, where he found Caridad dumping files into cardboard boxes. She looked as if she hadn't slept, her face sculpted by fatigue. "There's an incinerator downstairs in the alley," she said, handing him one of the boxes.

He found the wire basket where ashes still smoldered, dumped the contents of the box, holding his lighter to the papers, then watching the flame catch and spread, the papers curling as they turned into sheets of carbon. The weather was fine, the air fresh from the night's storm. He found a stick to poke the papers, then went back upstairs to see if there were more. Caridad was sitting at the table, going through files, a cigar burning in an ashtray. She looked up when he sat down on the battered green sofa.

"Tomorrow night you'll be in New York."

She nodded, the slightest frown flickering at the edge of her vision.

"How long will I need to stay here?"

"A month, six weeks," she said, not looking up.

"That long?"

"You can go off mountain climbing if you want. We just don't want it to look like you ran."

"And what comes after that? Do you know what we'll do?"

She turned a page, reaching for the cigar. "No, but if this goes as planned, we can write our own ticket."

"Sure?"

"We will have plucked a very large thorn from Stalin's side."

"I'd like to be assigned to New York."

She raised her eyes and studied him for a moment. "Let's see what happens tonight."

# THIRTY-FIVE

The sheet of lightning flickered off and on, a canopy of white that gathered itself into a bolt, unfolding, one joint after another, a long finger jutting down to stab the city. The windshield blades thumped methodically as the rain splashed softly against the undercarriage of the Buick, the headlights probing the dark street, drops of rain falling at a slant.

"*Hijo le!*" said Ramón as the thunder cracked.

"It's letting up," said Eitingon. "It won't last much longer."

"Yes, and a good thing."

They were driving slowly through a slum where water stood in the streets. At the edge of the headlights, a man scurried along, hugging the buildings in an attempt to stay dry. "That's the place," Eitingon said as the man disappeared into a tenement.

"Should I come in with you?"

"No. That's not necessary."

Ramón watched Eitingon go into the building, then drove on to the intersection of Cuba and Chile streets. Dousing the lights and killing the engine, he got out and pulled his gray fedora down as he climbed the steps of a tenement. The long narrow hall smelled of kerosene and garbage. The murmur of voices came through the thin wooden door. When Ramón tapped on the door, the room fell silent. Fear. Caution. The door opened a crack, and a Spaniard looked out. "*David me mandó,*" said Ramón.

"*Sí, sí, pasale! Pasale!*"

The poverty of the room was plain, a cot with a dirty bare mattress pushed against one wall, a torn paper shade hanging over the window, a flimsy table, a sardine can filled with cigarette butts. Two men got up from their game of dominoes, a third from the cot. From the next room came the hush of women and children herded out of sight. Ramón took off his fedora and gabardine raincoat, then passed around his pack of Lucky Strikes.

"David has been here?" he asked.

"Yes, with Pujol."

Ramón made an effort at conversation, but the distance was too great between him and the men. War refugees, they had lost everything in Spain and had nothing in Mexico. Ramón was a boss, a rich guy in fine clothes driving a car, riding above the fray.

The men smoked their cigarettes in awkward silence, then, as if a tourniquet had been released, the domino players went on in low voices among themselves. "Now the French will get fucked in the ass by Hitler," said one, indulging in a bit of schadenfreude.

"Yes, but Hitler will fuck the French then leave. Franco will never stop fucking Spain."

Thunder rumbled in the distance as the storm left the valley. Time passed with the minute clicks of dominoes, the sound of water dripping from the eaves. The men's anxiety kindled Ramón's. He didn't want to think about what was about to happen, about Sheldon opening the gate or Alfred and Marguerite asleep in their beds.

A car stopped in front of the tenement just before two. Doors opened and slammed. Men's voices filled the street.

"*Es el Packard de David*," one of the Spaniards reported from the torn window shade. Moments later they heard the knock at the door and a voice ordered, "*Abra la puerta! Es la policia!*"

One of the men tried to open the door a crack but fell back as Siqueiros pushed his way in, disguised as an army officer. He wore a major's tunic, a visored cap, jodhpurs, riding boots, dark glasses, and a fake mustache. Antonio Pujol and the Arenal brothers followed, carrying cardboard suitcases.

"*Muchacos, como me queda?*" Siqueiros demanded, pirouetting one way then the other like a fashion model. Boys, how does it suit me?

"*Muy bien!*" the men cheered with relief. "*Se queda muy bien!*"

Siqueiros was having a fine time. He was a hero to the men—a soldier, a revolutionary, an internationally famous muralist—and they were off on a lark. Siqueiros opened the suitcases and started passing out arms and uniforms as if it were Christmas.

By the time they reached Coyoacán, the clouds had opened on a pale white moon floating in a ring of haze. With Eitingon and four of the other men in the Buick, Ramón parked on Calle Abasola, a block back from the compound. There was no movement on the street. He could see the shape of the eucalyptus tree looming above the compound walls until the collective heat of the men began to fog the Buick's windows.

At ten till four, they eased out of the car, quietly shutting the doors. Jacques opened the trunk so that the men in army uniforms could get their weapons—a machine gun, rifles, a knapsack of thermos bombs. A dog close by began to bark, then another on Churubusco, and a third on Viena. Dodging puddles of water, Eitingon, bearlike in his trench coat and homburg, led the way, staying close to the walls.

A chill in the early morning air made Ramón shiver. He told himself that he was on a night raid in Spain, but with all of the planning and all of the waiting this was worse. He knew who was on the other side of the wall and what was about to happen. Even so, he felt a jolt of fear when he saw policemen emerging from the shadows on Calle Viena.

Eitingon held the two squads at the corner, waiting as Siqueiros and his men came sneaking from the opposite side of the compound along the front wall. When Siqueiros reached the policeman's hut, he stood up straight and walked in, followed by two of his men. He switched on a flashlight. There was a murmur of voices in the hut, then Siqueiros came out.

"Drunk as dogs," he whispered, swaggering up to Eitingon in his major's uniform. "They think they're under arrest. In a moment, they'll be bound and gagged."

"Ready?" Eitingon asked, taking Ramón by the arm.

Eitingon had chosen two of the men to accompany Ramón. One would crouch on each side and slam through the door the moment the iron bar was moved.

Ramón felt Eitingon's hand moving him into place. "If it's not Sheldon," the Russian whispered, "don't let them see your face."

As Ramón tapped softly on the metal door, he pictured the American sitting in the chair, paging through a magazine. He heard movement, then Sheldon's voice at the door. "Who's there? Is someone there?"

"Sheldon, it's me."

"Frank! What are you doing out there?"

"My car broke down. Let me in!"

The slot for the peephole opened and the floodlight came on. Sheldon's eyes moved from side to side, then, seeing Ramón, he snapped the electric lock. "Just a minute," he called, as he moved the iron bar out of the way.

When the heavy door began to open, the two men burst through, springing upon Sheldon, pinning his arms. He looked as if he were about to laugh—this had to be a joke—until a hand clapped over his mouth. Then, panicking, his eyes moved from side to side, trying to see his captors, until, bewildered and betrayed, they settled upon Ramón.

Ramón leaned close—close enough to smell Sheldon's breath, his skin and hair. "Sheldon, do what they say, and they won't hurt you. Do what they say, and everything will be all right."

The young American began to struggle as he was dragged out of the way and more men in uniform started pouring through the door.

Eitingon took Ramón's arm. "All right, let's get out of here."

Ramón and Eitingon walked quickly toward the car, listening to the muffled sound of running on the opposite side of the wall. The machine guns opened fire, shattering the morning stillness with a long and violent roar that stopped with a resounding silence. Voices called back and forth. A single shot was fired. Another. Then the dogs in the neighborhood began to howl.

## THIRTY-SIX

Natalia Sedova woke to a shattering roar, a concussion of noise, heat, and fire, bullets flying from every side of the room, the thud of lead popping the plastered walls, the sting of sand, the smell of sulfur. Her husband moaned at her side, trying to surface, to break the narcotic web of his sleeping pill. *They have come,* she thought. *What we have dreaded for so long has finally begun. Stalin's men have come to kill Trotsky.*

Struggling beneath sheet and blanket, she pushed her husband off the bed beside the wall and slid on top, shielding his body with her own. They lay so close, she felt him wake as the torrent of machine-gun fire rained down. Squirming, she pushed closer, pressing them into that angle between floor and wall. *Seva was in the next room. Stalin had killed both her sons, and now Seva!*

The silence came suddenly, waves of shock ringing out into the stunned night. Outside, voices in Spanish and English called back and forth across the patio. "Keep down! Keep down!" shouted one of Trotsky's guards.

"If you keep out of this, you will be all right," an assailant shouted, then sprayed the front of the guards' quarters with machine-gun fire.

Her frail body trembling, she heard a scrabbling at the door to Seva's room, followed by a whump of explosion that sent flames leaping as the room filled with smoke. Seva screamed when an exterior door opened to his room, then they heard footsteps coming, boot heels ringing on the wooden planks. From beneath the bed, Natalia Sedova watched the door to Seva's room swing open, flames flickering on the riding boots.

They knew what was coming. The executioner would switch on the light and yank back the covers. That was procedure. He wouldn't leave until he saw that the job was done. He would shoot them where they cowered on the floor.

The assassin approached, the boots coming to the edge of the bed, so close they could have reached out and touched them. But rather than switch on the light and rip the covers from the bed, he fired four rapid shots from a revolver into the mattress—the bullets hitting the floor beside them—then turned and walked out of the room.

Voices called back and forth in the garden. Men were running. "*Vamonos! Vamonos! Ya! Ya! Vamonos!*" a Mexican shouted.

They were retreating, heading for the garage. Car doors opened and slammed. Someone started the Ford. Another driver started the Dodge. The big garage door rumbled open.

"Seva!" Natalia Sedova whispered urgently. She knew her grandson was dead in the next room. She imagined the carnage outside on the patio, the bodies of their friends riddled with bullets, the blood.

Wedged into the corner, they listened as the Dodge pulled out of the garage followed by the Ford. The transmissions shifted from first to second, the gears winding out as they drove away. Natalia Sedova and Trotsky lay in stunned silence. A wave of tremendous violence had crashed upon them but somehow they had survived.

"Marguerite!" Seva's voice called out, high and sweet. "Alfred!"

Natalia Sedova gasped. "They're alive! Seva! The Rosmers! They're alive."

"Come!" Trotsky said, helping Natalia Sedova up. Turning on the light, he could see blue smoke hanging in the air and the ravaged plaster walls.

"My God! My God! My God!" Natalia Sedova moaned in Russian. In her nightgown, her gray hair falling down her back, she picked up a rug from the floor and threw it over the flames. Trotsky put on his robe and slippers and got a pistol from the nightstand. He tried the door to his office, but it had been jammed from the outside. Imagining his Stalin manuscript in flames, he shouted for help and banged on the door.

Their faces ashen, all but trembling, Jake Cooper, the big burly guard from Minnesota, and Otto Schüssler opened the door from the office.

"Where's the boy?" Trotsky demanded. "Is he injured?"

"A bullet grazed his ankle. Marguerite and Alfred have him."

Trotsky walked out onto the patio, where he saw the Rosmers huddling over the boy.

"He's fine," Marguerite said in French. "A little nick."

"Seva?" He touched the boy's shoulder.

Seva nodded bravely.

"What about everyone else?"

"No one else is injured. But Sheldon's gone."

"What happened?"

"They had us pinned down in our rooms," Schüssler answered. "They set up a machine gun by the eucalyptus tree. Someone turned on the patio light so they'd fire if we stuck our heads out."

Two more of the guards, Charles Cornell and Harold Robins, appeared, joining the others on the patio. The two Mexican women who worked in the house peered out from their quarters, their eyes wide with terror. Dogs all around the compound howled while the neighbors pretended to sleep.

"Where's Sheldon?" Trotsky demanded.

"Gone," Robins answered. "He was behind the wheel of the Dodge."

"Who had guard duty tonight?"

"Sheldon was at the gate."

"Who else? Who was on the wall?"

"After midnight, just Sheldon. I've had the crud all week and had to get some sleep. We're stretched pretty thin, boss."

"How'd they get in?"

"They didn't break down the door or come over the wall."

"Sheldon let them in."

"Was he one of them?" wondered Cooper. "An inside job?"

"Sheldon?" Trotsky repeated. "He's been here for weeks. He could have killed me with much less trouble. What about the police out on the street?"

"They're bound and gagged out in the guardhouse," said Cornell.

"You let them go?"

Cornell shook his head.

"Well, go out there! Let them go!"

The young men looked at each other, one to another. None of them had been to war. "Boss, there's that corn patch across the road. There could be a machine gun in there."

"No! They left. We heard them drive away. It's over."

The men balked, afraid to move.

"You can't leave those men tied up. If you don't let them loose, I'll go out there and do it myself."

He put his arm around Natalia Sedova. "The boy is fine. We all survived. Soon the police will be here."

He walked to the trunk of the big eucalyptus tree where brass casings glinted in the damp grass. It was obvious what had happened. Stalin had sent the GPU to kill him. The GPU had made its play and failed miserably.

"Should we have tea?" Natalia Sedova was wondering aloud.

"Tea or something. We'll be up all night with the police here."

# THIRTY-SEVEN

"**O**h *la!* The commotion you can't imagine! One minute we were sleeping soundly and the next I was sure we were dead." Marguerite paused a moment as a waitress placed a flan before her. "The inside of that bedroom is riddled with bullets. How they survived is a mystery."

She picked up her spoon and touched the surface of the pudding, the skin trembling beneath the metal. They were eating at Sanborn's, the same restaurant where Jacques took Sylvia not long after she arrived. The waitresses wore colorful Indian dresses with long full skirts. A crowd of men in dark business suits were pouring in for their large midday meal.

"You know," Marguerite continued, "Natalia Sedova saved him. He'd taken an extra sleeping pill and couldn't wake up. He thought the villagers were setting off fireworks to celebrate another feast day. Somehow, Natalia Sedova managed to drag him off the bed and into a corner of the room. He says that she was trying to shield him with her body."

"That makes no sense."

"Yes, but that's what they say. And neither of them exaggerates; they are always factual, very precise. But oh, it sounded like a scene from hell. When the shooting stopped, the door opened to Seva's room where a fire had started. Trotsky knew what was going to happen. The man would switch on the overhead light and rip back the covers off the bed. And when he found Trotsky and Natalia Sedova, he would shoot them like rats. That's how it's done. But no, he didn't turn on the light. He emptied his pistol into the mattress, turned around, and walked out."

"He didn't turn on the lights?" said Jacques, his voice filled with disbelief.

"Perhaps he feared the sight of blood."

"Who knows that?"

"Knows what?"

"That . . . the assassin didn't switch on the lights."

"Colonel Sanchez, I imagine. What difference does it make?"

"I can't believe it. To go that far . . ."

"Squeamish, I suppose. A squeamish thug. But if you saw the bullet holes, you could hardly fault his logic. It's a miracle those men didn't kill each other, firing from opposite sides of the room."

"And Seva?"

"Just a scratch on his ankle. He was grazed by a bullet."

For a moment, Ramón lost track of what she was saying. His mind was throbbing with the knowledge that Siqueiros, after months, years of preparation, had been so careless. Had he only looked, it would all be over now.

Marguerite tasted the flan. "Trotsky was so relieved afterward. Almost ecstatic. Stalin's thugs had made their play and shown what fools they are. They didn't even touch Trotsky's office, his precious manuscript of his Stalin biography. They made fools of themselves and Stalin would have mud on his face. But then that idiot Colonel Sanchez decided it was an inside job. I don't believe you know the Colonel."

"I saw him one day at the house. He was in uniform, looked like a kind of martinet."

"Lev Davidovich is in a state of fury with Colonel Sanchez. An inside job! What could be more preposterous? What *tonterias*!"

"Sanchez is in charge of the investigation?"

"Yes, he's head of the secret police in Mexico. He's known Lev Davidovich and Natalia since they arrived. It was his job to protect them."

"What is he thinking?"

"Who knows? Who knows if he thinks at all? He arrested the maids. He threw poor Consuela and Lupita into some prison called the *pocito*." Her nose and mouth wrinkled with distaste. "I gather it's some sort of jail where the police torture suspects. Mexicans hear the word *pocito* and their blood goes cold. If I'm not mistaken, it means 'little well' or something."

"Yes, that's correct," said Jacques. "Almost the same as French."

"Poor Consuela and Lupita, the two most vulnerable people in the house. The Colonel kept them for one night, long enough for them to recall that there were suspicious activities going on at the house before the attack. Then the inspector arrests Trotsky's secretaries, Otto Schüssler and Joseph Hansen, and throws them into the *pocito*."

She looked up from her flan to Jacques, her eyes filming with tears, the lines in her face more pronounced. "Is it possible this Colonel Sanchez truly believes that Trotsky would organize an attack on himself as some sort of propaganda stunt? Perhaps he's a Stalinist?"

"The inspector?"

"Yes, of course. Who else?"

"He could be a Stalinist," Jacques agreed. "It's difficult to know. But what about Schüssler and Hansen?"

"They're in jail. Trotsky spoke on the telephone this morning to one of President Cárdenas' secretaries. As luck has it, the president is in the city and will read Trotsky's letter this afternoon."

She took another bite of the flan, gazing around the dining room. "And poor Trotsky!" she continued. "He was sure Stalin and the GPU were going to come out of this with a black eye, and now they're howling with laughter. Trotsky gets blamed for his own attack! Stalin couldn't be happier."

"I doubt that Stalin is altogether happy."

"Oh. I see what you mean. Trotsky isn't dead. I suppose that's some consolation."

"A considerable amount, I would think. Particularly for Trotsky. But no one suspects Sheldon?"

"Trotsky insists the boy was kidnapped. He told the Colonel that if Sheldon wanted to kill him he could have done it weeks ago without so much trouble."

Jacques took a deep breath, crossing his arms casually over his chest. He was about to speak, to say that he was sure Sheldon was innocent, when, with a loud and startling crash, a tray of glasses, plates, and silverware hit the tile floor, bringing the room to a momentary halt. A busboy in a white jacket scrambled to his knees, frantically shoving the shards together as one of the waitresses in her Indian costume stood over him angrily.

After the moment's pause, the conversation resumed. Jacques broke off a piece of *bolillo* left in the basket, then put it aside. "Did you hear that Diego Rivera has fled the country?" he asked.

"Yes, I read in the papers that he's hiding in California. Such vanity! He was afraid the GPU would target him next. Such foolery. And poor Frida! I couldn't believe the Colonel threw her and her sister Cristina in jail."

"Frida?" He frowned. "I didn't know that. She was in jail?"

"For two nights."

"I don't envy the jailer. Whatever for?"

"The Colonel suspected that she was part of the plot, I suppose because of the rift between Trotsky and Diego."

"That's absurd! He's grasping at straws."

Marguerite scraped off a bit more pudding. "Alfred and I feel terrible that we're leaving just after this happened."

"Ah, that's right! You're sailing Wednesday."

"We've stayed so long, and we can't afford to forfeit our tickets. We've no income except for the little Alfred makes from writing. But you needn't worry about driving us to Veracruz. We can take the train."

"I want to. As I told you, I have to go to Veracruz at least once a month for my boss, so it's no trouble. Do you know what you'll do in New York?"

"What can we do but wait for the war to end? We can't go back to France."

# THIRTY-EIGHT

Harold Robins waved from the turret, and the gate snapped open before Jacques had quite reached it. "One second," Jake Cooper said as he moved the iron bar to open the door. "I guess you heard about the commotion here."

"Yes, I read about it in the papers. And Marguerite filled me in."

Cooper smiled. "Colonel Sanchez personally delivered Schüssler and Hansen to the house last night. *El presidente* must have given him a good ass chewing. He was bowing and scraping, begging the Old Man to forgive him for taking the boys. Trotsky was cordial, but Natalia Sedova made it clear how she felt. It was quite a little scene."

"And Sheldon?"

Cooper shook his head. "Nothing. No news. They must be holding him hostage. At least that's what we hope. You can go on in. They're expecting you."

Jacques followed the path up to the house. The library was empty, but laughter and the sounds of a celebration came from the dining room. Jacques glanced in at the gathering at the dining table, and, seeing Trotsky with a big scratch on his forehead, retreated to wait near the entrance. A moment later, Alfred came looking for him. "Come in! Come in! Lev Davidovich was just reading a letter from John, one of the American guards who was here. Come and join us!"

Jacques felt a slight internal lurch when Trotsky stood to shake hands. Man to man, the Russian was both larger and younger than Jacques imagined, as tall as Jacques and heavier through the shoulders and chest. The goatee and mustache made his mouth prominent, his lips protruding from the whiskers. With his silver hair and strong aquiline nose, he looked like an eagle, his eyes, behind the lenses of his tortoiseshell glasses, a penetrating blue. He clasped Jacques's hand. "Yes, Sylvia's husband," he said in French. "I've heard about you from Alfred and Marguerite. And my grandson." He smiled warmly. Unscathed but for the scratch on his forehead, he appeared to be in excellent spirits. "Natalia," he turned to his wife, "perhaps Mr. Jacson would like breakfast."

Jacques assured everyone that he had eaten, but accepted a cup of tea, taking a chair beside Marguerite.

"And Seva?" Jacques asked her.

"He had to go to school," said Marguerite. "We said our goodbyes before he left."

The feeling of celebration was suddenly dying away, the laughter. Jacques had come for Alfred and Marguerite. He was taking them away.

"*Alors*," Marguerite said, "I should make the last preparations."

As she started to push back from the table, Natalia Sedova grasped her hand, tears coming to her eyes. "Marguerite, I can't say goodbye!"

"Oh, my dear!" Marguerite replied in a sweet maternal voice, wrapping her arms around her friend. "I know we will see each other soon."

"No, we don't know that." Natalia Sedova shook her head. "We know nothing of the sort. I'm going with you to Veracruz so that we will have another day together."

"But Nata," Trotsky objected. "How will you return?"

"With Mr. Jacson."

Frowning, Trotsky spoke to his wife in Russian.

"Then I'll come back on the train. Or Ellen and I will follow them in one of our cars," she said, referring to an old-maidish American at the table. "Yes, Ellen and I can drive together." Drying her tears she got up from the table. "Ellen, you don't mind, do you? I'll pack a small bag for the night. I will only be a moment."

Jacques was waiting on the front steps with Alfred when Trotsky joined them. He placed a hand on Jacques's shoulder and smiled, his blue eyes twinkling. "Mr. Jacson, everyone here seems to know you, everyone but me, that is. When you are close to so many of these people, I begin to wonder why you aren't one of us."

"I'm afraid I know nothing about politics."

"But if you are in business, much of business is politics. Economics and politics are two sides of the same coin."

"I'm sure you're correct."

"We could use a man like you—someone who understands how the world works. I feel sure you could make an important contribution."

"Do you mean with money?"

Trotsky laughed. "No, but that is always welcome. You might like to write something for our publication. Sylvia said you worked as a journalist in Paris. I don't believe in telling people what to think, but I always encourage everyone to write. As you know, when you sit down with pen and paper you see things in a different way. It might be something that you've observed, something that you've been wanting to say."

"I don't know what to say."

"You needn't say anything. But think about it. Perhaps something will come to mind."

# THIRTY-NINE

He's very possessive," Marguerite explained. "And he's very proper. In his mind it simply isn't appropriate that his wife should travel alone with an attractive man and spend a night in a hotel. After all, what would people think?"

"I thought he didn't trust me," said Jacques, looking into the rearview mirror to make sure that Ellen Reed and Natalia Sedova were behind them.

"No, no, he doesn't trust *her*," said Marguerite. "Ever since he had that little dalliance with Señora Rivera, he's been wildly jealous of Natalia. Isn't that curious?"

"He doesn't trust himself," Alfred suggested.

"When you've been married so long, isn't it the same thing."

Jacques watched the old Ford in his rearview mirror. "Has he changed?"

"Trotsky?"

"You've known him a long time."

"Oh, yes," said Alfred. "When we first knew him in France, he was a charming young man who showed a great deal of promise. He became famous at a very early age, during the '04 uprising in Moscow."

"I don't see that he's changed that much," Marguerite differed. "He's always been the same person."

"But his life changed so dramatically. To live for years as a political writer, an intellectual, then become the commander of the Red Army. To be one of the great leaders on the world's stage to become what you see now—an exile living in obscurity. Now that was a dramatic fall!"

"He was vain," Marguerite interjected. "That was a problem."

"Yes, vanity was his great failing," Alfred agreed. "He believed, as did so many, that he was Lenin's only possible successor. When Lenin started having strokes, Trotsky did nothing. He wouldn't fight for power the way Stalin did. Whether Stalin poisoned Lenin is unclear, but there is no doubt that Stalin was always plotting, putting all of his people into key positions. No, for Trotsky to rise to the zenith of power then be driven into exile, that had to be a terrible experience."

"But he isn't bitter," Marguerite added.

"No, he's found a place in Mexico. He could have gone into hiding, completely disappeared, but he insists that he has to be able to speak out, hold his ground."

"Where could he disappear?" asked Jacques.

"The United States, of course. That's the only place he could be safe. Friends of the Fourth International own great tracts of land in the West. It would be a simple matter to smuggle Trotsky and Natalia Sedova across the border."

"He does seem different now," Marguerite added. "Before, he had no interest in the people who worked for him, never seemed to realize that they had families and lives of their own. He didn't notice them in that way and wasn't interested. But he's very fond of these young Americans working for him. He still grieves for Sheldon. I think living in close quarters with these Americans has changed him."


They were on the highway to Puebla, and as they climbed the flank of the volcanoes, the monsters dropped out of sight. They stopped in Puebla for lunch, then headed south and east through the Sierra Nevada. The mountains reminded Jacques of the Pyrénées, green pine forests, the air crisp and fragrant. Having told Marguerite and Alfred that he drove to Veracruz once a month for his boss, he had to bite his tongue when a glowing white triangle appeared in the clouds like a kite that, as he stared, slowly revealed itself to be the peak of a massive volcano dominating the landscape. "It's so big," he finally said. "It's bigger than Popocatépetl."

"Pico de Orizaba," Alfred commented.

With the snowcapped peak floating above the landscape like a remote ideal, the two-lane highway took them higher and higher until they began to drop down through gray clouds into the provincial city of Jalapa, wreathed in mist and gentle rain. Jacques found the zocalo, where there were two hotels. "I usually stay at the other place," said Jacques as they unloaded their luggage, "but I've been told this one is better."

After checking in, Jacques went for a walk in the gray mist, returning to the hotel to find Natalia Sedova and Marguerite talking on one of the sofas in the lobby. After an early dinner, they went to bed. The following morning as they were leaving, Jacques noticed a puddle of liquid on the garage floor beneath the Ford. After arranging with the manager of the garage to have the radiator repaired, they all continued in the Buick, the women sitting in back, Marguerite and Natalia Sedova happily chatting in French. Once again the drive was dramatic, the grades steep as they made their way down from the Sierra Nevada to the flat coastal plane, where, at the end of May, the air was already hot and humid. They drove through fields of sugarcane and saw rows of swaying palm trees.

Jacques had consulted a map of Veracruz before leaving Mexico City, but missed a turn coming into the city. Alfred and Marguerite grew tense as they circled through a sector of low adobe houses where vultures walked the streets as if they owned them.

"*Finalement!*" Marguerite gasped when they slipped out of the maze to find the ship waiting at the pier. A breeze blew off the Gulf of Mexico. Gulls swooped and squawked over the gentle waves. The pier was festive, filled with travelers and vendors, a marimba band playing. Jacques helped Alfred with the tickets and luggage, then they followed the women to their cabin, a small compartment, stuffy in the afternoon sun.

"Why don't we go up on the deck," Alfred suggested to Jacques. "We'll have a smoke."

Standing at a railing, Alfred filled his pipe, then cupped his hands to light it. "I'll be in New York soon," said Jacques. "We can spend time together there."

"Coming for a vacation?" Alfred asked around the stem of his pipe.

"No, for good, I believe. My boss is finishing up his business here in Mexico."

"That's good news. It will make Sylvia happy. And Marguerite! She feels very close to you, as do I. You know we never had children of our own. With the war and so much uncertainty . . ." His voice trailed off.

They walked slowly, companionably around the deck. "Do you remember that night you and Marguerite came to the hotel?" Jacques asked. "You were going to tell me something about Spain."

Bemused, Alfred Rosmer smiled. "Spain? No, I don't remember talking about Spain."

"We were talking about Trotsky and Stalin, what happened in Spain."

"No, I don't know what I was going to say, unless it was my usual heresy."

"What's that?"

"That the civil war in Spain would have been a revolution if not for Stalin."

"What do you mean?"

"Spaniards wanted a revolution. It was exactly the sort of spontaneous uprising Marx predicted and wrote about. The Spanish people knew Franco would reinstate feudalism, that they would once more be under the heel of the church and the aristocracy. They were willing to fight and die for a cause. If you remember, the peasants and workers were seizing land, killing priests, and burning down churches. Peasants would get into taxicabs with sticks of dynamite and attack machine-gun nests."

"But Stalin supported the people."

"No, Joseph Stalin supported the Republican government, which was the status quo. And that wasn't worth dying for. Instead of a revolution, Spain got a civil war. And that was something very different. For Stalin, the only revolution is the Soviet Union. Comintern won't support revolution outside the Soviet Union. That's official policy."

"But Franco won because Trotsky split the Left in Spain."

"You've seen Trotsky's headquarters. He can't defend his own house. Do you think he was telling trade unions and anarchists what to do in Spain?" The older man drew on his pipe, exhaling a fragrant cloud of smoke. Squinting in a thoughtful way, he looked inland beyond Veracruz. "Funny you can't see it from here," he said.

"See what?"

"Pico de Orizaba. I guess we're too close, but that's the first land that ships see way out on the Gulf before dawn. The snow catches the first light."

# FORTY

Sylvia watched as the Pan Am plane taxied up to the terminal at Idlewild. She was wearing her prettiest summer dress, but it was always stressful meeting Jacques after a separation, seeing him in a crowd as a stranger, separate and self-contained, fearing that he had changed, that he might see her without the kindness of his love.

The plane came to a standstill, the engines were cut, then, as the blades of the propellers were becoming visible, two workers ran out with chocks for the wheels. Jacques came down the stairs, wearing a suit and dark glasses, carrying a raincoat over his arm.

"There you are!" he said, taking her in his arms, leaning down to kiss her. "You can't imagine how glad I am to see you. What a dreadful flight!"

"Was it rough?"

"Yes, some bad weather."

Hand in hand, they went into the terminal, following the crowd toward the baggage claim. "Look at you," he said. "Is that a new hat you're wearing?"

"Yes, do you like it?"

"Very becoming, *très chic*. How are your sisters? Have you seen Marguerite and Alfred?"

Sylvia suddenly stopped. "Oh, Jacques, I was so excited to see you I forgot the worst news. The Nazis marched into Paris this morning. The reporter on the radio said Parisians stood on the streets weeping."

"Everyone knew this was coming," he said, suddenly looking tired and worried.

"I telephoned the Rosmers but their line was busy."

"At least they're out of it. I want to see them while I'm here."

Jacques claimed his luggage and hailed a cab. It was a fine June day in New York. Soft white clouds floated in the blue sky. A pleasant breeze whipped through the windows of the taxi, the skyscrapers and bridges rising before them. Jacques told the driver to take them to the Pierpont Hotel on Fifth Avenue between Seventeenth and Eighteenth Streets. "I'm going to be slaving on Wall Street," he told Sylvia. "Lubeck is already here and I have a meeting this afternoon."

"So soon? I hoped we could spend the day together."

"I'm sorry but not today. Lubeck says we're going to be in meetings all week. He's moving the business here and is setting up an office in New Jersey."

"Here?"

"Yes, it's good news. I may be able to hire your sister." He took Sylvia's hand. "And even better, you and I can finally get a place together, have a real life."

At the hotel, Jacques registered as Mr. and Mrs. Jacson. They followed the bellman to an elevator; standing behind him in the car, Jacques put his arm around Sylvia's waist, drawing her to him gently, playfully. The bellman led them to their room, insisted on demonstrating how the radio worked and asked if they would require any other services. "No, no, no," Jacques said, handing the man a folded bill.

"Finally!" Jacques exclaimed when the door closed. Loosening his necktie, he kissed Sylvia, pulling her close as he shed his jacket. "Do you want a shower? I have to wash. I must smell like a beast."

"No, dear, not a shower. I've just been to the hairdresser."

"We don't have time to draw a bath."

"Go ahead," she said. "I'll wait."

"I'm starving! For you and for breakfast, an American breakfast—eggs, bacon, toast."

"Should I call room service?"

"No, not yet. We might want more time." He took off his shirt and pried off his shoes. Kissing her again, he began unbuttoning her blouse.

"Go on, you beast!" she said, pushing him away.

"That bad?"

"No, not at all. You smell lovely. I love the way you smell. Go on, I'll be making myself at home."

He showered and shaved with the door open, calling to her, asking about her afternoon, her job, news of her family. When he came out, a white towel around his waist, smelling of soap and aftershave, she had turned down the bed and was propped against the pillows in her pale ivory slip. He sat down to face her and smiled as her hand reached out, stroking his chest. "I'm so glad to see you," he whispered. "I've missed you so much."

He began to lean forward but hesitated, suddenly distracted, his mind in another place.

"Jacques, what is it?"

"Oh, sorry. It's this meeting this afternoon. Lubeck is making a mistake. I know what he should do, but I'm not sure I can make him listen to me."

"He must be a reasonable man. And you're persuasive."

"We'll see. I don't want to think about it now."

Jacques began to kiss her once more then, discarding the damp towel as he slipped beneath the sheet.

After making love, they lay in bed talking, listening to the maids in the hallway. "This makes me feel wanton," said Sylvia.

"Wanton? I don't know that word."

"Making love in a hotel room in the middle of the day."

"It isn't the middle of the day." He frowned, reaching for his wristwatch.

"No, not yet. But if you're going to have breakfast, you should probably call room service."

After breakfast, a mood settled upon him as he dressed, a somber feeling of resolution.

"Which way are you going?" he asked as they left the hotel.

"I suppose I'll go home."

"A taxi, uptown," Jacques told the hotel doorman.

After seeing Sylvia into the cab, he asked for another going downtown. "Wall Street," he told the driver when he got in. He let the driver go five blocks, then told him he had changed his mind. He wanted to go to Washington Square.

After getting out of the car, he walked under the arch into the park and sat on one of the benches, feeling anxious yet hopeful. He had found the solution to their problem. It was so obvious, glaringly obvious.

The packed gravel paths had been recently sprinkled and raked. The people in the park looked happy in ordinary ways, mothers pushing strollers, little boys spinning tops, old men playing chess. He daydreamed about living in New York, having a job, an apartment with Sylvia. Then, checking his watch, he got up and walked around the inner circle of the park as he had been instructed, and, after a moment, saw Eitingon and Caridad sitting together on one of the benches. Eitingon was wearing a white Panama hat. Caridad wore an olive green suit with a small, dashing hat that looked like a bird's wing.

Eitingon gave him a warning glance as he approached. "Sit down and keep your voice low," Eitingon said in French. "We're probably being watched."

Ramón did as told, making a point not to look around.

"Who is watching?"

"Our people. The GPU, the NKVD."

"It's that bad?" Ramón said in French.

"The situation isn't good and could be much worse. We've been assigned to an NKVD agent here. We're going to meet him in a few minutes. Let me do the talking unless he asks you a question.

Everything will work out." Eitingon stood, checking his watch. "It's about time. We're just up Fifth Avenue."

"But before we go, I have something to say."

"Ramón, not now." Caridad looked impatient. "We're going to be late."

"But I think you should hear this."

"You have all week to tell us."

"Just one thing, a point of fact that should make a difference. At the house, after emptying his pistol in Trotsky's bed, Siqueiros didn't turn on the lights."

Caridad looked to Eitingon.

"He didn't check to see if Trotsky was dead," Ramón elaborated.

"That bastard!" said Caridad.

"How do you know this?" Eitingon asked.

"Marguerite Rosmer told me."

"Did this come out in the Mexican press?"

"No. Not that I know."

Eitingon shook his head. "It's disgusting but changes nothing,"

"It has changed everything," Ramón insisted.

"Not now. Don't bring it up. Your mother and I will be blamed. We were in charge of the mission. They'll say we failed to adequately train Siqueiros."

"But . . ."

"That's the way it works."

"There's something else I want to say."

"Later. This will be just the first meeting. I'm afraid this will last all week."


The building was unremarkable. The gold letters on the frosted glass door said Smith & Klein. Beyond a small waiting room, there was an office with windows that looked out on the street three floors below. Gaik Ovakimian had thinning blond hair, pale blue eyes, a bad complexion, and steel-rim glasses. His nose was oddly formed, hooked, the nostrils so small they appeared to have been added as an afterthought with a paper punch. He was wearing a cheap, badly cut suit, and was clearly unhappy to see them.

Eitingon launched into Russian, his voice rising and falling, while Ovakimian remained impassive, occasionally shrugging slightly, tapping his long fingers on the table. Ovakimian finally said something conclusive and cleared his throat, taking a very small green spiral notepad from his shirt pocket and glancing through it a moment. "Not good. Not good," he said in English, shaking his head back and forth, then giving them a baleful look. "Trotsky has already named David Siqueiros as his assailant."

Caridad glanced to Eitingon.

"How could he possibly know?" Ovakimian demanded.

"Pure speculation," Eitingon suggested.

"And David Siqueiros is giving Mexican newspapers interviews to make it appear he's still in Mexico City? What is the point of being so provocative? He's calling attention to himself."

"It's his way."

"Yet he remains in Mexico?"

"Yes, he's hiding in the mountains."

"In a place that's secure?"

"He says he won't be found."

"The Mexicans will find him unless they choose not to. He's involved too many people. We've had reports that two of the men who took part in the attack are here in New York. Leopoldo and Luis Arenas are going around the city, calling on expatriate Mexican artists and intellectuals as if they're on some sort of cultural tour."

"They're David's studio assistants. He must have given them money."

Ramón started to speak—he had been waiting for his chance—but Ovakimian inhaled sharply through his nose, a sort of snort in reverse. "None of this looks good by the light of day. Who in his right mind thought it would be a good idea to have a famous Mexican artist lead a secret mission?"

"Sudoplatov, Beria, and Stalin all endorsed that choice," said Eitingon.

"Yes, and none of them will remember that in the end."

He glanced at his notebook again. "And this American who was taken? Robert Sheldon Harte?"

"Siqueiros took him."

"Why involve this sort of person. His family is rich. His father went to Mexico to look for him. They've called the American ambassador in Mexico. Next they will call the FBI."

"The FBI would be helpless in Mexico," said Caridad.

Ovakimian consulted another page in his little green notebook, shaking his head and biting his lips as if confronted with a formula he couldn't solve. "Well, and what now?" He looked at Ramón. "You stayed in Mexico after the May twenty-third attack. Do you think anyone suspects you?"

"No one. Far from it. They're trying to recruit me to their side. Trotsky wants me to write an article for their publication."

"But that's very good, very useful."

"Yes, I would like to say something." Ramón looked from Caridad to Eitingon. "I've observed the situation in Mexico closely. And in Paris, I met the people who are running the Fourth International. At this point, I know Trotsky's organization better than anyone in the Kremlin. I know his guards and his secretaries. I have observed them closely." Ramón hesitated, taking a deep breath. "I'm confident that Trotsky and the Fourth International pose no threat to Stalin or Soviet Union. There is no reason to kill him."

"Yes, very good. Fortunately, we have a contingency plan in place. We need to adjust to the current circumstances and make the most of what has happened. The Kremlin wants Trotsky to be the author of his assassination. The assassin will be one of his followers, a disillusioned Trotskyist."

"But wait a moment," said Ramón.

Caridad shook her head. "This isn't the time."

"Plan B always called for an insider," said Eitingon. "So this would be a slight refinement."

"Yes, to take advantage of the current publicity," Ovakimian agreed. "What we need to do is write a letter, an alibi for our agent that will be found on his body, placing all of the blame on Trotsky."

"On his body," Caridad repeated.

"On his person, in case he should be captured."

Ramón looked from Caridad to Eitingon. "And who is this person, this disillusioned Trotskyist?"

Ovakimian's eyebrows went up.

Caridad met Ramón's eyes. "You understand what confidence we have placed in you. This is your great opportunity. Stalin, the Kremlin, everyone will be watching."

He started to speak, but her eyelids tensed, that warning look he knew from childhood.

"We should also think about this article Trotsky wants you to write," Ovakimian went on. "We must work on that as well while you're here."

The conversation moved past Ramón, around him, his head buzzing. He, the assassin? And they had never bothered to even tell him. Caridad looked at ease. A breeze came through the open windows, the sound of traffic on Fifth Avenue below.

Ramón waited until he felt sure of his voice. "Now that the time has come, may I ask what the contingency plan is?"

Ovakimian made an empty-handed gesture. "What do you mean?"

"You're planning the propaganda, but how does the assassination happen? Has that been planned?"

Eitingon leaned across the table toward him, smiling encouragement. "You know the situation best. The final plan will come from you, but we will help you. This sort of operation can be quite simple. Operatives in Bulgaria recently eliminated an ambassador there. They went in as moving men delivering a rug, cracked the ambassador's head with a lead pipe, rolled him up in the rug, and carried him out. No one missed him till the end of the day."

Ovakimian sneezed violently, then shifted in his chair to extract a folded handkerchief from his hip pocket. He opened the handkerchief, blew his nose into the white cotton fabric, then refolded the handkerchief.

"When?" asked Ramón.

Caridad and Eitingon looked to Ovakimian.

He took a small calendar from his wallet to study. "In August, surely. Before the end of the summer."

Ramón waited till the meeting was over and he was out on the street with Caridad and Eitingon. He searched his mother's face as they stood together on the sidewalk with pedestrians eddying around them.

"You didn't tell me?"

"I didn't know that this would happen."

"But if this was the contingency plan from the very beginning."

"The plan was fail-safe. If not for David Siqueiros, Plan A wouldn't have failed."

"Didn't you think I should have at least known what might be in store for me?"

Her mouth tightened and her sternum lifted as she straightened her shoulders. "You had no need to know. I wasn't going to leave you in Spain. I needed you with me. I'm your mother. I needed you."

"What kind of mother are you?" he asked in Catalan. "What kind of mother would do this?"

"I saw what was possible, but I didn't want you to have false hopes, to be disappointed. If that fool had done his job, you still wouldn't know."

Ramón felt his face growing hot, mottling with anger. "I don't want to do this."

"Of course you don't but it's too late to back out."

"I'm not sure I can."

Caridad gave him her most withering look. "Don't speak to me that way."

"Not here, not on the street," Eitingon hissed. "You're drawing attention."

"Do you think I care? Do you think any of these people are going to notice? You two have dragged me into this fiasco. You misled me and lied to me. You're both incompetent! You completely fucked up the operation, and now you want me to rescue you."

"Ramón, son, you're going too far."

"Not far enough," he answered, turning on his heel and walking away.

# FORTY-ONE

"You left your car with the guards?" Sylvia asked, leaning back and smiling at Jacques with a look of surprise, a daiquiri in her right hand. She was giving a party for him and was rather satisfied with her efforts. "Darling, whatever made you think to leave your car with Trotsky's guards?"

"I knew they could use it," he explained, smiling for the benefit of Sylvia's sisters and for Walta and Manny, and a few of the others from Paris. "That Ford of the Old Man's is always breaking down."

"But that you even thought of it?"

"I spent so much time waiting for you in front of the house, I got to know some of the guards pretty well."

"And you were there the night of the attack," said Walta.

"I was in Mexico, but no, of course I wasn't at the house. If I had been, things would have been different. I don't like to criticize others. You never know what you will do in an emergency, but what happened was shameless. Trotsky's guards didn't fire a shot to protect him. Not one shot!"

While Jacques talked, Sylvia slipped into the kitchen to check on the dinner. Clemmy had made her fried chicken, and Jacques had provided the daiquiris and several bottles of wine. He had seemed different to her in the few days he'd been in the city. He not only listened when everyone discussed politics but had begun to enter into the argument, referring to Trotsky as the Old Man.

His visit had started badly. His first day in town Jacques had come home furious from his meeting with Lubeck, so angry that he couldn't talk. He refused to tell her what had happened, but she gathered that he had been betrayed by Lubeck and was thinking about leaving his job. He seemed better now, as if he had made an important decision.

Hearing the Rosmers arriving, Sylvia returned to the living room. Marguerite carried the same black handbag; Alfred was wearing his dark suit and tie. *"Mon cher! Mon cher!"* Marguerite said, holding Jacques's face in her hands, her eyes alight with pleasure. They started speaking French, something about a journey and mountains. Finally, Marguerite turned to the others, taking Jacques's arm. "This dear man drove us all the way from Mexico City to Veracruz. Remember when we got lost in that terrible arrondissement. Oh, it was terrible. Vultures walked the street."

Jacques laughed. "Marguerite, we weren't lost. It was only one wrong turn."

"Yes, but we had a boat to catch!"

"You exaggerate terribly. Let me get you a daiquiri. Wine? Alfred?"

"Oh, you cannot imagine what this man meant to us!" Marguerite told the others as Jacques left the room. "Always so thoughtful. Such kindness at every turn."

"And you're moving here?" she said to Jacques as she accepted her drink.

"Yes, in a month or two. We're opening an office in New Jersey."

"Have you found an apartment?"

"No, I will let Sylvia handle that. She knows what we want."

"Marguerite, the news from Paris," said Sylvia. "I was so sad."

Marguerite shook her head, tears coming to her eyes. "Yes, it was ghastly. This is such a wretched world we live in. The news is always ghastly."

"Tell them about the telephone call you received today," Alfred prompted.

Marguerite put her hands to her face. "Natalia Sedova telephoned this afternoon! The extravagance, I could hardly stand it! They had just found that young American, Sheldon Harte."

"Natalia Sedova and Trotsky found him?" asked Jacques.

"No, the authorities, that foolish Colonel Sanchez and his detectives. Oh, it was gruesome. They found him in a little village out beyond Coyoacán."

"But that can't be true," said Jacques. "He was in the mountains with Siqueiros. They took him to the mountains."

Sylvia, Marguerite, Alfred, and the others turned to Jacques.

"In the mountains with Siqueiros?" Sylvia repeated. "Jacques, where did you hear that?"

"Someone in Mexico told me. I don't remember who. Everyone believes Siqueiros is hiding in the mountains and that he took Harte as a hostage."

"No, they killed him while he was sleeping," said Marguerite. "He was wearing his underpants and a blue sweater over a shirt just like a little boy."

Jacques listened in horror as Marguerite told how the police had found a bloodstained mattress on a cot in the little house that Siqueiros had rented in the country beyond Coyoacán. Siqueiros' *escondite!* The killers had slashed the mattress trying to get rid of the bloodstains and poured lime on the floor where blood had run into the cracks. They carried Harte's body down to the cellar, where they buried him in a shallow grave, covering his body with lime. To the Mexican police, Harte looked alarmingly white, like a white giant being unearthed.

The Arenal brothers, Jacques remembered them shooting the dog with such foolish cruelty. Did they taunt Harte? He must have been terrified alone in the shack with the Mexicans, unable to understand what they said. He must have been terrified just as Pablo was in Spain when he was strapped with dynamite and marched in front of the tanks.

"Colonel Sanchez brought the body to the Palacio Municipal in Coyoacán," Marguerite went on. "Trotsky went to identify it. Natalia Sedova said that after that had happened he finally broke down and wept when he saw the boy."

"I can't believe it," Jacques moaned, shaking his head.

Marguerite glanced at him. "That's right. You knew Harte, didn't you? I remember introducing you to him when Alfred was in the hospital."

"Why did he open the gate?" asked Sylvia.

"He had no idea what he was doing," said Marguerite. "Those people used him, then killed him so he couldn't talk. They tossed him away like a piece of trash."

# FORTY-TWO

Weeks later, after Jacques disappeared again, Sylvia kept coming back to the packets of money. The narrow manila envelopes tied with a green string, sealed with red wax had to be some sort of clue. Black-market pesos, Jacques explained. He'd bought pesos in New York and would make a killing in Mexico.

The day he left, he sent his luggage ahead to the train station, then asked Sylvia to go downstairs with him to his safe-deposit box at the Pierpont. With the door closed, he removed his jacket, placed the packets on the table, and rolled large rubber bands up over his striped shirtsleeves. He slipped the envelopes beneath the rubber bands. Nothing showed when he put on his jacket, and she didn't think about the pesos after they got in a taxi to Grand Central. The mysterious packets, the production of hiding them was in character for Jacques. She saw him board the train, then, the faithful wife, stood and waved from the platform as he waved back from his compartment.

Jacques telephoned from San Antonio two days later to say that he was catching a flight to Mexico City. The heat in the South had been brutal, and San Antonio was an inferno. The following day his telegram arrived: ARRIVED SAFELY MEXICO. ALL WELL. WILL WRITE SOON. LOVE, JAC.

Then nothing.

Sylvia knew a letter from Mexico could take weeks or even months to reach New York. She knew telegrams went astray. She didn't begin to worry until two weeks had passed, but then the old anxiety returned, the memories of his disappearance in Paris.

Only then did she focus upon the strangeness of the manila envelopes. Why did he make such a show of hiding them? Why did
he even bother? He knew he wouldn't go through customs in New
York. He wouldn't pass through customs until he landed in Mexico
City, where one's luggage was rarely checked. She began to dwell
upon the envelopes as a clue to his disappearance. She began to
count the days since he'd gone missing, to race home to check the
mail, to jump when the telephone rang. At night, she jolted awake
to the knowledge that Jacques had disappeared once again. He was
in trouble. He was sick or dying. He had been robbed and killed for
the pesos.

Or perhaps he didn't love her. There was always that.

Then, finally a telegram arrived: AM VERY SICK AND NEED YOUR
HELP. PLEASE COME. I'M AT THE MONTEJO. LOVE, JAC.

She called an international operator and placed the call, person-
to-person. "We will call back when we have your party," the woman
said. Thirty minutes later, the telephone rang. Over static and hum-
ming on the line, Sylvia could hear the operator asking Jacques to
identify himself. His voice was weak, a hoarse whisper. "You may go
ahead," the operator finally said.

"Jacques, what's wrong? What happened to you? I've been frantic
about you."

"Can you come?" he whispered, each word heavy as a stone.

"Yes, but what's the matter?"

"I'm sick." He paused to gather strength. "I got sick in a village
near Orizaba, too sick to leave." The line began to hum, a strange
voice emerging. "I'll explain when you get here."


The following evening, a bellboy let Sylvia into the suite at the Montejo. It was raining outside and the bedroom was dark, the shades
drawn. She could make out Jacques's dark hair against the pillow.
"Jacques," she said, stopping to turn on a lamp. She sat down on

the edge of his bed, putting her hand to his forehead. His skin was clammy, his hair matted, his face gaunt, his eyes sunk into their sockets. "Jacques, I'm here."

Eyelids flickering open, lips chapped, a white film in the corners of mouth, he rasped, "Thank you for coming."

"What happened?"

"The water, food, I guess. I couldn't get away. I thought I was going to die. I'm still so weak."

"Has a doctor been here?"

He shook his head.

"Oh, Jacques! Why ever not?"

She was telephoning the front desk to get a doctor when Jacques began to moan. "My stomach," he said, struggling to get up. She helped him to the bathroom, then, hearing the liquid onset of diarrhea, went back to the phone in the living room.

"I'm sorry," he apologized as he came out. "I can't help it."

"The hotel is sending a doctor."

She helped him back into bed.

"Where are your clothes, the rest of your things? There's nothing here but a knapsack."

"Everything is in storage at the Shirley Courts."

"I'll call them in the morning. You're going to need a change of pajamas."

"Yes, I'm filthy." He closed his eyes, drifting off. She sat with him until the doctor came, a portly Mexican who spoke broken English. "Amoebas," he decided after examining Jacques. "An amoebic infection." He called prescriptions in to a pharmacy and gave Sylvia nursing instructions. After he left, she asked room service to send ginger ale and soda crackers. She gave Jacques his medicine and sat with him through the night, holding a glass to his mouth, and helping him into the bathroom. When he had fever, she sponged his face with a damp towel. When he had chills, she covered him with a blanket.

"No, no, no," he would moan, thrashing back and forth.

"Did I talk in my sleep?" he asked in a lucid moment, when he found Sylvia sitting in her chair, reading a book.

"A little. Do you feel better?"

He watched her. His eyes followed her as she brought a glass of water.

The following day while he slept, she arranged for his belongings to be sent from the Shirley Courts and rounded up tins of soup. She began to unpack his luggage, helped him into a shower and a clean pair of pajamas, made sure that he took his pills on time, fed him soup and juice. She dozed in a chair by his bed, listening to him breathe, watching the shadows on his face.

The fever began to let up; the bouts of diarrhea and cramps came farther apart. But his cheeks and eyes were sunken in, his skin an unhealthy shade of green. Late in the afternoon when he seemed stronger, she asked what had happened.

He shook his head. "I decided to climb Orizaba before I left Mexico. I went up to a village to adjust to the altitude. I didn't tell you because I knew you would worry. There were flies on everything. I must have eaten something bad. I got so sick I couldn't leave."

"You're still sick. When you feel better, you can tell me what happened."

The third day, he put on his robe and slippers to eat a bowl of soup in the living room. "You've been bored," he said.

"Not really. You've kept me busy. And I've been reading."

"Yes, I kept seeing you with a book. What is it?"

"Freud, *The Interpretation of Dreams*."

The spoon stopped halfway to his mouth. "And did you interpret my dreams?"

"No, you haven't told me your dreams."

"Did I talk in my sleep?" he asked, suddenly anxious.

"Some, but you never said anything that made sense. You kept saying the name Ramón. You sounded as if you were very concerned about him. Who is Ramón?"

Jacques hesitated. "I'm not sure. It's a common name. There was probably a Ramón in the village where I was."

"I still don't understand what you were doing in that village, how you got there."

"I went with a group I met when I first got here. Carlos Patiño, the manager of the Pan Am freight office, organizes expeditions. We climbed to about forty-five hundred meters but the altitude was too much for us. The others left, but I decided to give myself a chance to acclimate. It was a poor Indian village, no running water, no electricity. I was going to try again, but I got sick. The Indians tried to help me, but I was too sick. I couldn't move and every time they brought me a cup of tea or soup it made me sicker."

"And how did you get back?"

"One of the Indians went down the mountain to the next village, where there was a man who owned a truck. I paid him to bring me into the city. It was the longest trip I've ever made. I kept having to get out of the truck and squat by the road."

The next morning, Jacques showered, shaved, and put on a suit. "You look dreadful," Sylvia told him. "You must have lost fifteen pounds. Your clothes hang on you."

"That bad?"

"You shouldn't go out."

"It's work, an errand I've put off too long."

Downstairs, he got a cab to take him to Coyoacán. On the way he felt cramping deep in his gut and feared he'd have to ask the driver to stop. He had dreaded the trip, that wave of sadness when they turned onto Calle Viena, where the yellow Buick waited in front of the entrance. The sound of hammering came from inside the wall. Joe Hansen waved from the turret and Jake Cooper opened the reinforced door. "We thought you were never coming for your car," said Cooper.

"Yes, I'm sure. What's all the racket?"

"We're reinforcing the place, beefing up security. The comrades in New York sent a big check. Hey, you don't look so good."

"I got sick in the mountains."

"I guess you heard about Harte?"

"Yes, in New York. The Rosmers told me."

"None of us ever believed he was a Stalinist. The Old Man took it really hard when they found his body. You heard how he was killed?"

"Yes. Yes. You know I'm not altogether well."

"I'll get your keys. They're in the library. Come on in and say hello."

"No, I'd better wait for you here."

Moments later, Jake returned with Otto Schüssler and Natalia Sedova following him. "Mr. Jacson, welcome home," she said, shading her eyes against the sun to see him better. "My, you look as if you've been ill."

"Yes, I'm afraid I've had dysentery. Sylvia came down to nurse me."

"Sylvia is here in Mexico? No one told us she's here."

"I've kept her busy, and it was an unexpected trip."

"We'd like to see her. Will you bring her for tea?"

"Yes. She doesn't know I'm here now. She would have wanted to come, and as you see, I'm not quite myself."

"I'll have one of the secretaries telephone her."

"Is your husband well?"

"Yes, but working too hard. He's put aside his Stalin biography to write an analysis of the GPU's assassination tactics. He believes that will do more to protect us than all of this construction work." She smiled sadly. "Seva has asked about you."

"Oh, Seva!" In his fever, he had almost forgotten about the boy.

"He has asked about you. It was difficult for him after Marguerite and Alfred left."

"Yes, I can't tell you how badly I feel for Seva."

"Seva? Yes, you and Sylvia spent time with him on your outings with the Rosmers."

Jacques winced slightly, the difficulty of choosing his words, the pain of remembrance. "I had a childhood with many disruptions. I know what it is to be a boy his age."

# FORTY-THREE

Eitingon nodded encouragement as Ramón brought a spoonful of the clear golden broth from the bowl to his mouth. They were sitting side by side at one of the banquets on the patio at the Bellinghausen. Eitingon noticed the young man's hand tremble and worried about the color of his complexion. He'd known him as a boy, watched him mature, and was now relying upon him. For a moment, he felt that it must be Ramón who was his son rather than Luis.

"Some lime juice might improve the flavor," he suggested. "That's what the Mexicans do."

"I don't want much flavor."

"Do you feel you're getting stronger?"

"Yes, the cramps come less often. It's only the nausea."

Eitingon took a swallow of his vodka, then linked his thick hands on the white tablecloth before him. "You should have some red meat. Steak tartar on toast."

"Or ground horsemeat with cognac?"

"Yes, something like that."

"I don't think so."

Eitingon's eyes drifted to the far side of the patio, where a famous Mexican comedian was arriving, causing a ripple to pass through the restaurant, heads turning, hands reaching out, waiters and maître d' bowing and scraping,

"You must eat something solid. I'll have them prepare eggs for you. Soft-boiled eggs and bread. Those Mexican rolls, *bolillos*, are quite tasty."

"I had eggs for breakfast. I'll be having tea soon."

"At four o'clock, you said."

"At four-thirty."

"That's good. You must observe everything. You know the physical structure. Now you must learn their habits. Does he close the door to his office?"

Ramón lifted his eyes to Eitingon's for a moment, then had another spoonful of broth.

"How long does it take to walk from his office out to a car on the street? Unimpeded, ten seconds? Silence will be critical. It's a large house but there are people all around him. This afternoon, talk to him about the article you're writing. Tell him that you will need his help. That will give you the opportunity to schedule an appointment. Perhaps two."

"I worry about being there with Sylvia. Before she left last time, she made me promise I wouldn't go to the house without her."

"But she knows that you are known there, that you often went to the house for the Rosmers. It's unlikely anything specific will be said."


"I'm afraid I'm dreading this," said Sylvia as Jacques parked their car at an angle to the wall.

"Why? You were so eager the first time you came."

"I know but Trotsky will want to argue politics, and I don't feel like an argument. Or politics. Marguerite says they haven't any money, that they're wearing the same clothes they arrived with in Mexico. Do you think Mr. Lubeck could do something for them?"

"Mr. Lubeck?"

"Yes, couldn't he include them in a deal?"

"I suppose if they have something to invest. Should I ask?"

"No, not today. They're so formal, they would probably find it improper to discuss business."

Jacques went around to open Sylvia's door, noticing the lightning flicker in the dark clouds bunched up against the volcanoes. The machine-gun turret was empty. The garage door rolled open as they approached. "Just come through here," said Jake Cooper, "I'm taking the Dodge out."

Cooper greeted them, then they followed the flagstone path up to the house, entering the library beneath the canopy of bougainvillea. Otto Schüssler, Walter Kertley, who was one of the secretaries, and Ellen Reed stopped their work to say hello, asking about Sylvia's sisters and the Rosmers in New York.

"We're having tea on the patio," said Natalia Sedova, coming in from the dining room, drying her hands on a dish towel. She embraced Sylvia, kissing her on both cheeks. "And Mr. Jacson," she said, offering her hand. "My husband is waiting for us outside. I think you'll find it pleasant."

A small round table had been laid with a blue-and-white cloth, cups, and saucers. "Ah, Sylvia!" Trotsky said, getting up to embrace her. "You are a welcome sight and an unexpected pleasure." He cocked his head quizzically when he looked at Jacques. "And Mr. Jacson, I understand you haven't been well. Goodness, your color is poor and you've lost weight. What medicines has your doctor prescribed? You have to be so careful with the water here. That's the first thing we tell our guests. We never drink water without boiling it first."

"I have something for Seva," Jacques said, touching the breast pocket of his suit. "Is he here?"

"He's in his room, the one at the end," said Natalia Sedova. "He'll be happy to see you."

Leaving Sylvia to answer questions about New York, Jacques walked to the three steps leading to the boy's room. "Esteban," he called. "I brought you something."

The boy came out, looking pale and shy, still wearing his school uniform. Jacques withdrew the long narrow package from his jacket.

"A glider," Seva said as he unwrapped the paper.

Jacques sat on one of the steps and lit a cigarette while the boy broke the thin pieces of balsam wood apart, inserting the long fragile wing into the slot cut into the body of the plane.

"Seva, what's that you have?" Trotsky asked as he joined them.

"A glider. Mr. Jacson gave it to me."

"Did you say thank you?"

"Yes, Grampa, of course. Thank you, Mr. Jacson."

Seva attached the tail wing and rudder, then threw the plane, which soared for a moment, defying the force of gravity. The two men stood watching as the boy chased after the plane. A breeze moved in the eucalyptus tree, the shadows swaying on the ground. The hens clucked softly in the chicken coop, the raft of dappled shade floating beneath the tree.

"I believe I've thought of something to write about," said Jacques.

Trotsky turned to him, his crystal blue eyes focusing, trying to recall what his guest was talking about. "Oh yes, tell me."

"I thought it would be interesting to look at how the war in Europe is driving up commodity prices in Latin America and discuss the issue of profit taking as opposed to profiteering."

"That sounds promising," said Trotsky as he gravitated toward his rabbits and chickens, Jacques following in his wake

"I've never written anything like this so I'll need your guidance— if you're still willing to help me."

"Of course," said Trotsky, peering into the rabbit hutch. "Bring me your rough draft. We'll go over that together. I can make suggestions then you can bring it back for a final read. That's the usual procedure." He placed his hand on Jacques's shoulder in an affectionate way. "This is a splendid development. I'll be happy to help you."

# FORTY-FOUR

She took a cigarette from the pack of Lucky Strikes on the table and pushed it to him. "It's time." She lit her cigarette, squinting against the smoke. "You don't need Sylvia here. Get rid of her."

Ramón lit his own cigarette, exhaling, not bothering to answer. Eitingon sat in a chair beneath a lamp to one side of the room, where he was going through a document.

"She's a distraction, and it's dangerous for you to be sleeping with her now. You could slip up, say something in your sleep. You shouldn't have brought her down here again."

Ramón's eyelids tensed slightly. "I was sick. I needed help."

"You could have gone to a hospital. That's what you should have done."

"I can't simply dismiss Sylvia."

"Of course you can. We're finished with her. You no longer need to worry about what she thinks or how she feels. We no longer need her. She's a distraction."

Ramón studied his cigarette, contemplating the smoke, the gray ash, the cinder slowly burning as if it were a very slow fuse. Against his better judgment, he had trusted his mother in Spain. He'd followed her to Paris and then to Mexico. She'd led him into the worst possible dilemma, a treacherous impasse with no feasible escape. He wasn't sure what he was going to do, only that he would have to find his own way and that he had no intention of sending Sylvia home to New York.

He raised his head, meeting Caridad's eyes. "I find that her presence keeps me calm."

"Leonid! Are you listening to this?"

Eitingon looked up from his document. "If she makes the boy feel better, what difference does it make? It's like putting a goat in with a racehorse. Ramón, when are you going back out there to show Trotsky your article?"

"On Friday."

"That's good. The Germans started air raids over England today. In a week or ten days, they'll start bombing London. We should do it before then. The timing will be perfect."

"Have you decided on the weapon?"

"I have an idea but I'm not sure."

"If only there were a way to silence a pistol," said Caridad. "Have you considered a garrote? You could conceal a piece of wire in your clothes."

"He would struggle. He's old but strong. If he kicked something over, the guards would come rushing in."

"There's always lead pipe," Eitingon suggested. "It's available in any hardware store."

Jacques grimaced. "I was thinking of something less crude."

"Yes?"

"A *piolet*, the kind I used climbing in Europe."

"A *piolet*?"

"It's an ice ax. The head has a sharp prong on one side and a blade on the other. I can cut the handle down and conceal it under my raincoat."

"It sounds like a grubbing hoe. You're thinking of going into his office with a farming implement?"

"No, it's very elegant and precise. Climbing in the Pyrénées, I shattered enormous blocks of ice with the prong."

"It would be easy to trace. Do you want to leave your calling card at the scene of the crime?"

"What difference does it make? They're going to know I did it whether they catch me or not."

"Do you have one of these elegant implements?"

"No, but I know where I can get one."

Caridad placed her hand on Jacques's forearm, gripping it firmly. "You must think positively about this. Use whatever weapon you want. You must take a pistol as well."

"Do you want a cyanide capsule?" asked Eitingon.

"No!" Caridad snapped. "This is not a suicide mission! That is not an option."

Eitingon gazed at her through the cloud of cigarette smoke undulating slowly in the room. After a moment, he sniffed audibly, then reordered the pages of the typescript. "Let's go over the letter again."

"I know it by heart. I'm Jacques Mornard, a Belgian aristocrat. While living in Paris, I joined a group of Trotskyists. One of the members asked if I would like to go on a special mission to Mexico, et cetera, et cetera, et cetera."

"Ramón, there is no et cetera," said Eitingon, getting up from his chair. "You're going to be under tremendous pressure. They'll grill you again and again."

"Yes, yes, I know."

Eitingon leaned down into his face. "Who approached you about coming to Mexico?"

Ramón felt his fury come boiling up. He wanted to grab Eitingon by the ears and slam his face into the table.

"Who? Who approached you?"

Ramón took a deep breath, trying to steady himself. "A member of the Fourth International. He said they would pay all of my expenses, but I had to assume a new name and travel under a forged passport."

"What was his name?"

"I don't remember. He never told me."

"What did he look like?"

"French, an intellectual."

"What were his instructions?"

"I was to keep my distance when I first arrived to avoid suspicion. After I met Trotsky, I became disillusioned. I saw that he was scornful of his own followers and despised the working class. He was a maniac who cared only for power. He wanted to send me on a secret mission to the Soviet Union to assassinate Stalin. When I realized that he had ruined my life by having me come to Mexico under false circumstances, I had no choice but to kill him."

"A secret mission?"

"Yes, he was going to send me to Shanghai, where I would meet with other undercover agents."

"And you swear your name is Jacques Mornard?"

"Yes."

"Where does your family live in Brussels?"

"They have a house in the city and an estate. A country estate."

"What is the address in town?"

Jacques looked to Caridad.

"She doesn't know. She won't be there with you. You're going to be alone. You'll be exhausted, desperate for sleep. You may be in pain, and they will come after you again and again, demanding answers, challenging everything you say. If you are an aristocrat, you know where your family lives. They don't move houses once a year."

"Why do I get the feeling that you expect me to be captured?"

"We don't. We expect you to walk out of that house and fly with us to the United States. But you have to be prepared because, given the chance, they will hammer at you, tear you apart. You must be able to do this in your sleep."

"Remember," said Caridad, "if the worst happens and you are caught, you will have the full support of the GPU. Sudoplatov has given me his personal promise that I will get all the money and men it takes to free you. This is Mexico, where everything is for sale. We can bribe the judges and prosecutors or, if worse comes to worse, we'll break you out of prison."

"But," said Eitingon, "you have to stick to the alibi. If you implicate the GPU, then you deprive Sudoplatov of a motive to rescue you."

"But that won't happen because you will be prepared. We will go over this again and again. I will not abandon you here in Mexico. Do you understand?"

Jacques nodded, taking a deep, nervous breath of air.

Caridad leaned close, her eyes a mirror of his, moving slightly, searching. "The way out is to go forward, son. You will walk into that house with confidence. It is a delicate operation but not impossible, no more difficult than threading a needle. Now, let's go over it again."

She unrolled a floor plan of the house on the table between them. "Here," she said, placing her finger on the plan where Trotsky's office was located. "The moment you strike him you turn and walk out the door. You don't run. You walk to your car and drive to here."

She switched to a map of the village, tapping her finger on an intersection two blocks from the house. "I'll be waiting for you with a driver in another car. You abandon the Buick and we drive to here." She tapped once more on an intersection at the edge of the village. "Leonid will be waiting here with yet another car. The driver will take us to the airport, where a pilot will have a plane ready to take off. By the time Mexican authorities realize what has happened, we will be out of Mexico.

"Do you see?" she asked, waiting for him to look at her. She held his gaze for moment, her green eyes intent, unmoving.

# FORTY-FIVE

"Jacques, do you realize that today is Saturday?"

Sylvia looked into the bedroom, where his trunk stood open, waiting for the stacks of shirts and sweaters and jackets laid out on the bed. Seeing that the door to the bath was closed, she went to the desk in the living room, stopping to open one of the windows to let in the fresh morning air. She was glad their suite was at the back of the hotel, protected from the sound of the traffic on Reforma. She sat down at the desk and began to make a list of all the things she needed and wanted to do before leaving Mexico. She still had gifts to buy. She wanted to see the Diego Rivera mural at the Bellas Artes that everyone in New York invariably asked about. They had tickets that night to see Carlos Chávez conduct the French Symphony. And of course, they would have to go back out to Coyoacán to tell the Old Man and everyone goodbye.

She was still writing when Jacques came into the room, freshly shaved, slipping into the jacket of his suit. "I was just wondering when we should have the hotel ship your trunk."

"My trunk?"

She got up and went back into the bedroom to survey the stacks of clothing on the bed. "Yes, it would cost a fortune to take it on the plane. Have you looked at what's going into the trunk?"

"Not really. I trust your judgment."

"Well, please come and look. Once we send the trunk, you won't see any of this again for two or three weeks."

She stood in front of the bed, pushing her hands through her short blond hair as she surveyed her work. "You've seen these." She picked up a small, toylike shadow box. Three sides of the box were made of some cheap wood painted chrome yellow, the front a piece of glass. Inside, a trio of skeletons played a trumpet, guitar, and violin. Jacques looked over her shoulder.

"I found these in the market and thought they would make nice gifts."

"Won't they seem morbid?"

"I don't know. I think the skeletons are cheerful in a strange sort of way."

"You see that sort of thing all over Mexico. Skeleton toys for children, candies shaped like skeletons."

"I do wish we were sailing. It would be easier and so much more relaxing to go by ship." She put the toy down and picked up a stack of shirts, going through them as if looking for something. "Is there anything here you'll miss?"

"What do you mean?"

"Something you don't want shipped?"

"No, I'm sure it's all fine."

"By the way, what are you doing with your car?"

"My car?"

She smiled indulgently. "Yes. You know, the yellow Buick."

"I hadn't thought of it."

"Well, you can't leave it at the airport."

"No, that wouldn't do. I guess I could give it to the Old Man."

"I don't know how he would feel about accepting that sort of gift."

"I could give it to the Fourth International. Or if they don't want it, I'll just drop the car at the agency where I bought it and let them sell it."

She put the shirts down and turned to him. "Speaking of skeletons, darling, you look like a scarecrow in that suit. It literally flops on you."

"All my clothes do. It can't be helped."

"I know, but we'll get you fattened up in New York. I'm arranging to have Clemmy come in to cook for you, and I've made an appointment with Dr. Blumenthal on Park Avenue. He'll know the best tropical disease man in New York. We'll spend a few days in the city, then we can go up to the lake for Labor Day."

Jacques picked up his gabardine raincoat and his gray fedora.

"Are you going out?"

"Yes, an errand for Mr. Lubeck."

"So late in the day?" She frowned. "I wish you could tell me what you're doing. You've been so nervous, I keep expecting you to jump out of your skin."

"I'm sorry. You know I can't talk about it." He hesitated. "It's just this last deal that has to be closed."

"Is it terribly important?"

"Yes. A mistake was made that has to be corrected."

"That is upsetting. What time do you think you'll be back?"

"Oh, by six anyway. Before the rain starts."

She put her arm through his, walking him to the door. "What about tomorrow? Can we drive to Cuernavaca? Have lunch at one of the hotels, go for a swim? You must give me a little incentive to keep me working. And it would be so good for you to get away."

"I don't know why not."

"You're taking your hat? You never wear a hat."

"Yes, but I thought I might make a habit of it."


As he got into his car, he felt a flicker of cramping deep in his gut. It was a little after four and his appointment with Trotsky was at four-thirty. Sitting behind the steering wheel, Jacques looked through the article once more that Ovakimian had had written for him in New York. He'd copied it in longhand, dropping a few sentences, changing the order to be certain that it would require a second draft. He worried that he had changed it too much, that Trotsky would reject it outright, but now it was too late and there was nothing he could do.

Taking a deep nervous breath, he folded the pages and pressed the car's ignition. He was going through the motions, putting one foot in front of the other. He stopped the car in front of Edificio Ermita, tapped the Buick's horn, and waited until Eitingon came down the front steps, wearing a hat, a raincoat folded over his arm.

"I could go alone," Ramón said in French as the older man got in the car.

"Of course, but you won't mind the company? I thought I'd stroll around the plaza while you go to the house. Coyoacán is such a charming little village. I might buy a few souvenirs while you're seeing Trotsky."

He settled into the passenger seat as Jacques pulled the Buick away from the curb. Having Eitingon along signaled a change, that he was being watched, wasn't quite trusted.

"You have the paper ready?" said Eitingon.

"Yes, I worked on it a bit more. I think it's right but it's rather a fine line. If the paper is too bad, he'll tell me not to bother and that will be that. And if it's too good, then there wouldn't be a reason for a second meeting."

"Yes, you have to have the second meeting."

Ramón pressed the lighter and felt for a cigarette without taking his eyes from the road. "It would be easier if it were spontaneous."

"How is that?"

"If I didn't have to think about it so much. If I didn't have to wait."

"But if you're going to get away a car has to be waiting, a plane. You're not going in with a weapon today?"

"No, of course not."

"That's good. We've made our plan and we don't want to deviate from it. We must trust our plan."

As they came up behind a large horse-drawn wagon, Ramón

slowed the Buick, remembering with a twinge of anxiety that he still had to get the *piolet*. The Shirleys' son had one, but he had to call and arrange to borrow it. He found his cigarettes and lit one, stepping on the gas to pull around the wagon. He felt another flicker of cramping in his gut as they entered the village, the cobblestone street bound by stone walls and lined with cypress trees.

He dropped Eitingon on the zocalo, then followed his usual route past the Rivera house until he saw the eucalyptus tree rise up over the walls, which always made him think of the sails of a schooner. In the distance, storm clouds roiled against the volcanoes. He felt detached turning onto Viena, as if he were watching a film. Two of the Mexican policeman stood in front of the brick hut as a peasant was coming from the riverbed leading a burro. A breeze rippled through the patch of corn across from the house.

Remembering Sheldon, he looked up at the wall, but no one was there. Where were the guards? How could they be so lax, so blind? How could they not see through him? Surely they would notice that he was wearing a raincoat and fedora. Surely that would tip them off.

As he got out of the car and slammed the door, the sound of hammering and sawing came from the opposite side of the wall. He pressed the buzzer; after a moment, Jake Cooper opened the door.

"I'm here for my appointment at four-thirty," Jacques announced stiffly.

Cooper smiled. "You have an appointment with the Old Man?"

"Yes, at four-thirty."

"Well, no one told me." Cooper consulted a clipboard, shaking his head. "There's nothing here about an appointment for you."

Jacques felt panic rising. "I called and spoke to Otto Schüssler about the appointment. I've driven all the way from the city."

"Take it easy. If the Old Man said he'll see you then he will. He doesn't always tell us about appointments if it's someone he knows."

Jacques squared his shoulders and passed through the garage into the brilliant sunlight, where Trotsky stood, watching as Joe Hansen and a Mexican covered the French doors to his bedroom with heavy steel shutters.

"Ah! Mr. Jacson!" Trotsky extended his hand, his blue eyes smiling. "You see what they're doing—turning my house into a prison. I think it's a waste of time. The GPU won't try the same thing twice."

"Yes, I'm sure you're right," Jacques agreed.

"I've never owned a house before and hate to see this one ruined, since I've rather come to like it. Hansen, will those hinges hold the shutter?"

"Yes, sir, I believe so, but we'll know for sure in a moment." Hansen and the Mexican lifted a long metal shutter and settled it in the frame. "There you go," Hansen said, moving the shutter, which made the hinges squeal.

Trotsky shivered. "That sounds like some of the prison cells I lived in."

"Where was that?" said Jacques.

"Before the revolution under the Czar. Prison isn't so bad if you can read and write. Your mind is free." He considered Jacques, the blue eyes attentive. "And how is your health today? Are you feeling any better?"

"Yes, much improved."

"And how is Sylvia?"

"She's well. The climate doesn't bother her. And your wife? Is she well?"

"Yes, she's gone out on errands. I'm afraid you will miss her. Well, let's go in and look at that paper you've written."

He put a hand on Jacques's shoulder, his grip strong, his hand reassuringly warm. They went through the library and dining room into the office, Jacques observing that Trotsky closed his door even when the outer rooms were empty. The office was at the dead center of the house, exposed on all sides. The sound of the men's voices came from the garden. The desk, a large wooden table, faced into the room so that Trotsky sat with his back to the dining room door, looking through the French doors to the front garden. There was a day bed covered with an Indian blanket in the opposite corner of the room, two chairs for guests, a Dictaphone machine, and a long, low bookshelf behind the desk that contained volumes bound in red and blue. Orderly stacks of periodicals sat on top of the bookshelf. The desk was bare except for a large black fountain pen, an inkwell, a clay cup sprouting sharpened yellow pencils, and a .25-caliber automatic pistol.

Trotsky rubbed his hands together in an agreeable way. "Well, shall we?"

Jacques had removed his hat when he entered the house, but now, encumbered with the raincoat over his right arm, he put the hat back on and reached into his coat pocket for the manuscript. "I'm afraid this isn't very good," he apologized.

"Don't worry," said Trotsky. "When you write you have an opportunity to see what you've done, then make it better. I'm sure we can solve any problems we encounter."

Trotsky frowned as he unfolded the pages. "You didn't have your secretary type it?"

"I'm sorry. I didn't have the opportunity."

"It's much easier to edit a document that has been typed. You can see what you're doing."

Trotsky sat down at the desk, squaring the paper before him—a habit of work—and started to read. Jacques saw that the situation was impossible. The room was too small. There was no place for him to stand, no place to put his hat. He couldn't pull the *piolet* from his coat while standing in front of Trotsky. The voices of the Mexican women came from the kitchen, the sound of the men working outside. He lingered by the door to the dining room, then, as if trying to look over Trotsky's shoulder, edged behind the desk, so close he could smell Trotsky's hair tonic, see the shine of his scalp.

Trotsky read for a few moments, then hunched his shoulders with irritation. "Mr. Jacson, do you mind?" He looked over his shoulder and for a moment their eyes met. Jacques felt the hair prickle on the back of his neck as he watched the expression in Trotsky's eyes change, as Trotsky saw through him.

Then, in some unaccountable way, the moment between them passed. "Your hat," said Trotsky. "Would you please remove your hat and take a seat?"

He read for a few more minutes, turning the pages before looking up again. "Well, you have some interesting statistics," he said, the warmth now gone from his voice. "You need to state your thesis at the beginning, and define your terms. You do that in your second-to-last paragraph, but it should happen at the beginning." He went through the pages, marking suggested changes.

"I see. Of course," Jacques kept saying. "Yes, I understand what it needs."

Trotsky folded the paper vertically, a conclusive gesture, then handed it to Jacques.

"May I bring it back? I'll make these changes and have it typed, as you say."

Trotsky hesitated. "If you must."


Trotsky was sitting on the patio reading a newspaper when Natalia Sedova returned from her errands. "Do we know who Mr. Jacson is?" he asked.

"Why, he's Sylvia's husband. Did he come for his meeting?"

"Yes, he left before you arrived."

"And how was the article he's writing?"

"Badly organized, the ideas commonplace. And he didn't bother to have it typed."

"Oh, that is annoying."

"But what do we really know about him?"

"Everyone met him in France. He's from an aristocratic family there. If I recall, his Christian name is Jacques, but he's traveling under a forged Canadian passport. Sylvia said he had some sort of problem getting a visa because of his military service in France. Why are you asking all of these questions?"

Trotsky recounted what had happened in his office. "I had the strangest feeling."

"You've always hated someone reading over your shoulder."

"It was more than that. He was wearing his hat."

"His hat?"

"He was wearing his hat in my office. When I looked up and saw that he was wearing his hat, I knew he wasn't French. A Frenchman would never wear his hat in another man's office."

"I believe he's Belgian."

"It is the same thing, Belgian, French. It's not done. A Belgian or a Frenchman would never wear his hat in another man's office. And if he isn't who he says, then he could be anyone."

"I see what you mean."

"And who is this fabulously wealthy Mr. Lubeck he talks about? I think it's time we make some inquiries."

## FORTY-SIX

Opening his eyes, Jacques saw the trunk standing open on the far side of the darkened bedroom, rows of suits and jackets on hangers, sweaters draped over the open door. He felt cold beneath the covers. A chill entered his back between his shoulder blades and ran down into his body. He knew he was sick. His bones ached; his breath smelled stale against the pillow.

He turned on his side, trying to recapture a scrap of sleep, a moment of oblivion. He'd been lying there pretending, his eyes closed, his body clenched. He had nowhere to go. He had no money. He had no escape. He was a fraud. Everything in the room—the trunk, the clothes, the room itself—taunted him with his fraudulence. He had no passport. His true identity was long gone, a recurring memory.

Curling up, hands to chest, knees bent, he becomes Harte sleeping on his side in underpants and sweater. He brought Harte to the gate. He caused him to open the gate to a reality of demons swirling through. Did he feel the cold steel muzzle of the .22 against his forehead, the circle of metal enclosing the dark spiraling infinity? Did Siqueiros pull the trigger? No, of course not. An artist, he didn't want those images in his mind, knew better than to switch on the light and pull back the covers.

The sound of traffic came from the street. Light crept up the wall between the valances and the curtains. The morning was almost gone. Sylvia was out seeing one of her friends. She always knew someone to call wherever she was. She had waited for him that morning, begged him to get out of bed. She was resourceful, always kind and sensible. Her perception of him as a normal, civilized man was what they were both clinging to. She wasn't a fool or stupid. If she didn't love him, if the truth weren't unspeakable, she would know who he was, what he was doing.

A future with Sylvia in New York shimmered like a mirage in the distance, a happy life beckoning from beyond an impossible barricade. The house in Coyoacán, Trotsky—Ramón could not thread that needle. He couldn't walk through the gate, kill in cold blood, and walk out again. That was a problem without solution.

Beneath the sheets, the toes of his right foot touched the heel of his left as the previous afternoon's disaster returned to him, the smell of Trotsky's hair tonic, the grooves of age on the old man's neck, the sound of the men working outside. In that moment of silent communion between prey and predator, he watched the understanding crystallize in Trotsky's clear blue eyes, cognition becoming recognition too quickly to separate. Breath caught, Ramón waited for Trotsky to press the button for the alarm beneath his desk or reach for the pistol in plain sight. He knew Trotsky knew. Driving back into the city, he was certain Trotsky's men would call the police, that detectives would arrive at the hotel. He waited for the hand on his shoulder, the knock on the door.

But instead, silence, an echoing, ringing silence. What did it mean? That Colonel Sanchez was preparing a case? That he would be arrested during the day?

Ramón lay there, his eyes moving back and forth across the ceiling.

Trotsky knew and nothing had happened. Trotsky knew.

Then, Ramón understood that Trotsky, rather than an insurmountable problem, was the solution. Trotsky needn't do anything but close his doors to Frank Jacson. He would ring the bell and Cooper or Robins would say, "Sorry, the Old Man can't see you." It was a drama with no climax.

He pushed the covers back, putting his feet to the floor. Switching on a lamp, he felt purged and lucid as after one of his fevers.

He gazed at the wonderful clothes in the trunk, then went into the bathroom, the tiles cold against his feet. He had to go to Coyoacán. He had to be sure. If Trotsky knew, the order would have been given. He could go to Coyoacán unshaven, his hair matted against his head, but such theatrics weren't necessary. He would go to Coyoacán to remind Trotsky.

He showered and shaved, wiping the steam off the mirror. As he dressed, he called to the desk to bring his car around. He felt better, more optimistic. He was deviating from the plan, taking matters into his own hands. When he walked outside, wearing his dark glasses to protect him from the brilliant sun, he was struck by how empty Reforma was and remembered that it was Sunday. No one was out. Everyone was at family dinners. He started the car, pulled out onto the street, then found himself turning back into the Zona Rosa.

He parked in front of the Ermita Building and climbed the steps—not sure what he would say but compelled to see Caridad. When he knocked on the door, he could hear her chair squeak. "*Momento! Momento! Quien es?*"

"*Yo, Ramón. Abra. Quiero hablar.*"

Dead bolts snapped back, a chain rattled. Caridad peered out, eyes narrowing. "What is it? You look like hell."

"I want to talk."

She pushed open the door and moved away, returning to her desk.

"You're working?"

She sat down, closing a file. "Yes, still cleaning up the mess Siqueiros left us."

He nodded, taking a chair. He avoided looking directly at her, frightened by the anger she aroused in him. "Something important happened yesterday. I wanted to tell you."

She listened as he described the encounter with Trotsky. "What do you mean, he knew?"

"He saw through me. There was this moment when we were both looking at each other and he understood what I was doing there."

"How could he?"

"I don't know."

She shook her head, squinting. "If he really knew, he would have done something. He wouldn't have let you walk out."

"I kept thinking he'd call the police. Last night at the hotel, I kept expecting Colonel Sanchez's detectives to kick in my door."

"Ramón, this is something you imagined. If Trotsky knew you were his assassin, you wouldn't be here now. You're letting your imagination carry you away."

"My nerves are bad, that's true. I've seen too much of Trotsky. I've spent too much time with the people around him. If he were a total stranger, perhaps I could do it, but I don't think I can walk in there and kill him in cold blood. I'm not a thug, a hired assassin."

"You can't back out now."

"What if I go to the house and the gate is closed to me? He tells his men he doesn't want to see me. That's all he has to do."

"Ramón, what are you getting at?"

"He's an old man. It's ludicrous to think that the Fourth International poses a threat to Stalin. I know those people. They're intellectuals. What will happen if I go to the house and am shut out? Will I be blamed? Siqueiros is still alive. How would you compare his failure to mine?"

"Ramón, you have to do this. There's no turning back."

"Tipping off Trotsky's guards would be an easy matter, an anonymous telephone call . . ." He was speaking rapidly, feverishly, alarming his mother.

"Sudoplatov would know what happened. He would waste no time informing Beria and Stalin."

"How could Sudoplatov know what happened here?"

"You don't think we're the only GPU agents operating in Mexico?"

"Is there someone in the house?"

"There could be and we wouldn't know. But you are talking about the kind of sabotage that would never go unpunished. Eventually the truth would come out."

"If only there weren't all of this waiting! That's what's killing me."

"It will be over before you know it, but stop thinking this way. Stop thinking about it."

"But how can I, with all of the planning?" He stood.

"Where are you going?"

"To Coyoacán. I have to see if he'll see me again."

"Tell them Sylvia wants to stop in to tell them goodbye. And don't do anything foolish!"

Like the city, the old villages Mixcoac, Tacubaya, and Coyoacán were wrapped in silence, somnolent, the streets empty. Ramón by now thought of Trotsky as the only person who could interrupt a terrible chain of events and save him from his fate. The boughs of the eucalyptus flew above the walls; the volcanoes stood in the distance, the snow blazing against the pure blue sky, a curl of smoke rising from Popocatépetl. The street in front of the house could have been a dirt road in the country, the policemen suspended in midday torpor. The guard tower above the street was empty.

Jacques rang the bell and a moment later Jake Cooper looked through the slot. "One minute! One minute!" he called as he opened the door.

"Mr. Jacson! Is someone expecting you?"

"No, I don't have an appointment, but I'd like to see the Old Man for just a minute."

The guard shook his head. "He's resting. He's not seeing anyone today."

"All day?"

"The doctor was here last night and ordered a full day of bed rest."

"I drove out just to see him. I only need a minute. It's about this article I'm writing for him."

"I'm sorry. There's nothing I can do."

"Is she here? Can I see Natalia Sedova?"

Cooper hesitated, uncertain. "I think she's around on the patio. Why don't you follow me and we'll see. But you need to be quiet. His bedroom's right there."

The dappled shade moved beneath the eucalyptus tree. A hen clucked quietly in the coop. Somewhere in the neighborhood, a dog barked. Natalia Sedova was sitting on the little porch above the patio just outside the dining room. She shaded her eyes when she saw the men, then stood and came toward them. "Mr. Jacson, I hope there hasn't been some mistake," she said in a low tone of voice. "We weren't expecting you."

"No, I was in the neighborhood and I wanted to see your husband for a moment."

"He's resting. Is there anything I can help you with?"

"I was here yesterday. He read the paper I was working on."

"Yes, so he said."

"I wanted to tell him that I'm making those changes. I'd like to show it to him tomorrow afternoon."

"Tomorrow? No, I'm sure he's very busy tomorrow."

"Then Tuesday afternoon?"

"I suppose that will be all right, but you need to call Otto or one of the other secretaries to make an appointment."

"Yes, of course," Jacques said, beginning to retreat.


He sat in his car feeling stymied and lost. He knew what had happened in Trotsky's office. The Old Man should have made a move. He wanted to go back, to bang on the door and insist that Trotsky see him. But instead, he pressed the Buick's ignition and started back through the village, slowing the car on Calle Londres. There was no one in front of the house, not a soul on the wide cobblestone street. On impulse, he stopped the car and rang the bell. The maid recognized him. "*Sí, la señora está. Que se espere aquí.*"

Inside, the large papier-mâché Judases still waited in the shadows while through open doors the garden beckoned. She emerged slowly from the gloom, walking with a cane. She looked ill, her face drained of color and animation, her spirit drained of energy. "*Ay! Dios mio!*" she swore. "*Que querés conmigo?*"

"I was passing by."

"Did anyone see you come in?"

"No, the street was empty."

"But that damned yellow car is out there. Now I'm fucked."

"I only wanted to see you for a moment."

"The police were here. They threw me and my sister in jail. They ransacked my papers."

"I'm sorry. I heard Diego had fled."

"What do you want, *muchacho*? Frida has nothing for you. You look sick, worse than me."

"I've got amoebas. This country is the shits." He laughed then he began to sob. "I knew you would understand."

"I understand. I understand very well, but you have to leave. I can't do anything for you. You have to go."

## FORTY-SEVEN

Jacques put off the errand till Monday, then, with the hours flying by and everything hanging in the balance, he drove to the Shirley Courts. He was well-known there, a respected Canadian engineer who always paid a week in advance and never caused the least trouble. A bell jingled on the door as Jacques went in, summoning Mr. Shirley to the counter that divided the small office from the lobby. "Mr. Jacson! Have you come back to stay with us?"

"No, nothing like that."

"Oh, too bad. We could give you your old room."

"No, I'm here to see your son. I want to ask him a favor."

"You want to ask Bobby for a favor?"

"Yes, I'm going for a climb and I've lost my ice ax. You just can't find them here in Mexico, and I was hoping Bobby would loan me his."

"Let me get him. He's in his room."

A moment later, the boy appeared in jeans and a plaid shirt. He was a sturdy fourteen-year-old with wide-set gray eyes and an earnest disposition. He smiled when he saw Jacques, who looked to be a rather ideal adult. "My *piolet*?" he asked.

"Yes, just for a day or two. I would offer to buy it from you, but I know you don't want to sell. I could give you a deposit in case something happened."

"No, that's not necessary." The boy retreated to the family's living quarters, returning a moment later with the ax.

"These are so well balanced," said Jacques, taking it in his hand. The polished oak handle was two feet long. The steel head was eight inches from the tip of the prong to the edge of the blade. He patted the side of the cold head against his palm. "You know, with one of these I used to shatter big blocks of ice in Europe."

"Yes, you told me that. Where are you going?"

"Ajusco. If it's a good climb perhaps you and I can go back."

"That would be swell."

Jacques took out his money clip and peeled off several hundred pesos. "Here, keep this in case something should happen."

"But that's far too much."

"Don't worry. You can give it back when I return the *piolet*."

With the ax in hand, Jacques drove back to Reforma then out to Chapultepec Park, pulling over in an isolated area. He got out of the car with the ax and his raincoat, which he spread on the trunk of the car. The blade would fit easily within the folded coat, but the handle was too long. He turned the coat one way then another, holding it over his arm, experimenting, deciding that the lining of the coat needed something—a loop—to keep the ax from falling out.

Jacques left the park to drive back down Reforma toward the zocalo, veering off in the direction of the city market, where small artisan shops lined the surrounding streets. From a distance, the market had the squalid smell of rotting fruit, the deeper funk of raw meat, fish, live and freshly slaughtered poultry. Meat, chiles, and onions grilled over countless kerosene and charcoal fires. The sidewalks were thronged, the pavement littered with trash. He cruised along slowly in the Buick until he saw crude, newly made pine chairs stacked in a doorway. He pulled to the curb, paid an urchin to watch the car then walked back to the *carpintero*, carrying the ax beneath the raincoat. He would be remembered—a European, wearing a suit, driving a yellow car.

"*Qué sería eso?*" the carpenter asked when he saw the ax.

"*Soy alpinista. Es para montar las montañas.*" Using his thumbnail, he showed the carpenter where he wanted the handle cut.

"*Pero no tendrá la misma fuerza.*"

"*Sí, pero suficiente.*" Yes, but enough.

The shop smelled of sawdust and wood shavings. The carpenter sawed through the handle slowly and methodically, then dressed the new edges with a rasp and sanded down the raw cut. Jacques asked the whereabouts of a seamstress and walked half a block to a similar establishment, where three women sat at sewing machines. A woman with thick glasses and an apron listened to what he wanted, a loop of sturdy cord attached inside the coat just below the collar.

The woman's eyes grew wider when he tested the contrivance by hanging the head of the ax in the loop, then hanging the coat over his right arm. "No, no, the cord is too short," she fussed. "It doesn't leave enough coat to drape over your arm."

She snipped away the first cord and sewed in a longer piece. "Now, that's perfect," she said when he draped the coat over his right arm.

He paid the woman then turned away to light a cigarette, and strolled down the street until he came to a vendor of knives. He tried the switchblades before settling upon an ornamental looking ten-inch dagger with a curving blade. "Do you mind?" he asked the merchant, raising the hem of raincoat to see if it was wide enough for the knife to fit.

"*Cabe?*" the man asked. Does it fit?

"*Perfectemente.*"

"*No caiga?*" It won't fall out?

"*Ojalá que no!*"

# FORTY-EIGHT

Jacques, we never went to the Bellas Artes," said Sylvia, gazing up from her guidebook.

He hadn't heard her. He was lost in thought, the cigarette in his hand forgotten, the smoke slowly spiraling up to the pure blue sky, his eyes hidden by his dark glasses. They were having breakfast on the patio at the hotel. There were big pots of red geraniums, and fresh flowers on the tables. A platter of fruit on a sideboard looked like a Spanish still life, a papaya sliced open to reveal the dark shining seeds that clung to the flesh. The sun shone brightly but it was too cool to be outside; a distinct chill emanated from the stones of the wall and the floor.

She continued reading the book, pulling a sweater closer around her shoulders. "Jacques, a penny for your thoughts."

He grimaced, tapping his cigarette in the ashtray. "I hate it when you say that. I wish you wouldn't."

"I'm sorry. I won't say it again. You were so far away."

The grimace twisted into a grudging smile. "I'm trying to work something out."

"Something to do with Mr. Lubeck?"

"Yes, I think I'm making a mistake, and I haven't spoken up. I have to tell him what I think."

"And he would want you to."

He raised his eyebrows indicating how uncertain that might be.

She took a swallow of tea and shivered slightly. "It's cold out here."

"*Quema, no calienta.*"

"What's that?"

"That's what they say, at this altitude the sun burns but doesn't warm."

"You are extraordinary." She smiled. "I know you don't feel well and are still working, but let's not waste this last day in Mexico."

"What do you mean?"

"This might be the last time we're together here. There are still so many things we haven't seen and done. There's a tendency to give up, quit before the game is over."

"Is there something you want to do?"

"I'd like to see the murals at the Bellas Artes. Do you have time?"

He was on the point of refusing then capitulated. "Yes, why not. I have to go to the U.S. Embassy to renew my visa, but that shouldn't take long. We can run up to the Bellas Artes then have lunch at that place you like. I'll drop you here before my appointment at three-thirty, and pick you up to drive out to Coyoacán."

"We don't have to go out there, you know."

"Yes. Why not?"

"It's out of the way, and, if you have a meeting at three-thirty, who knows when it will really start? This is Mexico."

"No, this fellow's at a bank. He's prompt. We just have to sign some papers."


Outside, Jacques hesitated on the sidewalk in front of the hotel. The avenue was so wide, like a river with its grassy esplanades, the traffic gliding back and forth, almost too wide to cross on foot. The morning felt and looked fresh after the night's rain, the mountain sky blue, the air sparkling, but the city had a harsh smell of petrol, sewage, and shoe-shine polish. Indians dressed in white swept the gravel beneath the trees with brooms made of twigs.

A long line of people had formed in front of the embassy, Eastern Europeans, Russians, refugees from the war. But for Jacques, a businessman from Canada, there was no line. He went straight in, then waited ten minutes for a clerk to look at his passport and stamp his visa.

He crossed Reforma once more, bypassing the hotel on his way to the Ermita building on Hamburgo. He felt as if he were trying to rouse himself from a deep sleep, break the spell of hypnosis, the force of inertia. Huddled into himself, rehearsing what he intended to say, he hardly noticed his surroundings. He climbed the stairs at the Edificio Ermita, tapped three times on the door, and let himself in with his key. Suitcases waited by the door. Caridad glanced up from a file she was dumping into a trash can and studied his face. "Did you take care of your visa?" she asked.

"Yes, I just did."

"I wish you wouldn't leave these things till the last minute."

"Is Leonid here?"

"Yes, in the next room. Leonid! Ramón is here."

Eitingon came in smiling, carrying a long white envelope. "Ah! There you are! I have your letter all ready for you. Now, you mustn't give this to Trotsky instead of the article, though by that time—ha, ha—it might not really matter. But should you be captured, and, of course, we don't expect that, but just in case, make sure they find this letter. It will direct the line of interrogation, make things much easier for you. It would be better if it were in Spanish rather than French, but that wouldn't have been right for a Belgian and they'll get it translated fast enough. You must stick to the story no matter what. You can say that you don't remember something or don't know, but do not vary. Do you understand?" He talked on for a bit, then turned to Caridad. "Am I missing something? Is something the matter?"

"Ramón," Caridad said, putting down the file. "This is going to be over before you know it. By the end of the day, we'll be on a plane for the United States. You will have proved yourself. You'll be a hero. You will go down in history as one of the great heroes of the revolution. Think of it! Think of the glory!"

He shook his head. "That's not right. None of this is right."

"Right? What isn't right?" She continued to smile but her face grew rigid and mask-like.

"What does *right* have to do with anything?" said Eitingon. "We're not paid to say what is right. We're here to complete our mission."

"What are you thinking?" asked Caridad, her alarm becoming palpable.

"I go out there this afternoon and they don't let me in. The door is closed. Someone has tipped them off. I can't get anywhere near Trotsky. What could Sudoplatov do or say?"

"That would be treason," she hissed, "going against everything we've fought for. You know what happened in Spain. If it weren't for Trotsky, we would have defeated Franco."

"That's propaganda, lies from the Kremlin. You've produced your share of propaganda. You should know the smell. The Old Man is harmless. What does he do after we go in and shoot up his house? He sits down to write an analysis of the attack. That's how he defends himself. He has nothing, no resources. He's broke. He has nothing except what he earns from scribbling. He keeps rabbits and chickens."

"Ramón," said Eitingon, "you don't want to end up on the losing side."

"As far as I'm concerned, we've already lost. We lost in Spain. I don't have a country. I'm like Trotsky, a man without a country. I will never see Barcelona again."

"Your brother Pablo is dead because of Trotsky," Caridad interjected. "You know that. It is because of Trotsky that we lost our country."

"No, I don't know that. I believed that at one time because that is what you wanted me to believe, insisted I believe. But now I'm beginning to think that you sacrificed Pablo to your ambition. You could have saved him, but you had to choose between your son and your standing in the Party. You sacrificed him, and now you're doing the same with me. "

Her eyes flaring, her hand snapped out, slapping him across the face. He felt the immediate sting, the involuntary tears in his eyes.

She brought her hand to her mouth.

"I was the one you loved," he said. "But you betrayed me. You lied to me."

"I didn't think it would come to this. I was trying to take care of you."

"Yes, well now I'm going to take care of myself."

"What are you doing? What exactly does that mean?" she demanded in a steely voice.

"It's none of your business." He turned to the door.

"You're like your father. You're a coward. You're not a man."

"Have it your way, because the truth is that I may not have the guts for this. Tell Sudoplatov that you made a mistake."

"Son," said Eitingon, his voice placating, "where are you going? The GPU will send someone after you. They will track you down wherever you go. Every time you hear a knock on your door, your heart will freeze. They will kill you. They will kill your mother. They will kill your younger brothers and your sister. And they'll probably kill me as well. They'll kill all of us."

"What difference does it make? Isn't the revolution greater than all of us?" Ramón heard his own voice as if another person were speaking. Could he betray Eitingon and his mother? Could he choose Sylvia over Caridad?

"Ramón, they will kill Sylvia as well," his mother warned. "She won't be spared."

"Think about what your mother said," Eitingon urged. "It will be over soon. We'll be on a plane together, safe, sound. Think of the welcome you'll receive in Moscow, the parades! You will be a hero of the revolution."

"I don't want to be a hero. I don't want any part of it."

## FORTY-NINE

**W**hat's wrong?" Sylvia asked when Jacques walked into the suite. "Nothing. Nothing's wrong."

"Jacques, you're almost trembling, and your face is splotchy."

"You know what embassy employees are. They're always slow and rude. They make you wait. I lost my temper."

"But you got your visa renewed?"

"Yes, I got it."

"Well, don't let a bureaucrat spoil your last day in Mexico." She was standing over two large suitcases that lay open on the bed. "These are ready. All I have left is our smaller suitcases, and my overnight case. Do you still want to go out?"

"Why not? What else is there to do?"

"If you're not in the mood . . ."

"Yes, let's go. You've dressed. It will pass the time."

The freshness of the morning had evaporated under the hot midday sun. The rows of eucalyptus trees along Reforma created a tunnel of dappled green shade. It was ten minutes by car to downtown, and at one o'clock they were climbing the steps to the Palace of Fine Arts, a mausoleum built on the backs of the peasants by the dictator Porfirio Díaz, a white marble building so ponderous it was slowly sinking into the earth. Sylvia and Jacques looked cosmopolitan climbing the steps to the entrance, both wearing sunglasses, she with her blond hair. They were sightseeing, and tomorrow they would leave. Cars roared past on the street. Indian women begged silently on the sidewalk.

The interior was cool, grand flights of stairs made of polished travertine in shades of amber. They found the murals in a large hall off a mezzanine, enormous paintings, outsize manifestations of heroic egos resting upon the backs of the working class. Sylvia's heels clicked on the polished floor as she studied the Rivera mural, a hymn to the Machine Age, at the center a godlike engineer transmogrifying by means of a turning propeller into an enormous dragonfly, an angelic creature. "See, there's Lenin," said Sylvia, finding his face in a crowd. "That's why they tore it down at the Rockefeller Center."

Jacques flinched when he saw Siqueiros's gigantic mural surging off the opposite wall in a violent wave of adolescent energy. Angelica, Siqueiros's wife, stood bare-breasted at the center of the painting, an Amazon warrior in a leather helmet, breaking her chains.

"Did you meet Rivera while you were here?" asked Sylvia.

"Only Frida."

"My sisters say he's charming."

"He has a way with women."

They were leaving the building, walking down the white marble steps in the midday sunlight, when Jacques, blinded by the glare, felt a man grab him from behind. Wheeling around, he came face-to-face with Trotsky's secretary, Otto Schüssler. Heart racing, Jacques knew that it had happened. They had sent someone to stop him. He had been apprehended.

Then he heard Sylvia saying, *Oh, Otto! What a nice surprise!* And Otto was grinning at him like a fool.

Furious, trembling from the shock, Jacques stalked away, pausing at the bottom of the steps, his hands shaking so badly he could barely light a cigarette. He watched Sylvia and Otto chatting happily, completely innocent of his reality.

"Sorry," she was saying to Otto, smiling apologetically. "Jac's not quite himself. He has to close some sort of deal and this is our last day in Mexico."

"Oh, I shouldn't have surprised him. I didn't know you were leaving."

"Yes, Jacques is trying to wrap up the last of his business today. What are you doing here?"

"Waiting for Trudy. I've got the day off. I'm on my way to a bookstore to get the newspapers from Germany. Then I'm going to the Alameda for an art exhibit."

"How lovely!" Sylvia gazed longingly at the park, the paths and fountains shaded by lush subtropical forest. "I'd love to see Trudy. We're going out to Coyoacán later in the afternoon for a last farewell, but it sounds as if you won't be there."

"No, not this afternoon."

"Sylvia!" Jacques barked. "We don't have time for this!"

Her eyes followed him down to the street. "I'm sorry I can't tell Trudy goodbye."

"You're coming back into town, aren't you? If you don't have plans, we could meet for dinner. We're going to La Blanca. It's right there on the corner at Madero and San Juan de Letran. Everyone says it's cheap and very good. But perhaps another time."

She could see Jacques waiting impatiently. "Otto, there might not be another time, and I do want to see Trudy."

"At seven?"

"That's a little early for Jacques, but we probably won't eat. He's having so much trouble with his stomach. But, yes, seven should be fine. We have a busy day tomorrow."

By the time she got to the Buick, Jacques was sitting behind the steering wheel. She considered asking him for an explanation but decided to say nothing. They had to get through the day. Tomorrow, everything would be better. "We can go back to the hotel, if you want," she offered as they pulled away from the curb.

"What about Salon de Quijote?"

"That's all right. I know you have no appetite."

"No, we have to eat."

He tried to make conversation, to make amends, as though he wanted Sylvia to enjoy the outing. The Quijote was a restaurant she liked. The interior was dark and romantic, pretending to be Spanish. A mural on one wall depicted Don Quixote jousting against a windmill, and the menus had little line drawings of Quixote and Sancho Panza. Jacques encouraged Sylvia to order a cocktail. "Will you?" she asked.

"No, I can't. My stomach. But perhaps a little beer."

She talked about New York, looking for an apartment, neighborhoods she liked. "You'll feel so much better after a long stay up at the lake. There's nothing to do except swim and lie in the sun."

At the hotel, Jacques told the doorman to hold his car; he would be right out. He took Sylvia's hand as they walked into the lobby, held her close in the elevator. He unlocked their door, then went into the bedroom. He still didn't know what he would do, but he returned with his raincoat and gray fedora. "Oh!" She gave a sudden start, putting her hand to her heart. "I just had the strangest feeling!"

"What was that?"

"I'm not sure, a premonition I suppose—that I wouldn't see you again."

He smiled sadly. "I won't be gone long."

"I suppose it's because it's our last day."

"Yes, and you always think I'm disappearing."

"Jacques, where are you going?"

"I told you, I'm meeting a man at a bank to sign a contract."

"I want to know where you're going. What's the man's name? Which bank?"

"Sylvia, what difference does it make?"

"I want to be able to find you if I have to. This is our last day in a foreign country. You could disappear."

He laughed, shaking his head.

"Please, just tell me. I want to know how to find you."

"If it will make you feel better." Jacques got out his agenda and a slip of paper on which he wrote two telephone numbers and an address on Reforma.

"I know I'm being silly." Holding the paper, she followed him to the door.

"It's having everything up in the air." He leaned down to embrace her, placing his face next to hers, feeling her arms tighten around him. "Yes, that's right! A good hug until I come back."

# FIFTY

He tipped the doorman, then got into the yellow Buick and started the engine, pulling out onto the tributary to Reforma, taking the first right, doubling back through the Zona Rosa to Calle Hamburgo. Arriving at the Ermita, he noticed two black sedans on the street and the two men in dark suits, strangers to him, waiting beside the cars. The trunk of the first car stood open, and, after a moment, Eitingon came out with a last suitcase, followed by Caridad dressed for travel in her olive green suit and her hat that looked like a bird's wing. She was carrying her handbag and a small overnight case. When she saw that Ramón intended to approach her, she raised her index finger, moving it slightly back and forth, a warning gesture he remembered from childhood, a gesture from Cuba.

Eitingon, his face gray, walked back to the Buick. "Are you ready?" he asked, shaking Ramón's hand.

"No. Not quite."

Eitingon nodded. "You see we have company."

"Yes."

"Don't think, just follow the plan. That's all you have to do. You're going to walk in and walk out before anyone realizes what has happened. Just put one foot in front of the other. Follow the plan. And don't forget, when Trotsky is reading your article, wait until he gets to the end of the first page and is turning to the second; that's when he will be most distracted."

Ramón opened the Buick's trunk where the *piolet* and dagger waited. He spread the raincoat flat on the floor of the trunk. He looped the ax through the cord inside the coat, then inserted the dagger into the horizontal seam of the hem. The coat, folded around the *piolet*, felt heavy but not cumbersome. Closing the trunk, he got in behind the steering wheel and placed the raincoat on the middle of the seat. Then, with the keys still out, he leaned forward to open the glove compartment, and took out his pistol, tucking it under the raincoat. So as not to confuse the two documents, he put the typescript of his article into one of the pockets of his raincoat. The alibi letter went into the breast pocket of his jacket.

Eitingon got into his car, which pulled away from the curb, followed by Caridad's, then the Buick. Jacques watched the back of his mother's head swaying stiffly with the movement of the car. She was smoking, her right hand going to the window at regular intervals. He felt angry and terrified. He wanted to weep with frustration. Caridad would not help him. She had led him into this trap and now had turned her back on him. His only hope was Trotsky, that the Old Man had seen through him, that the gate would be closed to him.

He lit a cigarette but his mouth had an unpleasant metallic taste. His body felt vile, his armpits damp, his stomach acid, his palms so moist they left prints on the steering wheel. He didn't see the road, just the car in front of him, his mother's head swaying back and forth. They passed through Mixcoac and Tacubaya, following the shoreline of the lake that was no longer there. On the outskirts of Coyoacán, Eitingon's car pulled to the side of the road. The Russian saluted as Jacques went by. Caridad's car led the way through the village, finally coming to a stop at an intersection three blocks from the house on Calle Viena. Jacques slowed to a halt beside her car. She met his eyes for a moment, pursed her lips in a kiss, then nodded, urging him on.

The eucalyptus tree came into view above the walls, then the volcanoes, a deep somber blue, the snowy peaks white against the enamel sky. The afternoon light was limpid, a touch of fall in the air, the smell of wood smoke from a fire burning somewhere in the dry riverbed. A donkey was braying in the distance, its ridiculous hee-haw, hee-haw making a mockery of laughter. A Mexican policeman slouched in the doorway of the brick guardhouse picking his teeth with the blade of a penknife. This was Mexico, where time stood still and nothing ever happened.

Rather than park in his customary way, Jacques made a U-turn in the street, pulling the Buick parallel against the wall so that it faced Coyoacán. He touched his breast pocket to make sure the letter was there, then slid forward on the seat so that he could shove the pistol into his back pocket. He put on his fedora and got out of the car, certain that the raincoat draped over his arm looked suspicious.

Joe Hansen, Charlie Cornell, and a Mexican were working on the roof next to the guard tower. Waving, Jacques called out, "Has Sylvia arrived?"

"No, but wait a moment," Hansen called back.

Cornell pressed the electric switch in the guard tower; downstairs Harold Robins opened the reinforced door. "I have an appointment with the Old Man," said Jacques.

"He's out at the ranch."

"The ranch?"

"With his chickens and rabbits. Go on back if he's expecting you."

Disappointed, Jacques looked from side to side as if he were missing something. "Is Sylvia here?"

"No, is she supposed to be?"

"She's meeting me, but I guess she's running late."

He walked around the wing of the house intensely aware of the weight of the raincoat and the pressure of the pistol against his buttock. A breeze whispered through the boughs of the eucalyptus tree, the raft of dappled shade swaying on the grass below. Trotsky, wearing his blue denim smock and work gloves, stood at the rabbit hutch with his back to Jacques. The hens were clucking, pecking at the ground. The rabbits rustled against the wire of their hutch. The smell of smoke drifted over the walls, along with the muted sounds of the village.

"Good afternoon. How are your rabbits?"

Trotsky turned, a quizzical look on his face. "Oh, Mr. Jacson." He smiled. "I worry about the rabbits. I can't find alfalfa here in Mexico that's been properly dried. If rabbits eat damp alfalfa, they get sick and bloat. I know there has to be a source for dry alfalfa but I can't find it. And how are you today?"

"Very busy," he answered, his mouth going dry. "Sylvia and I are leaving tomorrow for New York, and we wanted to stop and say goodbye. She was going to meet me here, but it appears she's been detained."

"You're leaving tomorrow?" Trotsky glanced toward the house, where his wife had come out on the porch

"Oh, that's you, Mr. Jacson," Natalia Sedova called, a note of annoyance in her voice. "I didn't recognize you with the hat."

"Yes, it's me," said Jacques. Hearing the disapproval in her voice, he gravitated toward the porch. She was the true gatekeeper. Like Sylvia, she would be intuitive. "I'm frightfully thirsty. May I trouble you for a glass of water?"

"Perhaps you would like a cup of tea?"

"No, no, I dined too late and feel that the food is up to here," he answered, pointing to his throat. "It's choking me."

"Yes, you don't look well. Not well at all. Why are you wearing your hat and raincoat? You never wear a hat, and the sun is shining."

"It's the rainy season. It always rains in the afternoon."

She started to point out that the storm wouldn't start for hours. But then she let it go. "And how is Sylvia?" she asked.

"Sylvia?" He was still worrying about his hat and raincoat. "Sylvia? Yes, Sylvia. She's always well."

"I'll get your water." She went into the house and returned with a glass.

"Thank you," he said, taking a long swallow. "I brought my article with the changes. I hope it's better."

"Did you have it typed?" she asked.

"Yes."

"That's good. Lev Davidovich dislikes illegible manuscripts."

She took the glass then walked with him out into the garden. As they approached, Trotsky spoke to her in Russian. She looked sharply at Jacques. "I didn't know that you're leaving tomorrow."

"Yes, yes, I forgot to mention it to you."

"It's too bad that I didn't know, I might have sent a few things to New York."

"I could stop by tomorrow."

"No, no, thank you. It would inconvenience both of us. Lev Davidovich wanted me to ask you to tea. I explained that I had, that you didn't feel well and wanted water."

Trotsky tilted his head, studying Jacques. "Your health is poor again, you look ill . . . That's not good. You should be in bed."

"I'll rest in New York. Besides, I wanted you to read my article. I made all of the changes and had it typed. I think it's much improved."

Trotsky started speaking again in Russian to his wife. Jacques heard something plaintive in his voice and understood that the Old Man didn't want to leave his animals to go in the house and read a paper. The garden was lovely, the afternoon sun filtering through the fragrant leaves of the eucalyptus tree. Feverishly, Jacques waited for Trotsky to say that he should leave the typescript. He would read it later at his leisure.

But then, reluctantly, Trotsky started removing his gloves. "Well, what do you say? Shall we go over your article?"

*Why wasn't he resisting? Did he want to die? He had seen through Jacques. He knew he was a fraud.*

Trotsky fastened the hutch and brushed off his blue blouse and started toward the house. Following, Jacques knew he was caught in some powerful chain of events pulling him inexorably forward. His heart throbbing in his ears, time slowed, then raced, his zone of vision narrowing to a cone just before him. Trotsky was holding his office door, then closing it behind them. He removed the smock to put on the worn jacket of his suit, and looked to see that Jacques removed his hat.

"Well, let's see how it went," Trotsky said, holding out his hand. Jacques touched the crinkle of envelope in his breast pocket, then remembered that the article was in his raincoat. "I don't want to give you the wrong document," he said, fumbling with his coat.

Trotsky sat down at his desk, squaring the typed pages before him. Men's voices and the sound of their footsteps came from the roof above. Through the open French doors, the strip of grass glowed a brilliant green, the bower of red bougainvillea dripping over the door. The office was tiny, claustrophobic. Trotsky's chair squeaked as he sat down. He cleared his throat once, twice, finally emitting a long sigh as he started to read.

The moment was rehearsed. Wait until he finishes the first page, Eitingon had coached. Wait until he is turning the page, when he will be most distracted.

His eyes misting, Jacques put his raincoat on the shelf of periodicals behind the desk and looked down at his hands, surprised they weren't trembling. Then, slipping the *piolet* off the cord, he gripped the handle of the ax in both hands and turned back to Trotsky, who would glance over his shoulder, who would reach for the pistol on the desk before him, and press the electric switch beneath the desk for the siren. But no, he began turning the page.

Jacques raised the ax over his head and brought it down with all his might, at the last moment shutting his eyes to imagine a block of ice shattering. He heard a nasty, wet popping sound, then felt the crunch of bone and something warm and sticky spraying on his hands. He opened his eyes to the horror of his hands on the ax, the prong buried deep in Trotsky's skull. The old man hadn't shattered like a block of ice, but sat upright and living, connected to Jacques in this ghastly moment. *The prong had to come out.* Giving the ax a jerk upward, Jacques unleashed a shriek of pure and unending agony. He froze as Trotsky rose up out of the chair like a wild animal, turning on him, grabbing the handle of the ax, grabbing Jacques's hand, biting down ferociously, breaking through the skin into the flesh. In a frenzy of blood, spittle, and sweat, he threw his arms around Jacques, grappling with him, until Jacques finally shoved him, the Russian sprawling toward the dining room.

Stunned, Jacques watched as the door opened and the old woman swooped down, wailing in Russian. She cradled her husband's head in her lap. The blood running down his face made his eyes look shockingly blue and naked without the horn-rims that had fallen aside. Holding his own wounded hand, trembling, Jacques stared at them, at what he had done. He heard voices, the sound of people running. He tried to remember what came next. He moved toward the French doors, thinking he would go over the little balcony. Natalia Sedova was muttering to her husband as she tried to wipe the blood from his face. She looked up at Jacques, an expression of profound consternation on her face. Frowning, trying to understand, she spoke to him in a language he didn't understand.

One of the guards, Joe Hansen, came in from the dining room to kneel on the floor beside the old couple. As he glanced up, Jacques remembered the pistol and pulled it from his back pocket as two more guards came rushing in. One knocked him to the floor, where they began beating him with their fists and the butt of a pistol. Sickening blows that broke his skin, his face, his eye, his mouth.

Sirens were wailing as he regained consciousness. The house was filled with people. Ambulance attendants gently lifted Trotsky onto a stretcher while his wife and Hansen hovered, assuring the Old Man he would survive.

When it was Jacques's turn to be taken out, a policeman handcuffed him and the attendants lifted him roughly. The house and the garden slid smoothly by, then he was in the back of the ambulance, the doors slamming shut. With sirens wailing, they made a parade through the city, a cortege. Through the windows, he could see people standing on the streets, staring. "He'll probably survive," the ambulance attendant told the cop guarding Jacques. "With head wounds, there's always a quantity of blood. The blow wasn't fatal."

Night, and the rain was falling. As they drove through the city, Jacques thought of Sylvia waiting for him.

# FIFTY-ONE

At four o'clock, Sylvia was dressed, ready for Jacques to pick her up. It wasn't unlike him to be late. Everyone was late in Mexico City. She folded the last of their clothes that hadn't been packed, then made a list of the things she would need to do in the morning. She started a letter to her sister Ruth, then put it aside remembering that she would see Ruth the following day, or perhaps the next. From time to time, she looked at the scrap of paper where Jacques had written the name Alfredo Viñas, a telephone number, and two street addresses on Reforma. At a quarter to five, she considered trying the number but instead called the hotel operator to see if perhaps Jacques had left a message for her.

The last night in a foreign city was always stressful, getting away; catching a plane only made it more so. She had been worried about Jacques for days and now as the minutes ticked past she began to fear that something terrible had happened. She called the hotel operator a second time, then a third. After six o'clock she began to worry that they would be late to meet Otto and Trudy. They were Germans. They were punctual and wouldn't understand.

Sylvia thought of herself as a rational person and kept telling herself that there was some sort of simple misunderstanding for Jacques's delay. He had been so distracted, half the time he didn't know what she was saying. She checked her makeup again, applied fresh lipstick, studying her reflection in the bathroom mirror. Of course, she finally thought, they were meeting Otto and Trudy at La Blanca. That was the misunderstanding. Jacques, having been held up at his business meeting, would expect to find her at La Blanca.

Feeling relieved, she got her handbag and picked up her fur coat. It would be cold out even at the end of August. Just in case, she left a note, *Gone to La Blanca, See you there, Love S.*

Downstairs, the doorman put her in a cab for the restaurant. She rarely went out alone at night in Mexico, but she sat back watching the city, thinking that in twenty-four hours they would be safely back in New York—the night, the missed connections a fading memory. The taxi followed the same route they took that morning, up Reforma, past the Bellas Artes and the Alameda. She paid the driver in front of the restaurant, and, adjusting her coat, went into La Blanca—really not the sort of place Jacques would like. Too modern, a bit garish, too big and modern. She smiled and waved when she saw Otto and Trudy sitting at a table near the door. Jacques wasn't there, no doubt because he would be trying to telephone.

"So sorry we're late! So sorry for the mix-up. We're sort of frantic, but Trudy, we wanted to see you."

"Is your husband coming?" asked Trudy.

"Isn't he here?" Sylvia craned her head around. "He thought we were meeting here."

Otto smiled. "No, we haven't seen him."

"But I was sure he would be here."

"We've been watching the door. We would have seen him coming in."

Hands in her coat pockets, her shoulders slumped, she said, "That man! Where could he be?"

"Didn't you say you were going to Coyoacán this afternoon?"

"Oh my goodness! He must have gone to the hotel. He just missed me and is waiting for me at the hotel."

"Did you call the house? Was he there?"

"Oh no, he would never go there without me. He's at the hotel. I'll call to let him know we're here."

She opened her bag to sort through her coin purse, then went to the pay phone in a hallway leading to the toilets. She dropped the coins in the slot and waited for the Mexican operator. Not understanding what the woman said, Sylvia recited the numbers in Spanish she had learned. When the hotel operator came on, Sylvia, sighing with relief, asked to be put through to the room. She listened to the number ring and ring until the operator picked up again. "Yes, this is Mrs. Jacson. Is my husband at the hotel? Has he left me a message?"

She took a deep breath to steady herself. She had been so certain. Otto and Trudy looked concerned as she returned to the table.

"I simply don't understand. I was sure he would be at the hotel. Poor Miss Noriega! I think I'm driving her crazy."

"Miss Noriega?"

"The hotel operator. I called her a couple of times before I left. I kept thinking Jacques had called or that something might be wrong with the telephones."

"Why don't I call Coyoacán to see if he was there?" Otto offered.

"No, don't waste your time. Jacques would never go to the house without me."

Otto cocked an eyebrow, skeptical. "Are you sure?"

"Yes, we have an agreement about that."

"He might have left a message for you there. People from out of town sometimes leave messages for each other with the secretaries."

"No, no, I don't want to panic. I must think. There's a logical explanation. This afternoon when he left the hotel Jacques said he was going to see a man at Banco Ejidal on Reforma to close a deal. It was a very important meeting. And I was so smart, I made Jacques give me the telephone number."

She opened her handbag to look for the slip of paper. "I know it's here. I put it in my billfold. Yes! Mr. Viñas. I'll give him a call." She excused herself and returned to the phone booth, which now held a plump bald-headed American, a salesman of some sort she was sure.

She waited impatiently, the slip of paper in one hand, rubbing two coins together in the other. When the man finally came out, she managed a crimped smile, then took his place in the booth. She picked up the receiver, dialed zero, waited till she heard the Mexican operator, then dropped a coin into the slot. Mustering her Spanish, she recited the first number that Jacques had written on the slip of paper. The line went dead for a few moments, then the operator came back, saying something in Spanish that Sylvia couldn't understand.

"*Como?*" said Sylvia. "*Como? Ingles, por favor.*"

Now another operator came on the line, a woman who spoke English. "I'm sorry," she said, "but this number doesn't work."

"Oh!" Sylvia sounded crestfallen. "But it's for a bank. The Banco Ejidal. The number must be good."

"Miss Lopez said the number isn't good."

"Could you try again?" asked Sylvia. "I might have said it wrong in Spanish."

The line went dead once more and after another brief pause the operator returned to say that the number wasn't functioning. Sylvia asked the operator to try the second number Jacques had written on the slip of paper. After yet another moment of mysterious silence, Sylvia heard an electric hum and static on the line, then a man with an American accent saying, "The Shirley Courts. This is Robert Shirley."

Jacques had gone to the Shirley Courts?

Confused, taken aback, she identified herself as Frank Jacson's wife. "I'm looking for my husband. It's our last night in town and I can't find him." She laughed. "He doesn't happen to be there?"

"No, he's not staying here."

"Yes, of course, we're still at the Hotel Montejo. But for some reason he gave me this number when he went out this afternoon. Do you expect him by any chance?"

"No, but he was here yesterday."

"He was?"

"Or the day before. He came by to talk to Bobby."

He muffled the telephone receiver to call his son, and in that instant, Sylvia imagined a little family room beyond the lobby of the tourist courts. After a few moments a boy's voice came on thin and a bit reedy. "This is Bobby," he said. In the background, Sylvia heard the deeper voice of his father. "He was here yesterday," said the boy. "He came by to borrow my *piolet*."

"*Piolet?*" said Sylvia.

"Yes, my ice ax. He asked to borrow it, but then he insisted on paying me for it. He was going to climb Ajusco."

"Ajusco?"

"The mountain west of here."

"Did he say *when* he was going?"

"Not exactly. But I thought it was today."

Beginning to tremble, wondering if she were losing her mind, Sylvia thanked the boy and replaced the telephone receiver. She was blinking back tears when she sat down at the table once more. "I don't know what's happening," she told Otto and Trudy. "The operator said that one of the numbers isn't good and the other number is for the Shirley Courts."

"Do you think he was going there?" asked Otto.

"No."

"He must have given you the number by mistake."

"But he went there yesterday to get an ice ax. He told them he was going mountain climbing today."

"There's some mistake," Otto insisted. "Let me try the number for the bank. If it's for a bank, it must be a working number. The telephone companies here in Mexico are crazy, but I know how to deal with them."

Sylvia felt suddenly weak as if she had started her period and her energy was bleeding away. She reached for her glass of water, then recalled she couldn't drink it. "Could I have a swallow of your beer?" she asked Trudy.

Trudy slid the glass across the table for her and smiled with sympathy.

"The Shirley Courts?" Sylvia shook her head then took a sip of the beer.

"Maybe he was sending you some sort of message," Trudy suggested. "It would be like a clue, in a mystery."

Sylvia clutched her arms and began to rock back and forth.

"Don't worry!" Trudy urged. "We will find Mr. Jacson."

"Yes, I know, I know. I'm not being entirely rational, but this brings back the time in Paris when he disappeared. Oh, that was the worst time in my life! Frantic, I was frantic. He was gone for weeks, but of course he couldn't help it. I didn't know where he was or what to do. I wanted to go home but couldn't leave, not knowing what had happened. It was the same when he got sick mountain climbing. I thought I was having a nervous breakdown."

Trudy smiled reassuringly. "These are such difficult times. So many are displaced."

Otto returned to the table looking perplexed. "I don't know what this number is, but it's not for Banco Ejidal. I checked with information at both telephone companies."

"It must be a separate line for the manager. Viñas is the manager."

"Do you want to go to your hotel?"

She studied the slip of paper once more. "No, he won't be at the hotel. He gave me these street numbers on Reforma. Viñas must have another office. I'm going there. I have to look for him."

"But how?"

"I'll take a taxi."

"But you can't go alone," Trudy protested. "We'll go with you. Otto, tell her."

"Yes, of course."

Outside, night had settled in the mountain valley, and the city had begun the process of shutting down. Stores were closing, metal grates rolling down in front of plate glass with ominous clattering. Office workers and clerks hurried to catch buses and trolleys; Indian women and children huddled on the sidewalks in front of buildings. The cold air was filled with the smells of exhaust fumes, kerosene, onions, and chiles frying. Traffic, pedestrian and automotive, eddied around the Bellas Artes on the corner of Avenida Hidalgo to flow past the Alameda. An age had passed since that afternoon in the blazing sunlight on the steps of the white marble palace.

At the bottom of the Alameda they turned on to Reforma, passing the Montejo and the American Embassy. Cars and taxis swirled around the Monument of Independence and past the Fountain of Diana. "There's the Banco Ejidal," Sylvia chirped.

"But it won't be open, not now." Otto asked the driver to stop the car. "What were those street numbers you had?'

Sylvia repeated the numbers, which he translated for the driver.

"*Esta bien lejos! Mucho mas alla!*" the driver exclaimed.

"He says it's a long way."

"Maybe Viñas has a private office," said Sylvia. "That would explain why it's taken Jacques so long. Let's keep going. I don't care how far."

Once Reforma entered Bosque de Chapultepec—the woods of Chapultepec, the city's great park—the mood of the traffic changed subtly, becoming domesticated and packlike, the cars filled with the affluent, the fortunate going home. A long river of red taillights streamed out through the night. Trudy began telling Otto something in German, and, after a few moments, he translated for Sylvia. "Trudy is saying this is like a story by Kafka. Do you know Kafka, a writer of German who lived in Vienna? His stories are very strange. You can read them again and again, and they never make sense. Something is missing or mistaken. There's a different logic to them."

Sylvia sank deeper and deeper into agitation, her mind spinning with possible scenarios. It had to be Mr. Lubeck, something to do with him. That or Jacques had had some sort of mental breakdown.

They passed the entrance to the zoo and on the far side of the park came to Lomas de Chapultepec, once a great hacienda on the hills overlooking the city, now an exclusive suburb filled with houses reminiscent of haciendas. The driver would slow down to look at house numbers, then speed up. They seemed to be reaching the edge of the city. Development gave way to darkness, Reforma becoming a gravel road. Finally, the car stopped and the driver turned to speak rapidly.

"He says this is the end of Reforma."

"Then we must have missed those addresses."

Otto didn't answer and no one spoke in the car for a while. They were now going against the traffic, and, as they drove through the park, the river of headlights coming toward them was white. Sylvia seemed to give up hope but then announced that she had to call the hotel the minute they got out of the park.

"We're going that way. Wouldn't it be better to just wait till we get to the hotel?"

"No, I have to call. Tell him the first possible place."

"Are you sure?" asked Trudy as Sylvia got out in front of the Café Swastia.

"It's okay. I've been around enough anti-Semitics. They'll think I'm German."

When she came out ten minutes later, complaining about that terrible Miss Noriega at the Montejo, Otto and Trudy were standing on the sidewalk waiting for her.

"I thought we might as well walk to the Banco Ejidal," explained Otto. "It's just a couple of blocks."

"But you said the bank would be closed," Sylvia reminded him.

"Someone might be working late. If Viñas is the manager, they'll know how to find him."

"Viñas might not be the manager. I'm not really sure." She pulled the fur coat close against the night. "And he might know Jacques by another name. His name isn't really Frank Jacson. It's Jacques Mornard."

There were almost no pedestrians on that stretch of Reforma—
an occasional Indian woman wrapped in a shawl holding a child
by the hand, men in white pajamas and sandals sweeping the pavement with brooms made of twigs. The avenue felt vast, a broad me-
dian running down the center, double rows of eucalyptus trees on
either side. The traffic—taxis and *colectivos*—seemed to pass now in
schools, as if there was safety in numbers.

The bank was closed as anticipated, but they could see a janitor
mopping the floor. Otto began to tap on the plate glass window
inside the steel grate. "Viñas! Viñas?" he shouted so that the janitor
came closer to the window. "*Señor Viñas! Es gerente del banco?*"

No, I don't know, the man gestured. The bank was closed. He
shrugged his shoulders and turned away.

"Well, that doesn't mean anything," said Sylvia. "He probably
doesn't know who the manager is and he wouldn't know the names
of businessmen who are associated with the bank. I suppose we
might as well go to the hotel. Jacques is probably there by now."

They continued walking and when they came to a telephone
booth Otto stopped. "I'm making a call," he announced. He dialed
the number for the house at Coyoacán, which was what he wanted
to do all along. He knew that Mr. Jacson went to the house without
Sylvia and didn't understand her confused objection. He deposited
his coins and gave the operator the number, then listened to the
recurring burr of the phone ringing at the opposite end. "*Bueno!*"
someone shouted at the opposite end.

"Hello! Hello! This is Otto Schüssler. Who am I speaking with?"

"Nilton. I live next door."

"What are you doing there?"

"No one is here."

"Where are Hansen and Cornell?"

"They're gone. Everyone is gone."

A wave of static came over the line as a school of taxis began to
pass. Otto could make out the word *hospital* and understood that

someone had attacked Trotsky. "What about Frank Jacson, a Canadian businessman? Was he there? We've been trying to find him."

"Yes, he was here."

"Do you know where he is now?"

"They took him to the hospital."

The connection was bad and with the sound of traffic from the street Otto wasn't sure how much he understood.

Sylvia shook her head, beginning to weep. "But who attacked Trotsky? And what was Jacques doing there? That makes no sense. Is the Old Man okay?"

"I don't know."

"We should go to the hospital."

"I don't know which one. We'd better go to the house to find out what's happening."

Sylvia wept quietly in her corner of the taxi, occasionally moaning softly to herself, ultimately sinking into silence, the strange city passing by in the night, all of her defenses unraveling. As they approached the house, people stood along the street talking, discussing something that had happened. There was an unusual glare of bright lights in front of the house, which looked like a film set with police cars blocking the entrance, neighbors and townspeople watching from the shadows. Sylvia felt as if she were floating, detached as they got out of the taxi and started across the dirt road to the house. The gate stood open. They followed the path up to the bougainvillea bower, where a yellow porch light burned. Sylvia felt weak, as if she were going to faint. She was terribly afraid. Afraid to ask questions, to find out what had happened. She noticed Otto speaking to a man wearing a dark suit, that they kept looking her way. She needed desperately to sit down. She needed to go to the toilet but the way through the dining room was blocked by a large dark stain on the jute rug.

"Yes?"

Otto was speaking to her now. Someone was touching her arm.

The man in the dark suit was taking her arm. She couldn't understand what Otto was saying.

*Was she married to Frank Jacson?*

That was complicated. Everything was so complicated. She tried to explain but the logic kept getting tangled.

"Don't worry, Sylvia! You will be all right," Trudy kept saying, patting her on the shoulder.

"The detective wants to know if your name is Sylvia Ageloff."

"Yes." She felt the pressure on her arm. "Otto! Tell him to stop!"

# FIFTY-TWO

The pain was excruciating, but it focused him on the present, oblit-
erating the memories that made him shudder and writhe—the
blood-curdling shriek, the crunch of bone, the spray of blood. "No!
No! It hurts!" he cried as the nuns in white cassocks worked over
him. Straps held him to the bed. No matter how he tried he couldn't
get away from the dabs of cotton, the stinging alcohol and iodine.
He could see nothing from his left eye, which had swollen shut. His
mouth was cut and bruised. His face and head ached within and
without. His hand throbbed where Trotsky sank his teeth into his
flesh. He felt alone as never before and frightened. Everything had
gone wrong. It was all a disaster.

He was thinking about Eitingon and Caridad when a familiar-
looking man came into the room, a Mexican with thinning hair
and that fleshy, vaguely feminine face of a villain, a distinctive mole
at the corner of his mouth. He wore a flashy chalk-stripe suit with
a matching vest. He looked at Jacques, amused. "*Quien te mandó?*"
he said.

Who sent you?

Jacques froze for a moment facing his adversary

"*Joven, quién te mandó?*"

Young man, who sent you?

"No Spanish!" said Jacques. "No Spanish." He winced, trying to
evade the sisters' hands, the stinging pain in the cut above his eye.
"English," he said. "English or French."

The Mexican studied him for a moment, then walked to the
window, gazing out. The rain was still coming down, and light-

ning flashed from time to time. "You wouldn't believe the throng of reporters down there," he said in Spanish. "The international press, every paper in the city, every radio station. The entire world is watching us tonight! We are at the center of the stage."

Jacques pretended not to hear, then noticed one of the nuns coming toward him with a large hypodermic needle. "No! Not that! No truth serum!" He struggled but the straps held him tight. Eitingon had warned him. If he talked, the GPU wouldn't save him. His eyes became very large as he felt the needle go in, then he leaned forward and bit the edge of his gown, his eyes working back and forth.

The man smiled. "*Es para la infeción. No vas a hablar.*"

The sisters proceeded with their work and began taping a large cotton pad over his swollen eye.

"*No hablas Castellano?*"

Jacques ignored the question, refusing to be tricked.

"*Entonces, espera me un ratito! No andas!*" The Mexican smiled again, amused by his humor, then left the room

Jacques waited for the drug to take effect but felt nothing. A few moments later, the Mexican returned with a second man, dressed in a dark suit with thick black hair. "This is Detective Morales, who will translate for me. I believe his English is excellent. He spent part of his childhood in Los Angeles."

He waited, giving Morales time to catch up, then went on in his amiable way. "And, of course, I should introduce myself. I'm Colonel Sanchez. Perhaps you have heard of me. I'm chief of special affairs in Mexico, which to most people means the secret police. You should probably know where you are, your general circumstances."

Jacques kept his face immobile, waiting for the translation. The sisters had begun to wrap his forehead in gauze, which covered his face a bit.

"This is the Cruz Verde, the municipal hospital," Colonel Sanchez continued. "And this floor is my jurisdiction. Officers are always posted at the desk in front of the elevators, and tonight two armed men are standing guard in front of your door. I've posted them there, not because we fear you will escape, but for your protection." He smiled maliciously. "We don't want one of your people to come in and kill you. That's how these things usually work, the surest way to keep you from talking. That is somewhat standard for the GPU. Of course, it wouldn't be one of your trusted comrades, no one who recruited you. It would be a stranger, someone you've never seen before. It might be an orderly, a nurse. Or even a police officer."

The Colonel took a pack of cigarettes out of his breast pocket and lit one, dropping the match on the floor as he waited for Morales.

"Trotsky is on the floor above us."

Jacques closed his eyes. "No, don't say that name! Please! I can't bear it!" The scream made his head swim and he and saw the old man and woman on the floor covered with blood.

"I see you understand something. But yes, Trotsky," again the malicious smile, "is in critical condition. His wife is with him, the poor old woman. You can't imagine her sorrow. She was covered in his blood when they came in. Now they're surrounded by their friends and comrades. The Fourth International is sending a famous surgeon from Washington. People are calling from the United States and Europe, all over the world.

"But you are alone. No one calls to ask about you. No one comes to the hospital. No one shows any sign of caring. That's always the way it is with the assailant." He removed Jacques's passport and the letter from his pocket, and made a show of studying both. "What is this?" he asked, holding up the letter.

"A letter," Jacques answered after Morales translated the question.

"Did you write it?"

Again the pause.

"Yes."

"What does it say? You don't know? Nothing? I'll have it translated into Spanish and we'll see soon enough."

The Colonel made a show of peering at the signature, then opened the passport. "This is signed by Jacques Mornard, but your Canadian passport is in the name of Frank Jacson. What is your name?"

"Mornard. I am Jacques Mornard."

"And the passport?"

"A fake I bought in Paris."

"We'll talk about the letter after I read it. You should know that we have arrested your accomplice Sylvia Ageloff. She's in a room just down the hall."

Jacques froze. He couldn't react, let them know he understood. But finally, "No, not Sylvia! She's innocent. She knows nothing."

"She was hysterical when they brought her in. She had been with one of Trotsky's secretaries and his girlfriend. She led them on a goose chase all over the city, looking for you. Kept insisting you had a meeting with a banker, that you would never go to the house in Coyoacán alone. The secretary said that Miss Ageloff became very quiet in the taxi, then went to pieces when she saw the blood on the floor in Trotsky's office."

Jacques closed his eyes. "No, Sylvia is good. She's innocent. Please leave her out of it."

The Colonel dropped his cigarette on the floor and stepped on it. "Reporters are waiting for me. I'll be back as soon as your letter is translated, and we can continue our little game of cat-and-mouse. We have much to discuss."

# FIFTY-THREE

Through the fog of fatigue and pain, Jacques groped toward some of the things Eitingon had told him, but he had nothing specific to hold on to, nothing more than the kindness in Eitingon's eyes and the tone of his voice. Caridad promised she would come to his rescue. It was Mexico, she'd said. They would bribe judges and break him out of prison if it came to that.

Despite the overhead light glaring into his eyes, he was dropping off when Colonel Sanchez and Detective Morales returned. "Let us begin again," the Colonel said, once more through the translator. "Your name is Frank Jacson."

Again, the pause.

"No, Mornard. My name is Jacques Mornard."

"But this says your name is Frank Jacson." Sanchez held up a passport, again waiting for the translator.

"That's false. I'm Jacques Mornard. I'm not Canadian. I'm Belgian."

"Where did you get a Canadian passport?"

"I bought it in Paris."

"Why did you want a false passport?"

"To come here. The man who sent me told me to get it."

"But who sent you?"

"A man in Paris, a member of the Fourth International. He asked me to come here to work for Trotsky. He made the arrangements and paid my expenses."

"What is this man's name?"

"I don't know. He never told me. It's all in the letter. I put it in the letter."

"But I don't believe you wrote it. I want you to tell me so that I'll know."

The lag between Spanish and English gave Jacques a moment to think, but it meant that he had to mask his reactions and endure the tedium of the back-and-forth, which was almost enough to make him confess.

"A man in Paris offered to pay my expenses if I would travel to Mexico to work for Trotsky," said Jacques. "Trotsky was my political hero, so of course I said yes. But when I got here, I began to see that Trotsky was a fraud. He cared nothing for workers. He said despicable things about the people who supported him. All he cared about was himself. When he asked me to go to Russia to assassinate Joseph Stalin, I explained that I couldn't abandon the woman I loved. That's when he told me that I was to break it off with her. That was when I was completely disillusioned."

"Who typed this letter?" the Colonel asked.

"I did."

"Where did you get a typewriter with French characters? You don't find them in Mexico."

"From a man I met at the Kit Kat Klub."

"What is his name?"

"Perez or Paris. I don't know."

"Who is he?"

"A guy, the type you meet in any big city who can get you whatever you want."

"Where is the machine now? We've searched your room at the Hotel Montejo and didn't find a typewriter."

"I gave it back to Perez."

"Where did you write the letter? In your hotel room?"

"No, in my car in the Woods of Chapultepec."

The Colonel put the letter aside. "I was with Madame Trotsky a few moments ago. I wish you could see her suffering. She's like a saint sitting at her husband's bedside, hoping he will wake from his coma."

Jacques's eyes became still as if he were cornered.

"Yes, a terrible thing for a wife to experience after all of these years. I've had the good fortune to observe them closely since they arrived in Mexico. People talk about Trotsky as the great intellectual and writer, but I always regarded him as a soldier and fellow officer. I'm not a Communist, but many of us think of him as a true hero." He smiled. "So strange that you would choose that weapon. When you struck him with the ax, you drove the prong two inches into his brain."

Jacques felt sweat breaking out on his face.

The Colonel held up thumb and index finger to measure the distance. "Perhaps he will survive. Stranger things have happened, but if he dies, then you are guilty of murder."

Jacques shook his head from side to side, once more hearing the horrible scream. "No! Please stop! No!"

"And you did it because of Sylvia Ageloff?"

"No! Yes!"

"And you love her?"

"Yes, more than anything. I couldn't abandon her. I couldn't leave her to kill Stalin."

"And she loves you?"

"Yes! She is innocent. She didn't know."

"Then you deceived her."

"Yes. I deceived her."

"The poor girl is still in hysterics, out of her mind. The doctors believe she's having a nervous breakdown. You know how delicate intelligent people can be. They tend to be anxious. They're susceptible to ideas, to psychological problems. You must have broken her trust in reality. They say that can happen when the mind has been deceived too long and too cruelly."

"No, not Sylvia. No! No!"

"Yes, Sylvia is in a room down the hall, and Trotsky is upstairs surrounded by his wife and his secretaries, all of the people you deceived. It's rare that a case comes together like this." The Colonel lowered his eyelids. "Yes, rather extraordinary; imagine the fun we can have. It's like one of those English mysteries, where the detective has all the suspects in the same house."

Colonel Sanchez glanced at his wristwatch. It was three in the morning, but he was only a few minutes' drive from Colonia Doctores, where he lived. He calculated how long it would take to feed the reporters clamoring for his attention and how long it would take to get home to bed. The Colonel took out a pack of cigarettes, extracted one, and offered another to Jacques, who winced with pain when he put it to his broken lips.

"Come, I can see you're a man of intelligence. Let's not waste time. We know David Siqueiros was working for the GPU. We even know where David is, hiding in the mountains near the village of Hostotipaquillo. He's been making a fool of me for months, planting articles in newspapers as if he's still in the city. The famous artist fumbled the job, so the GPU sent you to finish it."

"No. I don't know anything about the GPU."

"The GPU hired you to win Trotsky's trust, to be the snake in the grass. When Siqueiros failed, they sent you to drive an ax into Trotsky's skull."

Jacques began to weep. Tears streamed down his face. "No! No! I can't stand it!" he cried, twisting his face to the wall.

## FIFTY-FOUR

"C*alma. Calma. No se sienta,*" the nun whispered as the needle slipped beneath the skin. A tiny bead of blood appeared, scarlet, shining like a jewel, focusing Sylvia's attention, then a dab of alcohol-soaked cotton and it was gone. Everything in the room felt distant and muted, enveloped in a haze; people came in, people left. She kept hearing the voice saying no no no no, a familiar voice, a voice she remembered. The nun was leaving, her white habit rustling softly. A voluptuous feeling came over Sylvia, a sense of floating away. Jacques was there, someplace close by. She heard his voice calling her name.

"Sylvia! Sylvia!" A hand squeezed hers. "Sylvia, it's me, Otto."

He drifted away. People came and went. She lost track of time, the hours slipping by. Natalia Sedova sat by her bed, holding her hand, her eyes so sad, tragedy written on her face. The two women looked into each other's eyes, sharing their grief. Sylvia could no longer evade the truth. She understood what happened when she arrived at the house and she saw the bloodstain on the jute rug. She had been waiting for Jacques since four that afternoon, fretting, hoping that all of her suspicions would prove unfounded one more time. She had been frantic at seven o'clock when she took a taxi to meet Otto and Trudy for dinner. She wanted Jacques to be waiting for her at the restaurant, for there to be yet another silly misunderstanding, for yet another nightmare to end. It was her last night in Mexico, and Jacques had disappeared once again. All she had was a piece of folded paper where he'd written a name and two street numbers. Viñas, that was the name, one she wouldn't forget easily. She'd made Otto and Trudy get in a taxi with her to make the long drive through Chapultepec Park and out to Lomas to an address that didn't exist. And all the while, she had insisted Jacques would never go to Coyoacán without her. Otto wanted to call the house, but she kept saying, No, no, he won't be there. And then, on the long drive to Coyoacán in the back of a dark taxi, she began to know.

Now she was waking to an endless sorrow, retreating from a future that no longer existed, a past that was a lie, a precarious existence on a razor's edge of anxiety.

"Sylvia, you have to wake up," Monte began to say. "They want you to wake up."

Her younger brother Monte had come from New York to represent the family, to take charge of Sylvia. Dressed in a navy blue suit, he looked out of place with his freckles and blond hair.

The doctors had stopped her sedatives. Her lips were dry, her mouth parched. A Mexican woman helped her bathe. Another dressed her in clothes sent from New York by Ruth and Hilda—a knit sailor shirt with horizontal stripes and dark pants. Their father had sent Monte because he was angry with the sisters; Ruth and Hilda were complicit in knowing Trotsky.

As Sylvia ate a bowl of broth, she felt she was being prepared for some ritual sacrifice. Monte came in with a Mexican newspaper, which he paged through in a pompous way, sitting in the armchair. He couldn't read Spanish but was looking at the pictures.

When he finished, he folded the paper and placed the front page before her. "There was a procession," he said, "Don't look inside. The pictures are gruesome."

Sylvia put on her glasses and squinted as her eyes focused. She stared at the black-and-white photo of men following a hearse down the street with thousands of Mexicans lining the sidewalks. "How long has it been?" she asked, feeling a swaying lurch of disorientation.

"That's today's paper so obviously it was yesterday."

"No, I mean how long have I been here? I've lost track of the days."

"Three days. This is your fourth."

Studying the photograph, she recognized Joe Hansen, Charles Cornell, and Jake Cooper walking behind the hearse—their anger and the drama were written on their faces.

"No, don't," Monte said as she started to turn the page. "The pictures inside are grisly, autopsy kind of stuff."

Putting the paper aside, she felt a numbing anxiety creep upon her, an impending attack of panic. "My mouth is so dry. Could I have some chipped ice?"

Monte left the room. When he returned, he avoided meeting her eyes. Moments later, Colonel Sanchez came in, wearing his uniform—a tunic, jodhpurs, and riding boots—and accompanied by a nurse and a police translator. Sylvia had a vague unpleasant memory of the Colonel interrogating her.

At first the translator confused her; she couldn't tell who was really speaking or know whom to look at. "*Muy, muy bien!*" said the Colonel, smiling and rubbing his hands together in anticipation. "*Veo que la señorita está despierta y que se sienta mucho mejor.*"

"Very good," the police officer translated. "I see the miss is awake and feel much better."

Another effusion of speech came from the Colonel.

"We have a friend of the miss you would like to see. It would be good for the miss to get out of the bed and take a little walk. Therapeutic, yes? Not far, just here."

The Colonel smiled broadly and held out his forearm to her as if for a dance. She looked from side to side desperately and grabbed the edges of the mattress. "Monte! What does he want? What are they doing? Please! I don't want to go."

"Sylvia, there's nothing I can do."

"No, I can't. I'm not strong enough."

Protesting, she was helped down from the bed. Barefoot, she looked elfin with her damp blond hair combed behind her ears. Smiling, voluble, the Colonel led his little procession into the hallway. The nurse was on one side of Sylvia, the translator on the other, Monte bringing up the rear. "It's not far," the translator was saying. "A little ways."

As the Colonel opened a door to a crowded room, flashbulbs popped, blinding Sylvia. Men in suits lined the walls of the room. A stenographer sat waiting at a small table. For a hallucinatory moment, Sylvia thought Trotsky was sitting propped up in a hospital bed, his head bound in a turban of white gauze, his face obscured by a patch.

When Sylvia recognized Jacques, she lunged for the door. "No!" she screamed, her knees giving. "I don't want to see him. Don't make me do this!"

"Please take her away," Jacques cried, burying his face in his hands. "Please spare us this." He was alarmingly close to her, lying in a soiled bathrobe, his face battered and bruised. Sylvia wept, tears flowing down her face.

Smiling, standing at the center of the room, the Colonel began to address the assembled journalists in a stentorian tone of voice, confident his words would go directly into print. "The Colonel has invited the most celebrated members of the press," the translator was telling Sylvia, "Mexico's leading crime reporters."

Seeing that she was about to swoon, the nurse swabbed the inside of her wrists with alcohol. Still smiling, the Colonel approached Sylvia, speaking rapidly in Spanish.

"Miss Sylvia," the translator said, "do you recognize this man before you?"

She glanced from side to side. The Colonel nodded rapidly at her, to encourage an answer.

"Yes, I know him."

Again the Colonel's Spanish. Again the translation. "What is his name?"

"Jacques. Jacques Mornard."

"He says you are the justification of his life."

Sylvia had no idea how to respond.

"He says you are the justification of his life," the translator de-claimed, the Colonel's stentorian tone seeping into his voice.

"He used me," she muttered, looking down at the floor.

"Please, you must speak up," the translator insisted.

"He used me."

"Very good! And how did he do that?"

The exchange was losing its semblance of reality. She was in a hallucination. She was in a drama, and they wanted her to perform.

"He used me to meet Trotsky," she answered, finding it easier as she spoke.

"Did you love Jacques Mornard?"

"Yes. I was his wife. He was my husband."

"Did you believe he loved you?"

"Yes, I was sure of his love."

"And Jacques!" The Colonel wheeled upon him. "Did you love Sylvia?"

Sylvia couldn't bear to look at him but heard bedclothes rustling. "Yes," he answered in a low, hoarse voice.

"Please speak up!"

"Yes, I loved her. I still do."

"Sylvia, what are your feelings for him now?"

"He murdered Trotsky. He killed my love when he killed Trotsky."

"But Jacques says that Trotsky seduced and betrayed him, that Trotsky was going to send him as an undercover agent to destabilize Russia."

"Trotsky scarcely knew that Jacques existed."

"You don't believe what Jacques says, that his ideological disil-lusionment was the motive of this tragedy?"

"He was working for the GPU. Why would Trotsky commission him to go to Russia? Jacques doesn't know anything about Russia.

He can barely find it on a map. Trotsky would have sent a man he trusted."

"You never suspected that Jacques Mornard was a Soviet agent?"

"There was one moment when I thought he might have been a British agent. I knew that something was wrong. But I loved him. I closed my eyes."

"Look at him, Sylvia. Look at your lover and tell me what you see."

Sylvia turned reluctantly.

"Sylvia, tell us what you see."

"This is not the man I loved."

"Jacques, listen to the truths your lover is saying. They are very hard, formidable. She has become a witness against you. You said she was the justification of your life."

"*Mon cher, Colonel!* For pity's sake, take her out of here."

# NEW YORK, 1960

Waiting, she listened to the rain, a gentle hush settling upon the city. The room was quiet; the morning light coming through the windows was gray, the air cool, almost liquid. Ten minutes had passed, and her patient was struggling to break the silence. She watched his black calfskin shoes move back and forth once like the blades of a windshield wiper. Cars passed on the street six floors below. It was spring and the park was green and lush. She was imagining the rain striking the trees when the light on the telephone began to blink silently as a call went through to the answering service. It was too soon for Fritz to call. He hadn't reached his office at Columbia.

"Yes?" she finally said to stir her patient.

The man sighed. "This is so difficult."

She resisted the inclination to ask why, to be led into a conversation, to be seduced. He shifted his body, lacing his hands together over his chest. "Last night," his voice faltered as if he were about to sing, "last night I dreamed about being in the park with the dogs."

He was bringing her a dream. A man and woman, a path through the woods, and two dogs.

She listened closely, for the repetitions, the patterns. The family names, the biographical data, the dreams all became part of a fabric, a piece of whole cloth woven together in her mind. She could imagine putting a patient out of her mind altogether, but if she had one piece of the fabric, it all came back.

"It was a cold day, and Lil was wearing her red wool coat, the one her mother gave her. We were over on the East Side close to our apartment. It was cold but sunny, you know, a nice day. We were walking up a hill when suddenly one of the dogs ran into a thicket. Lil got upset and wanted me to chase him, but I said he would come back. We called and we called. . . ."

Why did he stop after telling the most concrete part of the dream when, if one waited, there was almost always more to a dream, a background of less vivid images, a context of shadows? He was still learning the process, to trust her, to trust himself.

"Dogs?" she finally asked.

"Yes."

"I believe you told me you had one dog."

"But in the dream there were two. Does that mean something, that there were two?"

"It might, but not necessarily."

"A friend told me that dogs in dreams always represent fidelity, that that's why they're called Fido."

"Dogs are faithful. That's how they have survived. But in a dream a dog can represent many things. It depends upon your life. It's your dream and will have a particular meaning for you. The path, for example; that could represent your analysis, the park or woods . . ." She let the sentence fall off. "But go on. Do you remember more about the dream?"

He shifted once more on the chaise. "No, I don't think so."

"Then what does the dream bring to mind?"

He was afraid to free-associate, to let his mind go and follow his thoughts. For some patients it was so difficult. It had been for her. As she waited, she remembered the photograph she'd seen that morning in the newspaper. Fritz had warned her when he brought the newspaper into the kitchen. "Perhaps you want to save this till after you see your patients," he said with a wintry smile. "Something from Mexico."

A German émigré, a physicist, Fritz had lost his family in the war. The past came back at regular intervals for both of them, something from Mexico, something from Germany.

She walked him to the door of their apartment, helping him on with his raincoat, giving him his umbrella. She had been lucky after all. He was the husband she wanted—an intellectual, a scientist and humanist. After he left, she went into the kitchen, where she put on the kettle and looked through the paper. Every year as the twenty-third of August approached, her friends and family tried to protect and distract her—from reporters, the news, the questions. But it was only May, the seventh of May.

She found the story on the fifth page: TROTSKY'S ASSASSIN RE-LEASED AFTER TWENTY YEARS IN MEXICAN PRISON. She knew in a vague sort of way that this was coming, that Jacques would be released after twenty years in prison, the maximum for murder in Mexico. The information was unsettling, but it was the grainy black-and-white photograph that took her breath away.

Jacques had been so handsome with his thick auburn hair and green eyes. But he was unrecognizable in the photograph. The young man she knew had been encased in a middle-age prisoner, a heavyset convict, his jaws hung with jowls, his small eyes framed by heavy black horn-rimmed glasses. He cared so much for beauty. She wondered if he could see how he had been transformed.

Her heart beating faster, Sylvia read the first paragraph—Ramón Mercader had flown to Havana and would proceed to Moscow. Then she scanned the columns of type looking for her name, hoping not to find it.

Chunks of Jacques's façade had crumbled and fallen away over the years. Reporters had called her in 1947 when his identity as a Spaniard was revealed, and again in 1956 when Khrushchev denounced Trotsky's assassination as a "vile and vulgar" crime. The political ground had shifted beneath Ramón Mercader while he was prison, changing the meaning of his crime. He had not turned himself into a Soviet hero, but rather, had become an embarrassing reminder of the past.

Sylvia's heart steadied as she came to the end of the last column of type. Jacques had never admitted to being Ramón Mercader or working for the GPU. And she had never given an interview. Her name didn't appear. She was fading from the story, referred to only as an American Communist, a New York intellectual. Soon few would remember. Her sisters might call her that day, but no one else.

She remembered falling in love in Paris, how desperate and confused she'd been. He seduced her, used and changed her in ways he couldn't know. She hated him, but slowly she understood what had happened. In the end, he had given her a mystery to solve, a puzzle to unravel.

She looked down at the blank pad in her lap, listening to her patient. He was talking about his wife and mother, his children. Most of what he said sounded inconsequential. She had to wait attentively for the patterns to emerge, for meaning. She believed she understood what he was going through, but she couldn't race ahead to a conclusion. She had to stay with her patient as he made his discoveries, allowing time for the transference to take place. Then, in this safe setting, they would relive the compelling drama of his life.

He lapsed into silence again. The hour was almost gone. Fingers laced on his chest once more, thumbs rotating slowly, he turned his head, attempting to see her face.

"This isn't what I expected."

"No?"

"When we started, I was afraid that something was going to jump out at me, some dark secret from the past, something buried."

"You're thinking of the anxiety attacks."

"Yes. But now I find myself worrying that there's nothing there."

She hesitated, aware that often it was her last words that resonated, defining what had just happened, setting the stage for what was to come.

"Nothing there?" She repeated his words. "Yes, many patients feel that way. They come, hoping to discover a key that will unlock the door of their psyche, the suppressed childhood trauma that will explain their lives. Such things do exist, events in our lives that are painful and frightening. But in most cases, neuroses are formed because as children we've misunderstood what is happening to us. We misinterpret something harmless that adults do or say.

"But you needn't worry," she went on. "There's always *something* in the past, just not what we imagine. And there are real things to fear, terrible things, but in an anxiety attack, it's usually not what we see that brings on the panic. It's the realization that we stopped looking."

# ACKNOWLEDGMENTS

I would like to thank the Museo Casa de Leon Trotsky in Mexico City and the Hoover Institution at Stanford University for access to their Trotsky archives. In Mexico City, one of the great urban mazes layered with history, I remain grateful to Pedro de Aguinaga and Víctor Nava for their hospitality and guidance.

Many friends and former colleagues read drafts of this novel. In Austin, Laura Furman deserves special thanks. A remarkable writer and editor, she became so familiar with the story and characters that she was able to put her finger on just the right title. Generous with time, encouragement, and wisdom, she always helped me see the next step.

The late Wendy Weil, faithful and unswerving, proved to be the perfect agent. I was lucky to have Wendy take on the novel and that Emma Patterson has seen the project to completion.

At Delphinium, I'm grateful to both Carl Lennertz and Joseph Olshan for their support and enthusiasm. I could not have asked for a better editor than Joseph Olshan, who at every turn challenged and inspired me.

# SOURCES

Immediately following Trotsky's assassination, the Fourth International asked everyone who had observed Ramón Mercader and Sylvia Ageloff to jot down what they knew and remembered. The result was a thin file of documents written by friends in Paris, Sylvia's sisters, Alfred and Marguerite Rosmer, and the guards at Trotsky's house that suggested a narrative path through a complex historical event.

One of the first and most compelling published accounts was *Murder in Mexico* (Secker & Warburg, 1950), by Leandro A. Sanchez Salazar, the head of the secret police in Mexico when Trotsky was killed. Sanchez focuses on his investigation of the crime.

Isaac Deutscher covered the assassination in *The Prophet Outcast* (Oxford University Press, 1963), the third volume of his magisterial Trotsky biography, as did Hayden Herrera in *Frida* (Harper & Row, 1983).

Other books that I found helpful: *Homage to Catalonia* (Mariner Books, 1979), by George Orwell; *Dreaming with His Eyes Open: A Life of Diego Rivera* (Knopf, 1998), by Patrick Marnham; *With Trotsky in Exile: From Prinkipo to Coyoacán* (Harvard University Press, 1978), by Jean van Heijenoort; *El Grito de Trotsky* (Random House Mondadori, 2006), by José Ramón Garmabella; *Stalin: The Court of the Red Tsar* (Vintage Books, 2003), by Simon Sebag Montefiore; and *A People's Tragedy: The Russian Revolution 1891–1924* (Penguin Books, 1998), by Orlando Figes.

Thanks also to Terry Priest, who provided valuable information about the jacket photograph of this book.

# A NOTE ON THE JACKET PHOTOGRAPH

The jacket image of Mexico City's Zócalo square was taken by Henry Schnautz, most likely in 1940 or 1941. Schnautz grew up on a farm in Indiana and taught in a one-room schoolhouse for three years in the early 1930's. Around this time he grew interested in socialist theories, and soon became an agent for *The American Guardian*, a socialist newspaper founded by Oscar Ameringer. He was a member of the Socialist Party in 1937 when the Trotskyists were expelled and formed their own Socialist Workers Party.

In 1940 he was distributing the SWP weekly paper *The Socialist Appeal* when he read of the attack on the Trotsky compound by dozens of gunmen. Trotsky survived, but Schnautz was stunned when he read that no shots had been returned. He wrote the main office in New York, volunteered his services—he stood six feet and was a good shot—and eventually got a reply: *We might be able to use you down there.* Off he went. He had been a guard for just five weeks when Trotsky was killed. He was in the tower when the assassin came in to the compound, and in his room when he heard Trotsky scream.

After leaving Mexico in 1943 and serving in Europe in World War II, Henry lived in New York until 1965 when he moved back to the family farm in Indiana. He died in 2010 at the age of 99.

# ABOUT THE AUTHOR

John P. Davidson was born and raised in Fredericksburg, a small ranching community in the Texas Hill Country. He studied economics and history at the University of Texas at Austin, then joined the Peace Corps, serving as a volunteer in Peru where he worked with agricultural co-ops in the desert south of Lima. Following the Peace Corps, he earned a master's degree at the University of Texas while teaching in a community literacy program.

He began writing at Texas Monthly magazine, where one of his early assignments was to follow Mexican workers crossing the Rio Grande to find jobs in Texas. He made the trip twice with two brothers and in 1980 published The Long Road North (Doubleday). He has held senior editorial positions at Texas Monthly, the Atlanta Journal-Constitution, and Vanity Fair. As a freelance writer, he has contributed to GQ, Fortune, Rolling Stone, Harper's, Elle, Preservation, and Mirabella. He received a National Endowment for the Arts grant, the Dobie Paisano Fellowship, and the Penney-Missouri Prize for Excellence in Journalism. He taught English at the Universidad Católica de Puerto Rico, and has been a guest lecturer at the University of the Americas in Cholula, Mexico. He travels frequently in Latin America and lives in Austin, Texas.

So here cometh
"Delphinium Books"
To recognize excellence in writing
And bring it to the attention
Of the careful reader
Being a book of the heart
Wherein is an attempt to body forth
Ideas and ideals for the betterment
Of men, eke women
Who are preparing for life
By living. . . .

(In the manner of Elbert Hubbard,
        "White Hyacinths," 1907)